A TALE OF TWO MAPS

Scott Bruce

Copyright © 2013 by Scott Bruce
All rights reserved. This book or any portion thereof
may not be reproduced or used in any manner whatsoever
without the express written permission of the author
except for the use of brief quotations in a book review.
Printed in the United Kingdom
First printed, 2013

ACKNOWLEDGEMENTS

I would like to thank some of the people who have given their time to help me put this book together;

My dear mother Joy who spent hours carefully listening to my ideas as they developed, my father Robert (Bob) who gave me a lot of support and encouragement when this book was started in 2007. Michael Hawthorne for the hours spent proof reading, Mark Jones of Praze Work for the cover design and George Mahood for putting the book into paperback.

Much appreciated.

TO MY LATE FATHER

ROBERT BRUCE

THE DARK MYSTERIOUS WORLD TRAVELLER

On top of a hill the dark cloaked Magician from the East stood in silence, his hands folded upon his long pointed staff.

From underneath the cover of his black hood, the glint of the dwindling setting sun, mixed with the flickering flames in the valley below, reflected in his narrow eyes.

He was not alone. Perched on a rock several metres away sat the old Druid Mahours.

The battle for the coveted throne of Britannia was about to begin.

The year was 420AD and the land was steeped in mystery in these times known as the Dark Age.

The first wave of Saxons had just arrived. Adrien was of Saxon blood and pagan background, making him the people of the south west's choice to be king. He was twenty four years of age, a man of average height with pointed features, blue eyes and shoulder length blond hair.

But General Darinus had been sent from Rome ten years after the Romans left to invade and retake Britannia.

The two armies had come face to face just outside Glastonbury.

This battle was being intently watched by the Druid and Magician.

Six thousand Britons (under the command of Adrien) on hearing the Romans were coming had dug themselves into trenches on the side of a large hill.

Five thousand Romans advanced shields up and spears pointed forward; from up high they looked like an army of regimented ants. As the Romans reached the bottom of the hill the battle began.

Echoes of haunted screams only made in the heat of battle could be heard from miles away.

The savage battle lasted five or six hours, during which time the two spectators remained still and quiet.

Six thousand were killed that fateful evening - three-and-a-half thousand Britons and two-and-a-half thousand Romans.

After the battle Adrien rode back to his residence, Gifle Castle, on the banks of the river Gir in the province of Mercia. Darinus rode back to Camulodunum. It would be only a matter of time until they met again.

In these times the Druids held a lot of power and respect. Mahours the Druid was part of the Gifle counsel and was said to be related to Merlin. He had met with Wei-Po-Yang the Eastern Magician who was travelling around the world, and who had been given his name after one of his forefathers Wei-Po-Yang the famous Taoist philosopher. He, also, practised the ancient arts of Taoism Magic.

Leaving Glastonbury they travelled to a secluded cave along the southern coast of Cornwall. These two men had little in common, but what they did find out, was that they had both been born in the same year and were both over four hundred years old.

Mahours asked the Magician for advice on what they should do to protect the throne, as it was evident that due to the number of casualties both armies would inflict on each other in constant fighting, there would be few left to defend the country once the barbarians decided to attack. After a few days with no food or sleep, Po-Yang came up with one of the cleverest and most unique plans ever thought of to resolve this problem.

He explained that the two enemies should face each other in the most extraordinary combat and fight for the throne in a game of chess.

The game Po-Yang invented for this epic battle was a mixture of a game that originated both in the land of Gupta and neighbouring Persia. So together the Druid and the Magician joined these two games together and introduced the game of chess we know today.

The next task was getting the two sworn enemies into the same place as each other; because they despised each other this was going to be a bit difficult.

The Druid went and met with both parties separately and with much persuasion and soul searching they finally agreed to meet.

Darinus refused to go anywhere that would favour the Saxon, so it was agreed that they would meet in a neutral venue, north of Hadrian's Wall at the Castle of Caledonia in a huge chequered courtyard, surrounded by round marble pillars.

Both the Roman and the Saxon were kept well away from each other, at either end of the courtyard, which was set up as a chess board with sixty-four squares divided equally into black and white.

Darinus stood on a white square whilst Adrien stood on a black square.

The Dark Magician from the East entered, his footsteps echoing off the cold stone floor and around the walls. The two rivals had never witnessed such a man. He was tall and finely dressed in a silk cloak that reached down to his feet, his face was hidden under the shroud of his hood and in his left hand he held a long black narrow staff that was pointed at both ends. He spoke in an ancient Manchurian language, stopping every now and then so the Druid could translate.

Slowly and in much depth he explained the game of chess, which at first baffled the two would-be kings.

Then out of nowhere chess pieces appeared, surrounding Adrien and Darinus on all sides of the square. They were transparent figures, which the Eastern Magician used to fully describe what was required of the players during the game. When he had finished his explanation, and the players understood the rules, the transparent figures disappeared into thin air and Po-Yang stepped away from the chequered floor.

The old Druid put the proposal forward, as he spoke Latin as did the two opponents. They would fight each other using the newly described game, which was not only going to be a fight of brute force but a battle of wit and brains. And instead of taking place on this old stone courtyard floor it was to be played across the whole world and across time.

After the initial shock at this bizarre plan and after screaming harsh obscenities across at each other they both agreed.

Both were to leave the Caledonian Court and return seven years to that day, along with a mixture of fifteen chosen pieces for their elite armies.

Their ranks would include eight Pignus (pawns), two Moenia (Rooks), two Equus (knights). two Pontifex (Bishops) and a Regina (queen). The selected warriors could be chosen from any given place, reaching to the four corners of the world.

Darinus travelled back to Calulodunum. He was to be aided by Po-Yang.

Adrien travelled back to Gifle castle to prepare and he was to be advised by Mahours.

The two kings could pick warriors from history dating over four hundred years into the future or four hundred years previous. The reason being that this was the age of both the magician and the druid and both having insight into the future were still going to be alive for another four hundred years.

BRONS

Over dinner that night in early spring, Adrien sat down with Mahours. Sometime soon they would have to leave Britannia and take to the seas. Adrien had never left Britannia before, let alone boarded a ship, but he was ready and willing; with Mahours by his side his confidence was like steel.

The next morning Adrien left Gifle and rode north back towards Caledonia and beyond towards the north east, and the land of the Picts, whom Adrien called Pictus, and whom he had met briefly in the past. Known as the painted people, they had no quarrel with Adrien and the people of the south, but they hated the Romans with a passion, and had been fighting them for decades.

Adrien travelled with his comrades, his cousin Godfrey and his Althing (commander of his army) Eals, for two weeks by horseback. Passing Hadrian's Wall they headed to Orcades in the far north east, the land of the Pictus, where the Picts had built many mysterious symbols using huge boulders unique to them.

The landscape was rugged and cold. As they drew nearer to the set of islands that made up Orcades they noticed many Brochs, the fortified stone towers of the Picts.

Before they got right to the coast, Adrien and his comrades found themselves surrounded by the painted people, all different colours, some with threatening symbols upon their faces, and speaking an ancient language Adrien and his comrades did not understand. They were taken down to the shore to narrow boats ready to cross over to the islands.

On arriving after forty minutes they were met by more Picts and taken up a steep hill to a fort-like castle with large stone symbols all around, it was getting dark as they entered the fort. There to greet them was Brons, the leader of the savage race.

Brons had already heard of the meeting at the Caledonian Castle between Adrien and Darinus and he was willing to aid Adrien in any way he could against Darinus. The Picts were a superstitious race, Brons knew that if Darinus ever gained the throne of Britannia in time he would attack his race once more.

Adrien, Mahours, Eals and Godfrey were taken into the castle. That night they dined outside by firelight inside the walls of the fort on wild boar and fresh heron. Mahours once again had to translate. After much eating and drinking (a drink that was totally alien to the southerners but would today be closely described as whiskey) Brons stood; the whole place fell quiet.

He was a massive man with a big Aruban beard and a loud deep voice. Being such a great warrior he would be an asset to Adrien. "What is it you want from my race, Adrien? Why does you come?"

Adrien replied to Brons saying, "Northerner, I need your help." And he explained what the magician had said at Caledonian Castle. Brons lifted his sword and swore an alliance with Adrien, agreeing to meet in seven years to take his place on the board at Caledonia.

Later that night Mahours took Adrien out of the fort and down to the rocky coast, where the sea was rough and the wind was fierce.

"Adrien, I agreed with the Eastern Magician, before the meeting took place at Caledonia that this is as far as I am to accompany you on your quest. This is your battle not mine. You will make the rest of this journey to choose your army alone, although I will be with you in spirit, if not in body."

Adrien just stared at Mahours in disbelief. Mahours had been with him since he could remember, always at hand to help with any decision he had had to make, and he trusted him with his life. Finally but reluctantly he replied, "Master, if this is your will, so be it".

From under his grey cloak, Mahours took out a canvas scroll and handed it to Adrien. "Keep this close, Adrien. Never let it out of your sight. For if it falls into the wrong hands it could cause disaster and put not only you but anyone with you in grave danger." Adrien, not knowing what the scroll was, took it and placed it into the satchel which he carried. After an emotional embrace they both returned to the fort.

The following morning Adrien was woken by Eals. Mahours was nowhere to be seen, for he had left in the night.

Adrien unravelled the scroll to find upon it a map of the world. Without studying it he quickly rolled it back up and put it back in his satchel.

The Picts had prepared a barge for the travellers to take them east across the sea as Adrien had requested. Brons arranged to send with the Saxons his own trusted cousin, Killgore, a great sailor, who was said to have eastern blood in his veins, although he was a Pict. Thin, with black hair and a small beard, he spoke several languages, which was unusual for such a savage.

When they set off the sea was calm, but during the four-week voyage Killgore had to sail them safely through storms and rough waters, which left both Adrien and his cousin seasick.

At one point the temperature dramatically dropped and without knowing it they sailed into the winter of 792AD. This is something that would happen to both parties at different times during their journeys, for this was part of the deep magic devised by the druid and the magician.

As they got closer to the land, well before their supplies dwindled, they spied what looked like huge trees, but as they got even closer the trees were not trees at all but a sight that sent shivers down Adrien's back. It was a fleet of Viking ships getting prepared to set sail.

ADRIEN IN THE LAND OF THE VIKINGS

As they passed the Viking fleet, they appeared to sail by unnoticed, after all their small boat was dwarfed.

Adrien, having suffered with seasickness, had lost weight but was feeling much better. Eals, his right-hand man, was in good health, but his cousin was seriously ill with fever; they would have to get help as soon as possible.

At the mouth of a wide estuary, Killgore steered the boat into moor at a quiet spot.

They had arrived in Tonsberg in Vestfold; climbing up the bank was a difficult task as Godfrey had to be literally carried.

The day was coming to a close and the sun would soon be disappearing. Reaching the top of the bank they found themselves in Tonsberg.

As they walked through the main street there were few people around. They needed help as Godfrey's health was deteriorating, and just ahead on the left-hand side of the road was a wooden barn, from where there was a lot of noise coming.

As they entered the laughter and the shouting ceased.

Now the barn-like building was narrow with long wooden tables with benches down each side; the place was packed with Norse warriors and Berserkers; it was actually a Viking navy drinking hole.

The Vikings were massive bearded men dressed in animal furs, most wearing helmets with horns sticking out of each side. They were drinking out of jugs, and were all fair skinned, most having blond plaited hair.

Fortunately the Vikings were all under the influence of alcohol and found the four strangers highly amusing. The silence turned into roars of laughter and the travellers were offered benches, and all sat down at the table. Godfrey lay down; seeing he was ill, he was covered with animal fur cloaks.

No sooner had they been seated when jugs of beer were brought out by huge-breasted blonde waitresses and given to Adrien, Killgore and Eals.

The main problem was the language barrier, but that didn't seem a worry after a few jugs of beer.

Adrien thought it polite to drink and Killgore was certainly making the most of it, after not having had a drink for a few weeks out at sea. Adrien suggested they wait till the Norsemen had drunk themselves stupid, then they could slip away or fight their way out, but this plan was halted as out of the blue an axe landed with a thud right in the middle of the table between them.

The Viking who had thrown the axe was obviously ranked highly as he sat at the head of the table up the other end.

With two fingers he summoned the travellers and the men either side of him vacated their seats on the bench. So, excluding Godfrey, Adrien, Killgore and Eals made their way and sat next to the Viking. One of the waitresses placed four jugs of beer on the table.

The Viking (whose name was Egor "the claw") picked up his jug and in one go guzzled the lot down before slamming his jug on the table. The other three, realising this was a drinking game, followed suit.

However, this would be a test as Adrien and Eals were used to drinking mead, on the other hand Killgore was a whisky drinker, but this was a drink of hops.

A busty pretty waitress brought back jug after jug; the first three went down ok, then for Adrien and Eals the room began to spin and on the fifth Eals fell back off the bench and, smashing his head on a pillar, knocked himself clean out. At this point Adrien was slumped with his head on the table;

Killgore carried on for another two thinking he could out drink Egor; however, failing miserably, he too fell from his bench.

Adrien woke next morning cold and wet to find shackles on his wrists and feet. He was in a dark room; the only light was from a narrow window high up. His head was aching and he felt dizzy; this felt like a bad dream, but no, this was reality – he was in a Viking prison.
His immediate thoughts were where his comrades were.
So one by one he called out their names, each replied in turn, Godfrey faintly. They also were shackled. All their weapons had been taken but more importantly his satchel, inside of which had been the scroll, was also gone. "No!" he moaned. He had been warned by Mahours that losing it would hold grave consequences for which Adrien would pay dearly. He had failed and his mission had gone completely wrong at such an early stage. What could they do? Well, current circumstances meant there was nothing they could do.

The previous evening after the travellers had fallen unconscious due to alcohol, Egor had ordered them to be robbed of everything they had - including their swords, Adrien's satchel (that contained a few Roman silver coins and the scroll) - and to be thrown into prison. Egor himself took the scroll. The following day, talk of the travellers spread like wildfire through Vestfold.

At that time Gudrod the hunter was king. He had two children, Olar Gudrodson, the heir to the throne, and his daughter Freyja.
Freyja is not spoken of in the history books, but she was said to be the most beautiful woman ever to have lived in the whole of Vestfold, and had been named after Freyja the Norse goddess, daughter of Niord who, according to Norse myth,

was the goddess of power and prosperity and was said to ride across the skies on a chariot pulled by cats.

Freyja, some say, had the spirit of her namesake and was a proven warrior herself, having fought in battles alongside her fellow Vikings dressed as a man so as not to give away her identity as a woman. She was a natural leader, well respected in her father Gudrod's kingdom, and many men had tried and failed to win her heart. She had fine, long, blonde hair, rosy red cheeks and the end of her nose was distinctly pinched upward at the point, and she possessed the clearest, bluest eyes.

When news came to Freyja about the previous night's events she immediately sent orders to meet with Egor, who was more than willing to meet with the princess.

At that particular time the Vikings were planning a surprise raid on Britannia early in the New Year; planning an attack starting at Lindisfarne monastery on an island just off Northumbria towards the north then to head south to attack the Wessex household. The ships were all in dock being prepared.

Freyja made her way down to the dock where she met with Egor, who dropped down on one knee, and kissed her hand. Then he began rattling on about the strangers from the previous night, indicating that a boat had been found and he thought these travellers could be spies.

He then produced the map and reluctantly handed it over to Freyja, who, after studying it for a short while, turned to Egor. "That will be my sea faring, lord," and she left taking the canvas with her.

Egor later tried to copy the map down, at least what he could remember of it. Interestingly some people say this is the reason the Vikings sailed to America at a later date.

Adrien felt completely helpless and blamed himself for the dire situation he and his men were in. The days passed, the dungeon was uncomfortable; all they had was just a few strands of damp straw for beds, and movement was limited due to the fact their chains were short and fixed firmly to the walls. Just before light each day two armed guards would enter the room, throw a piece of dried bread at each captive and place water in the centre of the room on a copper plate. Godfrey was still suffering.

Freyja took the map to her father who took little interest as he had other things to attend to. Freyja kept the map herself and she would spend many hours just looking at it.

On the map, what interested her most was a small Viking ship that marked where Vestfold was. After a month had passed, the map had dramatically faded, so the princess decided to go down to the jail and see the travellers for herself.

On arrival, the prison guards instantly knew her; she ordered to be taken to the travellers' cell. One guard unlocked the heavy door and Freyja entered. Adrien tried to stand and hoist himself up, but fell down; his eyes met Freyja's.

He had never witnessed such a beautiful woman.

From her bosom she took out the canvas; as she drew closer to Adrien, to her amazement the faded map became more legible.

Still looking into Adrien's eyes, she placed the canvas back into her bosom and promptly left. On the way out, the usually cold-hearted princess ordered the guards to unshackle the prisoners' chains.

As the days and weeks passed Freyja could not escape thinking of Adrien and it unnerved her. At dinner time she would not eat much and seemed pale in complexion. Now this did not go unnoticed, especially by her brother Olaf, who had heard of her visit to the jail and was concerned.

Adrien felt the same, but at least he and his comrades had lost the chains. He had not a single doubt, that he must make this beautiful woman his queen and escape.

Whilst in prison he was losing valuable time but the walls were high and the guards no longer brought food and water into the cell, instead they now used the trap at the bottom of the door. How he wished to see this woman again. On the floor was the straw so he decided to weave together a small straw boat, a replica of the long Viking ships they had passed when they had first sailed into the harbour. If she came again, he would give this to her.

The year was now early 793AD.

Freyja, one night, fell into a deep sleep and had a dream. The dream was crystal clear. She found herself standing on top of a castle tower looking down onto a black and white chequered courtyard. At either end, standing opposite each other on the different squares, were great warriors as if ready for battle, some dressed in garments that she had never seen before.

On one side, on the black square in the middle sitting on a throne was the traveller (Adrien) with a small crown on his head. She recognised him immediately. Next to him on the white square was a queen almost screaming out. She realised the queen was herself.

Taking a deep breath and stepping backwards there standing next to her was a white-bearded man in a long cloak (he was Mahours the Druid). "Freyja," he said, "What you see before your eyes is your destiny. Your brother Olaf seeks to execute the prisoners tomorrow before noon, you must save them."

Freyja replied, "How do I know this is not just a dream?"

"Make haste and go to the jail, where the Saxon will respond to his name Adrien. He will give to you a present, a straw boat like the one in my hand." At this the Druid held up a small straw boat. "You ought to return the canvas to Adrien and advise him and his men to head north without delay. You have to let them go alone and however long it takes, he will return to you."

Freyja woke with a start. Sitting bolt upright she took the map from under her straw pillow and to her amazement it was lit up and glowing. She dressed in her thick furs immediately.

It was still dark as she slipped quietly out of her quarters. It was bitterly cold outside and the snow was thick, but it was not too long until she reached the prison gates and was knocking on the huge door. The guard, on opening up, recognised her immediately and let her straight in. However the guards had been drinking heavily and sat lounging around. From under her furs she took a vessel which she had filled with a strong sleeping medicine.

Now Olaf, because of his concern for his sister, had assigned three of his servants (Berserkers) to keep a close watch on her whereabouts at all times. These servants were armed as Vestfold was a dangerous place. They had seen the princess leave and followed her footprints in the snow to the doors of the prison.

Freyja encouraged the jailers to drink out of the vessel proclaiming it was strong alcohol. Before long all the guards were comatose and asleep.

She took the keys from the jailer, a candle from the table and made her way to the dungeons and stood outside the traveller's cell.

Quietly she whispered the name "Adrien". After a few seconds she heard Adrien's reply (conversely they both spoke in different languages) "My lady, it is me." Before she opened the door she lifted the small hatch at the bottom of the huge door.

Adrien made his way across the room and proudly pushed the straw boat through that he had made; recognising the boat from the dream, Freyja instantly unlocked the door then, out of character, she hugged Adrien tightly.

Quickly she ushered the prisoners out.

They followed her back up the dark corridor. At the top they passed the sleeping jailer. Eals and Killgore stole two of the guards' swords and they made their way to the courtyard. Just as they were about to exit Eals noticed the flash of a sword in the moonlight outside across the courtyard. "Stop, comrades, this is a trap we're about to fall into." But it was too late. Godfrey being at the front stepped outside. One of Olaf's Berserkers was hiding next to the door and he bludgeoned his sword straight through Godfrey's stomach.

Godfrey fell to his knees as his blood dripped on to the crisp white snow; immediately, Eals and Killgore flew into action, swiftly disposing of two of the Vikings. As the third ran, Freyja herself drew her sword and hurled it through the air and straight into the back of the fleeing Viking's head, killing him instantly.

Adrien knelt down and anxiously picked up his young cousin. Godfrey died in Adrien's arms that night.

Nevertheless there was not a moment to spare. Eals and Killgore stripped the dead Vikings of their furs and took their weapons.

Killgore picked up Godfrey's lifeless corpse. Once outside the prison gates, Freyja produced the map and handed it back to Adrien. She pointed north to the hill. Adrien kissed Freyja softy on her cheek; he knew he would return and that she would sit as his queen next to him at the Caledonian Castle.

Before he left, the Viking princess took her sword, cut a plait from her hair and handed it to him.

Quickly the three warriors headed for the hill. Once beyond the hill they followed the coast and it wasn't long before they came across a small narrow boat, which they boarded and Killgore, taking hold of the two oars, steered them out to sea and away from Vestfold.

They sailed northwards for the few remaining hours of that dark night.

As the sun rose they sailed up a wide fjord; the landscape was stunning, with green mountains either side. Not far in, Killgore steered the boat in towards a cave; despite their exhaustion they pulled the old boat up the beach and disembarked.

Physically exhausted and emotionally drained, they slept on the beach for most of that day. Late in the afternoon, Eals and Killgore collected firewood from the pine forest surrounding the cave. Adrien stayed quiet and sober on the beach. Godfrey's corpse had been left in the boat.

That night they filled the boat with white cedar wood and placed pine branches upon the cedar and then they lay Godfrey's body on top.

Eals started a fire. Earlier he had cut down a pine tree using his sword. Making a wooden block out of wood from the tree, next he cut up a narrow stick, roughly ten inches long, then cut some stringy bark from the pine. Making a loop at the end of the stick he could use the stringy bark to hold the stick on the block of wood and began twisting it back and forth.

After some time the friction produced a spark which eventually started a fire. The pine wood on the boat was lit, and after a lot of spitting (because that's what happens when you burn pine wood) the fire consumed the wood around Godfrey.

All three of them pushed the boat out to sea; emotionally Adrien bid his dear cousin goodbye.

That night as they sat sombrely on the beach, they saw green lights like crystals dancing across the sky from the north.

JOURNEY BACK TO ROME

Darinus, on arriving back to Camulodunum, decided to leave Britannia, as it had become a hostile place to stay for the Romans. So, wasting no time, he collected his army of fifteen hundred men and headed to Felixstowe, where his fleet of seven vessels was docked. Po-Yang was with the Romans.

As he left, Darinus took one look at the beautiful coast of Britannia, knowing that one day he would return and be king.

Darinus was a forthcoming, well-educated young man with a neatly trimmed beard and shoulder-length brown hair. About five foot ten in height, he was a serious character and had a manner of authority about him and was particular about his men staying in line. Away from the battle ground, he had a softer, more emotional side to his personality.

When they arrived in Gaul, Po-Yang explained to Darinus, "It is time for me to now leave." He said this in Manchurian, however somehow Darinus understood. He handed the Roman a canvas map rolled up into a scroll, identical to the one Mahours had given to Adrien – there were only two in the whole world.

On this canvas was a map showing all the countries in the world. Even Darinus, who was educated, had never witnessed such a document. To him the Roman Empire was the world; all of a sudden there were many countries and places that had not even been conquered yet.

Wei Po-Yang said farewell and Darinus marched on foot with his men (they had only a few horses) eastwards through Gaul towards the great Renos River where Roman roads ran directly towards Rome. On average they would march up to thirty miles per day.

One night, after marching a long way, they set up camp near a Frankish-Germanic settlement.

That night, after Darinus had retired to sleep early, word came to camp about a warrior, Gregor, who was a great Frankish-Germanic warlord. Gregor came from the nearby settlement and his whole family lived there. Gregor was at war, engaged in battle with a Roman army in Gallia Cisalpina, the other side of the Alps near Rome.

Julian, who was a centurion and in charge of Darinus' personal bodyguards, took twenty five out of the fifty bodyguards, marched two miles to the settlement and burnt the whole town to the ground; killing and destroying, raping and pillaging everything in their path. By the next morning the place was utterly annihilated and unrecognizable.

Darinus woke the following morning and on hearing of the night's slaughter, was furious; he wept in his tent without anyone knowing. He could not show his reaction in front of his army as this would have been a sign of weakness. He could not even look at Julian.

The Romans marched towards the Renos where they crossed over.

Gregor soon got wind of the destruction of his home people and was enraged. He had just beaten his opponents and was closing in on Rome from the west, he and his army were on the brink of seizing Rome, but he pulled his army of forty thousand back to avenge his homeland.

Darinus knew this would happen and marching on, sent Julian and another officer on horseback, ahead to make sure the road was clear. They rode on the Roman-made road down the Germanic side of the Renos. As they rode, the landscape changed. Up until recently, Roman legions had been stationed at checkpoints at various boundaries. With these checkpoints there had been permanent camps, but now they lay silent as the Roman armies from the west had been called back to fight and protect Rome from the barbarians who were attacking her.

After two-and-a-half days riding, the hills were gradually turning into mountains. The two officers were approaching the Alps and came to the edge of a cliff which looked down into a valley. There was the Germanic army only a few miles below stretching out as far as they could see. Julian's initial thought was that Darinus' army would not stand much of a chance if they met these barbarians in straight battle.

Julian could not make out how big the army was because the road wound through the mountains and out of view. The army was moving at quite a speed, as they seemed to be on horseback.

The two officers turned about swiftly. They had to get back to Darinus and alert him as quickly as possible as nearly all the Romans were on foot.

Julian and the officer rode as quickly as their horses could carry them without stopping. They met Darinus a day later as Darinus' army had marched over one hundred and fifty miles in the time since Julian had left.

On arriving, Julian informed Darinus of Gregor's huge army. Darinus had to act swiftly as time was not on their side. Gregor's army would be upon them very soon. The Romans were tired, so Darinus decided to cross the great Renos and shelter in the Black Forest. The other option was to fight, but as Julian pointed out they were outnumbered by far. Only a few miles south was an old Roman border outpost where, if they could make it there in time, they could use an old bridge to cross the river to the other side, but to their horror, the bridge had been burnt and was impossible to cross.

As Darinus stared at the bridge in disbelief, he noticed three old roman rafts moored down the bank. Thinking quickly he ordered his men to take off their armour.

These old Roman outposts had a network of secret tunnels under the buildings and this is where they hid their armour. The men could not hide there as there was not enough room for fifteen hundred soldiers, plus it would be too dangerous. Each man was to keep just his sword.

The rafts were big enough to escort twenty to thirty men across the river at a time. The river was high that time of year as much rain had been falling and the currents were strong. The first three raft loads crossed with much difficultly; the first raft was worn and not strong enough to take the weight of the men and so halfway over the river it buckled and collapsed; twenty five men were swept down river and lost. Only three survived, swimming their way to the other side.

Darinus waited on the shore till all the men had crossed. It was dark by the time the last raft crossed (which took hours). Getting to the opposite shore the Roman's burnt the remaining two rafts and sent them down the river. The few horses they had were unsaddled and set free; all who had made it to the other side lay down and waited in the forest. It was pitch black. Darinus ordered every man to rub earth on their faces to camouflage themselves.

Two hours passed. Then in the distance the sound of horses and the rumbling of the Germanic army marching could be heard.

As the minutes passed the noise grew louder and louder. Within two hours Gregor arrived at the Roman border post. Stopping to dismount his horse he ordered his men to search the deserted camp from top to bottom for any sign of Roman life. Fortunately they never found the hidden armour; if it had been light they may have seen the fresh footprints of the Romans in the mud leading to the river.

Darinus could just about see what was happening, as the Germanic warriors held big stakes lit with fire.

Gregor brought his horse down to the river to drink as did many of his men with theirs. The Romans lay perfectly still and quiet, hidden away in the dark night, waiting for some kind of signal from their leader.

After a while, Gregor ordered his men to burn the deserted camp to the ground; the Roman Eagle Crest which still flew over the ghost camp was ripped down and with the place ablaze, the army left.

The army was so huge that it took what seemed a lifetime to pass. After a while quiet was restored. Darinus and his army lay low until light. The next problem was the river; the advantage now, was that the army were free from their armour and could move faster and more easily.

Eventually, after a few miles, they crossed a bridge back over to the road. Over the next few days they crossed the Alps through to Gallia Cisalpina, and finally went on to the Eternal city, Rome herself. On approaching the great city, Darinus' heart was filled with awe.

Making their way through the Salarian gateway, Darinus and his men were welcomed into Rome.

Caesar, on hearing of Darinus' arrival, sent for him to come to the Imperial Palace. The rest of the weary soldiers were given leave to take time out to rest, and some were even reunited with their families.

Darinus had only ever met the Emperor once, just over a year ago when he had been made a General on being assigned the task of taking the island of Britannia back.

The Imperial Palace was a magnificent building set in the heart of the city. Darinus, on entering the palace, was taken to the Emperor. As he walked down the large corridors, his every foot step echoed; on either side of him were large marble statues of past rulers of this awesome Empire. He met Caesar in a rather extravagantly decked-out room on the top level of the palace, where there were shazlongs and expensive furniture made from different types of wood found in various places around the Empire. Caesar stood out on a balcony overlooking the palace gardens.

On coming face to face with the Emperor Honorius Caesar, Darinus fell to his knees and head bowed trembling.

Caesar walked over to where the General knelt and placing his hand on Darinus' head, said in a shaky voice, "My son, Rome is being shaken to her foundations. We must be strong. Rome needs warriors like you. Welcome home. Arise and let me gaze into your eyes."

"Again we are under attack by the barbarians who come from the north and the west but the gods see all this and will strike them down".

"Alaric, the king of the Visigoths, is getting stronger and growing in popularity. I hear he is likely to attack Rome when he feels the time is right. Darinus I want you to take charge of an army of one hundred thousand men, and using the element of surprise, I want you to crush his army and bring Rome Alaric's head".

To Darinus this would be a great honour to serve Rome in this way and to lead this army, with this promotion given to him by Caesar himself. All this time there had been another General standing next to Caesar, whom Darinus immediately recognised as an old friend; Brutus from Britannia. Caesar at this point turned to Brutus. "Brutus will be the man at your right hand, he will ride with you."

These two young generals were to take on this role in a matter of weeks; Darinus was too afraid to tell Caesar of his mission and left the palace.

THE AMPHITHEATRUM FLAVIUM

Darinus got away from Rome and finally had time to think; all his life he had dreamt of leading such an army, but to rule Britannia, which was the jewel in the Roman crown, would be a price worth sacrificing anything (although he would need the Emperor's blessing).

Darinus had been friends for many years with Brutus. He was originally from Camulodunum from a very wealthy family but had moved to live in Sicily.

Brutus invited Darinus down to his home.

The following day, Brutus took him to the Amphitheatrum Flavium, set up high on a hill; the greatest and largest amphitheatrum in the whole of the Roman Empire. It could fit fifty thousand spectators inside. The roar of the crowd inside would be deafening when the games commenced. Because of their high rank, the two friends sat in the senator's area near to the front of the arena, where they were sheltered from the sun and given an endless supply of wine.

The amphitheatrum filled quickly. The noise of excited spectators was soon drowned out by the sound of trumpets.

In the arena, the high wooden doors at one end opened and slaves were the first to be brought out; they were made up of Gaul and Aryans, twelve in total.

On the opposite side two other portcullises lifted, and out came three young Roman gladiators, nuctorati (volunteers) fresh out of gladiator schools.

Both parties came (the slaves in chains) to the front of the senator where the politician who had arranged the event for his close friends (Brutus included), was sat in his seat at the top of some steps.

To oversee and referee was the harenarii who, with a big set of keys, unlocked the slaves' shackles, and handed each slave in turn a weapon, from sharp swords to ball and chains with pointed spikes on the balls.

The three gladiators were handed blunt swords; this would be their big chance to prove their worth on the big stage.

Now the slaves were political men who had been captured during these times of unrest. Their prize, if they survived in this arena, would be their freedom from the senator. The politician stood and as the crowd fell quiet again, he raised his right hand and hailed for the games to commence.

Both parties stepped back twenty yards from their opponents.

On the signal, the slaves in no particular fashion ran towards the nuctorati gladiators, who stood their ground until their opponents were almost upon them. Almost immediately two of the slaves fell due to a Gaul who had obviously never handled a ball and chain before. He had taken aim at the Romans, swung round and with the sheer weight of his weapon took two of his comrades down, killing one and seriously injuring the other.

The nuctorati instantly showed their skill, dodging weapons and easily evading attack; their aim was to disarm the barbarians.

The battle lasted ten or so minutes, during which time the first nuctorati had skilfully avoided an Aryan, stealing his spear as he passed, the second was caught in the thick of the fight and was fending off three fighters (only a few prisoners were properly trained). An Aryan straight behind him lifted his sword, driving it through the young gladiator's heart from his back; on seeing this, the first gladiator, taking aim hurled the spear he had just stolen, hitting the Aryan and piercing through the slave torso to the other side.

At this point, the harenarii stepped in to stop the fighting, ending the contest there and then. To lose a young gladiator in such circumstances was not in the script; to lose another could cost due to the investments made in their training.

At this point the arena opened, letting in Roman guards who surrounded the prisoners who were taken back out as none had earned their freedom: maybe another day, who knew? The two remaining nuctorati gladiators had shown their worth, and were summoned to the bottom of the steps to the officials' box, each in turn ascending the steps to the politician who handed them a palm and a bag of gold coins.

Different games took place during the day and as the day got hotter, eunuchs were on hand to bring Darinus and Brutus refreshments.

At lunch break it was clear the crowd wanted bloodthirsty entertainment, therefore deserters from the Roman army who had been caught and rounded up were brought to the arena to be punished: twenty were brought out.

The harenarii placed ten swords in the middle of the arena and briskly left. All the deserters could do was wait. The gates from the north opened and ten starving male lions were unleashed. The frightened Roman ex-soldiers raced to grab the ten swords. Only the quickest and I should say the most fortunate managed to get armed. The lions had obviously not eaten for some time, and spotting the prisoners, wasted no time in indulging their appetites. What happened next was too blood curdling to write in this book. The ex-soldiers put up a good fight, leaving three lions dead and five badly injured, but only one deserter survived.

After the lions were rounded up, and the sole survivor taken out and set free, the dead bodies were removed, as everyone was getting ready for the main event of the day.

The contest was to be between two unbeaten gladiators: Pothiponic, a Greek who had been unbeaten for several years, and Oct, a rookie who was from the flat lands of Abyssinia. He had been a gladiator for just over one year with already over fifteen kills at three different coliseums.

Both warriors were paraded before the crowd whilst their statistics were read out by the harenerii.

First out was Pothiponic, who was wearing lavishly decorated gold armour with a blue velvet cloak, and was aboard a chariot drawn by two white horses. The crowd showed their approval at having such a great warrior (if not a legend and one of one of the greatest of that time) in their midst. Saluting the politician the Greek gladiator left by the north gate.

Oct arrived on foot a few minutes later from the south gate, followed by a harem of beautiful Abyssinian women. He was a solid man with big muscles, black skin and beaded colourful locks. All he wore was a skirt and strapped boots. He walked round the arena bowing as he passed the politician before also leaving to prepare.

During the rest of the break, Persian dancers came out to entertain the crowd.

The main event of the day was about to take place and the scorching heat from the sun was burning hot. Out came Oct first, still in his attire from earlier. To the beat of Abyssinian drums he swaggered over to the bottom of the senator steps, standing in front of the politician, legs apart, hands behind his back and head bowed. If you could get close enough, you would be able to see the pure concentration on his face, although outwardly he seemed very relaxed.

The drums ceased as the northern gates opened and Pothiponic entered the arena, this time on foot. The lavish cloak was gone; he now wore a gold helmet and his right arm was covered with a gold armoured sleeve.

Suddenly the noise from the crowd became deafening, along with the sound of trumpets. Both gladiators stood before the senator, as the harenarri stood between them. The politician stood, showing his approval for the games to begin.

The atmosphere was electric as both gladiators made their way to the centre just twenty yards apart. Both were handed two of their own choice of weaponry. Pothiphoics chose a Greek sword and a shield, Oct a spear and a sword, which he hung on a belt he wore.

Both gladiators stood ready to face each other. The harenarri was still in the arena; raising his left arm he stepped back. Oct took one look up to the top of the coliseum to acknowledge the harem of women who were at the back, as that's where the women would be.

Then the famous words in Latin were screamed out by both gladiators. *Pro nos quisnam es super morior tutus vos!* (We, who are about to die salute you!)

The fight began as they moved towards each other slowly, circling round.

Oct was the first to lunge directly with his spear towards Pothiponic, who skilfully directed it away with his sword. This happened three times and on the fourth Pothiponic revolved round full circle and swiped at Oct's left leg. Oct was quick and moved out of the way although this was the first sign of blood as the Greek had sliced his leg.

With the back end of his spear Oct struck Pothiponic on top of his helmet; the Greek replied using his shield to disarm Oct's spear. Oct moved back, drawing his sword from his side, and they were now engaged in a full on sword fight. Pothoponic seemed to be the most skilful, although Oct was more athletic but could not get passed the Greek's shield, after ten minutes of hard fighting in the searing heat the harenarri called an interval.

Pothiponic had come out of the first bout almost unscathed, but Oct had been slashed several times across his torso and chest and had received a huge gash to his right shoulder. Both gladiators left the arena for a few minutes to recuperate and a doctor was brought to tend to Oct's shoulder.

On re-entering, both had new weapons. Pothiponic's was a double-sided axe. He had removed his gold helmet and sleeve and had two gladii (2x30ml daggers) which were kept in the straps of his boots. Oct appeared with two ball and chains in both hands, which he skilfully spun round like fireballs.

The fight commenced this time much more fiercely and faster; they were now at the edge of the arena. Oct spun the two chains round his head before striking Pothiponic's right thigh. Pothiponic staggered backwards but soon collected himself, turning full circle. As Oct spun the chains again, Pothiponic's axe took one of the balls straight out, severing one of the chains in two with such force it flew up into the crowd (maybe maiming or injuring someone). At this the crowd were all on their feet roaring with excitement. The fight continued for some time with both warriors fighting to the best of their ability. Then all of a sudden the Greek cleverly raised his axe and disarmed the Abyssinian, and in the same move kicked him to the ground.

Oct, now unarmed and helpless, made an attempt to dive towards the Greek, who raised his axe, bringing it down aiming it at Oct's injured shoulder with the blunt edge. It looked like this was the end of the duel as it seemed the fight had been won. The force of the blow was such that it was heard at the back of the arena.

Oct seemed to be lying lifeless. Pothiponic raised the axe with both hands, circling his opponent slowly, looking around the arena with such arrogance. Then he knelt down next to Oct and said something nobody else could hear. (What he said was in his Latin tongue, "You dog, how dare you challenge me? For this you must die.) He then stood. The crowd were roaring "Misso, Misso, Misso," (mercy). They had grown to like Oct. As Pothiponic lifted his axe, he looked up to the crowd, and as he did this Oct mustered up enough strength to swiftly slip the two gladius from his opponent's boot straps. As the axe came down, Oct move quickly out of the way and drove one gladius into the Greek's side and the other into his heart. The fight was over; Oct the Abyssinian was the victor.

Badly injured, Oct managed to get to his feet. Whilst watching this, Darinus was suddenly haunted by Britannia and the task set for him at the Caledonian Castle. After witnessing such a fight his mind was made up; he wanted to make this gladiator the first piece on his side of the chess board.

He told Brutus he wanted to meet Oct, which was arranged a couple of days later in the house of the politician. Oct was still badly injured, however he was being looked after by his harem of beautiful women, and was well enough to talk.

So Darinus explained briefly about the game.

The challenge of such a battle was too good to miss. Oct agreed, and was to make his way to Caledonia in seven years' time. All he had to do was stay alive.

Darinus did detect that this man had a bad attitude to go with his huge ego though, and realised he might have to sort that out.

After a few weeks Darinus and Brutus left Sicily to head back to meet Caesar in Rome. How would he explain that he could not lead the Roman army against Alaric? Nobody ever questioned the Emperor!

THE FIGHT ON THE GHAT

The three comrades awoke on the beach in the cold morning; the fire had burnt itself out during the night.

Adrien stood, letting out a wide yawn. "Men, we must move on. There is no time to grieve; my cousin is gone and no amount of sorrow will bring him back. We carry on our journey."

Studying the map, Adrien decided it would make sense to go south towards the warmer weather. He had no idea of the distances shown on the canvas map; after all he had lived his whole life on the island of Britannia, where to get from one place to another really was not too far, so now being unleashed into the big wide world he was in for a shock.

Having no transport, (for the boat had been burnt) and with no horses they set off on foot. At first they headed north. After many hours they found a crossing through shallow waters at the narrowest point over to the other side of the fjord, before hiking south.

There was no way Adrien was foolishly going to risk his men's lives by taking them immediately south past Vestfold again.

Near the Baltic Sea three horses were acquired. The fair-skinned travellers and the painted Pict lived off the land by fishing and setting animal traps.

The route they had chosen took them past Kiev, the Black Sea and the Caspian Sea, picking up the Silk Road that ran from west to east.

Adrien and his men took a right turn off the Silk Road, passing through Parthia on to the land of Pashua, a mountainous region where the terrain was torrid.

On the map a part of the world caught the Saxon's eye – the Gupta Empire.

One night, whilst journeying through Pashua, as it was getting dark, they set down in the shelter of a cave, high up above a village.

During that night another time line was crossed, and they went back to the year 499AD.

Waking up and stepping out of the cave the next morning, the first thing that became noticeable was that the village below had vanished, as settlers had not yet arrived in that area.

Moving on, it was not long before they crossed into the provinces that came under the rule of the Guptan Empire.

The capital of Gupta was a city called Pataliputra.

Adrien and his two comrades still had a long way to travel; the mountains became smaller and turned to deserts, where they witnessed breath taking sunsets.

The people of this land were brown in colour and well dressed, and the whole place had a peaceful air about it.

The travellers must have looked very strange, still dressed in Viking furs (especially the painted Pict).

A few more days' riding and they entered Pataliputra. Here the architecture was a fascinating treat, each building unique to itself.

But this was a city in captivity. This was soon made clear by foreign soldiers patrolling the streets. These were Hunnic soldiers from the north; Gupta had just been invaded and the Guptan army defeated.

Adrien, Eals and Killgore got off their horses and walked through the streets, following the crowd, which every now and then were all pushed to the side as yet another patrol passed. Before long they found themselves in a busy market place. Although dressed the way they were, nobody seemed to pay them much attention, as the place was full of foreigners anyway, mainly due to trading.

The market was bustling, tradesmen shouting, and different activities taking place, including a man who was sitting in a corner playing an instrument (it would be the nearest you would get to a sitar of that day; a long-necked Indian lute).

Slightly further along was another man crouching down and playing a flute. In front of him was a woven basket, inside which, moving from side to side, was a rattlesnake, its movement synchronized along with the flute music. Cows were roaming free; some with coloured and decorated horns.

More or less in the centre of the market a crowd had gathered. Being inquisitive Killgore handed the reins of his horse to Eals and went to see what all the fuss was about.

Adrien and Eals began discussing where would be a good place to pick another warrior for the chess game from. When Killgore returned he said, "I think you should come and see."

Adrien, too, gave the reins of his horse to Eals and followed Killgore, pushing their way to the front of the crowd.

In the middle sat two men perched on stalls at a table opposite each other. Both were native brown men, with red coloured marks on their foreheads and both wore turbans upon their heads, but the most interesting thing was the game they were playing on a chequered board similar to the Caledonian courtyard floor.

The tiny pieces on the board were lovely carved wooden statuettes.

The two foreigners got close enough to make out that the carvings were made up of miniature elephants, horses and chariots, and foot soldiers. The two players were using dice to play this game.

No sooner had Adrien and Killgore got to the front than a massive commotion erupted. Through the middle of the gathered spectators came Hunnic soldiers, brushing people out of their way, grabbed the two participants, arrested them and knocking the board to the ground, they marched them away. There was uproar from the people that had gathered to watch the game, but these relatively peaceful people were soon silenced as the soldiers drew their curved swords.

The two travellers looked at each other. Then Adrien shouted out at the top of his voice, "Does any person here speak Latin?"

To their surprise a brown man standing next to them in a turban replied, "My friend."

Adrien replied, "Who are these men that they have taken away, and where have they been taken to?"

The brown man, shaking his head, said, "The great Aryabhata and Byaskari. Oh, oh I now fear their lives are in danger. Our oppressor Toramana has banned Caturanga (the name given to the early form of chess played in Gupta). Any two persons showing disobedience will be put to death."

Adrien whispered to Killgore, "We must help. These are our men."

Eals had tied up the horses and had found his way through the commotion to his leader.

Adrien said to Killgore, "Did you see where they went?"

"I was not looking, my comrade," said Killgore.

"Whom do you seek?" asked Eals.

Adrien turned to Eals. "We seek two men with brown skin stolen away by the soldiers."

Eals answered, "They passed me that way." He pointed to a narrow street that led from the market.

Wasting no time, Adrien bid his two companions to follow; briskly jogging, they followed the route Eals had seen the soldiers take, down a narrow street.

But it appeared others had also followed the soldiers.

A lot of people were gathered at the end of the street. They soon saw why the crowd had come to a standstill.

Over the top they could see six soldiers spread out in a line across the end of the street facing the crowd ready to prevent anyone from passing. Quick thinking Adrien thought it would be best to split up to get past the soldiers.

He ordered Eals to go to his right and Killgore to his left and to make their way down the edge of the crowded street.

He himself pushing his way forward, squeezed his way to the front. Once at the front he found himself face to face with a Hun soldier. The soldier was slightly tanned, and wore loose clothing with a loosely tied turban wrapped around his head. Slung over his left shoulder was a long bow and in his right hand he held a curved shaped sword.

Behind these soldiers were what is known as Ghats; extremely steep steps leading down to the Sacred River of the people of this land – the Holy River Ganges.

Once at the front, Adrien could see exactly what was going on. Just along and towards the bottom of the steps, a few soldiers were gathered. Next to them were the two men from the market square, hands bound and with heads held low, sitting on the steps.

Surveying the situation, Adrien decided to take matters into his own hands. After seeing the chess game being played in the market he felt he needed to talk to these men. The only thing that stood in his way was a small matter: their Hun captors.

So the Saxon knelt down on one knee. Almost instantly the people around pushed back leaving him space. Adrien's sword was hidden under his furs. He slid his right hand onto the handle of his sword. On seeing this, the soldier directly in front raised his sword high, ready as if to strike. In a split second Adrien drew his own weapon, and with two hands he took the full force of the Hun's curved sword as it came crashing down. He then kicked out his right foot behind the soldier's knees which sent the guard stumbling backwards down the Ghats steps.

Whilst this was happening, Eals had squeezed his way to the front on the right-hand side of the street (at the left the crowd was dense, slowing down Killgore's progress). Eals witnessed the soldier stumbling down the steps.

The other five guards on seeing this happen to their comrade, turned to attack Adrien. The soldier closest to Eals, swung the bow from his shoulder, as did another guard on the opposite side, taking an arrow from his quiver, loading his bow and he aimed an arrow straight at Adrien. Eals, thinking quickly, just as the Hun pulled his bow back and fired, gave the bow a firm push, which caused the arrow to just miss his leader's head by a whisker and fly past straight into the opposite bowman's chest.

This sent the crowd into a panic. Being peaceful people of Buddhist and mainly Hindu faith, as were the people who had followed Aryabhata and Byaskari, the crowd dispersed and tried to escape the fighting.

Eals then grabbed the bow from the back, strangling the Hun with his own bow.

Killgore eventually made it through the mayhem to the front.

Out of the six Hun soldiers holding back the mob two lay dead, three ended up at the bottom of the Ghats steps and one had fled.

This all happened very quickly. Of the few soldiers standing on the Ghats, two with swords drawn came to meet the travellers, and one ran away in the other direction.

Adrien fought through the middle of the oncoming Huns on his way to the prisoners, leaving Eals and Killgore to finish the job; he then set about cutting the Hindu prisoners free.

After setting the two men free, the next thing was to get back to their horses, or would that not be wise? That option was soon quashed as an arrow landed in the sole of Adrien's shoe. The first soldier who had fled had returned with more men.

Speedily ushering the two prisoners along, they all ran in the other direction with arrows flying past. Then to their horror, in the other direction the other Hun that had fled, had also returned with reinforcements; they were now trapped on the Ghats steps. Behind them on the top of the Ghats overlooking the river were towering buildings. Again the quick-thinking Adrien led the way up the steps towards an entrance of one of the buildings, where there was an open doorway.

All five ran up the steps and into the doorway, with arrows flying thick and fast from both directions; thankfully no one was hit.

The building was derelict inside; outside it was now dusk and the daylight was beginning to fade, so inside it was pitch black.

Once inside, either side of the doorway, was a small wall behind which Eals and Killgore took up post either side. Adrien shepherded the other men further into the darkness; it was not long before arrows relentlessly rained through the open door for several minutes.

Then the first Hun, bow at the ready, slowly crept through the doorway, followed closely by another. Eals and Killgore waited until the soldier was just inside, before hacking him and the second Hun down. More Huns attempted to enter but Eals and Killgore fought them back.

Meantime Adrien was trying to find an escape route in the dark.

After a while everything outside the front of the building went quiet; it looked as if the Saxons and the Pict had held their own.

The building was tall and the windows were high up.

All they could do was wait, but they would not be able to hold out for long. During all this time, Aryabhata and Byaskari had stayed silent and co-operative.

As darkness fell outside, nobody could be ready for what happened next.

A single arrow alight with fire flew into the building.

Adrien had an idea; he picked up the lit arrow, calling out to his comrades, "hold fast". He ran through to the back of the building, using the fire as a torch. The place was completely empty and right at the back he found a step, which was very worn and so surely had been much used over time. It wasn't long before the torch went out.

All of a sudden a barrage of fire-lit arrows flew into the building; the whole place was lit up. Adrien could see a wooden door above the worn steps; shoulder barging it he fell straight through the old rotten door. He shouted out to Eals and Killgore (who could hardly breathe), "follow me".

Leaving the blaze behind, all five swiftly made their way down a damp passage. Adrien had picked up another torch. The passage was long and led downward quite a way before leading back up a steep incline. The heat in the confined walkway was sweltering and almost unbearable and the passage was roughly about two hundred metres long. Before too long, and now in complete darkness, they came to another locked door.

After feeling around, a bolt was found and easily unlocked. Opening the door they found themselves stepping out onto a deserted street.

Knowing the city well, the two natives took the lead and signalled them to take a left turn. No sooner had they walked a few metres, they heard the sound of Hunnic soldiers on horseback up ahead. So they hid in the shadows while they passed by.

It did not take too long to get out and away from the city.

Once away, the communication between them was slow going as Aryabhata and Byaskari spoke Sanskrit (an Indo-Aryan language). But they were well educated students both extremely clever and could both speak a little Latin. They explained that they had come to Papaliputra to study in the university.

Both men were uncannily similar in stature and height; both were smallish but could be distinguished by their different-coloured robes; Aryabhata wore faded orange whilst Byaskari wore olive. Their garments were wrapped round their legs like a dress and draped up over their left shoulders; both had long beaded necklaces around their bare chests.

As Byaskari was from Lanka, an island that lay many miles south, they decided it would be wise to leave this city and go to his homeland.

They made their way south to the island of Lanka, which was a beautiful place. The weather was hot and humid, which was hard for the Saxons and the Pict from the tiny island of Britannia to adjust to. On the crossing over to Lanka they were met by beautiful palm trees and yellow beaches.

Byaskari lived a long way into the island on the edge of a jungle; to get to the village they had to ride on elephants.

The village was small and the Hindu's mother still lived there. He came from a line of scientists. His grandfather and father had come from Papaliputra. His father had moved to Lanka before he was born, but had died only a few years ago.

There was much Adrien wanted to learn from these men, which is why he had travelled south with them. On reaching Lanka he decided to stay for a while.

The house was more like a shack. It had two rooms, the door to one of them (which was just a couple of planks of wood) had not been opened for some time. In fact it had not been moved since Byaskari had left a couple of years previously.

Byaskari took away the two planks. As a young teenager, before leaving to study in the Gupta Empire, this is where he had done his work, as had his father before him.

It was full of weird instruments and writings, written in inks made from berries, insects and other ingredients.

The travellers didn't really understand the significance of many of these, but there was one thing Adrien did understand, a chequered board with simple carved figures, so unlike the elaborate pieces on the board at the Papaliputra market place.

The travellers were glad to change out of their hot heavy Viking furs; their host gave them thin simple robes to wear.

During their stay (which ended up being a couple of months) the Hindus taught their visitors to count using an abacus, and to write simple sentences, which helped the two lesser educated Saxons, but what Adrien really enjoyed was the late afternoons when they would play caturanga (their form of chess).

Aryabhata taught clever strategies, but this was a different game to the one in Caledonia and it seemed as if it were only half the game, as to make a move you had to use a dice.

Whilst playing against Byaskari one afternoon, Byaskari told Adrien of his grandfather (as he spoke he constantly wobbled his head from side to side) who had told him when he was younger that many years ago he had taught a Magician from the east that travelled the world in 418AD, who had learnt a similar game in Persia. This Magician had spent time arguing with his grandfather about how he thought both games could be rolled into one.

Adrien realised that this Magician was the same Magician who had explained the game of chess in Caledonia on the big chequered courtyard floor. It was in fact none other than Wei Po-Yang himself.

Early one evening Byaskari took Adrien and Aryabhata to a lake nearby where they rowed out to the middle in a small boat. The bright moon was just coming up and they spent many hours in the boat. Aryabhata showed how the moon and the stars slowly moved across the sky from one side of the lake to the other, before disappearing.

The following evening they took the boat out to exactly the same spot as the previous evening. Then Aryabhata explained that he had discovered that the Earth was round, and the moon and stars had moved full circle around the world during that day, to the same place where they had started, and the sun lit up the moon as it too moved round; he described this as the Earth rotating on its axis.

He also referred to midnight as ardha-ratri. They talked of his works on the Zodiac, and the Elements, referring to them as Water, Fire, Earth, and Air.

A lot of what the two scientists discussed – geometric and alphabetical letters – went over the Westerners' heads.

The time soon came for the travellers to move on. Byaskari was very interested in going to Caledonia and learning about the game. For Adrien he would be a major asset on his side of the board. Aryabhata decided he would go back to Gupta. So it was agreed Byaskari would join the Saxon to take his place as a Pontifex (Bishop) on the back row of the board.

So they all left Lanka and headed north.

THE KING AND THE BENGAL TIGER

Back on the mainland, the mode of transport they used to travel was by elephant. Aryabhata had instructed and paid for two local guides to accompany the travellers on their journey through this land.

Adrien was interested in heading east, but first they had to go northwards for many days. It wasn't long before the already uncomfortable elephant back began to take its toll, leaving everybody irritable.

A few days later they began to hit woodland that gradually turned into endless jungle.

One day, whilst trudging through the sticky jungle, the elephants became restless, especially the one mounted by the guide at the front, and after a few more paces it came to a standstill, refusing to budge any further and waving its trunk furiously from side to side. The guide started beating his stick on the side of the beast but to no avail as it still refused to shift.

Soon everyone realised why, as a massive tiger appeared pacing towards them. After all, this was Bengal tiger territory.

Eals, who was next in line behind the guide, drew his sword.

As the majestic animal fearlessly padded forward, not making a sound, the elephant with the guide at the front suddenly bolted away to the side, leaving Eals looking into the tiger's eyes, which burned like fire; strangely it had blood all down the front of its coat below its neck.

With Eal's elephant trying to back up, the tiger suddenly crouched as it was now close enough to attack, and Eals decided to slip off, sword at the ready. In a split second the tiger pounced towards the Saxon, both clashed in mid-air; Eals managed to swing his sword and swiped at the giant cat, before hitting the floor with a huge thud – his sword had cut straight through the air! The tiger had completely vanished before the travellers' eyes. The Saxon lay on the ground badly winded; fortunately no blood had been drawn, but you would have thought the clash would have at least left Eals injured.

The elephants calmed down once the tiger had gone. Adrien and Killgore helped Eals to his feet; still in shock he said, "Sire, did I kill the cat?"

Adrien replied, "Not exactly, but we did see that you should have. I think we should move on hastily from this cursed wood before this creature returns."

Continuing on, the dense tropical forest began to thin; it was then that a startling noise was heard a bit like a horn being blown, and a party of five or so men came into view. The men were dressed in animal furs, and had obviously heard the elephants lumbering through the jungle.

The leader of this small group yelled up to the Westerners in Latin, "Morning. What a beautiful day to go hunting." This man was of average height and had straight black hair and a darker skin tone, with a slight high-bone structure and a visible scar which ran down the left side of his face. He wore a tiger fur with a belt loosely tied round his waist, and his feet were bare. He was a charming, cheerful fellow with a likable smile upon his face as he spoke.

Adrien yelled back, "We come in peace. I am Adrien and these are my friends. We are from the island of Britannia far away beyond the Roman Empire."

The man looked puzzled and replied, "I am King Taung. Welcome to my delightful kingdom. You will be guests at my palace. Come, follow me!"

Eventually they came to the grounds of the palace, which was surrounded by a brick wall that they entered through an opened archway, and which backed onto the jungle.

Taung turned to his visitors. "Welcome to my humble abode. Adrien and your friends get down from your animals; they also look like they need rest." Clapping his hands three young servants appeared whom he ordered to prepare food.

Taung's palace was enormous and the surrounding gardens were very well kept, the grass was short, slightly yellow in colour having been scorched by the hot sun of that land. The palace itself was built of bricks (much larger than the manufactured bricks of today).

They were actually at the rear end of the palace. Round the perimeter ran a sheltered path, which they followed round to the front; the sheltered roof was supported by pillars. At the front of the palace was a large statue of a tiger carved out of a single jade stone.

Inside the palace they were taken through a circular shaped room, from which a stairway ran up to another level, but their host took them to a very big hall, with a long wooden table with seats on both sides, which was laden with many exotic fruits from papaya to grapefruit. Servants stood next to the table. Taung sat, inviting his visitors, "Be seated, weary travellers and enjoy the fruits before you."

The Saxons and, of course, the Pict were glad to get a break from the uncomfortable elephants.

Taung had a lot to say for himself, in fact he didn't really seem to be interested in where his visitors had come from, but at the same time he was extremely hospitable.

He went on, "My new friends, feel free to stay for a while. Today you may join me. Shortly, I have some business to attend, then we shall hunt for tonight's feast."

As they possibly could, a servant came running into the hall and bowed before the king, before shouting out, "Myarajas is here, your majesty".

Taung promptly stood and bid them follow, as he made his way to the front door. Just before stepping out he turned to

Adrien. "Excuse me this is the business I need to resolve. My mother's personal guard, an old Nanzhao soldier from Yunnan, has many faults."

At this Taung casually strolled outside shouting, in ancient Pyi, the spoken language of the land, "So, old man, I hear many stories of your idle, loose tongue, of your hatred for me and my house and of how you wish to dispose of me forever, whispered around the dark corners of Sri Kesri. Remind me of what pay is owed to you and I will gladly let you leave after enjoying the duel which will give you the chance you desire to take my life as well."

The old guard Myarajas screamed back, "I have waited for this day to rid this land of such an evil. After I have taken your life, I will burn your palace, and the evil that lurks behind its walls, to the ground. So come! I am ready." Taung's challenger was tall and looked quite athletic for an older man. He wore a red bandana wrapped around his head and a tight belt wrapped around his grey tunic. Adrien couldn't help but think this old warrior was going to kill. Besides he obviously looked like he had a chip on his shoulder. In his hands he held two short thin swords, one side of each having a sharp edge.

A servant ran up to Taung and gave him two similar short swords, both sheaved, with ivory handles.

Taung walked past the tiger statue to the big open lawn to face his foe. A servant shouted for the duel to commence. Myarajas drew both his swords, but Taung left his swords still sheathed.

The old man screamed, "Even now you insult me," before launching himself forward with furious venom raining.

Round and round they moved, covering much of the lawn as they fought. Taung soaked up the pressure; twisting and turning, both moved swiftly and for several minutes the duel continued before Taung unleashed a flurry of powerful hits which overwhelmed and disarmed his opponent, knocking him to the ground. The bout was over. Taung was the victor.

The old man lay on the ground. The king walked over to the same servant who had orchestrated the contest, and who held a small velvet bag in his hand. Taung swapped his weapons for the bag, walked back and threw the bag at the guard saying, "Get up, Myarajas. Inside are ten silver coins. Now get out of my sight. Tell anyone in the city who disrespects me or my household, that next time I will draw my swords from their sheaths."

Myarajas got to his feet and staggered out of the palace grounds.

Taung walked back to Adrien, Eals and Killgore. He was so calm and had not even broken into a sweat. He then said casually, with a wry smile on his face, "Adrien and your friends, let's go hunting." A servant brought a small knife and a short hollow pipe and gave them to the king.

Taung led them back to the rear of the palace and back out of the open archway into the jungle, taking them a different way than they had originally come. They wandered round the outside close to the palace walls, where much of the jungle had been cut away, leaving massive open areas, and the travellers found themselves looking down onto the most amazing immense irrigation system, with small narrow streams running downwards dividing the hillside into different sections, looking like what could best be described as a patchwork quilt.

Adrien questioned Taung, "What is the meaning of this?"

The king replied, "These fields have fed the Pyi people of Sri Kestri for a long time and was built by my forefathers."

They continued past the fields and back towards the jungle. Following the edge of the jungle, Taung dropped his voice to just above a whisper and he walked slowly. Turning to his visitors he uttered, "At this point we must no longer talk." No sooner had he said these words, he froze like a statue and lifted his right hand, signalling the party to halt. Ahead in the thicket, grazing in the long grass, they spotted a sandy coloured deer with a black-and-white tail.

Taung slowly crouched, urging the others to do the same. He then disappeared quietly into the long grass, and all Adrien, Eals and Killgore could do was wait to see what happened next; the deer still continued to graze. After a while they heard beyond the deer a series of low calling noises, which they soon realised was the sound of Taung's pipe. Startled at the noise, the deer lifted its head; the noise came again. Strangely enough the deer stopped grazing and made its way through the undergrowth towards where Taung was lying in wait. Although quite a way off, the travellers could see clearly then. To their amazement, in the blink of an eye Taung leapt out of the grass and slit the dear's throat, killing the animal instantly. Adrien was in awe at how skilfully the king hunted his prey.

Taung hoisted his prize onto his shoulders and, with great pride, he carried it back to the palace.

That evening they dined on the rich venison, soaked in various spices, at the table in the big hall. The king commented on how good it was to catch one's own food. Apart from that, he remained silent until the food was finished and the servants had cleared the table.

Then the king crossed his right leg over his left and slouched back in his tall chair with a vessel of wine in his hands. In his low deep voice he began to talk. "So, my friends, let me tell you my lonely story. I have always lived here in this palace. My father, the great Taung, ruled the Pyi people of Sri Kestri, as did his father before him. His household was set in the centre of the city and he came to the throne at a tender age. He was deeply religious, as are the people of this land, and much loved by his subjects, until he met and fell for my mother, who was herself a Pyi, but agnostic towards the faith. They soon married and due to these circumstances the monks advised my father to leave the blessed household. It was then he built this palace on the edge of the city. He remained the king as it was his birth right.

"Shortly after moving into the new palace, I was born and named after my father. It soon came to light that my mother practised both black and white magic and was deeply interested in the occult. She tried to block me from being ordained into the faith of my forefathers, so secretly my father took me to be blessed by the reluctant monks. As I grew, my mother, behind my father's back, tried to teach me in the ways of her dark magic."

Taung took a sip of his wine. The sun was now setting outside, throwing its last rays of the day through the open windows, and the statue of the tiger on the lawn, which could be seen from the hall, glistened and shone in the light. Servants came and put lit candles on the table.

The king continued his story, keeping Adrien and his companions transfixed. "One morning, my father was found dead. I was immediately taken to my father's original household, where I, barely a grown man, was crowned king of Sri Kestri.

"With my father dead, my mother now freely practised inside the palace walls. She was a very domineering force, especially towards me, and sometimes I had to ask myself who was ruling this land. She had many enemies in Sri Kestri and, fearing for her life, she decided to employ guards to protect her from across the northern border; Nanzhoa warriors from Yunnan.

"During these times I made myself scarce, attending to matters of my people and hunting in the jungle. On one of these days whilst out hunting, I found a lone tiger cub next to its dead mother, which I brought back to the palace. My own mother saw favour with the cub, tending and nurturing it whist letting it roam the grounds. It was not long until the cub's father, a majestic tiger, found the cub and boldly entered the garden. The reunion between the two cats was heart-warming. The tiger would visit the cub every few days.

"Things in the palace were not good. Myarajas, my mother's own personal guard, did not agree with my mother's open use of black magic and she refused to pay his wages within the time permitted. As you have witnessed, Myarajas and I never saw eye to eye."

Taung's voice now grew slower, pausing between sentences.

"Then one day I woke to the screaming of my mother's voice out in the gardens. I hurried down to find my mother tightly holding the bloodied, lifeless body of the tiger cub; during the night someone had killed the cub with a sword. To this day I have never found the culprit. My personal view is that it was a Pyi who resented my mother inviting down the Nanzhoa warriors. I ordered the men from Yunnan to leave the palace, and I left the palace to seek the culprit in the city.

"Whilst I was gone, the cub's father returned. Finding the cub dead he took revenge, killing my mother and a servant. Picking up the lifeless cub, he returned to the jungle.

"Coming back to the palace later that day, I found the body of my mother. Although I felt little remorse, I took my sword and went alone into the jungle in search of the cat. For three days and two nights I searched, and on the third day before sundown the tiger found me in a clearing on the jungle floor. I was tired and hungry and feeling weak.

"The tiger's eyes met with mine. This was going to be a duel between two kings. What happened next was a blur. As the tiger pounced towards me, I thrust my blade deep into his heart whilst he left me permanently scarred. As the beast died that night, I looked deep into his sad eyes into his very soul;

they say animals do not have souls, but this tiger did. Rumour has it, his spirit haunts the jungle." At this the travellers all looked at each other.

Taung continued, "On my return, my heart felt heavy for what I had done, so I had the stone in the garden cut in his memory. After all these events took place, I have tried to look after my kingdom, serving and strengthening her in the best way I can, for I know the day will come when the people of Yunnan will invade. The Pyi people still see no favour in their eyes towards me, and for me this is a lonely place. At times, I have wanted to hand the land over to the monks, leave this cursed palace and seek my fortune elsewhere."

It was now pitch black outside and the candles inside gave little light.

"Friends, it is now time to sleep," Taung went on. "There are many rooms in my palace. I would advise you sleep together in the same room. Be not alarmed by any unusual happenings that take place within these walls."

Adrien was left uneasy by these words but said nothing.

The king bid them goodnight and disappeared out of the hall and up the stairs.

The three travellers followed a servant (who held three candles) up the stone stairway. The noise of their footsteps on the stone floor gave out a dull echo. Once up the stairs, Killgore whispered to Adrien, "I prefer to sleep alone." With a humorous tone, Adrien replied, "I agree with you Pict. I want a good night's sleep!"

The corridor was long with rooms either side, some with doors and some without. Eals opted to take one of the first rooms with a door, and the servant gave him a candle. Closing the door behind him, he found himself in a simple medium-sized room, with an open window; on the floor was a bed made up of long grass covered with deer fur.

Nevertheless, it was the picture that hung above the bed that caught Eals' attention. And so he held the candle up to take a good look. The picture of a tiger, woven in silk and encrusted with jewels set on a black background, shone in the flickering light. After inspecting the tapestry, the Saxon lay back on the comfortable bed.

The one thing all three of the travellers were trying to get used to was the constant, sometimes unbearable, heat. Taking off most of his clothing Eals fell asleep.

Moments later he woke to the feeling of clawing down his naked back. Writhing in agony, he reached for his sword. The candle was almost burnt out, but he could see that there was nothing or nobody in the room. The pain was excruciating. Reaching his arm up his back he could feel the drip of blood trickling down. This is impossible, he thought, sitting down on the edge of the bed, and looking up at the picture he noticed the claws of the tiger now had blood on them. In a furious rage he slashed the picture with his sword, cutting it into tiny pieces.

After a while he settled back down, still smarting from his wounds.

The patter of raindrops could now be heard outside; the moon was high in the sky. Just as his heavy eyelids were beginning to shut, the candle now burnt out, he noticed at the end of the bed the figure of an old woman. All of a sudden he was wide awake and terrified. In his left hand he still held his sword, but he froze with fear. He was trying to talk but the words never came out. Because of the dark he could not see the face of the old woman.

Eals finally collected himself and stood to his feet, and the figure of the woman vanished, gliding straight through the door. Still in shock, Eals told himself, "Keep calm. You are Eals, commander of his lordship Adrien's army.

He lifted up the wooden handle to the door and gingerly stepped into the pitch black corridor, feeling his way along the brick wall, when suddenly the corridor was lit up by a flash of lightning, and Eals saw in that split second the figure of the woman standing on the top of the stairs. The lightning was followed by an almighty clap of thunder.

Adrien and Killgore had taken separate rooms further up the corridor. The storm had woken Killgore, and he had heard the creak of the door to Eals' room open and shut, so he decided to get up.

He, too, stepped out into the pitch black corridor and made his way towards the stairs, feeling his way along the corridor wall.

Eals was moving along the wall cautiously, sword drawn at the ready. He had the fright of his life when Killgore touched his hand and they both nearly jumped out of their skin; fortunately the second lightning flash lit the corridor just as their swords met. They were now at the top of the stairway.

Killgore questioned Eals, "Why are you moving around in this darkness?"

Eals replied, "This palace is more cursed than the jungle."

Both warriors stepped silently down the stone stairway.

Halfway down lightning flashed again, and once again Eals saw the woman, this time at the foot of the stairway. Killgore saw nothing but commented to his friend, "This house has a very bad feel. I can sense evil all around."

Eals replied, "When the light flashes, can you see the old woman?"

Killgore said, "Comrade, I see nothing."

Once down the stairs, they entered the hall. Although still pouring with rain, the moon lit the hall through the big open windows.

Suddenly, as they were walking past the long table and looking outside, they both gasped in disbelief, as there on the lawn pacing up and down was the tiger from the jungle. Eals whispered, "That's him; that's the ghost of the tiger Taung was talking about and that is the same cat that attacked us in the jungle." Just as he was finishing speaking, the majestic tiger stopped and looked straight at them. They swiftly moved to the top end of the hall and through to where the kitchens were.

Not even these brave men were ready for what they were about to witness next. In the middle of the large kitchen, covering most of the floor, was a circle drawn out of chalk. Inside the circle was drawn a six-pointed star and at the tip of each point was a long lit candle, but the most frightening thing was the old woman standing in the centre. She wore a hooded cloak which covered her face. This time Killgore saw her as well. The lightning outside became more frequent. Both soldiers were terrified; at the same time they turned and ran back through the hall to the stairway, almost tripping in the darkness over the first step. They clambered up; reaching the top they stopped and got themselves together, but this only lasted for a minute as the lightening flashed again and there stood the old woman at the bottom of the stairs.

Eals spoke, "We must wake his lordship Adrien."

Finding his room, they woke their leader. Eals said, "Your lordship, we must leave here; this palace is full of evil spirits."

Adrien trusted his friend and could tell by the sincerity of his voice he was telling the truth. He replied in his tired voice, "Eals, I will not leave until I have spoken with the king. We must find him!"

The last time they had seen Taung he had been walking up the stairs. So they decided to continue up the corridor.

Quietly, Adrien called out as they passed each room in a deep voice, "Taung, Taung."

The corridor came to an end and a closed door hid a flight of narrow stone steps winding up to the roof. On reaching the roof the rain had now subsided. The travellers saw before them several tall objects, triangular in shape would be the best way to describe the objects which were in fact stupas made mainly of gold.

Beyond the stupas was a flat roof. To their surprise, in the centre of the rooftop was a purple–and-green fire. Drawing closer, they saw the fire was burning in a circle around what looked like a human. It was indeed a human – none other than King Taung. Adrien started shouting out to wake him but he didn't even stir, so Adrien then tried to step through the flames but he couldn't even get close due to the immense heat. Looking round, he found a stone to throw but it never broke through the fire wall.

Turning to his restless companions he said, "Men we still have some time till the sun rises. We will stay here and try and get some sleep."

The Westerners were woken by Taung, who was surprised to see them on the roof. The sun was already getting hot.

Over breakfast, Eals told of the night's events, about which Taung seemed uninterested, until Eals showed the ten deep claw marks which ran right down his back, Taung called for a servant to tend to the wounds. Adrien asked Taung, "Why is it you sleep on the roof of the palace surrounded by flames?"

The king answered, "The fire, which comes from oils found in the northern mountains, protects my soul from the demons and evil spirits that roam these walls from the twelfth hour."

Adrien told the king that it was time for them to move on but he offered Taung a position on the chequered floor at the Caledonian castle. Taung accepted without hesitation. After all, with his hunting and fighting skills and knowledge of the dark side he would be a great asset to the Saxon's army.

Before leaving, Taung ordered his servants to bring the three travellers leather-soled shoes for their bare feet, held together with straps, as he insisted that walking barefoot through the jungle would not be wise. Unfortunately the elephants had been taken back by the guides the previous day to their own land.

THE COUNT

Darinus was dreading facing Caesar. But all the same he returned to Rome with his friend Brutus.

The morning before the afternoon he was due to meet Caesar, Darinus met with Julian, "Julian, I need you to meet me at the gate of the Imperial Palace. Select ten of my most able bodyguards who fought under my command in the battle for the island, ready a worthy horse for me. I will be holding council with the Emperor Honorius, may he be blessed by the gods. On my signal, be alert and ready to depart. Now make haste."

Once inside the palace Darinus was again acquainted with Brutus, who had been elsewhere in the city that morning.

Together they walked through the long echoing corridors (a messenger had gone before them to inform Caesar his visitors had arrived). Brutus questioned Darinus' cold silence, "Why are you mute, my friend?" The Roman general chose to ignore this question and remained silent. He had far more important things on his mind than the concern of his friend.

Once again they met Honorius Caesar on the balcony that overlooked the palace gardens; both generals knelt down on one knee before the Emperor.

In a deep voice he said, "Look at this glorious city. Its fate is in your hands, my generals."

At this point Darinus stood. He was trembling from head to toe; in a shaky voice he mumbled, "My Caesar may you be blessed by the gods, your humble servant regrettably cannot accept this blessed offer of leading your army."

He then produced the map and held it out to Caesar.

Shocked at what he was hearing, Caesar turned to face the Roman general (up until now he had been staring out of the window). His face was turning redder by the second. Snatching the map, Caesar briefly studied it. "Explain," he commended.

"Emperor, I acquired the canvas map whilst on my quest to take back our island when I met a man from the east." Darinus continued to tell the story.

"Games and trickery" (games) Caesar roared. "Games, traitor." Next Honorius called for the guards.

Immediately four guards entered the room, two from just outside the door and two from the balcony, but Darinus was ready for the reaction from Caesar, lunging forward he grabbed the map from Caesar and drew his sword.

"Guards, arrest this traitor," Caesar ordered. Darinus was too quick for the guards and managed to fight his way out of the room without injuring anyone. He tore through the Imperial Palace corridors and out of the front gate and down the steps, where Julian and his very own bodyguard were waiting. "Let us make haste," Darinus screamed as he leaped up onto his horse.

One guard who had given chase had kept up with Darinus and was just a few yards behind. As the guard ran down the steps Julian jumped off his horse and charged towards him. Raising his sword he struck the guard, killing him with one blow.

The twelve soldiers rode towards the North gate galloping through the streets of Rome. The gate guards, on seeing Darinus' purple cloak, let him and his men out of the gate without delay.

The party of twelve rode north eastwards for two days solid. Fortunately events that had taken place at the Imperial Palace had happened so quickly that they had managed to leave Rome, giving Caesar's men little time to follow.

Darinus was furious with Julian for killing the guard, which meant they would now be banished from Rome, with no chance of them returning whilst Caesar Honorius was in power.

Eventually they arrived at the banks of the Danubus River; Darinus was now using the map to guide them.

On arriving at the banks of the huge river, they set up camp on the south side.

It was a pitch black night. Little did they know that during that night the year had changed and they woke the following morning in the spring of 445AD.

They crossed the Danubus River not knowing that they had entered the Empire of the Hun.

On reaching the other side, they turned sharply to the right, and headed east.

Darinus planned to get to Colonia where he could recruit more pieces for his side of the chess board. He would not have to wait too long.

After a day or so, the landscape became flat, and they found themselves on the edge of a marsh. Darinus and his men were now in what is known nowadays as Transylvania.

Coming the other way towards them, also on horseback, was a band of about fifteen Hun. The Huns were as shocked as the Romans to see the opposite party, as this was now their territory. There wasn't any time for negotiating; swords were drawn on both sides. Darinus was a bit confused, as he had never seen such men dressed in loose clothing with such headwear before.

The Hun fought better than the Romans on horseback. As the fighting commenced, both parties were eventually drawn into the marsh.

Darinus soon found he was engaged in combat with the leader of the Huns. Both leaders slipped off their horses, and the fighting took them further and further into the marsh.

Darinus was an excellent swordsmen, probably one of, if not the best, in the Roman army, but he found his opponent to be relentless and his sword was made of stronger metal than his own.

During the fighting, the thick fog was making visibility difficult, when something extraordinary happened – just above their heads a swarm of large black bats appeared, startling the fighters.

Almost in a blink of an eye, the bats disappeared and a tall knight appeared dressed in gold and silver armour. Twisting and turning, he weaved in and out of the fighters, killing and maiming only the Huns.

Darinus was still in full combat when his opponent's sword struck with such force it shattered his own sword into several pieces. In the next instant, the gold and silver knight turned to fight the leader of the Huns, who seeing his comrades lying dead, ran for his horse.

Darinus turned to watch him run, then he spun back around, but the knight was gone. Up above the swarm of bats had reappeared then disappeared, and the fog was now so thick you could hardly see your hand in front of your face.

Darinus called out to Julian, who instantly responded. Only two Romans had been killed.

After a short while, the fog lifted slightly. There was not a single sign of the Huns' dead bodies, all the horses had bolted and the marsh underfoot was making it difficult to walk.

It seemed Darinus and his men had lost their sense of direction and did not know which way to turn, as at every step the marsh was getting deeper. After hours of aimless wandering, the fog began to thicken.

Then, just yards in front, in the middle of nowhere there appeared a beautiful woman, tall with long jet black hair, almost naked, she stood on a stone and behind her was a path.

She beckoned to the weary troops, and then she turned and walked up the path. The Romans followed her in silence. After a while she reached a door. Both Darinus and Julian's eyes were transfixed on this beautiful creature. She opened the door and entered.

Above the doorway was a silver plaque which the Latin-speaking Romans did not understand as the language in which it was written was Transylvanian. It read CINE AR TREBUI SA INCHEIE PAL DATORIEI SALE CU CONTA SAU SA PLATEASCA CU VIATE SA (he who enters should pay his debt with the count or pay with his life).

Once inside, they found the woman had vanished. In front of them was a long corridor dimly lit by candlelight. Swords were drawn (except Darinus who no longer had his). On entering, the door swung shut behind them.

With no sign of the woman, they slowly crept along the corridor, which opened out into an octagonal-shaped room. This was the most extraordinary room, with mirrors all round the outside. Except these were not ordinary mirrors, they were made of smoke, not glass.

The Romans could see their own reflections through the smoke, looking back at them. Whilst gazing at himself, and trying to touch the mirror, Darinus noticed the beautiful woman from the marsh standing directly behind his right shoulder. He swiftly turned, but she was nowhere to be seen.

Glimpsing the opposite mirror, he once again noticed the woman standing, this time behind his left shoulder. Again he spun round and once again she was gone.

"Men! This domain is cursed. We must depart." They attempted to leave the way they had come in, but the corridor had changed and it now led to some steps.

Julian took the lead, down the corridor and up the steps, which led up into a massive square room with a high ceiling, where hung a wooden chandelier laden with lit candles.

Seated at the far end of the room on a throne-like chair, was a man dressed in black with a gold star-shaped medallion around his neck. He had long black hair; the reflection of the candles could be seen in his black pupils.

On one side of the room was a roaring fire and either side of this man were beautiful dark-haired women, three on one side and four on the other.

"Romans, why were you in the marsh"?

Darinus stepped forward and replied, "We desire to find our way to Colonia."

This man spoke good Latin, although his accent was guttural. "Colonia! Why would a Roman want to go to Colonia? It is a Hun stronghold. You need many more men."

At this point Darinus realised that he and his men had crossed a time line, as the Chinese magician at Caledonia had explained would happen.

Darinus asked, "Sire, in which year are we?"

"You are in the year 445, Roman."

Darinus continued to question the man, "Pray tell me your name."

"My name is ISTVANIA, you and your men owe me a debt you must pay. I saved your lives whilst you wandered into the marsh."

At this Istvania stood. He was extremely tall. He walked over to a table, on which stood a gold goblet.

Although he was now dressed in a long black robe, Darinus realised this was the gold-and-silver knight they had encountered in the marsh. "Istvania, who were the men in the marsh and why did you spare the leader his life?"

"Roman, I am a Gepid, and come from a long line of Gepid gypsies who emigrated to this land. As a child, my parents were murdered by the Hun, the heathen Pagans you encountered in the marsh are the Hun, Attila is the chief of the Hun Empire along with his brother Bleda. Their empire stretches all the way to the Baltic sea. Attila plans to assassinate Bleda at an opportune time this year, leaving him sole Emperor of this huge empire. When he succeeds, life for my people will become easier as Attila will take his fight to Gallia.

"Roman, it is clear you have crossed a time line. I do not know how or why, but now in Rome your people fear the Hun tribes and most of all Attila the Hun. The Roman Priscus tells of Attila's sword and how it came to his hands by miraculous means."

Darinus could not take his eyes off the beautiful woman from the marsh that stood to the right of Istvania's chair. Istvania had noticed.

"Roman, these are my concubines." He picked up the gold goblet from the table. Lifting it up to his lips, he took a sip and as he tipped his head right back, his blood shot eyes started to roll, then with a deep sigh, he groaned, "This warms my cold heart; the taste of the Huns." The goblet was filled with the blood of the dead Hunnic fighters he had slaughtered in the marsh.

Striding over to the Romans, Istvania held out the vessel. Julian stepped forward and took the cup. At this, Darinus drew Julian's own sword and held it up to his throat, forbidding him to drink the human blood.

Istvania took back the vessel and handed it to his concubines to drink.

"Romans, tonight you can rest here by the fire, for tomorrow you will pay your debt."

At this, he left the room, taking his concubines with him.

The following day, before sunrise, Darinus and his men were woken by Istvania. Bleary eyed, they followed him outside to the front of the mansion (the marshland was towards the back) and up a rugged rocky path. Because it was still dark, they had to follow the outline of Istvania; the path led uphill and into woodland.

All of a sudden, the quiet was broken by a high shrilled howl close by, which was met by another howl; there was a pack of wolves very near.

Then, as they passed a clearing in the wood there stood the pack of wild wolves. Istvania stopped and the wolves ceased howling; seemingly to be very comfortable in his presence, they lay down.

The party moved on, and eventually arrived at a hole in the hillside, which was the entrance to a gold mine. The hole was narrow and either side was rock. Istvania owned this massive mine; most of the people in the country worked in the mine. He looked after, and protected the country and the people, mostly from the Huns with whom he currently traded gold and silver. He was widely acknowledged as the Count of the land.

Parts of the mine's corridors were very narrow. The soldiers were taken a long way down under the ground; the mine was very deep due to many years of digging and mining the ore.

"Romans, you shall dig for gold until your debt is paid." This was the first time Istvania had spoken that day. At this he left.

A worker gave them the required tools to smash the rocks and dig with, and Darinus ordered his men to start work. So with picks they hit away at the stone, Julian in a half-hearted way. The day dragged on until Julian threw down his pick and snarled, "Darinus, we cannot work as slaves. We are Romans. Surely this is not acceptable?"

At this, Darinus placed down his pick on the floor and replied, "Julian, for once you speak with sense." The general was an upright man and true to his word. As far as he was concerned they would repay their debt by other means. He said, "Men put down your tools."

They had been working in a large open area; the entrance to this part of the mine was narrow and only one person at a time could fit through. Darinus went to walk through, but was stopped; it was as if he had walked into an invisible door. He tried again, but with the same result; next Julian tried, but he couldn't get out either.

All this time, sitting next to the exit, was a grubby young boy. He had sat there all day; if a candle had failed he had lit it and he had also brought water throughout the day for the workers.

Darinus crouched down next to the lad, and in a soft voice he said, "Istvania, I need to talk with Istvania." The frightened boy stared blankly. Darinus repeated, "Istvania, Istvania." Then inexpertly Julian leaned over his leaders shoulder and shouted at the top of his voice, "Istvania! Istvania!" At this, the young boy leapt to his feet and ran straight through the exit.

An hour passed, and then the boy returned and whispered, "Istvania." This time, the Romans were able to walk through the opening, and they followed the boy through the narrow twisted walkways of the mine. Surely if the Romans had attempted to escape from the mine, left to their own devices, they would never have surfaced again.

When reaching the opening, the moon was high – they had been in the pit for the whole day.

On arriving back at the mansion they found the Gepid once again in his hall with his concubines. Darinus said to Istvania, "I will make an offer to pay the debt which we owe. I offer you a coveted square in my chosen elite army on the chequered Caledonian courtyard floor. Should you accept you will stand high on the back line as a Pontifex." Darinus went on to explain, showing the map. Istvania had already realised they had crossed a time change so it did not take much persuasion; he would take his place at the Caledonian Castle when the time came.

That night Istvania allowed the Romans to stay one more night. He gave them Hunnic clothing to wear, as the Romans attire would not be appropriate as they were planning on going to Colonia. He also handed Darinus a new sword to replace the one Attila broke in the marsh.

Darinus woke early before light. Julian, who usually slept by his side, was gone. He woke the rest of his bodyguards, and then set about looking for Julian who was finally found in one of the towers. To Darinus' horror in the concubines' quarters, Julian had woken to see Istvania leaving for the mine, and had taken his chance. The general was livid and immediately ordered Julian to dress.

The Romans exchanged their dress for the Hunnic garments and left the count's mansion. On leaving the mansion, they found ten horses had been left for them.

TRAVELLING CIRCUS

The city of Colonia lay to the east. Drawing nearer to the old capital of the province of Darcia, the roads which had been Roman built grew wider, but recently they had become overgrown in patches. Obviously, since the Romans had left, the upkeep and maintenance had become slack to non-existent.

As the party got closer to the city, Darinus halted at a fork in the road. Observing the map, he decided to turn south. It was clear Colonia would be overrun with the Huns, and Huns were leaving and entering the city continually.

The Roman general would take his men south to pick up the Silk Road that linked Konstantinopel to Asia; a popular trading route.

Darinus was excited at the possibility of stepping outside the borders of the Roman Empire; he might even make it to the end of the world and look over the edge.

After many days on horseback, the landscape was changing. Konstantinopel was given a wide birth as, dressed as Huns, it would be unwise to pass through the gates of the great city.

The Silk Road was busy, and the travellers only stopped to sleep and eat. Food was easier to find once on the Silk trail for their gold Roman coins went a long way.

The road passed through Armenia, Media, Parthia and then on, crossing the wide Oxus River that runs into west Asia. The road dipped down a slope towards the Oxus, where a narrow bridge spanned the river.

The Romans found themselves passing the most unusual convoy of brightly coloured wagons along with brightly coloured people in a long procession - the front almost on the bridge. Just as they passed a bright blue wagon in the middle of the procession, a young man dressed in a burgundy velvet top, baggy shorts and a dirty white turban upon his head, walking barefoot next to the wagon, shouted, "Stop!" in a language they didn't understand. This was echoed by other voices, and the convoy came to a grinding halt. Darinus and his bodyguards also stopped.

A voice from inside the wagon bellowed out, again in Arabic, "Alad-Kazac? Why have we stopped?"

The young man who had been walking beside the wagon replied, "Father, an ambush appears imminent."

Inside the wagon the curtains opened and then quickly shut again.

After a moment or so, the door opened, and a hunched man stepped out. He wore purple satin clothes with a purple turban upon his head, had a short beard and wore shoes turned up at the end of his toes.

Although he was almost doubled over already, he bowed further in front of Darinus. "We are only humble circus folk from Mauretania Tingitana, who are making an honest living. Please do not steal from us." The man spoke relatively good Latin; being from a travelling circus he would have to speak many languages.

Darinus declared, "Stand straight old man. Be not afraid. We are not your foe. We wish not to engage you in conversation in why we are dressed this way. We desire to trade with you"

As soon as Darinus mentioned the word trade, the old man straightened up, stroking his beard, "Splendid," he gasped. "I am Abiy-Kazac, the master of this famous circus. Oh, honourable general, let us commence with the talk of trade, and what you have for me."

Darinus got off his horse and followed the old man into the blue wagon; the young man who had been standing next to the wagon, held the door open for the two traders, then closed it behind them.

Julian and the other soldiers were left outside. Julian decided to trot up to the front of the now stationary convoy; he had never seen a circus prior to this, as he had been trained to join the army from an extremely young age, and had swiftly reached the rank of centurion, becoming the leader of his own legion.

Just in front of Abiy-Kazac's wagon was a trailer pulled by a single horse; chained to the side of the trailer was a massive male grizzly bear, next to which there was a dwarf who held a whip.

In the next trailer sat four brightly dressed men. All had painted faces and all were wearing different shaped hats. As Julian passed, they cackled and threw fruit. These were obviously the circus jesters.

On the back of the next trailer was a lion with a shabby mane, locked in a cage. In front of the caged lion was yet another wagon, and on a step at the back, there sat an old lady.

Julian pulled lightly on the reins of his horse and dismounted. He felt drawn towards this woman. In her hands she held sheets of thinly shaved wood (close to paper of that time), each with different pictures on them. Holding them up, the woman spoke in broken Latin, "Tell your life, tell your life."

Julian sat down next to her on the step. With the pictures face down, she placed three of the sheets on the step between her and Julian, and took Julian's hand. Holding it closely to her, she briefly studied the lines, then she started to shake her head. Frowning she scowled at him under her eyebrows.

The lady took the first sheet to her left and turned it over face up. On the sheet was a picture of a sword with crimson blood dripping off the blade. Sternly the woman uttered, "Cruor." (Blood.)

She turned over the second sheet, which revealed a Chinese prince with a black leaf in the corner (best described as a knave, the jack of spades). The woman uttered, "Ultionis." (Revenge.)

The third and final sheet was turned and the old women swiftly pulled her hand away as if she had just been stung. She gasped at the picture, which was of just a single black leaf (the Ace of spades). "Decessus," (Death) she murmured.

It took a few seconds while Julian mulled this over in his head: Blood, Revenge, and Death. Not a good combination: What could she mean?

Standing up, in an angry tone he screeched, "Witch!" and walked back to his horse.

Meanwhile, Darinus was sat in the wagon on a comfortable seat opposite Abiy-Kazac, who had a scared little monkey, dressed in a red coat, sitting next to him. Every time the old man moved his hand, the monkey flinched.

Abiy-Kazac proceeded to talk in his croaky voice, annoyingly uttering the word, "splendid" before each sentence: "Splendid! Oh honourable general, what is it you desire? We possess expensive silk acquired from Asia, medicine, purple dye from Mauretania Tingitana, and ivory from the Gupta Empire." Finishing the sentence, he picked out an apple from a bowl of fruit. As he chomped with his mouth open, the little monkey watched every bite longingly. When he finished eating, he opened the wagon door and threw the core out and the monkey leapt out of the door after it.

Darinus replied, "It is not possessions we desire; it is medicines, nourishment and wine if you possess any."

Darinus reached down for his wallet that hung on his belt. It was then he realised that the button that held it together was undone and all the gold coins inside were gone. "I have been robbed, I declare. My coins are gone!"

Abiy-Kazac leapt up, opened the door and shouted, "Alad–Kazac, Alad-Kazac!" Alad was still standing just outside the door, with the little monkey on his shoulder. Abiy held out his left hand, and sheepishly, Alad handed over the gold coins he had pickpocketed from Darinus, as he had brushed by him whilst entering the wagon. When he had given back every single coin, he received two blows to the top of his head from his father. Abiy-Kazac gave Darinus back the coins. "I apologise for the insolence of my bastard son. I found him as an orphan child, begging on the streets of Tingis. I clothed him and gave him my honourable name. Having no son of my own, he is to inherit this great circus when I am gone and this is how the wretch repays me."

Darinus brought food and medicine, left the wagon, and climbed back onto his horse. The circus convoy began to move again.

All of a sudden, the earth shuddered; up ahead the lion in the cage started frantically running around in his small jail and growling loudly, and the grizzly bear stood on his hind legs only for the dwarf to crack his whip bringing the bear back down to all fours.

The vehicles rolled onto the bridge, but just as the wheels of Abiy-Kazac's wagon hit the bridge the ground began to tremble, and the shaking underfoot grew more violent until the earth began to crack. The river was thrown from side to side, just as if it was in a tub. The bridge snapped, and the swell of the river hit the bank, causing a huge wave, forcing both Darinus and Julian off their horses and sucking them towards the river.

The earthquake lasted no more than thirty seconds, but the damage it had caused was devastating.

A crack in the ground two metres wide had appeared between the river bank and the Romans. Darinus and Julian found themselves hanging over it, just holding on by their fingertips. Fortunately, they both managed to hold tight and were pulled to safety by the other soldiers, although their horses had both been lost, falling into the gap.

Abiy-Kazac's wagon was left rocking on the thin line of ground between the deep crevasse and the drop down to the river. Alad-Kazac, who had been behind the wagon as the wheels had rolled on to the bridge, acted quickly. Abiy-Kazac called out to him, and Alad took a run and leapt over the gap. At any point, the wagon could fall. Abiy tried to get out of the wagon, but dared not move, as on opening the door, and seeing the sheer drop, he realised the predicament he was in.

Alad, balancing himself, leaned over and grabbed his stepfather's arm with one hand, while with his other, he slipped out a set of keys from inside Abiy's satin jacket.

Then he pulled back his arm and callously pushed his father away, before giving the wagon one final push. With Abiy-Kazac inside, it slid forward towards the river, smashing as it hit the rocks jutting out from the sides of the bank, and disappearing into the water below.

The bridge, and the rest of the circus convoy that had been unfortunate to have been on it, had disappeared into the Oxus River. Alad-Kazac then stood, braced himself, and dived out as far as humanly possible, disappearing into the river.

Darinus had been watching the young man's actions since he had been hauled from the crack.

A couple of minutes later, the lion from the cage appeared, followed almost immediately by Alad's head that again disappeared. The lion frantically splashed to the bank.

This time the young man was under water for much longer, and the Roman general was beginning to become concerned. Then further down river a figure was seen at the edge of the bank, and on the other side of the Oxus, the grizzly bear was spotted.

Alad staggered back towards the remaining party. First to greet him was the little monkey, who leapt on to the exhausted hero's shoulder. The youth had saved both the lion and the bear.

He had really impressed the Romans, and without knowing, he had won a place on the chessboard at Caledonia.

AMBUSHED

Leaving Sri Kestri, the Saxons went south; this time the adventurous Adrien was eager to brave the considerable distance down to the huge continent standing all on its own, surrounded by a deep sapphire sea; this was the unknown red land of the Aboriginal people.

The three Western warriors travelled for three months solid and covered nearly four thousand miles.

They crossed both land and sea, much of the land was covered in fascinating landscapes with much thick forest, mainly rain forest and monsoon forest which wasn't much fun, but the varied fauna and flora were fantastic; they encountered attractive looking butterflies, lizards, spiders and friendly geckos. The abundant forest had a lot to offer when it came to provisions; being particularly rich in a diverse range of fruits, wild animals, and wood for fires.

One of the main things the trees provided was an umbrella from the searing sun. It certainly was a different world to what they were used to; at times the terrain was almost impassable, but they managed to cross the straits by boat and canoe.

Towards the bottom of the Islands, Adrien took the decision to turn east, where the channels between the islands were much narrower to cross.

To get to the red land of the Aboriginal people the largest most easterly Islands, sat closest.

They arrived on the big island; here the forest was not as thick as it had been and they were able to walk more freely. They followed the shore line but stayed slightly inland as it was easier.

A few days in, and they could not have been too far from where Adrien wished to find a suitable place and some kind of vessel to cross over.

It was mid-morning when they found themselves wandering single file along a thin track, which ran along the brow of a steep bank that disappeared into the shrubbery below on the right. On their left-hand side, the bank continued upwards.

Killgore, who was at the front, came to an abrupt stop, and turned to Adrien, who was directly behind, and in a low voice said, "Saxon, I believe I sense something is with us; eyes have been burning me since we awoke."

From the rear, Eals sarcastically quipped, "Pictus is it a painted man like yourself? Or maybe it is another ghost!" The Pict had been known to exaggerate dramatically from time to time.

The painted Pict ignored Eals' comment and the three pressed on. But Adrien, too, had begun to feel uneasy; as a person he was slow to judge and he too began to check his surroundings a bit more carefully.

Time ticked by, and by noon it became apparent that they were being followed, as each in turn would see movements in the undergrowth out of the corner of their eyes, but as soon as they turned to see whatever it was, they would see nothing.

Adrien did not even have to give the signal, as all three swords were drawn, and they began to move more cautiously and they opened up the gap between them. Eals at the rear walked backwards.

Then Killgore stopped, as ten or so yards in front a dark-coloured man appeared from behind a tree. He was completely naked, but the most noticeable thing about this strange man was his size, he was obviously a full grown adult, but in height he would only have measured up to the average Westerner's chest.

This strange man had a hard, unfriendly look upon his sour face, and by the looks of it he was not amused to see these tall, pale men in his domain.

The peace was soon shattered as Killgore yelled out a painful yelp, as he felt a sharp sting prick his neck. Automatically he reached to the point of the pain, where he yanked out a tiny dart; before he could react, both his comrades screamed out, as they too had been stung with tiny darts, and it didn't stop there as more and more darts shot the pale men; they came from all directions; up above and down below.

Adrien screamed his orders but nothing came out; just a vague murmur and a sour taste consumed his dry mouth. This was not his only concern, as he felt a leaden sensation take over his now heavy legs, which refused to move. He was stuck fast to where he stood, like a helpless statue. His two companions were in the same state.

At this point, more small, dark-skinned, naked men appeared from the undergrowth from all directions. These menacing tribesmen all held short bamboo sticks, which were the hollow weapons they had used like pea shooters to blow the deadly darts.

The darts were tipped with poisonous oil which temporally paralysed humans and animals.

The tiny pygmy men came and bound the three intruders' hands together, using thin strips of bamboo leaves, which surprisingly enough, when used to bound, are as effective as rope. They then tied the captors with an extra rope round the neck, tied in such a way that if the Saxons or the Pict tried to resist, then the jungle rope dug deeper into the skin.

Although temporally paralysed, the three victims could still feel and the Pygmies were not gentle to say the least, as they bound the Western men.

After binding the men, the Pygmy men stood back and just stared awkwardly at their vulnerable prisoners. Twenty minutes passed, and the paralysis wore off enough for the Westerners to walk again, and they soon found themselves being marched forwards. Adrien felt aggrieved at the ease in which he and his loyal men had been captured, and by men that were as small as children. He felt so ashamed!

The captives were hauled down to the beach that was nearby, and led forward on the hard, dark yellow sand. This unpleasant and somewhat painful journey lasted a good two hours, and the tiny men remained silent throughout.

In due course they reached a place where half-a-dozen thin, shabby two-man boats were lying on the beach, up away from the calm sea. The Pygmies made a sharp turn into the forest, which here had changed and become denser, and the party had to duck under the branches of some low trees. You could say that this place was more of a jungle, for this surely was the dwelling place of the tiny men and their people; as they advanced under the low trees it was as if they had entered another world.

One of the Pygmies, using a large bamboo cane, lifted the branches and held them up, which shed a bit more light into the dreary jungle.

There were women busily bustling around, and a handful of children, all of whom seemed to be occupied in some way or another.

Up above were unusual tree houses, which looked like giant nests, and scattered around the jungle floor were weird looking structures like half-domes, made from bamboo and covered with large bamboo leaves.

But a little way in was a clearing, and in the clearing, there were heaps of thick bamboo canes. But the most harrowing thing for the captives was the bamboo cages to their left, which were placed in a solitary row.

The Westerners were thrown into these miniature cages, which had not been made for men their size. After they had been forced in, the cage doors were securely fastened and their weapons were removed and placed on the floor a few yards away.

The thick bamboo cages were solidly built, and all the uncomfortable prisoners could do was helplessly look on and ponder their miserable fate.

The women started to build a fire. Adrien found them quite fascinating, as they too were almost naked, but wore painted bamboo leaves to cover their nether regions. Nearly all of them had amazingly big bottom lips, as if they held some kind of round plate in their mouths, and their earlobes were stretched with gaping holes. Some had small bones pierced through their noses.

The fire was most odd, as short thin canes were built into a small pyramid out of a hole in the ground and the inside was stuffed with green leaves, and the bottom of the perimeter was surrounded with more leaves.

The men stood around drinking a kind of cava out of halved coconut shells.

Being stuffed into these cages was agonising, as none of the cramped prisoners could stretch out. Every now and again the children would walk by and poke the odd stick in.

The indignant Killgore called out to Eals, "Eals, you should have listened to me in the forest when I warned you."

Mockingly the Saxon replied, "I apologise, Pict. Next time I will use my extra eye!"

Killgore retorted, "Saxon, I trust I will taste sweeter than you!"

As you can imagine, the captives were now resigned to the fact that these Pygmies were going to cook them and eat them.

As the two bickered, Adrien, whilst considering an escape plan, was gazing out to the blue sea; he spotted two boats out on the water not too far from the shore.

From above, one of the Pygmy men, who was on look-out duty, slid down the branchless coconut tree and started whacking the base with a short stick. This clearly was a signal of invasion.

Within seconds, the whole settlement flew into defence mode; the women and children disappeared: some up trees, some retreated into the jungle, and the men took positions hiding in various hideouts, all with their darts ready to attack, and amazingly within one minute the whole place looked as if nobody had even been there at all; the only thing that remained were the boats on the beach.

The two vessels arrived and several massive men hauled them out of the water. One was a large catamaran and the other a waka. Once ashore, these men meandered up towards the jungle.

Adrien was thinking these were among the fiercest race of people he had encountered on his travels so far; they were massive, all with golden brown skin, but you could hardly tell this as they were covered from head to toe in tribal tattoos. Hanging from their sides they all had short clubs, and a couple had longer, thinner club- like weapons.

As they approached the trees, the little Pygmy men came out from their hiding places and, huddled together, nodded to address the new visitors. Obviously they had been acquainted with these men before.

Soon it became clear that the huge men had come to trade. The leader of this barbaric tribe was a man mountain; he was so thick set that his neck was thicker than his head, his black hair was shaven round the sides and on top but round the back it was long and tied up in a kind of a bun, with a single stick through it.

He walked past the Pygmies, who all stepped out of the giant's way, and over to the pile of bamboo. He lifted one of the poles and gave it a close inspection, before raising his hand as a gesture of approval.

Then the Pygmy men picked them up and took them down to the beach, where the other huge tribesmen took them and stacked them onto the waka. After every last one had been carried, another of the huge men collected something from the catamaran, and brought it back to his leader.

From where Adrien was positioned, he could just about see everything that was going on; fortunately, he and his men had not been seen yet. He saw the tribal leader take four lovely looking shells out of a leather bag, then he had to bend right down to give it to the Pygmies, who looked extremely pleased to be trading bamboo for shells.

Then, to the Westerner's dismay, just as the fierce tribal men were about to depart, one spotted the cages and bellowed out in their strange language something that brought his leader to a stop, and he turned and came over to the cages.

His reaction on seeing the pale men caged up was surprising; he fell to one knee, as did his men. He then frantically shouted in his harsh tongue at one of the younger warriors, who raced down to the catamaran and returned with something in his hands.

The tribal leader then presented this beautiful transparent shell to the Pygmies; Adrien figured that he was trying to use this extra special shell as a bargaining tool to buy him and his men.

But simultaneously the tiny men shook their heads in disapproval; finally, after two more trips to the catamaran, the deal was settled and the Pygmy men reluctantly untied the cages.

All three prisoners fell out in great pain, and it took a couple of minutes to stretch out their painful limbs. Then all three picked up their weapons and left with their new masters, but they were not treated as slaves, as the Tribal men, who were Polynesian Maoris, gave them food and water. They left on the big catamaran and sailed out to sea, not knowing what their fate would be, and not knowing whether the Tribal men would be good to them or not as they kept nodding at them as if they were some kind of gods.

These giant men rowed for days at a respectable pace; there were seven in all. One of them had a green stone knife, and he just sat on the front of the waka, sharpening the tips of some of the newly acquired bamboo.

Both vessels were decorated with intricate carvings and were made from wood. At the helm of the waka canoe (which had been carved out of a hollow log, and could carry several men) was a fearsome figure-head, which these people obviously took great pride in.

It didn't take long for Adrien to rediscover his annoying sea sickness, and the second day of the voyage was spent with him vomiting over the side.

He was contemplating getting out the map to have a look which direction they were heading, but decided against the idea.

In the centre of the catamaran there was a tiny room that was full of provisions for the journey. These great sea faring men were very focused as they drove the two vessels forward. The voyage took seven days.

The leader was called Hiahia, and he and his men were originally from the island of the long cloud many miles south east. Their tattoos were works of art, and all had a meaning and a story to tell. They made these warriors even more intimidating than they already looked.

Adrien, Eals and Killgore were very well looked after, although they tried to stay out of the rays of the bright sun by moving around and keeping in the shadows of the wide sail.

On the seventh day, the outline of a group of islands came into view a few miles ahead, and a sudden whooping sound went up from the excited sailors. Adrien now decided it was safe to take a quick peek at the map, so he opened up the rolled-up canvas; a border had lit up around some islands, highlighting where they were. This was not where the Saxon had planned to be, but he didn't seem to have a choice at that moment in time.

Approaching the islands, they were met by coral atolls that poked their heads out of the clear blue water and were covered in crystal white sand. Some had the odd solitary palm tree upon them. Sailing through, they approached a much larger island, home to a picturesque volcano. The coastal strips of this island were sheltered with mangroves and coconut trees; there were other green islets dotted around but much smaller than the volcanic island.

The sailors knew exactly where they were, as they had recently made this their new home; they brought the vessels round to a small hidden away estuary. At this point, three of the warriors said farewell to the rest of the party and continued on (in the waka containing the bamboo canes) sailing round the island, whilst the remaining Polynesians slowed down and leapt into the shallower waters. Wading through to the side, they pulled away some of the mangrove branches and uncovered, hidden neatly away three small waka tiwai (smaller vessels used for fishing and river travel).

The catamaran was hoisted up and hidden where the three new waka tiwai had been. Once in the smaller vessels, they paddled up the narrow creek. Adrien went in with Hiahia and another of the warriors at the front, whilst the other two followed. Hiahia was making crossed arm signals to the Westerners, and it soon became obvious why, as the creek passed through open swamp areas which were infested with crocodiles. The pale men had never seen crocodiles before, but just the sight of these long, armoured skinned predators was enough to register that they were not at all friendly, so the best option would be to keep their hands away from the water.

The trip, though, was a refreshing change from the repetitive sea. Further up creek, they pulled into a little cove on the right-hand side, now nearing the foot of the volcano, where the dense lowlands had been cleared and cultivated.

It was mid-afternoon and incredibly hot and sticky. The relationship between the Westerners and their new companions was incredibly calm, although to be fair there had been little communication. The Polynesians had treated their counterparts with utter respect and not at all like slaves. Adrien thought that either these people were genuine, or they had another motive, but he held comfort in the fact that at least he and his men were armed.

In this cove, Hiahia and one other warrior disembarked, and they pulled the front waka tiwai ashore. Adrien was bundled into the second waka tiwai, along with Killgore, and the party sailed on up the creek; twenty minutes later the creek became so narrow and shallow that the waka tiwai could not continue, so they all got out onto dry land. One of the Polynesian Maori stayed with the Westerners, and the other two took the two boats back down the creek.

Not much happened over the next few days. They spent six days relaxing and keeping a low profile at the bottom of the dense lowlands of the volcano. But from where they were, they could see below them the Maori settlement. They could see the small bay off to the right-hand corner, where Hiahia had disembarked, next to a neatly cut sprawling green. In the centre of this green, was a raised area, surrounded by elegantly carved, short wooden posts.

This area was a Marea, a communal sacred place.

On the near side of the Marea, were several smartly built houses made from dark wood, with sloping rooves; if inspected closely you could see that every single piece of wood had some kind of carving on it. One building, the meeting hall, was twice as big as the others and this stood alone off to the left of the big green.

These Polynesian Maoris had arrived at this new set of islands only two years previously, bringing their families with them, having left their original homeland for some unknown reason. They were all relatively young, and had arrived here to build a new home.

Hidden away in the dense undergrowth above, the Westerners spied on the village in the late afternoon; from where they were they had a superb view.

The Maori men of the village would all meet inside the Marea, where they would pray to different gods and engage in other activities, but the thing that the Westerners found intriguing was that before they did anything they started off with a Maori war dance, similar to a Haka, which was practised and perfected by these warriors. It was incredibly intimidating, as they chanted and made bizarre noises throughout.

Adrien observed that Hiahia, who, to his surprise, was not the chief, stayed close to the chief, and they were inseparable. The women, following the chief's young wife, would join the men before dark, and they would all go to the meeting house.

The two Saxons and the painted Pict spent five days with their Polynesian comrade, who let them get on with things and didn't say a word; the only thing he did do one day, was prevent the visitors from attempting to build a fire.

On the sixth day early in the morning before sunrise they were woken by an unusual sound, similar to a chirping noise. At this, the Polynesian's ears pricked up, and he waved the Westerners to follow him. They ventured through the thick scrub back to the creek, as this was where the chirping noise was coming from, and there, waiting for them, were the two Maoris with the two waka tiwai that had dropped them off several days before. One of the Maoris had been making the rude noise with a reed between his lips. The bored lone Maori was thrilled to see his fellow countrymen, and greeted them by rubbing their noses together.

As they rowed back down the creek, they came to the cove at the edge of the big green, where they stopped paddling and just floated quietly, passing the cove. Adrien and his men were fully aware that something secretive was taking place.

They followed the creek all the way back down to the sea, and then they turned right, and with their smaller waka tiwai staying close to land, they rowed around a hundred or so metres and coming round a tight bend, they were met by a sandy bay. In the bay there were two catamarans, one of which they recognised straight away, but the second was a tidy looking vessel made from bamboo.

Adrien suddenly realised, as he saw three familiar characters – the three warriors who had left with the bamboo-laden waka days before - that this new vessel had been built from the bamboo traded from the pygmies.

On the sand lay three fair-sized waka.

All the vessels were stocked up with provisions, as if they were getting ready to go on a long voyage. The two tiny waka tiwai that had been used to sail the creek, were hoisted ashore, and once everyone was out, flipped upside down before holes were bored into the bottom of the boats. Then they were flipped back over.

Everyone now seemed to be waiting for something, and as time slowly passed, the Polynesian Maoris started to get nervously restless and the atmosphere in the cool morning light began to get more and more tense.

Then, from the corner, another waka tiwai appeared, and on it was Hiahia along with a female, and this was not just any female, but the chief's wife.

As soon as this boat came into view, the rest of the warriors flew into action, pushing the three waka into the water and boarding the catamarans.

As soon as Hiahia arrived, he greeted the Westerners as if they were old friends, by rubbing his nose together with theirs.

Adrien now realised what was going on, and he felt sick to the core. Hiahia had run away with his friend, the chief's wife, and they had deceitfully planned to leave the islands together, whilst all this time he had pretended to be the chief's close friend. And the reason Hiahia had brought the Westerners, was that he believed the white people had been sent by the gods to bring him good luck in his dark quest.

As they sailed away from the shore, it became apparent that they had been followed by the chief's men, as he had woken up to find his wife Aoatea gone.

These warriors, seeing the three waka timai on the beach, pushed them out and jumped in to chase the traitors, but the pursuit didn't last long, as soon their vessels sank due to the holes bored by Hiahia's men.

CROSSING THE UNFORGIVING SOUTHERN SEA

The catamarans glided on, with their sharp tips cutting through the white foam waves, as the powerful Polynesians rowed forward at a great speed.

These vessels were very well designed and constructed with robust and flexible joints; the double catamaran was made up of two hulls connected by lashed crossbeams, roughly six metres or so across. The bamboo base in the middle at half-mast was a matted sail, and a long steering paddle was used to keep the catamarans sailing on course when the sail was erected. A wooden enclosure was built in the middle to shelter passengers and supplies for the voyage. This is where the three travellers sat.

In convoy with the catamaran, were an identical vessel and three other long waka.

The island behind was rapidly growing smaller, and it was not too long before it disappeared completely. Once way out to sea, the waves became choppier, but the fearless Polynesians rowed on and on, each side in sync with the other. The cool spray from the waves was very refreshing.

What a day! But now, away from the island, and with the tense events behind them, they felt they could relax and get ready for what the southern ocean had to throw at them. But still Adrien could not look in the direction of Hiahia or Aoatea; he strongly disagreed with their immoral behaviour. Fortunately, Aoatea rode on the other vessel.

They passed many days out on the lonesome waters; all that could be seen was miles of endless blue. The navigational skills of this great sea-faring race were astonishing.

They used the sun, the moon and the formation of the stars and the ocean swell to guide the way, acting as their own natural compasses. For the journey, provisions had been prepared, and leather skins were used to store water and were refilled when the rains came.

From time to time, mostly during the day time, when the sea was calm, the Polynesians would rest, and if the wind blew eastwards or northwards, the sails would be lifted. At these times, nets would be lowered into the water to catch fish, which would not take too long to fill as there were shoals of fish in abundance.

Adrien was getting used to the sea, and was beginning to conquer his sea sickness.

On one particular day, the swell of the sea became more restless and intense; up ahead the sky was beginning to turn black. The three waka and the two catamarans were all brought together and tied tightly next to each other; the Polynesian sailors all began to tie themselves to their positions.

Hiahia left his position at the helm on the right-hand side of the catamaran, and made his way over and stood on the beam next to the three passengers, to whom he handed rope. They used the rope to tie around their waists, attaching themselves to the beam. Adrien and his companions felt uneasy; they knew a storm was brewing, but did not know what to really expect.

The sky blackened and the rains began to fall; at first very gradually, before the heavens opened, and the waves became higher. The vessels rode them up, then down, up, then back down; it was enough to turn your stomach. Eventually the sailors pulled in the oars.

Then up above, the first deafening crash of thunder rolled, followed shortly by electrifying lightning, imitating jagged daggers across the dark sky. As the storm began to rage, the catamarans and wakas were tossed up and down and from side to side. The blue sea had turned black from the reflection of the harsh, now charcoal-coloured sky. The storm raged on and on and the thunder clapped continuously.

Hours later, the Saxons and the Pict became weaker and had to rely purely on the tight rope wrapped around the beam. At times, the high waves would take them underwater, but every time the sturdy catamarans and waka would find their way back to the surface, before being dunked under again and again. Every time they resurfaced, they would have to take deep breaths.

The unforgiving storm went on for two whole days and one night, not that anyone could notice. Adrien never thought he would escape, and that they were surely doomed. Then on the second night the storm threw them out onto a calm tranquil sea.

Adrien lifted his weak head. The moon had been switched on, and up above he saw the beautiful stars that made up the Southern Cross, flickering brightly in the night sky. They had survived and come through what can only be described as the abyss. He was humbled on witnessing how vast and powerful the ocean really was; this situation had been completely out of his hands. His two friends were still tied on next to him. Laying his head back down, he fell asleep.

The next day, as the sun rose, in the quiet morning, the damage was calculated. All the robust vessels had come through unscathed, and amazingly, only two oarsmen had been lost. Everyone was dehydrated but there was still water in the skins. The sail was put up, the other catamaran and the three waka were untied, and the convoy sailed on eastward.

Nobody knew how long they sailed, but the voyage took what seemed like a lifetime.

The travelling passengers were not clear on the destination, but Adrien could see, dotted on the map, small random islands, and further east, another large continent.

So he was not too alarmed.

One morning, a speck of land was spotted on the thin line of the horizon. Hiahia shouted out, "P-whenua" (land), followed gleefully by, "Te Pito o t e henua," for this was their destination – the island which stood on the south-easternmost point of the Polynesian triangle, and the most isolated inhabited island on earth, surrounded by eight hundred leagues of vast emptiness. It was a small triangular volcanic mound, only fourteen miles in length and seven miles wide.

As the pointed vessels swiftly drew nearer, the green land got bigger, revealing a mysterious isolated island, which looked eerie, with many extremely solemn-looking, tall carved statues of stone faces in a row, which rose up above the green vegetation. What were these immense figures? Were they gods?

Circling half-way round, the sailors found an appropriate spot to land by a neat bay. Here, they were met by long empty canoes, hollowed out of large palm trees, which was a bit unnerving, as how were the locals going to react to the uninvited visitors?

Cautiously, they landed the waka on the deserted beach alongside the unmanned palm-tree canoes.

The island was green, and rich in vegetation with massive palms twice the size of usual palms; some even rose fifty foot, for these were Paschalococos Palms. There were a lot of these Paschalococos stumps around as noticeably many had been cut down. Beyond, at the foot of the volcanic hill, were the fearsome statues they had seen whilst out at sea.

Even the ardent Polynesian Maori seemed somewhat apprehensive at the sight of these strange massive figures. Eals quipped (as he always found time to make some smart remark), "Giants, Adrien. This is what you need for your entire army." The now serious Adrien just threw back a cold glare, as he was as concerned as the Polynesians were right now, and for all they knew this looked like it might actually not be too far from the truth.

Then a harsh silence fell upon the visitors, as way up high on a ridge something was happening: one of these massive statues was slowly moving along the ridge. Everyone just froze.

After all staring in disbelief for a moment or so, they quietly walked forward toward the statues. There were only five, all raised up on a stone platform long enough to hold many more. The nearer they got the bigger these stone monuments became.

On a closer inspection, they found the monuments were all facing inland, oddly with their backs to the sea. They all had oversized heads, three-fifths the size of their bodies, with huge brows and distinctive curled-up noses. The lips protruded in a thin pout, and the noses and the ears were elongated and oblong in form; the jaw lines stood out against the thick necks, the torsos were heavy and they did not have any legs. They were all carved from solid volcanic rock, and each had a slightly different face, with some bigger than others.

What a strange place! However there was no time to hang around and the party pressed on up the hill. Now, at this point, Adrien would have done things a bit differently, and would have stopped to devise a plan, but not these Polynesians, who, taking the bull by the horns, swiftly scaled the hill, making their way fearlessly to the top of the ridge.

The walk up was a bit of a hike, and took quite a while. All this time, they could see the monument gradually moving along the ridge, constantly staring ahead and, luckily, never once turning to look down.

Finally, all a bit flustered and out of breath, the party reached the top of the ridge, where they crawled the remaining five or so metres, towards the giant head.

Pretty much simultaneously they peered over and this was what they saw, to their relief, the giant stone head was not moving of its own accord, but was being heaved along by dozens of men; some pushing, whilst others pulled at the front on long ropes. Underneath, the statue was being rolled on colossal palm-tree logs, which explained why so many of the Paschalococos palms had already been chopped down. The logs never ran out, as other men would pick up the logs at the back, and hurriedly carry them to the front; the mechanics of this conveyer system kept everything running like clockwork. Adrien and the other two watched in sheer admiration of this impressive show of pure man power. The Polynesian Maoris stood upright, but the workers were so engrossed in their work, that none were aware of the visitors.

There were two different races working and living side by side; the more native were of Polynesian ancestry, who were tall with dark bronze skin, black hair and flat noses, and they were called the "Short Ear", and there were the "Long Ears", who had not long arrived on the island. They had ginger hair and pale skin with pointed noses and were shorter in height. They had clearly earned their name as their ear lobes were abnormally long, due to the fact that they were weighed down with rings and all kinds of decorations through them. Some had been stretched so long it would have been possible to have tied them right round the back of their necks.

Between these two races was a feeling of jealousy and bad blood, and it would only be a matter of time before all these bitter feelings would eventually boil over.

Maybe it was because the visitors didn't look too far out of place (except the painted Pict, of course) that they were not so noticeable.

It was getting late in the day, and Hiahia made a decision; rather than following where the workers were taking the giant statue, he decided to trace back to where the natives had come from, which wasn't hard to find, as the giant logs had crushed everything in their wake, leaving a wide path that followed the ridge off to the left.

Looking over the other side of the ridge, the party found themselves gazing down into an old, redundant, grey volcanic crater; to look down it too long would send anyone giddy.

Following the flattened path for a few hundred metres, it suddenly swerved off and disappeared into the crater. At this point, it was just about feasible to carefully walk backwards down the slope, and how the locals had hoisted it up this steep ravine was unbelievable. Not too far down though, they entered a quarry and inside the volcanic quarry were workers, all totally absorbed in what they were doing.

There was a big hole in the stone floor, where the new Moai, which was now being hoisted along the ridge, had been sculpted. Two more had already had work started on them, one out of a big boulder in the middle of the quarry, and another out of the rock in the wall.

It was fascinating just watching these men at work. There must have been fifty or so skilful sculptors, hammering away at the rocks, who were mainly the Long Eared and the Short Eared were doing the hard work and clearing away any loose stones or rocks that fell to the floor. The whole operation was very efficient. Hiahia, the rest of his men and the Westerners, sat themselves down and watched for a while.

This quarry was a relatively new site, and only a small part of the volcanic pit had been mined, as only a handful of these statues had been sculpted so far.

Centuries later, these peoples' obsession to make hundreds of the Moai would take them to the edge of extinction, and cutting down all the trees to transport them, would wreck this budding paradise's eco-system.

Something caught Adrien's eye. Leaning up on the side, was a long piece of slate with chalk symbols on it, and standing next to it was an older man, who ever so often would add a new symbol, using chalk. These hieroglyphics were the unique system of writing these people used, called the Rongorongo script.

If you watched the workers long enough, you would see that they all glanced at the slate to see what the old man had just added. Then another symbol was added to the slate, and the workers working on the single boulder in the middle, downed tools and finished for the day. The man had just given them their knocking- off orders.

The sculptors were easy to identify, as each one wore a slate belt around their waists, on top off their loin cloths, made up of tiny bits of square slate all tied together with a piece of string. Shortly after the first knocking off symbol was added, another and another was added until eventually all the workers finished for that day.

Hiahia went to talk with the older man, who, on seeing the rest of the party started to panic, especially looking at the Westerners, but Hiahia defused the situation, and although they spoke different languages, many of their words were similar, as they were all originally from the Polynesian world.

The old man calmed down, and led them all out of the crater, intent on taking them to meet the chief. They took a different route from earlier, and further down the hill, came to a village, where the stone houses were made with basalt slabs and covered with thatched roofs, that resembled overturned boats.

Adrien decided he and his men would disappear and spend a bit of time alone so, consulting with Eals and Killgore, they slipped away.

GAZING INTO THE FUTURE POOL

Some days after the wide Oxus River had tragically swallowed up most of the Mauretania Tingitana circus, Darinus and his men had stopped for a break.

Alad-Kazac had joined the party, as it happened he had seemingly been unaffected by the loss of his step-father (clearly there had been no love lost).

He sat there, cleaning the dirt out from beneath his long grubby fingernails using a short, three-pronged dagger. As Alad could not speak any Latin, communication between him and the Romans was limited.

Alad's little friend, the mischievous monkey, had stayed by his side most of the time perched on his shoulder. But this particular day he was pestering the Romans; grabbing at anything shiny; at one point, Julian threatened to chop off its tiny hands.

The reason Darinus had decided to take a break at this particular point, was that the Road came to a fork, the wide Silk Road ran to the right but a thinner road wound to the left.

As it happened, Darinus took his troops left. Up ahead, the region became hillier and large snow-capped mountains rose up in the distance. They rode for many hours with the young Mauretanian riding on the back of one of the Roman soldiers' horses.

The hills became steeper and more rocky, and the further and higher up they travelled, the chilly air became thinner and the path narrowed, which forced the party to follow behind Darinus in single file. It was not clear whether he thought he had taken a wrong turn; none of the others ever questioned their leader's judgement; not even Julian this time.

After an uncomfortable night's sleep, they continued on their way up the steep path, and before long, the crunch of snow could be heard under the horses' hooves.

Later on, the pathway levelled out. It was then Darinus came to a grinding halt, as on the path below he saw a print in the snow which looked like the print of a human, but was almost twice the size. He spoke out to his men "Men, be at the ready. We may have entered the land of myth and monsters. This surely is not the print of a human".

Moving on breathing became slightly harder due to the thinning air. Further on, patches of green grass could be seen, next to them a stream babbled and up above an eagle flew by. Higher up still, white mountains towered. The travellers trudged on, barely speaking. As the day pressed on, the shadows of the mountains grew longer.

Looking up, Julian spied the flickering of a fire out the corner of his eye. He informed his captain, "Look, Sire. I see the light of a fire".

They continued towards the flickering light. The path again wound steeply upwards and so they all had to dismount and walk in single file.

All of a sudden, Darinus stopped. Out of the shadows stepped a small bald man with a round face and narrow eyes, wearing a cerulean-coloured robe and sandals With his arms held out, he walked towards Darinus, speaking in broken Latin. "Darinus, you are late; for many moons I wait."

Poor Darinus was shell shocked and speechless, as the man embraced him. "Come, before it gets too cold. I will guide the way."

As they walked, the man spoke, "I am Ravarda, a follower of the eightfold path" (He was, of course, a monk.)

The climb upwards took a good twenty minutes or so; the sun had now faded. Once at the top, the path led to a strange building; a square temple. Either side of the path, candles lit up the way and to the side, a small fire glowed. Ravarda told them to leave the horses and accompany him into the building.

They followed up three steps. There was no door, just an opening through two sturdy wooden pillars, and inside there were more men dressed the same in cerulean robes, all sitting crossed legged facing a gold statue and meditating in silence.

As the travellers entered the temple, Ravarda signalled for them to remove their shoes.

The Romans and Alad sat down at the back. All around the sides of this strange place were upright scrolled-shaped wheels. After a while, two of these meditating men got up and left, returning minutes later with bowls of food and small wooden vessels which they handed to Darinus and his men.

Inside the bowls was rice and hot vegetables with a slice of yak butter on top, and inside the vessels was yak milk. The bitter taste of yak milk did not bother the hungry travellers; they were all more than grateful.

After eating, they were given sheepskins, and that night slept where they sat, as did the monks, of which there were twenty-four in total.

Many hours later, as it was just getting light, Darinus was woken by the sound of a cockerel crowing, at which the monks rose, then sat down again in the meditation position. When the sun had fully risen, they all got up and made their way outside. As they passed the Romans, they slightly bowed their heads, and left to go about their daily business.

Ravarda beckoned to the Romans, Alad and, of course, the monkey (who had been behaving itself) to leave the temple. Once outside, Ravarda spoke, "Darinus, this day you will follow me alone; your soldiers can stay here and rest."

Julian piped up, "Sire, I will not leave your side."

Darinus replied, "Julian, you shall remain here and await my return."

The monk and Darinus left. They took the same path which they had taken the previous night. As they walked, Darinus meekly questioned, "How is it you know who I am?"

Ravarda answered, "This is what I intend to show you, my Roman friend. I have watched you since you left the castle at the commencement of your journey."

They came to the point at the bottom of the steep path where they had met, and, turning left, they carried on walking. It wasn't too long till they came across a pool, which was cut out of the side of a rock with a fog hovering over the surface. Getting nearer, Ravarda lifted his arm and the fog lifted, leaving the water crystal clear, mirroring the reflection of the mountains and light blue sky above.

"Darinus, this is where I first saw you. I have followed your journey through this pool of water."

The puzzled Darinus spoke to the monk, "But this is nothing but a pool."

The reply was, "No, this is much more than that, it shows the past, but more importantly it shows the future. What you are to see, very few men have seen. You will see things you do not understand and it may disturb you; if this is so step away. I am the only being that holds the key to this water; with great honour it was passed down to me from the Elder of this land and from his Elder before to him. So, Darinus, brace you!"

Ravarda sat down and crossed his legs in the lotus position resting his two elbows on his knees! He pressed his fingers together and closed his eyes.

Darinus stared deep into the water. The reflection of the mountains and sky died away and the pool turned a pale shade of white.

Then, to his amazement, within the pool, he vividly saw the chequered courtyard inside the castle at Caledonia. Wei Po-yang the Magician, and Mahours the Druid were there, and his sworn enemy Adrien the Saxon was standing on a black square on one side! On the opposite side he could see himself standing on a white square. He could not hear a thing, but could only see the figures moving around. The Magician and the Druid each held a scroll each; looking closely he saw they were the two maps; one which he had himself and the other that had been handed to his adversary.

This picture faded and was replaced by another. This time he saw himself standing before Honorius Caesar in the Imperial Palace in Rome. He saw Caesar turn to face him, his face red with rage and the guards entered the room and he saw himself fighting his way out, before escaping.

This vision too faded, and was replaced by an army racing down a hill into battle. Instantly he knew this to be a Roman army, with the Roman crest held high. The army was massive, with tens of thousands of men. Darinus recognised the general as none other than his friend Brutus. He watched in awe, the opposing army coming to meet them. They were clearly people from the north and the west, as the men were fair skinned. The battle was fierce and furious. Then he saw to his horror, another army closing in from behind the Romans.

It suddenly dawned on him that this Roman army was none other than the army Caesar had appointed him to lead alongside Brutus, and the opposing army was led by Alaric, King of the Visigoths.

In utter despair, Darinus watched as the Romans were absolutely annihilated. Clearly they had been betrayed, and sent like lambs to the slaughter. This was meant to have been a surprise assault. His dear friend Brutus soon lay dead on the field.

The General took three steps back from the pool. The blood in his veins went cold, and he was in a state of complete shock, knowing that that should have been him.

Eventually he got himself together, (Ravarda remained in the same position) and moved back to the pool, which had changed back to the chequered Caledonian courtyard. But it was now different, with the squares either side full of different-looking characters; he counted sixteen on each side.

Darinus saw many more things in that pool: ships sailing from Gaul towards Britannia, and Gaul taking Britannia, defeating their army. A large book was opened; recorded inside were all the names of the people on the island along with all land owners and cattle.

He saw a knight dressed in white with chainmail armour, who held a sword and shield. On the white shield was a red cross. He fought a green and purple dragon, which the knight slew, thrusting his sword through its heart.

After every scene, the picture would fade and disappear and another would reappear.

Then he saw a map of the whole world, and a great battle between many countries; each country had its own flag and was surrounded by its own boundary.

The country he knew as Germania was represented by a red flag with a white circle and a crossed black symbol in the centre. They fought a battle, unfamiliar to Darinus, with sticks and explosions of fire. Germania was defeated and a great wall was built; splitting the country down the middle. Then the iron curtain was lifted, and the wall was ripped down.

He saw many smooth roads covering the map. Transport was different to horses and carts, the vehicles still had wheels but they had lights and were many colours, and they raced at high speeds on these roads. He saw men travelling in the bellies of beasts that travelled on tracks, metal ships, and to his amazement, giant metal birds in the sky.

The pool showed a man in the dark putting a flag on the moon. The flag had white stars with red-and-white stripes on it. He saw the Earth far away from the Moon. The Earth was slowly turning and on one side a great wall was visible.

The vision moved on to the country with the stars and stripes. Two high identical buildings could be seen on an island, both made of glass. Two metal birds flew into each of the towers, and, like a pack of cards, the towers crashed to the ground.

Again the vision in the pool faded. Another map appeared; the separate flags over Britannia, Germania and the Roman Empire, and beyond, were replaced by a blue flag with gold stars representing all the different countries. A building stood out towards the north-east of Germania, where the wall had once divided her, and was clearly the centre of this new Empire.

The world became under a new world order.

Then, far away, he saw a red planet, from where soil was brought back to earth in a long glass tube, which caused a reaction, and many people lost their lives.

In one country, a nation could be seen digging for black gold. When the oil was found, in the distance, a huge red army was seen marching towards this country.

But it was the last vision Darinus saw, which interested him the most. A knight on a black horse was seen riding at night across the draw-bridge at the Caledonian castle. He dismounted from the horse, and walked briskly to the chequered courtyard, and in the middle of the courtyard was a table with a crown sitting upon a cushion. The knight walked towards the centre, and out of his pocket he took out a shiny stone. Then the vision vanished. Darinus was left baffled; he knew this knight was either himself or his foe, Adrien, but due to the darkness, he never got to see the knight's face.

The pool returned to normal, with the reflection of the mountains and the light blue sky.

Ravarda got to his feet and spoke to Darinus, who was shaking and drenched in sweat, "What you have seen is the future of this world; much you will not understand but you will witness many of these event some of which you will take part."

They both wandered back up the steep hill to the monastery.

Both had been gone for a good few hours. On returning, much of the day had passed, and most of the other monks had returned from their labour. The main entertainment had been the little monkey that had sat on the side of the steps sulking, as he had received a severe telling off from Alad.

Just outside the monks' square building, on top of the hill, or small mountain, a thin rope, which was pulled tight, ran from the side of the wooden structure to a tree, and hanging from it were the monks' prayer flags (flags that the monks had written prayers on and these prayers were taken by the wind to heaven). The monkey had climbed up onto the rope and had pulled off several of the flags.

Darinus was very quiet, after all, he had experienced a very traumatic day, and Julian was very concerned.

The Romans stayed one more night. The following morning they said good-bye.

Darinus asked Ravarda to join him and take his place on one of the squares at the courtyard. Ravarda replied, "It would be an honour, my friend. I have been waiting since my youth for you to ask. This surely is my destiny. I have never seen further than you saw in the pool yesterday."

They both agreed that Alad-Kazac should stay there with the monks. After all, the monks had already grown fond of the mischievous little monkey.

Ravarda pointed the travellers in the direction to take them back to the Silk Road, back down the hill, past the future pool and beyond.

THE LADY AT THE LAKE

The way back to the Silk Road was easy to find.

Soon they were heading east on the popular, well-used trail once again.

For many days, the party travelled eastwards; the mountainous regions turned into grasslands and further on became a desert. The road continued for some days by the edge of the sand. Fortunately, Ravarda had urged them to take the sheepskins along, as the nights were bitterly cold.

Not knowing how long the road would lead them by the desert, Darinus made a decision, they would rest during the day under any possible shade that could be found out of view of the scorching sun, and travel through the cold nights.

One particular night, after galloping hard for hours on end, a thin line of red appeared in the east up ahead, signalling the sun rising. Shapes could be seen on the horizon, and this prompted them to continue. As the sun rose, it threw its rays onto the grey sand that turned yellow, and began to twinkle as if it were littered with diamonds.

Not a single bird could be heard to welcome in that morning, and the shapes, which looked like lumps, were mountains, now looking within touching distance.

Pushing on through the blistering heat, hours passed. Roman determination spurred them forward. However, when travelling through a desert, things can look nearer than they really are. On their way with the mountains in view, a clump of tall jagged rocks broke the journey. They made their way to the rocks. The glare of the unyielding sun made them squint and the horses were breathing hard and foaming at the mouth. The rocks gave little shelter, but there was a shallow pool of water, at the sight of which they fell off the horses to take a drink. A family of lizards lay on the rocks bathing in the sun.

Riding on at a slower pace, hours later, the sun began to set behind them in the west. Finally, under foot they were met by green vegetation and long coarse grass. At long last they could relax, as they had reached the edge of the desert.

These mountains were different, being thin and high; in the dusk they looked blue. Little did they know that whilst they had crossed the harsh desert, they had ridden into 542AD. Burnt from the sun, exhausted, but at the same time elated, the warriors collapsed and slept.

When daylight arrived, they could now see their new surroundings. They had reached the northern plains, vast yellow and grey flatlands, bordered by these blue and grey mountains, but what was more noticeable was a huge wall, just metres away, made from yellow and grey stones. A smooth path ran next to the wall. On seeing this, Darinus realised he had led his men off the route they should have taken (as this smooth path was the Silk Road). In being careless, he could have caused them all to perish in the harsh, unforgiving desert. What had really happened was that because he had chosen to travel at night, somewhere along the way he had navigated them in the wrong direction.

In this place, there had clearly been little rainfall for some time; the grass was dry, and the odd cacti were dotted around, and nearby, a brook was now just a series of nearly dried-up puddles, which provided a little water for the thirsty travellers.

Back on the Silk Road with the high wall on the left casting a shadow over their already burnt skin, they rode on.

It wasn't too long before other travellers were passed; sometimes the odd person carrying a bag, or sometimes groups of people, all going the same way as the Hun-dressed Romans. The unusual thing was that not one single person passed by in the opposite direction; all the time previously spent on that road, people had passed in both directions.

Every few hundred or so metres, up on the wall stood watch towers manned by soldiers. Both Julian and Darinus were paying much attention to the wall, as on the other side of the path, the land was barren. That was until they came across a man with a stick sitting weeping on a stone, his face hidden under a pointed straw hat with a dog lying beside him, its balding fur sucked into its ribs. But the most alarming thing was a herd of cattle, lying dead strewn around on the ground. These emaciated animals had wasted away due to lack of food and water, as the brook that had once babbled next to the road was now bone dry.

A couple of years previously there had been a great famine, especially affecting the countries in the west.

It was still early morning when they came to a gateway in the wall where many people had gathered, and the huge doors underneath the archway were closed.

They didn't have to wait long before the beating of a drum was heard above the gateway upon the wall. At this sound, the people surged towards the doors, which slowly creaked open, and a smallish man stepped out, holding out at arm's length a white sheet of white paper, which looked like a canvas with the single black symbol for trade.

In some kind of chaotic queue, the people lined up.

The people waiting were from different countries; some had travelled for weeks, some dressed richly, some were clearly poor and bedraggled, most carrying goods or at least something to trade.

In turn, they showed their wares to the man in the gateway, who either showed approval by letting them pass through, or shook his head and turned them away.

Darinus and Julian left the other Romans and joined the line on foot.

Eventually, after waiting patiently, their turn arrived. Feeling very awkward, Darinus produced a few Roman coins and handed a couple to the man, who looked puzzled but waved them on through.

Julian called to the other troops to join them, bringing the horses, which caused a bit of commotion amongst the others waiting in the queue. Each in turn also had to pay their way through.

Inside were many soldiers, smaller than the Romans, all with high cheek bones and with a slight yellowish complexion, who glared at the strangers as they passed by. The Silk Road continued winding its way up and away into the distance; the wall had been built by these people to protect their land.

As the days passed, the flatlands became richer. They rode across the province of the western Wei dynasty. Darinus was intent on getting straight to the coast, and on entering the province of the northern Wei dynasty, he decided to break the monotonous journey and take another road, off which they stumbled across a quaint village with simple grey roofed houses all made from bamboo cane.

The people of the village all looked like the soldiers at the great wall (as did all the people of this land) and wore hats like the sad man who had lost his herd.

Using sign language to communicate with an elderly woman, Darinus managed to barter for somewhere to stay; at a small cost she gave them a rundown hut at the edge of the village which all the Romans crammed into.

Darinus woke early whilst the others slept apart from two Romans who stood on guard just outside. He left the hut, deciding to take a walk and spend some time alone, still troubled by what he had seen in the future pool weeks before. The village stood on the outskirts of a dense wood; once inside the wood, the quiet was eerie, and every time he stepped on a stick the noise echoed off the trees.

A nightingale flew by, obviously late for its bed.

Wandering deeper in, Darinus found himself next to a lake, around which a thin beach ran. The clear air was warm. He loosened and removed his boots, and as he walked, the feel of the soft sand was very soothing.

He came to a point where bamboo impeded his way along the sand, so he decided to wade through the water to get round. It was here he stopped in his tracks, when the peaceful quiet was broken by the high pitch of women's laughter. Peering round the bamboo, this is what he saw: sitting on the end of a short jetty, dangling their feet in the water, were three Eastern women; two wore plain white and one was dressed in a red silk tunic with two sticks holding up her raven-coloured hair.

Darinus crouched in the water, hiding out of view. He was only a few feet away and could see everything clearly. At the sight of this woman, his heart missed a beat; she was elegantly beautiful.

He had not seen such a woman in the whole of the Roman Empire, her beauty was so different to that of the women from the West.

The General felt guilty watching. What he saw next, almost took his breath away, but he could not look away.

The woman got up and started unwrapping her red silk tunic, taking the sticks out of her hair and shaking it free. She stood naked on the jetty; her skin was pale, and she was slight in stature. She sat back down at the edge, before elegantly lowering herself into the water.

All Darinus could do was wait, as any movement would surely attract their attention. His eyes transfixed, he watched as she splashed around in the water. At one point she swam close to the bamboo, but after a while she swam back to the jetty and pulled herself back up. Darinus noticed that on her smooth back, at the top of her left shoulder blade, was a tattoo of a red and black dragon.

He had seen enough, or too much! So quietly, he slipped away and went back to his men.

The troops were all up. Later on, in the early afternoon, Darinus, Julian and two of the soldiers went off to explore their surroundings. Secretly Darinus wanted to find out more about where the women from the lake came from. So they all went back through the dense wood. In some places swords were drawn to cut through the thick undergrowth, but soon they came to the lake, where they followed the thin beach round, wading past the bamboo to the jetty. A walkway had been cut through the trees, leading to a road, which they followed round to the other side of the lake, where they came to the outskirts of a town with grand houses.

On entering this unusual town, they saw bunting strung across the road overhead from house to house. People were frantically running around, no doubt anticipating some event that was to take place, and a few were waiting outside a particular building.

Getting closer, Darinus and his men were inquisitive and wanted to find out what was going on. They stopped to look at this grand official-looking building, which had a yellow roof and its outside was decorated with exquisite lattice work windows. On either side on the slats there were paintings of good luck symbols with different animals, birds and flowers.

Whilst standing and admiring near the entrance, the Romans failed to notice a rickshaw pull up behind them. The light, two-wheel rickshaw was pulled along by a servant holding two straight handles on either side. Stepping out from his seat was a man dressed all in black from head to toe. Making his way to the entrance of the building, he had to walk around the gawping Romans. Just as he passed, Julian stepped back, treading on the man's black shoe. "Pardon," said Julian apologetically. The man looked the Roman and the rest of the party up and down as if they were dirt. In disgust, he spat on the floor and calmly strolled into the building. Once again Darinus had to stop Julian from over reacting.

Shortly afterwards the four of them wandered into the building. Inside, they found themselves walking through a corridor with open windows with neat gardens on both sides. Following other people, they entered a hall in which the floor was covered in sand and around the outside were benches, in rows of three. The travellers went over and sat down on the second row on one side. They stuck out like a sore thumb, and the locals just glared at them as if they were from another planet.

The hall covered quite a big area. At the far end there were two chairs, one slightly taller than the other. As the room filled, the front benches remained empty. Some older people brought in cages with exotic coloured birds in and a cock strutted by, followed by two chickens. Darinus and his men waited in anticipation to see what was about to take place, as the local people were getting more and more excited.

THE BIRDMAN CHALLENGE

Across time, and many miles away, Adrien and his two companions were on the Island, in the middle of the Pacific ocean, and they had managed to get away from the untrustworthy HiaHia and the crowd, and had found a secluded spot, right back down by the sea. Meandering along a short beach, they passed a giant turtle that drew their attention for a bit.

Eventually, they perched on a huge round boulder right next to the sea. The early evening air was clean and the fresh wind stung their pale faces. The waves gently lapped against the rocks below.

Killgore had started to re-paint his face, as the original face paint had faded a bit since they had spent so long out on the ocean.

As usual, Adrien was deep in thought. He needed to hatch a new plan. Like it or not, they were pretty stranded in the middle of nowhere, and between the three of them it would be some feat to sail anywhere and survive in the great vast blue, especially with their lack of sailing experience (apart from Killgore).

As they sat on that boulder, a red-head surfaced the water a few feet away, and whoever it was swam to the shore and hoisted themselves up out of the sea onto another boulder nearby.

This pasty skinned man was slight in stature and very thin. He was paler than the Westerners, which was saying something (or maybe just at that time, as they had spent a lot of time in the sun over the past couple of years or so), he had carrot-coloured hair which was shaved to the skin on the sides and longer on top; in fact if it had not been wet, he would have styled his spiky hair upward making it flat at the top. He wore the common Tapa loin cloth made from thin bark.

Unmistakably, he had the traditional long ear lobes, in which he had coconut rings embedded, making him a "Long Ear". His nose was thin and long, and his lips were tight and thin. If you looked close, you could see he had weak-coloured orange eyes, topped with wafer-thin eye brows. Freckles gave him a unique look, sprinkled over his bluish cheeks. He was recognised as one of the sculptors, due to the fact that he wore a slate tagged belt around his waist.

The "Long Ear" sat there for a time, fiddling with his toes, unfazed by the visiting Westerners. After a time, he clicked his fingers together, clearly to get the attention of the others, and with a mischievous look in his eyes, he pointed to the water. Then in a flash, hands pressed with finger tips together, he dived into the sea so perfectly, that he glided into the water without a single splash.

Minutes later, the red-head bounced out from the water again, and with his right hand, clicked his fingers together; obviously his way of gesturing for the Westerners to join him in the water.

At first, the conservative warriors chose to ignore the gesture, but the playful "Long Ear" continued clicking his fingers. In the end, the more adventurous Pict stood and encouraged his friends to join him.

It would have not been the same if the talkative Eals hadn't made some kind of comment. So, keeping with the trend, he remarked, "Go on Pict! If you can see anything interesting, Adrien and I will join you."

To that Adrien returned in a stern voice, "Let us all make the plunge, if one goes, all go."

So stepping out of their garments, they all in turn splashed into the water.

They could all swim, but none that well. Once in, the initial thought was whether they could touch the bottom, and to their horror they couldn't.

The red-haired Long Ear had been swimming around like a dolphin, seemingly pleased the Westerners had joined him, before he disappeared into the depths.

The realisation that they were in deep waters was causing Adrien and his friends to inwardly panic but sheer pride kept them from being the first to climb out and so they just stayed there treading water.

The sea was a nice temperature at 22 degrees, and not too choppy.

Killgore was the first to dip his head downwards into the brackish water, to see if he could see the long-eared local. His jaw dropped as his eyes saw, through the crystal clear water, the amazing water world below, causing him to swallow a gulp of salty sea.

Lifting his head back out, and through the coughing and spluttering, he urged his comrades to do the same, and they cautiously obeyed.

The stunning visibility in all directions was unbelievable, as they were all introduced to a wonderful sea garden hidden away in the depths. Little was known of what existed underneath the sea.

There, swimming beneath them, (or should I say gliding) was the red-haired water boy, darting around like a fish.

The bottom was a long way down, but just seeing the water baby below them made the whole scenario less scary; in a funny way it was a bit of an adrenalin rush. He was still clicking his fingers, indicating for them to come deeper down, which they all attempted but only managed five or so metres before resurfacing, gasping for breath.

Eals gave up and returned to the comfort of the boulder.

After a couple of attempts, Adrien and Killgore could manage fifteen metres down, three minutes at a time, before coming up for air. But for the water boy it was a different story, as he had been under the water for more than an impressive twenty minutes; his ability to hold his breath for that long was astonishing.

When they were a bit more used to the water, they found they were surrounded by tropical fish. The garden floor was covered with boulders that created mini hills and perched on these hills were endless coloured corals.

A family of rays passed by undeterred by the alien humans, then a school of silver fish swam by in such a fashion it looked like they were making some kind of a symbol. The marine life was fascinating. The excited water boy led them through arches a bit higher up and they passed openings to underwater caves. It was a terrific experience.

High up, the rays of the evening sun that had been piercing through the surface above began to dwindle, letting them know that it would soon be setting. After a thrilling encounter, it was time to leave.

On surfacing they noticed that they had drifted further out than expected and were a little way from the shore. The ginger-haired Long Ear, on seeing that they were not accustomed to sea swimming, stayed with them until they reached the boulder. There, he turned and disappeared back into the sea.

Back on dry land, they met the impatient Eals who had been out of the water for a good half an hour.

Five minutes slipped by and water boy returned, loaded with three fair-size rock fish and a few oysters. He fed the fresh sea food to the hungry visitors, who had never tasted such raw ocean delicacies before. The oysters were a bit of an acquired taste, but the rock fish was sweet and good.

The Long Ear went his way and the three tired visitors slept further up the short beach near the giant turtle.

Two days went by and Adrien, after consulting the other two, had decided that they would fully recharge and revitalise, before acquiring one of the canoes and taking their chances back out on the open sea.

They didn't hide, but just kept a pretty low profile down by the coast, but on the third day in the early morning, the sleeping Western men woke up to strange mixed thumping noises up on one of the volcano ridges, on the south west of this smallish island. The urge to go to investigate was too strong to for these adventurous warriors, so they set off and climbed back up the steep hill to the ridge. Getting near to the top, they saw that many people were gathered. It was the annual festival and there was a lot going on. The festival was held to celebrate the Birdman Challenge. It was apparent that the majority of the people there were the Short Ear race.

They were situated at one of the most dramatic parts of the island next to a pointed ridge. Lots of different music was being played, using all kinds of weird and wonderful instruments; from people whacking a maea, which were round sonorous stones that were beaten rhythmically using a long mallet, shaped like a thin paddle, to playing the conch, a shell trumpet. In time with the conch, were dancers in long grass dresses and grass head-pieces leaping provocatively on flat stones, performing the rarest of dances.

But the most prominent instrument being played, and not to be ignored in the background of the musical din, was the hio; a sort of bamboo flute with holes that gave the most pitiful melancholic sound.

The Birdman Challenge that was to take place was a contest between all seven clans that were on the island, who were to be represented by two of the fittest men from each clan. Whoever won, would see their clan's chief be made the ultimate chief of the whole island, and the members would be given special rights, like being able to fish in the best places and have different privileges given to them over the rest of the islanders.

The birdman winner himself, would have his name written on the sacred rock along with all the other previous winners, and he would have the whole year off work. This was a heavy burden to put on the contestants, as a lot was a stake, and to lose was not an option.

The original birdman challenge of that time was very different to the one historians have recorded happening centuries later, as with time the rules changed.

The people knew it was time for the competition to start when the flocks of sooty birds had come to nest out on the three close-knit islets that were situated off the main island. In those days, the flocks of birds were massive, but as the eco system of this island deteriorated, so the numbers of these birds declined.

They would lay an abundance of eggs, and the challenge would be that whoever got to one of the islets, stole an egg, and returned first with the egg intact, would be the winner.

But it was one of the harshest and deadliest races, for these fine men to compete in, as it started with them all standing in a line at the thinnest point of the ridge on the rim of the crater, with the volcano behind and the rocky vertical slope before them. Once down this dangerous slope, they would have to swim through shark-infested waters out to one of the islets, obtain an egg, then complete the race back in reverse. On reaching the top, the first contestant would give his egg to the waiting high priest, who would then present the prize egg to the chief of the winning clan. Now, all these chiefs were direct descendants of Hota Matu'a the legendary first settler and Ariki Mau (supreme chief) of the island.

The fourteen contestants appeared to great applause, as they were all blessed in turn by the high priest. To distinguish which clan they were from, they wore different coloured loin tapa cloths. Amongst these men were, surprisingly, two of the pale Long Ears. As they passed the priest, he ignored them, and the crowd fell silent as they passed. The three on looking visitors recognized one of the Long Ears straight away as he was their new friend the water boy.

The men competing in the race walked out to the narrow rim and awaited the signal for the race to begin. The whole place went quiet. You could cut the atmosphere with a knife as the tension began to mount.

The Westerners had found a good position from where to watch, a bit further down the slope. Their friend, the Long Ear's name was Mezsel (which meant sculptor); it was a traditional long-eared name, which was very common. He stood there, much smaller than the other tall Short Ears, who all had tattoos like their Polynesian cousins, but their tattoos were different as they were all writings from the Rongorongo hieroglyphic script.

From the side of the narrow rim, a man appeared. This was the supreme chief who had held the prize for the previous year. In his hand he held the winning egg from last year's challenge. He raised his arm back and threw the egg as far as he could. When it hit the ground, that was the signal for the start of the race, but before it hit, some of the more eager contestants had already set off.

The crowd erupted; the Birdman Challenge was underway.

Two of the cheating contestants foolishly sprinted down to get a head start, and this method may have worked for a short distance if they had not collided, causing them both to lose their footing and bounce down off the rocks to their certain death below.

This race was a marathon not a sprint.

Mezsel had waited for the egg to drop and therefore started right at the back.

Different men used different techniques; the most effective was to scramble down backwards on all fours, the other to slide down on their backsides.

Mezsel had his own method, staying relatively close to the central bunch, he moved diagonally from left to right, backwards, holding on to the odd tree shrub or rock.

The first fifty metres was carnage, as some of the contestants were almost scrapping with each other and small rocks were being unearthed, causing mini avalanches which fell and the front runners and caused slight injuries. It took on average twenty minutes, or there about, for most of the challengers to reach the bottom and a couple more fell to the curse of the perilous slope on the way down.

The other Long Ear was right at the front with two others who had a bit of a lead; Mezsel was now in with the middle bunch. In turn, the contestants entered the water, most jumping in. Mezsel was seen diving in.

Eals joked, "Adrien, I thought some of the things you make us do are mad, but this really is madness." At this comment, the nearly always serious Adrien, gave a wry smile for once.

Off shore, the three islets could be seen. All that lay between was the shark-infested ocean, and it didn't take too long for the baying crowd way up on the ridge to quieten down, and the mood to change. Amongst the bobbing heads swimming over to the islets, fins appeared circling round; even the somewhat naive Westerners recognised this awful sight, as the sharks arrived in their droves.

Slowly, a few unfortunate contestants disappeared and were briefly replaced by crimson patches against the deep blue; these would have been the ones that had suffered cuts or injuries whilst scaling down the dangerous slope. Three contenders perished in that shark-infested playground.

After some time, the first two contestants could be seen clambering onto the first pointed islet (which was the smaller and denser of the three). In dribs and drabs the other challengers climbed out of the water; one of the first being the other Long Ear who had opted to take the second islet, and was not far behind the leading swimmers.

Then, with a yell of delight, Killgore shouted, "There he is!" and he was right, as the smaller frame of Mezsel could be seen scrambling onto the far islet. He was the only one that had decided on the furthest one away.

Only eight had so far survived the hazardous slope and the jaws of the finned predators. Vaguely, they caught glimpses of the men rushing around on the islets, and up above them were the very annoyed Sooty birds flying around screaming down at the intruders stealing their newly laid eggs.

An hour passed, the scattered crowd up near the top of the ridge had settled down, and the constant shouting had died down for a bit. Then the first contestant was seen leaping back in the sea from the second islet, and this was the other Long Ear. A minute later, the crowd erupted as two more from the first islet entered the water. And, to the thrill of the Westerners, Mezsel dived in seconds later, the others following shortly after. Everyone had found an egg. Different methods were used to hold the egg; the most popular being to wrap them in their loin cloths at the back.

The race was now on, and although the front three had the advantage the race was wide open. Mezsel was the only one that seemed a bit too far behind and had an awful lot of ground to make up.

A couple more fell into the jaws of the merciless sharks, but the first to reach dry land was the other Long Ear, closely followed by a Short Ear, and then thirty seconds later, Mezsel appeared for the first time since he had been spotted leaving the third islet. He had made up so much distance with his most incredible swim, which he must have accomplished underwater as he hadn't been swimming above the surface with the others.

It was now noticeable that the contenders were weary, as the sharp pace at which they had started earlier, had turned sluggish; you could see that this climb back up was going to be a battle of endurance and pure stamina. The first thing each racer did on reaching dry land was to unravel the egg and carry the prize in their hands.

The other Long Ear was really setting the pace, and was now starting to make the climb near the foot of the slope, with the first Short Ear two paces behind, and Mezsel ten paces behind him; once more he had his own technique where he zigzagged upwards rather than scrambling straight as the others did.

Then something peculiar occurred; the other Long Ear, who was opening up his lead at a steady rate, unexpectedly fell face down, banging his head on a rock. He lay there for a short while, before pressing on, still holding the lead. Then, after climbing a metre or so, he jolted and fell to the side, arching his back as if a spear or something sharp had pierced him from behind. For him the challenge was over as his egg crashed to the ground, shattering as it hit. Up on the ridge the crowd screamed even louder (the last thing they wanted was a Long Ear winning the Birdman Challenge).

Adrien, talking to his companions, said, "He has surely been afflicted by some evil."

Killgore replied, "Yes, Adrien. Look up yonder," and the ever-alert Pict pointed up to a group of old men huddled round an hunched-up old woman, not too far up from where they were perched, who had suspiciously cheered and cackled both times the Long Ear had suffered, and a bit louder when he had dropped the egg.

Meanwhile, the race continued, and the second Short Ear took the lead. Mezsel was hot on his heels, and closing in fast. As they reached halfway up the torturous slope, it was hard to judge how close Mezsel actually was, using his unorthodox method (which meant he was covering more ground than that of the others).

The rest of the contenders were now a long way down and at that point it had become a race between Mezsel and the tall Short Ear (who was identified by his dyed blue loin cloth). Subsequently, when next Mezsel diagonally crossed the Short Ear's path, he had taken the lead. The crowd above hushed, and he looked like he was gaining momentum, holding his egg tightly in his left hand.

Next something alarming happened, as out of the blue the ginger-haired Long Ear halted, clasping his left wrist. The crowd above erupted.

Killgore, who had been watching the contest along with the other two, leapt up and started scrambling up the hill himself. Meanwhile, Mezsel too fell to the side, arching his back like he had been speared between his shoulder blades. Writhing around in pain, he suddenly lost his grip on the egg, which flew up high in the air. Surely that was the end of his race? Everything that happened next appeared to happen in slow motion. The egg spun round and round, and just as it was about to smash on the floor, Mezsel managed to muster enough strength through the pain, to throw out an arm and catch it just in the nick of time.

But the blue-tagged Short Ear passed by, taking back the lead.

Killgore had shot up the slope to where the old hunched woman was surrounded by the now excited old men. As he approached, he saw that the hunched old woman was holding a straw man in one hand, and a sharpened piece of flint in the other, and every time she drove the flint into the straw man, more pain was inflicted on whomever she directed this evil tool towards, for this was a voodoo doll.

Seeing the painted Pict hurdling towards them terrified this cowardly gathering, they screeched out and all the old men ran, leaving Killgore face to face with this voodoo witch. In a flash, Killgore drew his sword and smashed it straight through the straw figure, before taking it away from the witch.

Mezsel had just managed to get himself back to his feet, but as Killgore's sword had taken out the straw man, he felt the blow right into his stomach; fortunately, Killgore had only used the blunt side of his sword, but even so it was a strong blow, and took the wind right out of his lungs and he fell to the floor badly winded.

He lay face down, clutching his tummy for a while, then to the Westerners' amazement, he shakily got to his feet, for this Long Ear was down but not out; the big hurdle he faced now was to try catch the front runner. This was going to be a mammoth task, as the blue loin-clothed man had only twenty metres to get to the crest of the ridge. Mezsel needed to dig deep to find the strength, and that is exactly what he did, and with sheer stamina and perseverance, he pressed on. Surprisingly enough, he chose to carry on with his diagonal routine. Adrien was a bit baffled by this, as he thought Mezsel would have just gone all out and scrambled straight upwards.

Starting off a bit shakily, Mezsel soon broke into his stride. As if something had breathed new life into his lungs, he tore up the remainder of the dangerous slope, moving twice as fast as the fading front competitor who thought he would surely win, with nearly all the crowd willing him to the top; even all the other clans, who did not want the Long Ear to win.

However, Mezsel had other ideas, and he caught up, crossing the flabbergasted Short Ear's path five metres from the top. As they were now pressed shoulder to shoulder, this was going to be a tussle to the end. The Short Ear was taller, and all he had to do was use his strength and muscle his opponent out of the race.

Both men were absolutely exhausted, and this showed on both their faces.

Mezsel was beginning to buckle; it looked as if he had used all his strength to catch up. Then, two metres from the ridge, the Short Ear lashed out with frustration and clumsily missed. What an idiotic error – all he had to do was use his weight. This was Mezsel's chance, and he took it indeed, as he threw himself to the top, being the first to reach the pinnacle.

This was a travesty for the majority of the islanders who were mostly Short Ears, for this was the first time in history that a Long Ear had won the Birdman challenge.

As was tradition, the exhausted Mezsel reached out and handed his egg to the disgusted priest, who had been waiting for the winner at the summit of the ridge. There was the most uncomfortable silence during this traditional occasion.

The priest walked along the narrow ridge to where Mezsel's clan leader was waiting. If you had been able to look closely at this new chief's face, you would have seen a wry smile out of the side of his tightly closed lips. The rest of the clan members were nearby, but due to this hostile atmosphere and the embarrassment that they had just been represented by a Long Ear, none of them made a sound.

Sadly, this champion had no one to cheer him on. He was like a fish out of water in this antagonistic environment, but he was the winner, and proudly he wandered along the ridge off to the right where the long stone tablet stood, holding the names of all the worthy winners that had gone before.

And by rights, his name was to be placed at the bottom of the list. Sadly for him, there was no one to inscribe his name, as the normal scribe had thrown his tool on the floor and refused to write his name; so Mezsel had to write his own name in Petroglifics.

The crowd bitterly drifted off in silence.

The Westerners decided to go and join the champion, and each patted him on the back to show their approval. As he inscribed his name, Adrien couldn't help but see that the red-headed water boy had tears of sadness in his eyes.

Adrien was so impressed with this heroic Long Ear, never having seen such a show of pure human stamina before, that he turned to his comrades and said, "Men, this unusual red-haired warrior has earned his place in my army."

During the next couple of days, the travellers managed to find Hiahia and his tribe on a quite secluded part of the island. Here they had set up camp and intended to stay.

The Westerners stayed with the Maoris for a few days, before Adrien decided it was time for them to leave. After much explanation, Adrien somehow reluctantly persuaded Hiahia to join him. He wasn't too pleased about inviting the adulterous Hiahia to join his army at Caledonia, but this rogue had saved his life, and he did owe him a debt.

Hiahia eventually agreed he would come, and Adrien managed to urge him to bring along with him the red-haired Birdman when the time came. Hiahia had also witnessed the exhilarating challenge, and knew exactly who Adrien was talking about.

When the time came for the travellers to leave, Hiahia had carved a long boat or canoe from a gigantic Paschalococs Palm which was long enough to sit five men, and sent two of the Polynesian rowers to go with them.

Before long they found themselves back out on the familiar lonely blue ocean.

Another long journey took them East, to where the centre of the two western continents met. They travelled for days and days but were glad to reach dry land again.

SACRIFICE ON THE PYRAMID

Stepping onto the soft sand was like heaven; weeks at sea had surely taken its toll on the weary travellers and trying to walk just a few steps, after being in the same position, was quite a task, so they collapsed on the beach for a while.

The two Polynesians pulled the long boat up the beach, away from the lapping water. Taking the empty skins with them, they went off on the hunt for fresh water.

The Westerners were slightly suffering; their lips were chafed from the constant sun and salt.

Jungle overhung the beach. Eals noticed coconuts lying on the ground everywhere. Picking three up, he used his sword to cut the tops off the shells, handing them to his comrades. The watery milk inside was so very refreshing. The Polynesians returned with the skins now full of soothing fresh water.

Adrien pulled out the map, which now showed a range of what looked like grey triangles dotted around on the new continent they had arrived at.

He got to his unsteady feet and said, "My good friends, let's move on." Killgore groaned, but he as much as anybody was ready for the next adventure.

The Saxon commander decided to head for an area to the East, where six grey triangles were clearly shown on the map

They set off, leaving the obedient Polynesians behind. Fortunately, the jungle was only dense in small areas, and they soon stumbled on a network of narrow pathways.

On the journey, they were met by black toucans with bright yellow necks and long orange beaks, amongst other exotic birds chattering away in the trees. Then, at one point they thought they were being followed, as spider monkeys swung from branch to branch up ahead. This was the first time they had seen monkeys, although they had heard much about them. You can imagine how alarmed they were.

Through the duration of the nights, howler monkeys could be heard calling out to each other.

After three days of brisk walking they arrived at their destination. They came to cultivated land; a small reservoir lay to the right and off to the left ran a stone road. High up ahead the first triangle came into view.

Just beyond the cultivated field were small houses. Killgore said, "Would it not be wise, to go stay here until nightfall?" Adrien and Eals agreed. So they decided to lie low, under the shelter of the jungle until dark, and then go and explore.

As soon as the cloak of darkness was thrown over the land, the travellers crossed the cultivated field and approached the houses. This was the outskirts of a city where the poor people, the craftsmen, farmers, and lower classes lived. The houses were tiny and made of adobe, with roofs made of branches; every house had a tiny yard, most with plants and vegetables all cramped in.

Just beyond these small buildings ran the road, which was made up of long flat stones that all fitted into each other like a puzzle, making a smooth surface. At the side, lighting up the road every twenty yards or so, were thin concrete posts and on top of these posts were thick burning pine logs.

The travellers kept in the shadows, moving one by one, from one house to another.

Few local people were out and about. The outline of the pyramids rose up in the night sky. The name of this awe-inspiring city was Mital; this is today known as the ancient city of Tikal.

Exploring the city they found temples, market places, big squares that would look beautiful in the daylight, public wells, and most impressively towering up to the sky, the six huge pyramids. The few people they did pass were much smaller than the trespassers.

One single pyramid stood on its own, away from the other pyramids. They decided to explore and climb the colossal steps to the top. The steep climb was deceiving and much harder than it looked, but fortunately they went unnoticed. Reaching the top, they found a small simple temple with a plain, stone altar inside.

The foreigners stayed up there and relaxed under the stars that shone like brightly polished diamonds glistening in the night sky; to see the stars at Mital that night was a phenomenal sight..

They chatted between themselves; Adrien expressed how he was surprised at how slack the security was. Not knowing what the following day would bring, they plotted to take over one of the tiny houses on the outskirts of the city to use as a base, whilst they were there.

Sadly, because of the dark, they never got to see an aerial view of this superb city from the apex of the pyramid; all they could see were small fires dotted around and the outline of buildings.

Before dawn, the two Saxons and the painted Pict climbed back down the steps and, leaving the pyramid, made their way back to the outskirts. The fires that lit the roads were now burnt out; the city streets were deserted. It was like a Mayan ghost town.

Stopping at the second house from the end, next to the cultivated field, Adrien whispered, "Right! This house looks like it will do." The house was only tiny and the wooden door had no lock, so with a slight push the trespassing travellers quietly entered.

The day was now beginning to break, so they could vaguely see inside the house. There were two rooms, but no door separating them, the second room was the sleeping quarters and the sound of deep snoring could be heard. Once inside, the soldiers closed the door behind them and waited, crouching down.

Eals felt some kind of rat-like creature scurrying around his feet. Looking closely he noticed it was an ugly looking little dog with no fur; it was just sniffing around, not making a sound.

When there was sufficient light to see properly, Adrien signalled it was time to attack the people in the other room. Swords drawn, Killgore and Eals entered the tiny room. On the floor lay two people; a man and a woman sleeping under a fur blanket.

Eals pointed his sword at the man's neck. As he slowly pulled away the blanket, the man awoke, and Eals put his finger on the man's lips to silence him. The tanned man looked absolutely petrified. His wife was woken by Killgore in a similar fashion.

The tiny house was sparsely furnished inside. They took the blanket and cut it up, using the material to make three hoods to hide their faces. It was not until the afternoon that the trespassers decided to venture out. Before leaving, they found some old rope and tied up the scared man and his wife.

The route behind the house was chosen in order to attract as little attention as possible. At the rear of the house a wasteland backed onto the back of other houses that ran in parallel towards the city centre. As they drew nearer to the centre of the city, they put the hoods over their heads and stepped back to the front of the houses and into the road.

The local people were mostly walking in the same direction, off a road to the left. So keeping heads down and hunching up to make themselves appear smaller like the local people, they followed.

The road became more crowded and next they were entering an exquisite ball court with four stands on each side, which rose up with steps at the side. The travellers climbed the steps on the right to the top, so they were out of the way.

The grass on the court was short. It was marked with chalk all the way round, and was divided by a single line into two equal sections. It was a bit like a soccer pitch, but much narrower and slightly shorter. The shadow of a pyramid was cast over part of the court. Adrien, Eals and Killgore did not have a clue what was going on, but the place was packed; there must have been a good four or so thousand people there.

These people were the Maya. They were short people, well built, with large thorax and short muscular limbs. Their faces were wide with steep cheeks, slightly oblique eyes and aquiline noses and their hair was straight and black. But the weirdest and most noticeable thing was the shape of a lot of their heads; some had long heads, some so pointed that they looked quite deformed, for these people re-shaped the shape of their babies' skulls from a young age.

There was an obvious class difference. The people nearer the front of the stand next to the court were well dressed, wearing a lot of jewellery, some had different animal heads and parrot feathers on their head pieces, but the poorer people, who sat higher up the stands, wore clothing made of bark material (which is beaten till soft and flexible).

The travellers kept the hoods over their heads and did not talk, as they needed to draw as little attention as possible. The crowd began to stir and everyone stood up.

On one side of the court a group of men appeared, at the same time another group appeared on the other side. Both groups came to the centre and standing a yard away from the line, they stood facing each other. On each side were roughly twenty-five men.

A very colourful man appeared and wandered elegantly down the centre line between the two groups of men, inspecting the men on each side as he went.

Adorned on the man's head was a decorated hat with long parrot and toucan feathers. He also wore a gold crown and had a cloak wrapped round him, for this was the Mayan king. He took his seat - a stone throne at the front of the opposite stand.

The game was ready to begin. Both teams started in their own ends. From the side of the court a man stood on the centre line holding a round rubber ball, just a little smaller than a football. Both teams were dressed differently; the team on the right-hand side from where the travellers sat high in the stands had been painted all over in a turquoise blue colour. All they had on was a loin cloth, on one knee they wore a leather knee pad and an elbow pad on either their left or right arm, depending on whether they were right or left handed.

The other team were dressed more colourfully and not one player the same as another, although they too wore knee and elbow pads, and two or three even wore leather saddles around their waists. Many had unusual headdresses, some with jaguar tails and snake skins hanging down their backs; one even wore a whole jaguar fur with the big cat's head still attached on top of his own head. Some even wore turkeys.

However, one man stood out. Taller than his team mates, he wore a head adornment made with feathers of toucans and shiny green Quetzal feathers (a native bird), and an extremely long tail hung down his back almost touching the floor. His name was Buluc Chabtan, and he was the leader of the Mayan army of that region. He was painted red with white lines across his face. Apart from the head-dress, all these men also wore loin cloths. Some of the players on each side held short, flat, racket-shaped objects made of wood.

The game began with the neutral ball man throwing the round rubber ball high up in the air towards the centre. Players from both sides jumped high to catch the ball, which was knocked over to the side of the blue team. One player caught the rubber ball, but before he had time to pass or get rid of it, he was bulldozed down by the opposition.

There was no referee and no fouls. The aim of the game was to get the ball over the opposing team's back line. The game was fast and furious; players fought with each other even if nowhere near play. The game only stopped when the ball passed the side lines and out of play, when the last player to touch it would stand on the line and hit it back in using his elbow or knee with the leather pad on. The pads were used a great deal during the course of the game to really whack the ball. Not one player stayed in one position, both teams bunched up and all chased the ball like five-year olds playing football.

Ten minutes in, the ball went out of play near the blue side's back line. The man in the jaguar fur elbowed the ball back into play, and a blue player with a racket in one hand intercepted it. He ran a long way, dodging his opponents and passing the centre line. Another blue man was out to his left, so the man with the ball threw it up in the air; using his racket he slogged it over to the unmarked man who ran the rest of the way and crossed the opposite line. The crowd remained quiet.

The brutal game went on with much blood spilt. It didn't take too long until the colourful team equalized, as a blue slipped near his own line and was robbed of the ball. As soon as the colours scored, there was loud applause from the approving crowd.

The game continued on, and within two hours the blue team were five to one up. After the fifth goal, the Mayan army leader, Buluc Chabtan, called the colourful team to the back of the court for a stern talking to; after drinking water, the game was ready to carry on. Things now changed for the colourful team, rather than being aimlessly bunched up, they were now strategically positioned, with two at the very back and six in a row just in front, with all the players at the back having rackets. The majority of the players were placed in the middle forming an arrow shape with Buluc Chabtan, the lone man at the point of the arrow; level with him were two men with rackets out wide to the left and right side.

The ball was once again thrown towards the centre by the neutral man. Buluc leapt high above the opposition to catch the ball, which he instantly released, pushing it back towards his team mates, despite taking a hit to his face by an opposing racket, splitting his nose. The game changed dramatically; the colourful team now moving as a unit, and with players holding their positions, they started to pass the ball round with great ease.

Buluc was involved in most of the clever play. Using the wide men, they crossed the opposite line, scoring three times in quick succession. The blue team was falling apart, and they were beginning to tire. This now became the clever army leader's show. Attacking from the front, he was running rings around the blue team and he scored twice more and set up the seventh to put his team seven to five up.

But he was to save the best till last. The blues piled on the pressure and had pinned the colours deep into their own half, when Buluc stole the ball, ripping it away from an opponent's hands. He passed it back to a player at the back near the corner, who hit it on the volley with his racket, sending it high towards the centre. Buluc had started running forward as soon as he had released the ball and, jumping up, he plucked the ball out of the air, landing amidst the blue team. Using sheer strength, skill and determination, he dragged himself, still holding the ball and taking a battering, away from the bulk of the blue team, and dodged his way forward, running the whole length of the opposing team's side of the court. There was just one man to beat nearing him, and using his padded knee he knocked the ball over the man's head, twisting round as he passed he caught the ball the other side of the last blue man and crossed the line; game over! The colours had been victorious, which was all down to the army leader's clever strategy.

The crowd was ecstatic as Buluc Chabtan was their favourite - a local hero. He had taken the Mayan army into battle and using his famous strategies, had out foxed enemies and won battles against the odds many times.

After the game the crowd dispersed; it was late afternoon – the game had gone on for a good four hours. Adrien and his two comrades came down from the stands and got in amongst the crowd, who were all going in the same direction. Following on, they came to a beautiful big square at the foot of one of the pyramids, and here the people began to just sit as if waiting for something.

The inquisitive trespassers were not content to sit, so they decided to get closer to the pyramid that now looked so different from the night before.

These pyramids were a symbol of testimony to this great Mayan civilization. Inscribed on the stonework at the bottom, were fantastic drawings of animals and vivid sculptures and symbols of the gods of this land, made of green volcano turf and painted many colours. This particular pyramid had steps at the front and the back, leading up to a temple on top.

A hundred or so metres down the road, in one of the buildings many people could be seen carrying things inside.

Adrien whispered to his comrades, "I think we should now leave." He was right. People were beginning to stare at the strangers. And here for the first time they saw soldiers; two standing, holding spears at the foot of the pyramid. So the foreigners crept from the grassy square and slipped away to the outskirts.

Adrien spoke as they sat next to a well, "I need the captain from the game. He is an intelligent leader of men, and so we must go and find this man."

As the darkness fell on the land, the dull beat of a drum began to hum, coming from the square they had left earlier. So, back the travellers went, having removed the hoods that had been covering their faces. The fire-posts on the sides of the road had been lit. Before they arrived back at the square, they passed the place that had been bustling with people coming to and fro that afternoon. All three were tempted to have a peek inside.

Two low steps led up to two terraces at the level of the building that turned out to be a temple. There was not a single man in sight, for everyone was up at the square. Looking inside the big temple, they saw several long tables in a row, set up for an enormous banquet. A few women were putting the finishing touches to the feast; clearly there was to be a kind of celebration for an event that was to take place.

Very seriously, Adrien said to his men, "I wish for you both to stay here and wait for me to return. I will go to the crowded place alone."

So he left his two companions and, keeping close to the shadows, he made his way towards the crowded square. The sound of the skin drum drew closer, thumping like a heart beating. Coming to the very last house which was a house for the priests, he stepped into the shadows out of view. From his hiding place he could see the whole square in front of him. Next to him was the pyramid and he could see the colossal stairway that was well lit by stakes, from the base, all the way to the temple at the top; it was an impressive sight. At the back of the square, behind the gathered Mayan people, the sky was lit up by an enormous fire. A pleasant smell filled the cool night air, coming from the pinewood fire; it was like liquorice and vanilla mixed with pine resin.

The people were swaying to the beat of the drum and the whistling of a flute-like instrument could be heard. As if they were all in a trance, some stood, some were sitting and a few lying on the floor, but all were moving to the beat.

Adrien watched intently. After a while, he realised he recognised the men at the front nearest the foot of the pyramid, for they were all the members of the colourful team from the ball court that afternoon. He hadn't recognised them earlier because now they wore masks made of jade and pyrite. One of the men held a chain holding a black jaguar, that seemed relaxed about being surrounded by humans, and stood contentedly with its master, who was none other than Buluc Chabtan.

There was no way the Saxon would be able to get near to this man; all he could do was take his time and wait. Looking up, he saw four bearded men coming down the stairway from the temple dressed in white, who were the holy men, one of whom held a book. The men stopped as they approached the bottom step.

Buluc Chabtan placed the jaguar's chain on the ground and followed the priests, who turned, and climbed back up the staircase, with Buluc now in the middle.

Right then, Adrien felt he had to act; he had a bad feeling about what was to take place. So he crept round to the back of the pyramid, which was deserted, and in the dark he started to swiftly clamber up the back stairway.

Meanwhile, Eals and Killgore, with their leader gone, decided it was time to grab some food. The women, putting the finishing touches to the feast, froze as soon as they saw the foreign trespassers. Eals raised his sword and used it to beckon the women into a corner, where the women stayed, falling to their knees with faces to the ground, for they automatically thought the Saxon and the Pict were gods.

There was so much food spread out on the tables: fruits from the forest, including mangos, papaya, squash, avocados, fish, yams, beans, maize, chillies and spices, cobs of corn, and many more delicacies. At the top of the temple hall was a throne, with a table laid out; the spread here was more elegantly decorated than the rest, fit for royalty, for this was the Mayan king's table. On this table were woven baskets and finely turned pottery to contain the food.

The two comrades made their way to the more attractive king's table and started enjoying the feast. Also on this table was a wooden cup sat next to a couple of pottery bowls, inside which was a thick brown liquid. Eals picked up the cup and dipped it in the brown liquid. It smelt delicious. Putting it to his lips, he took a sip; the taste was sweet yet appetising, so he drank the whole cupful. This was the drink the Mayans made from the cacao bean, known today as chocolate. The first bowl had honey added to it. Eals urged Killgore to taste some and he too gulped it down. The other bowl was a little different, as the chocolate had chilli peppers mixed in, making the beverage spicy.

Adrien reached the top of the pyramid before Buluc and the four priests. He crouched, staying just below the top steps. Coming from the other side, he heard a noise like rain falling into a bucket coming from the staircase; the structure had been made in such a way that when anybody got near the top, their footsteps would sound like the pitter-patter of rain and this would echo around the base of the pyramid.

The men appeared at the top. Buluc Chabtan willingly lay upon the solid stone altar, the men in white robes gathered around and the man holding the book opened it and started chanting in an alien language, verses from the Popol Vuh, their religious book. After each paragraph, he would glance up to the sky, to acknowledge the different gods he called upon.

The temple was bare; four columns held up a sloping roof above the stone altar, but it very well lit by the wooden stakes.

The priest reading the book, picked up a long obsidian knife, and held it over some flames to heat it up. He then took the heated knife over to the altar, where Buluc Chabtan was lying completely motionless, as if he had already accepted his fate, his eyes fixed on the night sky.

The other priests took up their positions; one on either side next to Buluc's arms, and one at the bottom of the altar near his legs. Then the priest holding the knife, lifted it up shouting the words, "Chaac, Chaac." Chaac was the name of the Mayan god of rain. As he repeated these, the heavens opened and rain began to pour.

Adrien had to stop this ritual ceremony, so he stood and ran up the last three steps. On seeing the pale-skinned Saxon, the priests instantly dropped to their knees, pressing their faces to the floor, as the women in the temple had.

Adrien offered his hand to Buluc who sat up. With a look of sheer disbelief on his face, he obediently followed Adrien, who led the Mayan back down the front of the colossal stairway, towards the crowded square below.

The beat of the drum thumped and the enchanting flute whined on. Since the rain had come, the ritual dancing had become more intense, and Adrien now noticed how some Mayans were cutting and piercing their own skin with sharp objects. This was a sacred act the Mayans did to please the gods, which was called bloodletting. They too, on seeing Adrien and Buluc descending the stairway, dropped to the floor.

Once at the bottom, the passive jaguar padded to his master and followed as the Saxon led Buluc away from the square. Passing the temple, Adrien called out to his companions, who on hearing their leader's voice came out immediately.

"Friends, we need to get as far away from this city, while all the people are hypnotized," said Adrien earnestly.

So that night they left Mital, taking with them Buluc Chabtan and his pet jaguar, stopping as they reached the tiny house on the outskirts where they had tied up the man and woman, to release them.

They got as far away as possible before stopping to sleep.

YIN AND YANG

Just when Darinus and his men started to think nothing was going to happen, a local man stepped forward to the centre of the room and shouted out some words. The hall fell silent, and everyone got to their feet and bowed their heads. Awkwardly the Romans followed.

A richly clothed man entered, holding the hand of a stylishly dressed young woman (Darinus recognised her to be the beautiful woman from the lake). They elegantly walked, the full length of the hall and took their places on the two chairs, the man sitting on the higher seat of the two. Once seated, the speaker in the centre shouted out their names and the rest of the people sat back down. The man's name was Shai-Tang and the young woman was his niece, Ki Sui-Tang.

The event that was about to take place was a contest Shai-Tang had arranged, in which to find a husband, worthy enough to take his niece's hand in marriage.

It was time for the contestants to arrive, warriors from dynasty's near and far.

First to enter the hall was the man in black, who confidently swaggered in. He took long strides, towards the right side of the hall, where empty benches stood, but instead of sitting on a bench he sat down upon the sand floor, crossing his legs into the meditation position. He was followed by six other warriors who all in turn made their way to the empty benches.

The last man to enter the room was dressed in white. He was identical to the man in black, only the colour of their costumes separating them. He walked over to the left side of the room, the same side as the Romans; he also preferring the sand floor rather than the bench.

There was a story behind the black and white warriors; the man in white was named Yang, and the man dressed in black was his twin, called Yin; they were the two sons of Chu-Song, ruler of a far north dynasty. The eldest was to succeed their father at the helm of this rapidly expanding province, but there was one major problem, for it was not known which one was born first, Yin or Yang, as at birth there was seven minutes between the twins, but due to complications with their mother, they were left on their own, and on returning to the new born twins nobody could remember which one had been born first.

Through the years that followed the issue caused many problems between the brothers. The quarrels and fighting became so severe that at the age of twelve, Chu-song sent them both away to two separate monasteries to be taught values.

It was during these times a prince called Bohdidarma, who was from a faraway country, travelled these lands teaching the monks. He had been spiritually enlightened, and as he travelled long distances, he developed repetitive exercises. He enlightened many, teaching what is known today as martial arts.

Yang and Yin in their two monasteries both grew and excelled in the arts.

This day within this hall, was the first time they had stepped foot into the same room as each other for eight years, since they had been separated.

There were eight contestants who wished to fight: a Xiang Pu wrestler, a local man with a Samurai sword, a sorcerer, a balding man, who had a long distinctive moustache, a stocky, rough-looking man from the north and a tall immaculately dressed guy, as well as the twins.

There was no surprise why these men were willing to fight, for the prize was Ki Sui-Tang's hand in marriage; she was popular, bright, beautiful and intelligent, and also had studied the arts - she came from the Tang family, an extremely wealthy family of good status. Ki's mother was a Sui and her late father was a Tang, Shai's younger brother. Shai-Tang himself was the civil governor of this dynasty, and had arranged this contest.

Although unable to understand the language it was reasonably clear to the Romans what was happening.

All of a sudden Darinus got to his feet. Undoing his belt he gave his sword to Julian and climbed over the bench, and joined the other warriors. Everyone in the room had their eyes fixed upon this foreign stranger.

Eventually the man in the middle of the room indicated for the contest to begin, and he pointed at Yang, the twin dressed in white, screeching "Ju," then turned and pointed to the weird little sorcerer man dressed in a dark kimono, who had a darker skin complexion than everyone else and his cheek bones appeared higher than that of the locals. This was because he was from the Eastern islands known as the land of the five kings. Darinus could sense that this sorcerer man had an evil presence surrounding him.

The men stood opposite each other. Yang bowed his head as a mark of respect. The tournament began, as they edged closer to each other, many combinations and punches and kicks were thrown, but the sorcerer seemed far too quick (for he was using an unexplained supernatural force). However he still could not penetrate through Yang's blocks.

Eventually the sorcerer took five long steps backwards and pulled out a Hira Shuriken (an eight pointed death star) from beneath his wide sleeve and threw it with great speed at Yang, where it hit him cutting deep into his left thigh. Just as quickly, the white twin ripped it out and threw it right back with equal force, and it landed between the vile sorcerer's eyes, instantly ending the fight.

The referee ushered two random men from the front row, who picked up the corpse and threw it out into the street.

Yang sat back down, resuming the meditation position, still deep in concentration, appearing to be unfazed by the blood seeping through his white garments from the wound in his thigh.

Julian noticed halfway through the duel that Ki had left the building.

The next two contestants to be called up by the referee were Yin, the black twin, and the similarly dressed local man with the Samurai sword (which he left on the floor near the edge). He was from a nearby village and wore a brown tunic.

This fight was a lot more intense, as they both fought with a comparable style. It soon became apparent that Yin was stronger; the Samurai man, realising he was going to lose made a dive and grabbed his sword, swiftly turning he lifted it high but as he brought it down to strike, the quick-thinking Yin stepped aside and putting his arm under his opponent's armpit in such a way it snapped the man's arm at his elbow. The noise of the bone breaking followed by the blood curdling scream was horrific. Yin finished the move by kicking away his feet.

Next up was Darinus. For once the fearless general was anxious, for the way these warriors fought in their unorthodox fashion was alien to him.

His adversary was the Xiang Pu wrestler (sumo). All he wore was strapped underwear around his waist; he carried so much weight his massive belly bulged, his hair was tied up in a bun sitting on top of his head. This man was so much bigger than Darinus.

As they faced each other the Xiang Pu wrestler crouched and looked the Roman in the eyes. He rubbed his hands together then, loudly clapped them, then he placed them on his knees and moved oddly around, stamping his feet on the ground (the reason the Xiang Pu wrestler did this was to crush any evil spirits). He progressed towards Darinus, who was the first to act by punching the big man straight in his face, as hard as he could, but this had no effect as the half-naked man put his huge arms around Darinus' waist, and, grabbing him by his belt, lifted him up and threw him high into the air. The shocked Darinus must have gone five metres to the edge near the crowd. Just as Darinus was getting his breath back, the Xiang Pu wrestler picked him up again and threw him just as far the other way. This went on a few more times, at one point Darinus flew into the crowd and whacked his back hard on one of the benches.

Finally he managed to get his breath back and get away from the big man's grasp. He ran around for a bit as he was too quick for his adversary.

He decided the only way to beat this man was to use one of his most effective moves which he had used numerous times in battle, and which was a move that these men of the arts would appreciate. He rushed at the Xiang Pu wrestler and, spinning round, he used his elbow to strike his foe's chin. Fortunately this worked as the big man fell to the floor with a massive thud, knocked clean out.

As soon as the battered Darinus had sat back down, the next fight began, between the skinny bald man with the long distinctive moustache and the nomadic warrior from the Xiongnu Empire in the north, who was a stocky, scruffily dressed unkempt man with wild hair.

This contest was vicious and the nomadic warrior acted like an animal, showing his opponent no respect, he fought in a more kick box kind of style, and he had long pointed nails which he cowardly used to scratch and claw with.

At one point he closely passed Darinus. Opening his mouth he revealed a set of sharply pointed teeth that he used to bite the bald man with. He ruthlessly broke bones and finished the bout by digging his claws into the poor man's collar bone and yanking it down, causing the most brutal death.

During this last bloody conflict a new warrior slipped into the back of the hall, they were small and wore a purple dress from head to foot with only their eyes on show. The referee noticed and put them immediately into combat against the tall, immaculately dressed man, who took off his top and to the surprise of the crowd he had a finely tuned figure, although he sauntered around in a rather feminine fashion though.

This fight lasted ten or so minutes, mainly down to the purple contender's fancy movements, using spinning kicks, flips and swift combination punches, which the tall man dealt with, seemingly with great ease, pushing forwards all the time. The fight ended with the purple warrior spearing his hand into the tall man's throat, followed by a spinning hook kick to the torso, before sweeping away his feet, thus ending the bout.

Still even at this point of the tournament there was no sign of Ki's return.

Soon the time came for Darinus to fight again; the referee pointed for him to step up, but before his opponent could be allocated, the small purple warrior hastily stood forward.

"Right then," Darinus confidently muttered, under his breath, "let me teach this little man my way of fighting." He lifted his clenched fists up.

Nevertheless, like a whirlwind the small fighter was all over him. He managed a couple of air punches before his legs were taken from under him and he hit the ground horizontally. The crowd started yelling with delight. He attempted to get to his feet but as he stood, he felt the full force of his opponent's foot directly in his mouth. This time he spun half a circle as he hit the sand floor.

He had never lost a one-on-one fight before. However this might be his first and people had died in that place already that day. If he didn't act quickly he might be the next, so with sheer determination he hauled himself up, spitting blood from his mouth as he did. Nonetheless the purple warrior was not going to give him time to recover as they swiftly moved in, driving their knee hard into Darinus' chest, which took the wind out of the Roman general's lungs. Yet with his right hand Darinus just managed to grab the floppy belt of his rival's tunic as they twisted away, which briefly stopped them in their tracks and gave the battered Roman enough time to unleash his left fist hard into their stomach, clearly this winded them. Without delay he landed another punch hitting his opponent's cheek and knocking them to the ground.

The shouting and cheering ceased, as Darinus pulled the clothing from his defeated opponent's face, revealing to all the spectators, and to his own amazement, the face of Ki-Sui-Tang, who had been temporarily stunned by the blow. Shai-Tang put an end to the contest.

Julian signalled to the Romans to leave instantly, picking up his exhausted master and swiftly leaving, managing to avoid any confrontation.

Back at the hut Darinus rested for the entire day.

The following morning Darinus woke (he had not slept too well). He could not get the thought of Ki Sui-Tang out of his head, and blamed himself for striking her.

Leaving the hut he made his way back through the wood to the tranquil lake. 'Just maybe she would return in the early morning to bathe'. He waited, once again hiding behind the bamboo canes, with the jetty in sight, and the water up to his knees.

He did not have to wait long, before the muffled voices of women could be heard up the trail, and then the three women came into view. They walked elegantly to the end of the jetty and sat down, dipping their feet into the lake. This time they acted more sombrely; once again Ki stripped and slid into the water.

Darinus had fallen under the spell of this beautiful creature. He felt helpless – he wanted to know her; the feeling came from deep inside his stomach. How could he tell her? She didn't even know him, how would she react seeing him again especially after yesterday's event?

Ki pulled herself back up and out of the water, and one of her maids gave her a towel.

She sat back on the jetty drying her hair. Darinus was all in a panic. He had always lived under the slogan; 'if you never act you might never receive, everybody's destiny is in their own hands'. He could not leave this land without letting his feelings be known.

So as the three women got up to leave he waded out from behind the canes. At first none of the women noticed him, until he bellowed out "wait".

They all turned as they were stepping off the pier. Darinus continued, "Please stop." Just then he lost his footing wading into deeper water. His head disappeared, and then seconds later reappeared. Spitting out a big gulp of lake water, he swam the short distance to the small pier. Hoisting himself up he slipped (nerves had got the better of him), banging his chin on the wood as he fell, he cut himself quite badly.

The women stood still like statues, shocked at what they were seeing. Once up onto the end of the pier, Darinus knelt down on one knee and raised his hands, as if surrendering.

The two servant girls turned to leave whilst Ki stopped, looking mystified at the humiliated Roman for a few seconds, before holding her head high and briskly leaving. Wiping the blood off his chin the sad Darinus got himself together and returned to his troops.

"Sire," Julian remarked, "who has attacked you? Show me and I will vindicate you."

Darinus replied in his calm manner, "All is well with me, Centurion." Gathering the rest of his men Darinus said, "I have made a decision. We shall stay here for seven sunrises then continue our quest." Nobody dared question the commander's decision.

The following day the Roman general (leaving his sword) returned to the lake. On his way through the wood he stooped down and picked a handful of wild flowers. He arrived earlier than the previous day. Once again he followed the beach, waded past the bamboo canes, through the deep water and climbed up onto the jetty.

Sitting on the side of the jetty, his only fear was whether she would not return.

Patiently he waited.

But thankfully she did, this time with only one maid for company.

On seeing Darinus the girls paused. Ki took charge, and they cautiously tiptoed passed him to the end of the pier. Ki was defiant, she would not be intimidated; ignoring the stranger they sat at the end dipping their feet in the cool water.

A few minutes passed. Darinus got up and slowly walked towards them, gently placing the flowers on the wooden deck next her, he turned to leave. His legs felt like jelly, he stumbled and in doing so stubbed his toe, causing him to cry out in pain. At this the girls started to giggle. Oh, good at least he had got a reaction, indubitably that was positive.

Darinus jumped into the water, and went back the way he had come.

On the fourth day, once again he made his way back to the lake. Ki was already there, this time alone. He sat down next to her at the end of the small pier, she did not appear to be at all fazed by his presence.

After some time the silence between them became almost deafening (all that could be heard was the water gently lapping up the small beech). Darinus decided to speak. Knowing they spoke a different language, he slowly introduced himself. "Dar...ii.n.us."

Ki glared at him before bursting out laughing.

They spent quite a while together, trying to communicate. Just before going their separate ways the general leant over, tenderly kissing her cheek (which had been bruised in the fight).

As the days passed the two spent more and more time together, walking in the wood and swimming in the lake.

One particular morning Ki brought her uncle Shai Tang to meet Darinus. Shai was accompanied by an older fellow, with thinning hair and a long beard, who was an interpreter. Translating between them, he said Ki had found favour with the Roman which was good enough for Shai (who had already witnessed the bravery of the general).

Shai moved the Romans from the hut in the quaint village up to the town with the grand houses. Two weeks later Darinus and Ki Sui-Tang got married with Shai's blessing.

The wedding was a low-key affair, held under a lovely pergola decorated with flowers surrounded by phoenix and dragon shaped candles. Ki was very much drawn towards dragons, maybe this was because she had been born in the year of the dragon. The pergola was next to the lake. The setting was stunning. Darinus wore the traditional red dress: a tunic with a sash and a narrow angle-length skirt. Ki also wore the symbolic colour red, along with a red veil covering her face.

Her hair was ritually put up, and she wore a thin white gold crown on the top of her head.

Darinus was content. He now had a strong and intelligent queen to sit next to him at the castle in Caledonia.

Comically, the one thing that began to annoy Darinus and Ki was the translator, who followed them everywhere.

A SURPRISED GUEST TURNS UP FOR DARINUS

After several blissful months, Darinus was really enjoying married life. His new bride Ki's uncle 'Shai-tang' had kindly given them a nice modern place to live, with a long garden, stretching down to the beautiful lake. At the bottom of the garden overlooking the water, was a platform neatly decked with wood.

The other Romans, including Julian, were all given comfortable accommodation in the town. They all even adopted the local dress, dressing in posh silk tunics.

Life was good, in fact it was that good that Darinus had almost forgotten why he was there and as for the Caledonian castle and the chess battle, they rarely entered his head, and if they did they were soon drowned out by the chores of everyday life.

One particular morning Darinus was dozing in his canvas chair out on the wooden platform. It was now the season of autumn, the tall trees that stood on the edge of the lake were many rustic colours: reds to oranges and different shades of yellow. Out on the lake the lilies had now closed, getting ready for the winter. This calm serene morning was suddenly interrupted, and the wind started to blow. Darinus heard tapping a few yards away. Drearily opening his lazy eyes he was all of a sudden fully awake. There to his dismay right before him was the magician Wei Po-Yang. At the sight of him Darinus almost fell out of his chair.

This time the magician looked far taller and more frightening than he had at the Caledonian courtyard. He did not look at all amused, in fact he looked so furious that his eyebrows met in the middle of his brow. Po-Yang spoke in such a voice his words seemed to echo across the water. "Roman, you appear to have abandoned your mission, you have allowed your vision to become clouded over." At every word the magician uttered, the gale force wind became more ferocious, and he stamped his pointed stick harder and harder on the decking.

One thing that did surprise Darinus was that this was the first time he had heard Po-Yang speak in Latin. But these words pricked at the Roman's heart. Looking down at the floor he hung his head in shame. The magician was oh so very right; after meeting and falling in love with his lovely Ki his sight had become jaded.

The magician continued tapping his pointed stick, turning away in disgust from the miserable Roman he gazed out onto the vast lake.

The Roman began to feel the hunger start to burn again, deep down in his belly. He stood up straight and said, "Sire, I understand I have failed myself, you and the good druid. I whole heartily apologise."

The magician replied, "There is not much time to lose, you have already lost enough, you must make haste. I hear there is trouble in the land of Chu-song, the northern dynasty. I hear you have already been acquainted with his sons Yang and Yin. You would be a fool to overlook these two exceptional warriors for your army. Go, Darinus. Follow your head."

Darinus, making haste, rushed through his house and over the road to where his Centurion, Julian, had moved in with a local girl. It was a small squared house typical of the town.

He burst straight through the front door. Julian had just got up from his bed and was still wearing his loose bed robe and was extremely surprised to see his commander so early in the morning, especially these days.

Darinus got his breath back. "Julian, I have been a fool, we must leave here and leave here immediately."

Julian could see that glint once again in his master's eyes. He replied, "Master have you gone mad? I thought we were going to leave all that behind. Besides you are now married and life is good for us all here. Anyhow, who desires that stupid island Britannia. It is full of pagans and heathens."

Darinus reacted crossly to this comment. "Julian, look at us what have we become! We are soldiers, Roman soldiers. I order you to meet me at noon together with my guards armed and ready to depart, and yes, we will build an almighty army and we will conquer Britannia. Before I forget to tell, I have had a visitor who at this very moment is in my garden – the magician Wei Po-Yang".

Julian was shocked, and now he would have to obey this order.

Darinus had to break the news to his new bride. Returning home he found Ki out in the garden practising yoga. Po-Yang was nowhere to be seen, and for a snap second, the general thought this was only a dream. He went and sat down next to his wife; speaking gently, "My beloved, the time has come for me to depart and continue on my quest."

Her eyes welled up. She knew of the battle, the druid and the magician and the Caledonian castle. She replied, "I know, my husband."

Darinus carried on, "Shortly we will be reunited, and you will take your seat next to me in the chequered courtyard, where I will conquer, and become the first Roman king to sit upon the throne of Britannia. You will be my queen and our line will continue to rule, long after I have gone to Elysia."

Not long after Darinus had departed, his wife found that she had fallen pregnant; months later she gave birth to a healthy son.

Darinus and his men rode northwards upon horseback, towards the north dynasty belonging to Chu-song. The Roman leader had noticed a bad atmosphere hanging over his men, especially Julian's attitude. He had been in a foul mood ever since they had left. You could literally cut the atmosphere with a knife. So the Roman Commander brought the party to a halt, swinging his horse round to face his men, he shouted, "I will not tolerate this insolence! I command you all to cease now. Each of you, have been personally chosen to accompany me on this quest. Life has become comfortable and I strongly regret allowing this to happen, but I now challenge each of you, if you no longer wish to follow me, to depart now."

Turning to Julian he said, "Centurion.", after a moment's silence Julian lifted his right hand, and pledged his allegiance to his master. In turn each of the bodyguards followed suit, those too pledging allegiance to their leader.

The party galloped on. In a matter of days they entered the borders of the far north dynasty. The path was marked on the canvas map all the way to Chu-song's castle.

In the distance the outline of the castle, with its sloped roofed towers came into view. As they got closer they could see that large patches of vegetation under foot had burnt and were dead, which was a bit unusual; you could sense something was not right in this land.

As they got a hundred or so metres away, a gang of well-armed men rode out to meet them. Darinus instantly recognised their leader: a warrior adorned in white from head to toe, with only his eyes showing; this was Yang the martial arts fighter from the contest for the hand of Ki.

Darinus called out in his broken accent (he had learnt a little of this language from his wife), "We come in peace."

To the Roman's amazement, Yang was calm. They actually expected this warrior to be hostile, but Chu-song's household had already been visited by the magician Wei-Po-Yang, who had told of Darinus's arrival. Yang said nothing. He just nodded to show acknowledgment, before turning to gallop with his gang back to the castle. The Romans followed.

Reaching the handsome fort, they were met by three banks of steps rising up between its high walls. Running down the centre of the stairs were many different coloured flowers for decoration.

On dismounting, Darinus ordered two of his bodyguards to stay with the horses, as he and the rest of his men followed on up. Once reaching the top they got a view of the whole castle, which looked bigger inside than it did from the outside. It was symmetrical and the long walls the same length all the way round. Four towers with sloped roofs rose up on each corner. Two flights of steps ran up and over the wall from both the north and south, where at each side were four more, smaller guards towers (those too with roofs), obviously for the guardsmen. There were various buildings dotted around inside the walls but the most prominent were the two in the middle, the drum tower and the lofty bell tower. Yang had brought the Romans up by the southern stairway and down into the fort.

Although there were many people around, the place was strangely quiet – not even the twitter of the odd bird could be heard. Undoubtedly something was terribly wrong.

They were led across an open sandy space, to a brightly coloured yellow building. When they got to the wide doorway Yang just stopped and pointed for the Romans to go inside; he himself chose to stand outside.

Walking into a long narrow room they were met by heavily armed soldiers packed down either side. Unmistakably in counsel; at the front a king was wandering from side to side with his hand on his chin as if in deep thought. This was Chu-song. Behind him at the top of the room standing next to a simple throne was another familiar figure, Yang's brother, the man in black, Yin. All that could be heard above the devastating silence was Chu-song's footsteps. He raised his bowed head and looked in the direction of the Romans.

Yin beckoned them to come right in. Turning to his father he said, "As the magician predicted, here is the Roman."

Chu-song wore metal armour, on his head he held a short black hat, and down either side of his thin mouth he wore a long, thin, jet black moustache.

Yin's attitude too was very different this time. Showing a meeker side, he spoke, "My father welcomes you and your men in these troubled times. We have come under attack by an invisible force. They entered our castle walls deep in the dead of night for the past two moons. During the first moon they stole all the virgins who live in the safety of the castle walls, leaving undetected, killing only the guards. Not one soul left alive witnessed this; the lower doors at the foot of the walls were left wide open."

Yin walked down nearer to the Romans and continued, "My father sent for myself and the other (by the other he meant his brother Yang), to come to his aid. On arriving we searched the land in vain for the virgins but to no avail. Before dark I took charge of the north end of our castle and the other control of the south.

"It was unclear if the enemy would return, but they did. I stood waiting on the top of the steps with many soldiers lined behind me. As I stood I sensed evil approach but even by the fire I could see nothing. It was then I found myself in combat with the invisible enemy. These cowardly warriors were much taller in height; the strength of just one was of that of seven men. Using meditation and the arts that I had been given I fought, holding my own ground, but the invisible army massacred most of the soldiers around me, breaking through our ranks. At daylight we found most of the ordinary women had now been stolen. I have never encountered such a formidable force". He paused and swallowed hard, and with a scowl upon his troubled face he continued.

"Checking myself I noticed my sword was soaked in thick black blood so I know I did cause some damage.

"My father has sent for the holy man from the mountains, mine and the other teachers of the arts.

"The invisible army has left our land scorched, we do not know who or what they are or where they come from."

Chu-song had remained quiet during Yin's speech, but now he lifted his bowed head, and facing Darinus, he spoke, "Roman, can you enlighten us?"

At this Darinus felt awkwardly put on the spot. He replied, "I have never encountered such an enemy, but I learnt of a force, that at the beginning of time, came to earth from Orion, known as the Nephilim. They saw that the women of our world were fair, and lived on the earth taking wives. These beings were giants but as far as I know they were expelled. This is all I know, but it may explain the disappearance of your women. Maybe they have returned but I believed they were nothing but a myth, but after hearing your unfortunate plight, of this I am now unsure".

Little did he know but Darinus was right. He continued, "We need to find how they arrived here and where they have set up their camp. My men and I will try and be of service to you, sire."

Bowing his head, Darinus then ushered his men out of the building.

Yang was still just outside. The Roman leader said to the White prince, "Show me the scorched land." This time Yang took them a different way out of the castle. Round the bottom of the castle walls ran several passages, which were used to let in horses and carts, and such like, and had thick wooden doors each protected by a portcullis.

Once out of the castle, Darinus began to inspect the scorched ground. Big chunks of the grass were withered but only in places; the conclusion was reached that this was where the invisible enemy had trod and the grass had died. They followed the tracks, up and over hills and eventually they came to a wooded area. Darinus conferred with his Centurion. "What do you see?"

Julian replied, "This is not a big army; I suggest twenty or so."

Darinus agreed. As they approached the woodland the scorched land came to a stop at the foot of the tall silver trees. The grass underneath the lush green wood remained untouched. This was somewhat puzzling. After wandering around for a bit and trying to figure this out, they decided to return to the castle, and prepare for the night's onslaught.

On returning they found the holy men from the mountains had now arrived.

The atmosphere surrounding the castle had now changed; these men wore single crimson garments, wrapped around them. They all had shaven heads. There were roughly about fifty in all.

Darinus and his accomplices quietly questioned between themselves how these religious men were going to protect this place, in such an hour of need; why had they been called?

Chu-song had been in counsel with the holy men. When he saw Darinus arrive, he beckoned him forward saying, "Roman now you have witnessed the damage our foe has caused, what is your conclusion?"

Darinus was quick to respond, "Sire, we must light up the castle and surround the north and the south with fresh hay and bushes, as this will alert us when the invisible army arrives, breaking their element of surprise, as we will see and hear their footsteps."

Chu-song walked the width of the room, hand on his chin, engrossed in thought before agreeing.

Before dark this had been done and stakes were lit and pushed into the ground alongside the fresh hay. After the final preparations were made, Chu-song and his men were ready, along with the aid of the holy men and the Romans, to defend their land from the Nephilim, the dark sons from Orion.

Darinus and four of his guards lay low behind freshly cut trees, just a few yards from the hay. Julian had taken the other four to the southern staircase to aid Yang.

Now the bodyguards were among the elite in the Roman army and had endured hard intense training, which included learning to fight in the dark, or with little visibility.

Darinus remembered as a child his father had taught him to fight using a wooden sword whilst being blindfolded. These were happy times. As his father had seldom been around during his brief childhood before he himself was enlisted into the Roman army, this was one of the few times he remembered. What brought this memory back were the holy men, who strangely all had black cloth wrapped round their heads covering their eyes. They were now all spread out, and staggered all the way up the stairway. Yang stood halfway up the second flight. At the very top were soldiers from Chu-songs army; they were all ready.

As Darinus lay on the soft turf, watching his own breath against the bitter cold, in the flicker of the firelight, one of his guards suddenly tugged at his foot, as the fires upon the stakes began to violently waver and the fresh hay and bushes began to be thrown about. In a blink of an eye the holy men were thrown into action; it was the most bizarre thing to witness.

Darinus remained in position, as did his trusting guards waiting for their leader's signal.

The first line of holy men was soon overwhelmed. If you really looked hard enough, every now and then the figures of the Nephilim could be seen; it was hard to estimate how many, but as they fought their way up to nearly halfway up to the flight of steps where Yang was waiting, it was then Darinus called to his men, "It is time, stay as a unit. Let's move." Getting to their feet, and a yard apart they marched forward, passing the lit stakes and over the hay (that had almost disintegrated). Concentrating hard they all raised their swords out in front of them. Yang and the holy men were now holding the stairway fast. All they fought with were small swords. Several holy men lay dead. Before long, the Romans were engaged thick in the battle. Darinus screamed, "Stay close, stay close." The first thing that struck him was the foul vile smell that these evil beings generated.

The unorthodox battle continued for a good few hours, but as the morning began to break, the Nephilim were eventually forced back. The Romans stayed disciplined and only one was lost that night. Many of the holy men paid with their lives defending the castle. The enemy got close but never reached the top of the south staircase. Yang fought valiantly along with Julian. On the north steps it was a similar story. Although the casualties were greater, Darinus and Yin, along with the other holy men had held their own too.

As the night began to fade, the beaten Nephilim turned and fled. Darinus and Yang gave chase, not being able to see the enemy they followed the burnt track over the hills to the woodland; on the way they were met by Julian and Yin who had also given chase.

As they approached the silver wood they saw a glowing bright light like a swirling hole, in between two trees. The huge grey figures could now be seen entering through into the sphere. The colours were fantastic, and it's hard to describe them, as they were colours from a different place, never seen before. As the last figure passed through, the doorway to the other world disappeared. The two Romans and the brothers were left standing alone in the still morning, all thoroughly exhausted.

Then pure emotion came over the twin brothers, who - besides the contest - had hardly set eyes on each other for many years. As they embraced and hugged each other they put their differences aside.

Darinus and Julian went to inspect where the door had been; a single tree lay horizontally across from one tree to another creating a door.

Returning to Chu-song's castle, they found the king back inside the usual building. On seeing his two sons enter the room arm in arm, the tears streamed down his old cheeks. All he could say was, "Well, if any good came out of this evil at least I have both my sons back together. How proud their fair mother would have been of them." It was the first time he had seen them in the same room, since they had been sent away at the tender age of twelve.

Much of the silver wood was burnt or cut down. Hopefully the Nephilim, the fallen sons of god (who live on Orion) will never return to our world again. The holy men over the centuries have kept watch over that wood; I understand they still keep a vigil to this very day.

Chu-song thanked Darinus for his help and wisdom, and he offered him saying, "Is there anything you want of me, Roman?"

The Roman said, "Yes, there is one thing. I desire to ask your sons for their services, to accompany me in the greatest battle this world will ever see." It took very little persuasion, Yin and Yang would relish the prospect.

DISASTER STRIKES AS ADRIEN GOES IN SEARCH OF THE GOLD CITY

It was a hot cloudy day, as the travellers sat waiting for Adrien to make a decision, as he closely studied the map. On the map, an X marked the gold city, which lay on a continent directly south. Although in his heart he knew it was wrong to attempt this journey, he was driven and consumed by greed.

He said to his comrades, "We are so close to the city of gold we shall go south before we head north, to the great northern pass."

Killgore, who was repainting his face, sternly interrupted. "Adrien, I must disagree. It feels wrong. I fear if we do this we might put ourselves in grave danger. There is a reason for the X marking on the map. Can you not see you have been blinded by greed? If you decide to take this journey I will have to depart and go to the northern pass alone."

The conversation became more heated, as Eals decided to get involved. "Pict, you were sent to travel with us by Brons your cousin."

Killgore replied, "No, if you remember Brons ordered me to accompany Adrien across the waters from my homeland. I have now, for a long time, followed the map with Adrien across sea and land and many dangers."

Eals stood up and lifted his sword. Killgore also jumped to his feet. At this point Adrien shouted, "Friends, stop! I need both of you. Eals put away your weapon. I respect my brother Killgore's decision. We shall go south in search of the gold city and I will point my good friend, the faithful Pict, the way to the northern pass where he can take the Mayan home to Britannia with him."

The Mayan warrior just sat upon the ground, unaware of what the Westerners were talking about, with the jaguar lying peacefully by his side.

So they said their goodbyes. Adrien put his right hand on Killgore's shoulder and said, "I will be glad to know you're beside me when the battle takes place at the Caledonian courtyard."

The painted Pict replied, "I am tired. I would advise you one last time to forget the search for the gold city and come with me. If you will not heed my advice then so be it, goodbye. It will be an honour to serve you at Caledonia." He turned to Eals, and they awkwardly embraced one another.

Adrien pointed Killgore and the Mayan warrior in the right direction, and the two Saxons set off southward, bound in search of the gold city. They made their way to the beach, where the two Polynesians were still patiently waiting at the long boat. Adrien showed them on the map the X that marked the city. The skins were filled with water and coconuts were gathered for the journey.

They followed the coast south. For days they sailed, coming into land only for supplies. The sea was calm, and the further down they sailed, the sea became warmer and turned turquoise in colour, and they could see through the crystal clear water the bottom of the seabed underneath them. Many beautifully coloured tropical fish swam around the boat.

They sailed as far as what is nowadays called the land of Columbia.

From this point Adrien decided to bring the boat into land, as the X on the map was now directly inland.

Leaving the Polynesian sailors behind, they ventured forth on foot. The terrain from the beach became very hilly, leading to vast lush open grasslands with pockets of Alpine forests dotted around. After hours of walking, Eals said, "Sire, surely we need transport?"

Sometime later they came across a herd of alpaca; well to cut a long story short, they actually captured two of these strange wild creatures and after a lot of patience and hard work the animals submitted and the Saxons were able to ride on the alpacas' backs.

Taking a look at each other, the two passengers found the whole episode rather amusing.

After a long and tedious journey they arrived at the edge of the greatest forest on earth: the enchanting Amazon. On the edge of the jungle they were met by axe breaker trees, with huge buttress roots that looked like claws coming out of the ground.

The two Saxons felt shivers down their spines. The creepy rain forest looked so thick and dark inside that the thought of entering it seemed rather daunting.

The alpacas were set free and the Saxons entered the jungle on foot. In some places the terrain was so dense that they had to use their swords to cut a path. Inside, although dark, the sun's rays shone through to the forest floor in narrow streaks.

Many unfamiliar noises could be heard: the cooing of birds and the howl of monkeys, similar to the ones in the Mayan forest. They saw big spiders' webs and ants under foot, five times bigger than the ones they were used to in Britannia.

On and on, sweating in the torturous almost unbearable heat they went, the dense forest began to thin. Then the torrential rain came. The travellers took shelter under a large tree until the rains decided to subside, the ground was left sodden, and thick swarms of mosquitoes appeared. Adrien and Eals began to feel the sharp bites of the insects, biting into their fair skin like tiny pin pricks; there was no way of escaping them so after a while they stopped trying to squat the little mites.

As the sun began to set, the travellers built a fire, which took a lot of effort struggling to get a spark in the damp jungle. Eventually they sat next to a small fire, and cooked some fish they had brought with them from the sea. They cooked them wrapped in leaves which made a hearty meal, and the fire scared off the mosquitoes.

The following day they wrapped their shawls around as much of their naked skin on show as possible to stop getting bitten.

Days later they came to the edge of a wide river, this must be the great river shown on the map that runs to the gold city. Next to the river they trudged through marsh lands in water up to their knees. This went on for a day or so.

Just as they were beginning to reach solid ground, a horrible thing suddenly occurred; it all happened so quickly they were taken off guard.

A monster leapt out of the marsh. It had a large black head with bright evil-coloured eyes, positioned on top above wide nostrils, followed by a thick, stocky, yellow-striped neck. Instantly, mouth wide open, it grabbed Adrien, and sank its sharp long fangs into his side, before dragging him under water and into the marsh. For five or six seconds Eals remained in shock. Adrien's arm appeared, sword in hand, thrashing around, but the sword came flying out, and his arm disappeared.

Eals swiftly drew his own sword and started blindly hacking into the murky waters of the marsh, raining down blow after blow. His only fear was that he would hit his commander. The anaconda was just below the surface, holding its victim tightly underneath the water, as anacondas do. They crush and drown their prey. Just as Eals was beginning to feel he was getting nowhere the water began to turn red, so he carried on. He was making progress as the snake loosened its grip of Adrien. Although now very weak, Adrien managed to escape and lift his head up for air.

The monster reared its ugly head out of the swamp, towering over Eals, mouth wide open. The Saxon general took aim and launched his sword into the bottom of its jaw; at this the anaconda fell dead, its full weight falling on the soldier, thus knocking him over.

Eals pulled his master out and away from the marsh on to solid ground. Adrien was bleeding badly, blood flowing from two deep fang marks in his left side, where the snake's strong jaws had crushed the bottom of his ribs, leaving him very badly injured. The general ripped his own cloak and tightly tied it round Adrien's waist to stem the constant bleeding.

Although in great pain Adrien kissed his loyal servant on his cheek faintly uttering the words, "Thank you my trusted friend. You have just saved my life."

Eals replied, "Quiet, you need all of your energy."

They tried to move on, with Adrien's arm round his comrade's neck to steady himself, but they only managed to get a few hundred yards past the marsh to the banks of the great river before the pain was too much for Adrien to bear. So they stopped where they were. Besides it was beginning to get dark. Eals gathered and built a fire.

But the worst was yet to come! As they sat next to the fire they both found they were shivering and sweating at the same time, and then Eals started vomiting. Nothing was said that night, but the mosquito bites were now burning and swelling.

The following morning the sun was already up when they awoke, having had little sleep with quite a start, there, a few feet away at the edge of the river, stood an extremely tall man holding a staff. His skin was even whiter than that of the Saxons, his strawberry hair was long; he was like a giant and his muscles were so toned he looked like he had been chiselled. All this man wore was what looked like woollen shorts. He held no expression upon his long face. In his left hand, he held a long thick nobly staff. He was from a race named the cloud people.

Adrien was too weak to even speak, and Eals' vision was slightly blurred.

The man came over and knelt down next to Adrien. Gently he took off the blood-soaked cloak, covering the fang wounds. He muttered some words neither Saxon understood. Lifting up Adrien's arms he took off the injured commander's clothing. Ripping it into sections he walked to the river, soaking it, and wringing the cloth out. Returning, he wrapped it round Adrien's wounds. Then he walked to a nearby tree. Using his strong bare hands he pulled away the bark. Underneath, oily sap began to run, and collecting it on the bark, he covered Adrien from head to toe with the substance.

Gathering more he brought this to Eals and covered Eals' skin in the same way. Both Saxons showed no resistance.

The gentle giant had obviously arrived by an odd-looking, simple, canoe-type boat, which calmly rocked on the mild waves (or ripples) of the great river.

The man picked up Adrien in a single swoop and carried him out to his canoe. Eals followed with the little energy he could now muster.

Using a single oar-like branch the fair man rowed out to meet the middle of the great river where the current was strong. The river ran from west to east, taking the boat at quite a speedy pace.

The travellers were getting weaker by the hour. Adrien was now vomiting, and Eals' joints were beginning to hurt from the inside. Not knowing anything about this alien disease, they had been struck down by malaria, caught from the lethal mosquito bites.

Unfortunately, the Saxons missed out on the beauty that surrounded the great river; they glided by the gateway to the gold city without knowing, and passed the almighty waterfalls that ran into the river near to the city.

The unusual white man rowed on and on; they will never know how long that journey took them. Adrien was nearing death's door now, slipping in and out of consciousness.

The strawberry-haired man had left the main river and was now rowing down a small, quieter river. He pulled the boat in to moor by a grass bank.

THE SAXONS ENTER ANOTHER REALM

On top of the bank there sat a man next to an orange fire. He looked a bit like an ape, and was old, with straggled grey hair. Wrapped around him was a patchwork cloak, made of different animal furs. This man was an Ido, also known as a shaman, a medicine man.

The strong white-cloud man lifted Adrien out of the canoe and carried him up the bank. Laying him down on a flat rock next to the Ido, he went back to help Eals up the bank.

Nothing much was said between the cloud man and the shaman for these men of that jungle are men of few words. They did acknowledge each other, though, in the ancient Aymara language. The white man said, "Laphil, kgochu," which means hello, friend, and the shaman replied in a high-pitched voice, "Laphil."

Mysteriously, the shaman was ready for the sick travellers. He knew the exact time of their arrival, for he had seen all this in a vision and had spent that day preparing. He shuffled over to the dying Saxon commander. Holding his wrist, he found a faint pulse, before opening his closed eye lids and studying his dilating pupils. Next he looked in to the weak Saxon Eals' eyes, before sitting back down next to the fire.

Hanging from a stick (that was supported by two sticks either side) over the flames, were three clay pots, one was filled with water whilst the other two with other rare potions.

It was now late afternoon before dusk. The shaman produced a leather bag, and from inside he took out a dart frog. Using his own bare hands, he held the poisonous frog - through years of practice he had become immune to its poisonous skin; any normal human would surely die if they were to touch a dart frog. The shaman held the frog close to his face and began to chant. Its skin became brighter and brighter, which is what happens when a dart frog meets predators, in which to warn them off and in the process produces more poison.

The shaman then held the frog over one of the clay pots above the fire, and a few drops of the venom, from its poisonous skin, dripped into the pot containing the boiling water. When enough had diluted the water he let the frog go.

The pot was taken off the fire to briefly cool down, and then the Ido brought the potion over to Adrien and opened his mouth enough to pour a little inside. He gave a little less to Eals. This potion acted as a strong painkiller and was almost two hundred times more powerful than morphine.

Inside the second boiling clay pot was a potion made from the embauba plant, the shaman had gathered from the forest floor. The whole plant was used to make this concoction, the bark, roots, sap, leaves, and trumpet-shaped flowers. The scent of this narcotic aroma could be smelt in the fresh jungle air. This potion was a dull thick mixture, which again he gave to each of the travellers.

Eals was vaguely aware of what was happening. His main concern was for his commander, whose health had rapidly deteriorated, but all he could do was trust this weird little man with his magical potions.

The third and final concoction that the shaman had brewed was an ancient form of ayahuasca (known as the sorcerers' brew). He had chopped up a jungle vine called banisteriopsis, and smashed it to a pulp, mixing it with cold water and adding various other plants. This potion had been boiling for a number of hours but was now ready, after it cooled this was given to the travellers, washed down by the embauba.

After a while, although still very weak, Adrien began to stir. The dart frog venom had taken away his pain. He felt extremely dizzy, then he came over incredibly sick and started to vomit; the vomiting continued for quite a while, until there was nothing left inside, and his stomach muscles were cramping. When the vomiting ceased all of a sudden he entered a euphoric state.

It was now dusk; the insects and the creatures of the night were beginning to stir. Adrien still lay sprawled on the flat rock. He felt waves of contentment coming over him. A dragonfly flew by, and he watched it turn into psychedelic colours. It seemed to magnify and he could see its face in great detail; it smiled at him before landing on his chest.

As darkness fell the hallucinations became stronger and more visual. He turned his face towards the river, where the trees on the opposite side had changed to an aluminous green, and were beginning to sway. They all had faces and their branches looked like arms, and seemed to bow towards the Saxon whilst dipping their long arms into the now purple river.

The shaman had begun to circle around Adrien, chanting as he moved.

The moon was full and getting higher in the night sky, its reflection rippled upon the river. To Adrien this looked like a stairway that reached up to the sky. He thought, if I climb this stairway I can make it to the roof of the world, and touch the stars.

He now felt the oddest experience, as he stood up, and leaving his weak body, he walked over to the river and started to climb the moon stairway step by step. As he got higher he felt himself reaching out and feeling for the stars that glowed brighter as he touched them.

As he got higher he peered back down below to see his own body on the rock, with the shaman now frantically shuffling round his lifeless frame. He then saw the unusual old man open his mouth and poured in a liquid; he saw an aluminous orange substance going down his throat. Even from where he was, he actually felt the warm ointment slipping down.

Later on, at different times of his life he would remember that experience; he often wondered whether he really died that night.

He found himself climbing on the spongy moon and reaching out to touch the roof of the world. As soon as he touched it he was sucked through to an unfamiliar realm. He now felt he was weightlessly flying through space; he saw galaxies and planets, some bigger than others, spinning round as he passed. He saw planets that had come to the end of their lives and disintegrated like amazing space butterflies before him.

He reached another universe, where he landed on a planet on top of a gaping live volcano. He looked down inside into the erupting furnace below. He had no feeling so the intense heat did not affect him; sporadically bright burning lava would be spat high up into the air above.

Adrien noticed, standing opposite him, not far away just the other side of the open crater, a familiar figure; it was that of the Druid Mahours.

The druid spoke. Adrien could hear and see the words leave Mahours' open mouth.

"Adrien you have disobeyed yourself once more. You were warned not to go to the gold city, yet you let your heart be consumed by greed when your instincts told you it was wrong. Have you not yet learnt? Next time it could be too late."

The druid vanished. Adrien was ashamed. He felt himself leave the volcanic planet, and be transported back to his own world, where he found himself pulled back into his own body. The shaman was still leaning over him; his face looked blurred and distorted. The Saxon commander could feel his body beginning to slowly heal and restore itself.

The hallucinations continued the whole of that night through the following day and into the next night.

The tall, gentle, cloud man stayed, faithfully by the two Saxons' side, protecting them from coming to any harm. The second night Adrien began to wander about, drawn to the psychedelic-coloured leaves on the bushes and trees, trying to pick and eat them. Every time he raised a leaf to his mouth the cloud man would gently take it out of his hand.

The cloud man certainly had his work cut out watching Eals, who had removed all his clothing and tried jumping into the river on several occasions.

One of the final visions Adrien encountered, was similar to that of what his sworn enemy, Darinus, had seen in the future pool. Of the hooded knight, riding through the night and entering the drawbridge at the Caledonian castle. Adrien did not recognise the man or the black horse he rode, but he saw the knight dismount and walk through to the chequered courtyard, where in the centre was a table holding a crown sat upon a cushion. The man produced a jewel, and the vision disappeared.

On the third day both Adrien and Eals came back round. The visions stopped and both men slept solid for twenty four hours.

On waking they both felt good; overall it had been a positive experience. The Odi fed their empty stomachs with piranha fish and fruit.

Adrien realised the value that this old man could be in the ranks of his army, so he tried to speak to the shaman, telling of the great battle that was to take place, and why he was travelling to recruit his army, and how he wished the old shaman to join him and make him his second pontifrex (bishop) on the board. Although he spoke a different language, the shaman understood, but never said a word. Adrien knew he would be there when the time came.

As they were getting ready to leave, the shaman spoke in his high-pitched voice introducing himself, "Auqui …..Auqui."

The two Saxons departed with the cloud man in his canoe. Adrien was still in some pain with his broken rib but his health had been fully restored.

Before they had left on the journey, the cloud man encouraged them to cover themselves from head to toe with tree sap, to keep away the insects - most importantly the dreaded mosquitoes.

Adrien was in awe of this white cloud man, who had a strong yet gentle nature. Throughout the previous experiences they had encountered he had stood by the Saxons, staying awake the whole time.

Adrien tried to communicate, saying slowly and clearly whilst pointing at his own chest, "I am Adrien (pause) Adrien."

The cloud man, who was standing at the back of the canoe and rowing, leant his head to one side and repeated, "Hdien, Hdien." Approvingly the Saxon nodded, then pointed at his comrade. "Eals, Eals." Once again he attempted to copy saying, "Ale, Ale," which was close enough for the Saxons.

Then the tall cloud man with great pride pointed at his own chest and said, "Icci Irachocha, Icci Irachocha." Adrien smiled and along with Eals clapped with approval, which was the first time the giant smiled out of the corner of his thin mouth.

However, they could now really appreciate the sheer beauty of this lush green rain forest from the river; the sky was a deep blue, the hum of insects and birds could be heard cheerfully chirping in the trees, pairs of exotic parrots were seen flying overhead, some blue, with red tails and yellow wings, and others green with yellow faces.

Eventually the small river flowed back into the great river.

This time the cloud man, Icci Irachocha, rowed his boat close to the bank; as he was now rowing against the current, to take the boat out to the middle of the great river would make rowing incredibly difficult. Once on the wide river a group of pink dolphins appeared, racing each other alongside the canoe, ducking under then playfully diving out of the water as they swam; it was an awesome thing to see these amazing creatures.

The tranquil journey carried on. A day later limestone cliffs broke up the bank overhanging the river. On these cliffs the Saxons noticed painted carvings ground into the limestone of fearsome faces. Most of them had been painted using red dye (the faces were not very detailed just used to deter trespassers). For this was the land of the cloud people.

In the distance the sound of crashing water could be heard, then the most fantastic waterfall came into view. The closer they got the higher it rose, it must have been roughly one hundred and fifty metres high; the sound of the pouring falls was very relaxing.

Icci brought his canoe beside the waterfall and sailed straight through, the pouring water drenched the travellers but because of the boiling hot day it was quite refreshing.

Inside the falls was a still pool. Icci beckoned the travellers to climb out of the boat up onto some smooth flat rocks; he then got out and lifted his boat out of the water onto the rocks behind the waterfall. It was just like being in a cave. Even more drawings had been carved out of the walls.

They followed Icci beyond the pool, to some hidden steps cut out of the rock, which twisted and turned upwards next to the cave wall. In places they had to be careful of sharp rocks jutting out of the sides. At some points due to the darkness, they could not see a thing, and had to feel their way up for quite a long way in the pitch black. They had to move quickly to keep up with the tall cloud man's strides, plus Adrien's still delicate rib was irritating him somewhat.

Reaching the top they came out, blinking, into the bright sunlight. Here they were met by two rather threatening tall, fair-skinned tribesmen, who stood either side of the opening, both with big staffs. Like Icci, these men towered over the Saxons; they too were cloud men. On seeing Icci they stood aside and let the travellers pass. The unusual thing was they said nothing to their fellow tribesman.

Before them, there ran a mud path next to a calm shallow river, wide but not as wide as the great river they had just sailed.

The calm river disappeared behind them and poured over a huge shelf producing the almighty waterfall. Having walked just a little way up the mud path, Icci made a sudden turn to his left through a tiny opening between some bushes. A little way through they arrived at a settlement. In fact it was so well tucked away that if anybody was to wander down the mud path next to the river, they would never know a settlement was even nearby. The whole place was surrounded by jungle.

Limestone round houses were dotted about the settlement, on top of these buildings were tall, pointed thatched roofs. The entrance doors were halfway up, with steps leading all the way round and up to a terrace. The underneath of these round houses was obviously used as storage areas. It was a peaceful place to live. All the people of that place had white skin with fair hair and were all so very tall. The women were attractive, and so gentle, which made them even more beautiful. The cloud people took little notice of the travellers as they seemed to be a placid, content race.

The cloud man was greeted by his wife, who was holding his young son.

The Saxons stayed for only one night in Icci's one-roomed house with his family. They were fed, with what could best be described as 'spicy soup'. Adrien showed his host the map, while the small child took a shine to Eals, inquisitively touching his face.

By early morning, the rain, that had been hammering down all night, began to ease off. They left the settlement with Icci, following back down the mud path. When they reached the opening in the rocks to the steps, Icci took them just a little beyond to the side of the waterfall shelf. The view from so high up was breath taking – you could see the vast rain forest sprawled out as far as the eye could see for endless miles beneath them.

Over the forest a blue mist was rising from the trees. This is how the cloud people had earned the name people of the clouds, because they lived so high up in the jungle where the mist rose.

From the fantastic waterfall a magnificent rainbow had formed; the colours were so vivid you could see every one of them. One end of the rainbow came out of the falls while the other end reached out and landed down river. And there it was, gleaming in the morning sun – the illusive gold city.

They say that at the bottom of every rainbow is a pot of gold.

This sight sent shivers down Adrien's spine. After admiring the surreal view for a time, Icci took them back through to the rocky steps and down. Reaching the bottom he lifted the canoe into the water. They went back through the waterfall, in the process receiving a good morning shower. Rowing gently down the river they came to the open archway to the gold city. The great river passed by, with the city to the left-hand side; a small river left the main river and flowed through into the city.

Two solid gold towers stood either side of the archway. Icci started to steer the boat toward the small river. Adrien started to panic. The tall cloud man saw and understood the anguish on the Saxon's worried face, so he turned the canoe back to the great river.

Eals glimpsed through the archway. He saw inside everything looked perfectly symmetrical, small pillars ran down both sides of the river which flowed into the heart of the gold city.

Icci Irachocha was one of the watchmen and protectors of the city, as were his people, who guarded her walls.

So with the canoe now back on the great river they headed west. It sailed past the solid gold walls that towered up above. Once the gold city was out of sight Adrien breathed a sigh of relief.

The tall cloud man took them further down river, much closer to the coast than they had come. When he dropped the two Saxons off Adrien felt a little sad to say good bye to the faithful, tall, gentle giant, but he had managed (I am not sure how he had got the message across) to convince Icci to join his side when the time came at the Caledonian castle. Maybe he would make the journey along with the shaman; who knows?

After quite a trek they found the way back to the Polynesians, who had once again waited patiently.

This time they were definitely going north to the northern pass, without getting side-tracked.

LOST IN THE MAZE OF DESPAIR

Darinus and his men left Chu-song's northern dynasty. After the appearance of the Nephilim the land was a mess, but in short this was not really the Romans' problem to help sort out.

On the positive side Darinus had gained two magnificent warriors in Yin and Yang. Although he was more than satisfied with all the men he had selected for his army so far, the problem was, due to all the months he had spent enjoying marital bliss, he had lost a great deal of time, which he now had to make up.

The party rode westward, where the terrain started to get rocky and the weather became rather unpleasant, too.

The Roman leader decided because of the time factor, he and his men would venture east no further. He studied the canvas, which showed the vast blue ocean and further to what we know today as the Americas.

They travelled for many days, even weeks. Slightly south they picked up another part of the silk route (there are many trails and roads that make up the silk route).

Eventually they reached the Indus River. The only way across was with an old man on a large raft. Safely across, horses and all, they disembarked, Darinus reaching for his wallet to pay the man (as he had agreed to only pay when they were on dry land the other side), he turned his back to the river for one second, when he turned back, to his surprise the man and his raft had entirely disappeared. Instead there stood a wide bridge just up river. Darinus exclaimed, "Men, this is ludicrous. I do believe we have crossed to another time. I do not understand."

He was indeed right. They had entered late spring of 560AD. This was the first time they had noticed a visible change whilst crossing a time line in broad daylight.

This time, the time change had pushed them past a fierce battle. As in this region two armies were at war: the Sassanids were fighting the Hephthalites.

A day or so on the travelling Romans entered the northeast border lands of the Sassanids' empire. This region was called Atropatene. To their right the White Mountains rose up. The attractive scenery made a fantastic picture.

They rode at a fast pace, galloping the horses on the now flat lowlands, which the horses loved, as for weeks on the rough terrain they had barely been able to break into a canter.

Away in the distance to the left a wall came into view. As they got closer it materialized that the sandstone wall was actually a handsome-looking fort.

Something off to the right, toward the beginning of the base of the White Mountains, caught Darinus' attention, where a clump of unusual tall green trees were gathered. But soon enough his attention was drawn back to the fort, as they were fast approaching the arched gateway.

The party dismounted to walk on foot through the entrance. Once within the walls the place appeared to be empty. This was the fortified city of Phraaspa, the capital of Atropatene. A wide road ran ahead of them before veering sharply off to the right; the reason being as further on was a massive pond. Just inside, next to where they stood, ran a thin passage between two sandstone houses. Coming from the passage the sounds of laughter and soft music could be heard.

"Darinus, shall we go and investigate, sire?" uttered Julian. After a pause, his leader agreed.

So cautiously they tiptoed up the passage, swords at the ready. The bodyguards stayed back to look after the horses. The narrow passage swung to the right. Turning the corner they were met by an open doorway. Peering in, they saw a familiar sight: set in a modern courtyard was a Roman bath, roughly ten metres in length and five metres wide.

The voices were coming from inside the bath, whilst the calm music was being played by a woman strumming on a harp in the corner.

The Romans hid out of view, but it was too late – they had already been heard. The voices stopped and the music ceased. After a moment or two's silence, a man's voice rang out from inside the bath. He spoke in a foreign language which the Romans had no knowledge of.

So Darinus and Julian (putting the swords away) came out from the passage and stepped through the open doorway, placed under a narrow arch. In the luxurious Roman-style bath was a man with light skin and short, neatly groomed brown hair with the odd streak of silver in it. He was frolicking with three semi-naked larger sized ladies, who had a darker complexion.

On seeing the Romans, the man changed his language to Latin. He looked rather puzzled as he spoke, "I do not know why you are dressed the way you appear. I see you are men of the crest, from the western realms. Why, I ask, are you here in such unstable times?" As he spoke he held tightly to a short, thin sword that lay on the edge of the bath.

Julian was more than excited to see the Roman bath; he couldn't care less about what the man was rattling on about, and he strolled over and sat down next to the water and started to unlace the straps on his boots before dipping in his feet.

The man continued, "Do you come in peace Roman?" Darinus assured him they meant well.

On hearing this, the man went on to say, "I invite you to come and bathe as your rude comrade already has." He frowned at Julian who just scowled back.

Darinus replied, "I am honoured by your invitation; I have seven men waiting at the entrance with horses."

The man said, "Invite them in. As you can see we have plenty of room; they can tie the horses. Besides, there are no men here, just women and young children as all the men are at war."

Darinus turned to Julian. "Centurion, go fetch my bodyguards and bring them hither."

Darinus had full respect for his men as they did for their master. Julian let out an irritable sigh, took his feet out of the water and swaggered out of the courtyard.

Boots off, the Roman commander stripped down to his loin cloth ready to get into the bath. The man introduced himself. "My name is Lanik. I am a Hephthalite."

At this Darinus replied, "I am Darinus. I command many Legions directly from Rome. I serve Honorius Caesar."

Lanik looked surprised. "Honorius. That's a Caesar I have never heard the name of, but Rome is only a small state, a mere shadow of her former self, over run by barbarians, who claim to be the new Caesar at every turn. Besides, I do see the mark of the Legion on you." He was referring to the mark tattooed on Darinus' right shoulder.

This luxurious Roman bath, although similar to the baths Darinus was used to, had an expensive Sassanid touch to it; sunk into all four sides were thin steps, the floor was made of clear alabaster squares, some were fused with expensive black alabaster writing, written in Pahlawi (the Sassanid language).

The reason wooden sandals were worn, was because the floor was red hot. In the basement underneath, there was a furnace that was constantly fuelled by slaves.

Julian returned with the rest of the bodyguards, all donned the wooden sandals and slipped into the bath.

Darinus questioned. "So how is it you come to own such a place with such a lavish tub?"

Lanik let out an annoyed laugh. "I do not own it. I have simply temporarily acquired it, along with the household whilst he's away; he being Akabijar the government adviser to Khosray the emperor of the Sassanid, who is away at war against my people the Hephthalite."

Julian interrupted. "So why you are here in your enemy's camp whilst your people are at war? Are you a traitor or just a cowardly deserter?" Julian had taken an instant dislike to him.

Lanik snapped back, "Oh, no, I would not use such a strong word as traitor. I see no use for war. Besides, look around. There's never been such an opportunity to indulge with so many fine women." At this he kissed one of the larger ladies next to him.

The thinner women in the corner had begun to strum on her harp. Julian had already noticed her. The woman who had handed out the wooden shoes had slipped into the tub and was flirting with the soldiers. She made a bee line for Julian, who turned up his nose and moved away, mockingly saying to Lanik, "You have an acquired taste in your women."

It was clear Lanik was a slimy character; one you could never trust.

He went on to tell that Phraaspa, was built centuries ago by Takha-e-Soleymen (King Solomon), who had built his throne here next to a flowing pond, which would be the pond they had seen when they arrived. He told the old folk legend of these parts that a big crater outside the fort walls was where Solomon used to imprison monsters.

Darinus questioned, "What is the meaning of the tall trees outside the walls?"

Lanik's eyes lit up and he rubbed his hands together. "Roman, I will show you myself. There is no time like the present – shall we go now?"

Darinus decided to leave his bodyguards to relax and enjoy the bath. Julian invited himself along, which seemed to please the Hephthalite a great deal, and he even had the audacity to ask to borrow a horse. Darinus obliged, whilst Julian made a comment under his breath, "No doubt the deserter will try and steal the poor beast." This time, instead of reacting, Lanik smiled.

And with a smirk said, "I am an honest man. Roman your beast looks finer than mine." No doubt if Darinus had not been present they both would have been at each other like hammer and tongues.

There was a slight chill in the afternoon air, as they trotted down toward the strange clump of trees. "So tell me the reason for the trees," said Darinus.

Lanik replied, "Hidden behind the trees lays the most magnificent palace. To reach the palace you have to walk down the corridors between the tall trees."

At this point Julian piped up, "Whoever built such a palace would be a fool. Why are the trees taller than the lookout towers?"

Lanik looked annoyed by this proclamation, and snapped back, "I would expect such a statement from you. All you think of is violence and are constantly paranoid about being attacked."

They soon reached the foot of the tall trees, and now, standing next to them, they looked enormous. They were lush green juniper trees, neatly trimmed and very well looked after. They had been densely grown together so there would be no way of squeezing between the branches. A gap through the trees was the obvious way in.

All three men dismounted, which was when Lanik paused and said, "Darinus (he only ever addressed the Roman general) I have left the key for the palace. As you might have guessed the owner is also away at war." He was very convincing, although his story did not make much sense. Lanik urged them to make their own way to the palace saying, "Go straight and follow the corridors and you will eventually find the palace. I will be with you shortly."

So the Romans stepped through the opening in among the trees. Before them ran a perfectly straight path two metres wide sandwiched between neat junipers either side. The green grass was short; you would be forgiven to think it had been cut only that morning.

The two visitors wandered up the pathway. Reaching the end they came to a T-junction so they took the right turn, both directions looked exactly the same, with juniper trees both sides; for they had entered a maze.

After a time and having taking a network of pathways Darinus said to Julian, "I think we have been deceived; I do not believe there is a palace."

He was right. The walkways were almost identical only varying in length and direction, but the same trees, same grass and same blue grey sky up above.

Julian mumbled, "Sire, you should have allowed me to deal with him."

Darinus said, "We shall return the way we came." He had never really been good with enclosed spaces and was beginning to feel claustrophobic. They had already come some way into the maze; to remember the exact route out would be virtually impossible - which they were about to find out.

By now Lanik should have returned, so Darinus yelled his name a couple or so times. What they did not know was as soon as they had disappeared into the maze, Lanik had waited a few minutes, before dismounting the horse and untying the two Romans horses and letting them go; without reservation they bolted and he himself left.

All that could be heard was the soft wind breezing through the top of the fir trees. Time wore on. The Romans searched in vain for the way out, but only found they were going further in the wrong direction, at every turn they were becoming more and more demoralised.

There was no sign of Lanik. Then Julian drew his sword and started to violently hack furiously at the juniper trees next to where they stood, but the bouncy branches were so densely grown that the sword was just swallowed up, having little effect and it soon became clear it was a pointless exercise; there was no way through.

Darinus said, "Centurion control your anger, this will solve nothing."

At the top of his voice and among other obscenities Julian screamed, "Lanik, may the gods help you if you fail to get us out of here immediately."

Two or more hours passed. For a while the frustrated Romans just sat on the floor. Between them they could not come up with a feasible escape plan, with Darinus struggling with claustrophobia and Julian battling with his temper it was hard for them both to think straight.

Up they got, and carried on, then turning to their left they finally saw an opening at the other end of one of the grass passages; almost breaking into a run they quickly reached the opening. They stopped; a spear, a belt and a thin brown cloak lay upon the floor. They found themselves standing on a cliff, looking down at a sheer drop. At the edge the grass had been worn away.

Darinus and Julian lay down on their bellies, so they could get a better look over. Peering over they found they were staring into a gaping pit roughly one hundred metres round the perimeter and forty metres in depth. The ledge dropped directly down, making it impossible to even attempt to climb down the smooth walls within.

Darinus said, "I believe this to be the baron pit the deserter talked of; where Takha-y-Soleymen used to imprison monsters."

Far beyond on the other side of the crater they could see the fortified city of Phraaspa. At the bottom of the pit they could see the remains of two bodies. One had almost decomposed to a skeleton, and if not been eaten by wild animals, had fallen into the rocky hole some time ago, whereas the other had fallen whilst trying to escape more recently, which would explain the cloak belt and spear.

Darinus retorted, "Centurion, this surely is a trap. It is not an escape route. To attempt this climb we would face certain death."

So they got back up off their bellies. Julian started yelling for help but this was no use; they were so far away his faint cries were pointless. Julian swapped his belt for the one that was lying on the floor.

So back into the maze, they wandered up more grassy corridors. A feeling of utter despair was beginning to creep into both the Romans' heads. Turning another corner and the feeling was accelerated as slumped on the floor face down was the body of a Sassanid soldier. Julian turned the corpse over; it had already started to decompose and the smell was horrendous.

Stepping round it they swiftly continued. The shadows of the juniper trees were getting longer. Now later on in the day, they found that out of the sun it was quite chilly; they had been lost for a good few hours.

Eventually the darkness fell and they decided to stop and sleep. The place they stopped was not far from where they had encountered the rotting corpse. Julian went and took the cloak for some warmth. So tired hungry and thirsty and feeling rather sorry for themselves and with their backs against each other (as they often slept so they could face any danger from all sides) they fell asleep.

Waking up, they had been beaten by the sun that had got up earlier than them and was now high in the sky.

Now they needed to form some kind of plan, rather than just aimlessly roaming around this network of grass corridors. So up they rose and were just about to hatch a plan when they stopped in their tracks as there just a few metres away was a small stool, on it was a simple clay jug, with two clay cups placed next to the jug.

Automatically Julian picked up one of the cups and with the jug started to fill the cup. Darinus all of a sudden halted Julian. "I forbid you to drink, this is not right. I feel in my heart that what you are about to drink is laced with poison." He grabbed the cup.

Julian muttered, "You truly are mad, sir."

This was hard as they were both so thirsty.

Taking the cup he slowly poured the liquid on to the blade of his sword; he was right, the substance was murky and bubbly. The Roman smelt it closely – it had a kind of toxic smell to it. To consume just one sip would have been fatal. Glancing at each other they now knew someone was out to kill them, especially as there were three other people who had lost their lives in this maze.

The spineless, lying deserter Lanik was nothing more than a conman and a cold-blooded killer. He had spied Darinus' wallet when he first saw them from inside the bath, plus he didn't really want the Romans hanging around anyway.

Since his arrival he had got to know the maze like the back of his hand, and had already used it as his weapon to trick, kill and rob any unfortunate victims that crossed his path. He had learnt that there were secret ways in and out of the maze. But once lost in the maze the likelihood of escaping was very slim.

Lanik had planted the poison in the night, certain that the Romans, being thirsty, would gulp it down before realising; this deadly poison caused a painful death leading to paralysis of the breathing muscles, before shutting down the rest of the major organs. Any quick movement would rapidly speed up this process.

As the two Romans were discussing their predicament, at the end of the long, grass corridor they had just come down stood a women dressed in dark brown, with a veil covering her face. She stood for a few seconds before disappearing into the maze.

Losing no time, the Romans sprinted to where she had been standing; turning the corner they were met by the familiar sight of nothing but juniper trees grass and sky.

An hour or so on they gave up looking for the veiled women, who had vanished into thin air.

Something bizarre happened next. Whilst standing at a junction debating cutting crosses into the grass with the swords (which they should have done the previous day rather than panicking) to the left they saw a fox. Different to the orange red foxes we know, it was a skinny, grey-white fox just meandering around oblivious to the Romans, until Julian moved. The fox looked as surprised to see the two humans as they were to see it.

It turned and scurried off, but instead of disappearing round the corner and into the maze it ran straight through the fir trees. This was the most encouraging thing they had encountered since entering this maze of despair.

Striding to where the fox had made its getaway, at first they couldn't make out where it had disappeared, then Julian found that the branches at that particular place, lifted up, revealing an opening a metre high through the trees to the other side. So lifting the branch the other side they found they were in the next grass corridor. As they crept through, to their amazement it was the same the other side of the next corridor and so on and so forth. They crossed through twelve grass walkways, which meant that they must have been deep inside the perilous maze.

They exited through the last juniper firs and found themselves at the bottom of the White Mountains. Darinus was extremely pale and ringing with sweat, but almost instantaneously the harrowing claustrophobic feeling lifted. But now free, they soon forgot about the burning hunger and thirst that had been eating away at them, they had other things on their minds.

It was early afternoon and to find the way back to the city all they had to do was follow the perimeter of the tall juniper maze. Soon they came across a spring with ice-cool, crystal-clear water that had dripped down from the beautiful White Mountains.

The walk round the maze took quite a long time, which gave some insight to how big the maze actually was. In due course they turned the corner off to the right-hand side, where the fortified city of Phraaspa came into view.

The walk back was quite a hike, as if you can remember they had come down the previous day by horseback.

On reaching the city, they sat down, backs against the wall, to rest for a while and recuperate. Instead of charging in like bulls in an arena, they thought about their next actions, though if Julian had had his way he would have charged in, forcing the Hephthalite into a slow, harsh, torturous death.

But the Roman general had other ideas for the deserter.

Finally they walked through the gate to the city. By the look on the two warriors' faces I don't think anyone would want to have been in Lanik's shoes.

Another concern was what had Darinus's bodyguards been doing? Their job was to protect Darinus.

At first the Romans ventured up the narrow passageway to the courtyard that held the bath. Here they found, lounging around in the tub swigging wine and frolicking with a few local women, three bodyguards who were so drunk they failed to notice their leader, until Julian harshly ordered them out. Darinus seethed. "Where is the deserter?" before snarling, "I will deal with you three on my return."

Searching the posh house, Lanik was nowhere to be found, and none of the women could help as none spoke Latin.

Lanik was eventually located, relaxing out by the flowing pond, again hanging out with two of his larger ladies. A look of sheer horror crept upon his face when he saw the two Romans briskly making their way toward him. At first he stuttered something in his own language, before deciding to make a run for it, and fled. The Romans gave chase.

Julian caught up with him first, tackling him to the ground, where he fell face forward into the pond, and Julian held his head underneath the water for a few seconds. Darinus had to order Julian off.

The pathetic deserter got on his knees and started to beg for his life, "I came to find you," he stammered.

Darinus strongly voiced, "Save your lies traitor," before ordering him to remove the light shawl he was wearing. At this Lanik obeyed and began to sob like a child.

Darinus then told Julian to take off the belt he had acquired in the maze, and he whispered in Julian's ear, "Three strikes, Centurion. Only three."

By now the two larger women had caught up and started to shout abuse at the Romans; one even threw a small rock that just missed. Julian turned to face them and drew his sword, at which they shut up and cowered away.

Julian administrated three savage blows to the lying deserter's back, who screeched out in agony at each stinging blow.

The compassionate Darinus knelt down next to Lanik and said, "Three strikes for the three dead men we found in the corridors of despair in which you left us to rot. The belt used to punish you is from one of the dead men."

Lanik, like the coward he was, cried out, "Please, kill me quickly."

Darinus replied, "No, deserter, I have a better use for you. I will give you a square on the chequered courtyard where you will serve me at the castle of Caledonia."

On hearing this, Julian was furious, and with great venom he said through his teeth, "Sire, have you gone completely mad?"

Darinus calmly replied, "Oh, believe me, Centurion, his shameful punishment there will be far greater than here."

Two of the bodyguards had been murdered, one poisoned and the other stabbed by a local women as he slept. The rest were given a dressing down, but knowing the cunning ways of the Hephthalite and how he had conned them they got away lightly.

Before the Romans left the city of Phraaspa, they came across a group of camel's tethered to wooden posts next to the water, they were already saddled, so did belong to someone, but since a lot of residents of this city had gone off to war, maybe their owner had gone too.

Climbing on was a feat in itself. The one Julian chose whined and bellowed the most, threw him off and spat putrid green saliva in his face.

THE ASSASSIN

Travelling upon these desert horses, was a sluggish affair as they only had one gear - 'slow'! - making the journey rather tedious. One positive thing about the one hump camels was their ability to travel great distances, pressing on without sleep or water.

Darinus, on searching the canvas, took an interest in the large southern continent that lay to their south west, known as the African continent. All through the Sassanid Empire the roads were kept in fairly good order.

The party crossed the empire; most of the men were away at war so not many people were on the almost deserted roads. The road passed the White Mountains then farther on meeting up with the Black Sea. It followed the water's edge and into the regions that belonged to the Byzantium Empire. The Roman general decided they would just drop into the capital Konstantin polis; he was intrigued to see what the other half of the Roman Empire was actually like.

A couple or so weeks on and they were deep inside the empire's borders. Unsurprisingly, one night whilst asleep they crossed yet another time change from spring 560AD back to spring 471AD; apart from the roads now not being so smooth, they failed to realise – they just thought this was due to border crossings between the different lands.

Off to the south against the skyline, the wall city of Konstantin polis eventually came in to view, away to the west the sun was slowly setting. This gave the most surreal picture of such an awesome capital; it was late in the afternoon and being early spring the weather was temperamental, hot and humid one minute, cold and chilly the next.

As they trudged down the road on the back of the dreary camels, a hooded man on a splendid jet black horse came charging past from behind them, followed shortly behind by four Roman soldiers in pursuit. Also on horseback, they galloped past, completely ignoring Darinus and his men, without stopping.

They were soon out of sight. An hour or so later, they caught the same Romans up, but now this was a different story as all four lay dead either side of the road, the horses were nowhere to be seen.

Julian said to Darinus, "I sense we have cause for concern."

Coolly Darinus replied, "No, Centurion, be aware we must keep a watchful eye and be aware."

The walled city of the Byzantine capital was drawing closer; off to their right in the twilight the faint flicker of a fire was spotted hidden away behind a small hill.

The faint sound of trumpets was heard coming from the city signalling the closing of the gates. This prompted Darinus to change direction, and being inquisitive, he decided to investigate the fire. So veering off the stony road they plodded onward, the slow camels were not the flavour of the month, especially for the impatient Julian who had made his feelings towards the one humped animals known on one or two occasions.

A short way from the small hill, they slipped off their animals.

Just beyond the hill was a tent besides a tired fire with the flames barely able to breathe through dying embers.

Once more Darinus left his bodyguards a few metres away with the animals, and crept forward with Julian.

The tent was supported by six wooden posts, four at the corners and two longer poles holding the tent higher up in the middle. Tied to one of the corner posts, was a ragged dirty old mule, accompanied by the most splendid jet black silk coated horse, for this was the horse belonging to the hooded man who had galloped past them a few hours earlier, and who had almost certainly been guilty of butchering the Romans who had been chasing him.

Venturing closer to the edge of the tent they could see covering the floor a unique, deep blue Persian rug (the pattern on it was not visible due to the poor light), but the rug gave the sparse tent a kind of homely feel; there were no sides surrounding the open tent. Tied between two of the support posts was a bulging hammock.

The bulge in the hammock was a man, snoozing. It was hard for them to judge much about this man as he was lying down. As they approached he opened one eye. They could make out he had shoulder-length, dark brown hair, with a stubbly unshaven face, not quite long enough to boast a beard. Across his body in both hands he held two razor-sharp, curved daggers that gleamed in the fading flicker of the fire; if you looked closely enough at these weapons you would see the engraved writing on each one written in ancient Greek - honour on the left, and power on the right; one side of each blade was sharp whilst the other was jagged.

Darinus was the first to speak, "Stranger, we come in peace."

The man gave a similar puzzled look as Lanik the deserter had.

After a short while, the man, in one movement, sprung out of the sling, and impressively landed on his feet. He must have been at least six foot tall, he wore what could be best described as a leather waistcoat, round his waist was a belt, held together by a large gold buckle, for trousers he had knee-length cotton breeches, around his neck he had a long thin gold necklace, and a gold bracelet round his left wrist.

The man invited all the Romans into his tent, and stoked the fire back up, and fed the tired Romans goat meat. This man was called Tariusas-Tolia; he was a mercenary and an assassin, originally a commander from the Isaurian army, and very well known in those regions and beyond; his price was extremely high.

Tariusas was intrigued by Darinus' story and showed a lot of interest. He himself was here on an assignment, and had been hired by Leo, the Emperor of Byzantine, to discreetly eliminate the Magister Militum (master of troops second only to Caesar), who was called Aspar, and his son, who was called Ardarbur, who were both guilty of planning to betray the empire.

They were plotting to kill a man called Zeno, a general who had intercepted letters of betrayal from Ardarbur to the Sassanid Empire and had informed the Emperor Leo. Zeno was also an Isaurian (Tariusas had fought alongside Zeno against the Huns). Emperor Leo was close to Zeno and desired to make him the Magister Militum in place of the out-of-favour Aspar.

Currently Aspar and his son Ardarbur were together in Konstantin polis. The problem was that as usual they were heavily guarded by the chief Roman guards, as there was unrest in the city, so this meant they would be difficult to get near.

After hours of discussion, Darinus agreed to join Tariusas-Tolia in his quest, secretly thinking, that if this mercenary is as skilled and as competent as he makes out, then he would be one warrior made for his army.

So, after a good night's sleep on the Persian rug, they woke refreshed at the crack of dawn, and started with the preparations. Two of the bodyguards were sent back to strip the four dead Romans of their clothing and to bring the clothing and the armour back.

The reason why Tariusas had killed the Romans was this - he had held up a convoy from the east and stolen perfumes and spices to use on his mission. The Roman Byzantine soldiers had been patrolling that area and had given chase.

Tariusas produced a scroll that he unravelled to show an outline of the city of Konstantin polis, with a map of a secret canal system flowing from a secluded point from the golden horn bay, running underneath the city streets. This had been originally built by the Greeks, but had been modified to be used as an escape route for Roman emperors and such like in times of need; very few people knew of their existence.

The Roman commander, the Centurion and two of the bodyguards changed into the dead soldiers' clothing and donned the armour (as the clothing they were currently wearing would cause a few unwanted eyebrows to be lifted when they entered the city). Julian, with a humorous sigh, said, "Comrades, how good it feels to be a Roman again even if it's just a foot soldier."

Tariusas the assassin donned his disguise. He started by putting a tight purple hat upon his head, hiding the wisps of his thick hair underneath, before tying a bright yellow shawl, to form a turban round the top of his head with the top of the purple hat showing through. He then took some black charcoal, and using it as a kind of eyeliner, he darkened the circles of his eyes, and then lined the edge of his lips. On to his left finger he slipped a broad gold ring set with an emerald stone, on his feet he put on some strapped sandals. When he was ready he slung on an uncomfortable bright yellow clock, hidden underneath he still wore his normal clothing with his trademark daggers clinging to his belt. Picking up a hessian sack filled with the scroll, a flint and a pyrite firestone, concealed underneath the perfumes and spices that he had required from the convoy he had robbed. Now they were ready to go. The mercenary wore his disguise well and was unrecognizable as the Isaurian warrior he actually was.

By the time they actually got going, it had already turned to mid-morning; the other bodyguard stayed at the tent. Tariusas, Darinus, Julian, and two bodyguards entered the west gate, which had been open for a good few hours since dawn, so if there had been any big queues there they would have dispersed by now.

The disguise Tariusas had adopted was that of a wealthy Persian, bringing expensive perfumes and spices to trade in the city market. In those days wealthy men would sometimes hire soldiers to escort them on their journeys, as many bandits and robbers stalked the roads that ran from east the west. So being escorted by four Roman soldiers was a perfectly normal scenario. Passing through the gates Tariusas was stopped and his bag searched (well just opening the bag to have a quick peek inside); seeing the Roman soldiers guarding him they didn't bother him too much and ushered him through.

As they had walked away one of the soldiers at the gate mockingly called out, "So I notice you soldiers from the west now have acquired slave work."

This was more than an insult to Darinus and his men, who each were ranked higher than this lowly gate guard; to Julian this was like a red rag to a bull, and he immediately turned round. Fortunately Darinus knew he would react in this manner so was quick to deter the angry Centurion, otherwise the whole ploy would have been thrown into chaos.

Tariusas knew this awesome city well. Darinus' first impression of the place was that it had a more relaxed and less regimented feel than that of Rome. The road inward took them up a steep short hill; either side of the road stood majestic colonial buildings with round white stone pillars and marble doors, giving a Roman feel to the place. The Mese (Main Street) ran straight from the west gate to the main colossal square called the Augustaion plaza, which was the main hub of this fantastic capital. A second hill followed on from the first and a third short hill from the second; further in, the Mese was beginning to become more crowded, with the majority of the people heading towards the main square.

As they were descending down the third hill, Tariusas-tolia turned left up a narrow street between two buildings. The rest of the party swiftly followed as they had all been informed of this part of the plan. The mercenary then (excluding Darinus) gave his instructions to the other three Romans, and they left.

Twenty or so metres up the tiny street one, individual building was raised up. Leading up to the front door was a flight of steps, and there were large flower pots along the front of the building. Tariusas stopped outside this particular building, looking up and down the road to make sure nobody was watching, he got down upon his knees and pulled away two of the flower pots, this exposed a gap under the building about one and a half foot high. The mercenary lay on the floor and rolled straight under the gap. Darinus, a tad confused, lay down and he too rolled under. A few rolls in and he fell off a shelf, not very high. He found they were in a space under the building not quite high enough to stand up in, which meant they would have to crouch as they moved.

Tariusas unravelled his turban, and taking off the rest of his disguise he left it all in the void. He opened up the scroll and took a look at the canal network diagram, to familiarise himself with which route to take, against the slither of light coming through the gap.

The mercenary had come well prepared; out of the sack he took a flint and firestone (a stone containing iron such as Pyrite), he then effortlessly struck a fire torch, and took a couple of other items which he had hidden under the perfumes and spices, before also ditching the bag. Making haste they moved briskly on, using the lit torch to show the way; surprisingly enough the torch gave out a great deal of light.

They came up against a low grid door, with eroded steel bars, which was firmly shut with a heavy-looking, rusty chain wrapped round the bars, held together with a thick lock.

Beyond they could see the flickering reflection of candlelight bobbing gently up and down on the rippling water.

The mercenary handed the torch to Darinus, and from under his belt he produced a long barrelled key. Placing it in the lock he turned it half way, but it refused to turn any further; it soon became evident that this was the wrong key. But the cool assassin showing no sign of panic, took the two clips he had in his hair he skilfully picked the lock. This impressed the Roman.

The creaky gate stiffly opened, and just through the gate, they stepped down three high stone steps onto a walkway next to the canal. The narrow path was just wide enough for a single person to walk on. A little way in and the tunnel turned left, steadily they ventured forth, the curved ceiling was just high enough for them to stand straight, the musty smell was almost overpowering, but the stale water was gently flowing, the sides were horribly damp and the constant drip of condensation falling from the ceiling echoed off the walls. The torch gave sufficient light, so they could observe their surroundings; the canal itself was only several feet wide.

They pressed on. In places the tunnels got thinner and the walk ways became narrower, if not non-existent, when they would have to wade through the ice-cold water; on two occasions the depth of the water changed and they had to literally swim. The network of tunnels crossed each other, in different places and the canals joined up.

Then they turned one corner, where this part of the canal became twice as wide as the others so far; they were now almost underneath the main Augustaion square, and at one point streaks of light came flooding into the tunnel from above, because just above, on the edge of the square, was a statue that had holes built into it, not noticeable to the public. They were now nearing their destination; they could hear vaguely the faint noises of people up above.

All of a sudden Tariusas stopped and froze. On the ledge just ahead was a tiny, cute-looking baby rat, who was just as startled as the scared Isaurian. It had been standing on its hind legs holding something with its front paws, that it had been nibbling on; now frightened to death it stopped nibbling and stared.

Darinus whispered, "what is the problem, Isaurian?".

In a shaky voice Tariusas whispered, "Rats! Rats! I cannot stomach the vermin." In fact this was about the only thing in the world the great mercenary was scared of.

So Darinus, putting his hands in the water and leaning past the assassin, splashed some water at the little rodent, which let out a screech of annoyance, and scurried off into the dark. The Roman thought, 'well you learn something new every day'.

Eventually they came across a small locked wooden door, on the same side of the canal they were on; this time the long barrelled key worked. Through the door was a flight of stairs, leading to a thin passage. The two trespassers walked up the stairs, where they found the thin passage was only short and blocked off by a big marble pillar.

Whilst studying the wall next to the pillar, Tariusas said to Darinus "Roman, hold your hand here on this stone." It was about waist height. He then squeezed back past Darinus and hurried back down the steps, putting the torch out in the canal water.

Returning in the pitch black he fumbled back past the Roman and placed his hand back on the wall next to Darinus. With his back supported on the opposite wall for leverage he pushed the stone, then something strange happened. There was a grinding noise, then slowly the pillar began to move to one side letting daylight into the dark passage; at the first sight of bright light their eyes hurt.

When the pillar had fully opened, they stepped out, finding themselves in a corridor in the Nagnailira, or Curias house (the house of the Senate) which was situated at the far side of the Augustaion Plaza. This corridor was kind of narrow and not too long; it had a stone floor and plain marble walls with a high ceiling. No sooner had they stepped out, than the sound of footsteps could be heard coming from down the left hand side of the corridor. Tariusas got down on his knees and hastily started feeling his way along the bottom of the wall next to the passage opening. Satisfied he had found what he was looking for he got back to his feet. Just in time, as a servant entered the corridor from a flight of stairs he had just walked down.

The servant was an Eastern man, maybe from the Gupta Empire or nearby, he was dressed with an orange sash across his bare chest, thin cream quarter-length shorts and a bright orange turban upon his head and on his feet he wore plain sandals. In his hands he was holding a silver tray, on which sat a silver jug and two silver goblets, along with an assortment of juicy green and red grapes. He was a bit taken aback to see Tariusas and Darinus lurking around in the corridor. As he approached, the two men stood aside to let him pass; both men looked a bit dubious as they were still a bit wet from wandering around in the underground canals.

The man had every reason to be suspicious; as he passed, Tariusas, quick as lightning, with two straight fingers poked the servant in the neck, instantaneously knocking the poor man out and in the same movement Tariusas grabbed the tray. It all happened so quickly not a single drop of wine in the jug was spilt.

Handing the tray to Darinus, the assassin speedily swapped his clothing with the servant, and bundled him into the dark passage. Then he got back on his knees and pressed the stone he had found before the servant appeared, and slowly the pillar moved back over the entrance, hiding the dark passage.

So far, everything they had planned last night was going accordingly. With Tariusas-Tolia dressed as the servant he continued up the corridor whilst Darinus took the opposite direction. On reaching the end of the corridor (just beyond the stairwell from where the servant had appeared) the passageway turned right; ten or so metres ahead were a pair of huge black double doors, either side stood two Roman guards.

Darinus pressed forward, thinking he must stay focussed. As he approached, a guard knocked on one of the doors. Now in any other circumstances these soldiers would have stood to attention and saluted the Roman Commander, but at present, dressed as an ordinary foot soldier, this respectful gesture was neglected. Darinus had always wondered what this would be like, now he knew. The two big doors were opened by slaves on the other side, and Darinus found himself walking into a huge familiar room, for this was the main Senate hall.

The oval shaped room, had an extremely high ceiling held up by thick marble pillars, making the oval hall look even larger. The floor was decked with black marble along with white tiles, signifying the shape of a large star in the centre. Set halfway around the room, were five rows of wooden benches, each stepped up a level from the front to the back, sort of set up in a tier system, like a modern parliamentary chamber. On the walls were paintings engraved in the marble walls, of chariots and weapons, but the most impressive was saved for the ceiling, a life-size picture of Constantine the Great, the founder of the Eastern Roman sector. He was standing looking over Konstantin polis from a cliff above the clouds. For an early painting from that century the intricate detail of this masterpiece was phenomenal. Also dotted around in true Roman style was the odd statue, and again the most prominent was a full-size statue of Constantine standing next to a marble throne, almost at the front of the room.

Darinus had entered the room from the rear between wooden benched tiers (where the walkway was at ground level), and crossed the marble floor to the front of the room.

Guards were stood round the edge of the room, every ten or so feet. High up windows were located each side of the main doors letting light in, although there were lit candles dotted around. Darinus went and positioned himself near to the main doors, and waited with his back against the wall.

An hour passed, then came a knock at the back door, indicating for the two slaves to open up. An old man entered; he had white hair and wore a white toga bearing a purple strip, and Darinus instantly knew him to be a man of the senate. This was Marcus Semis; the Aerarium Militare (central war finance minister); he wandered down and sat on one of the benches at the front.

Ten minutes later the doors were knocked again; again the slaves obediently opened up, and two pompous men entered, one wore a red robe, and one wore a purple robe, both were deeply engrossed in conversation. Darinus knew them both to be Arians, and figured out the older one in the purple was Flavius Aspar, the Magister Militum, and the younger in the red was his son Ardarbur; they were followed in by two Roman guards. But where was Tariusas? The men greeted the Aerarium Militare, who stood and kissed them each on both cheeks.

The door knocked again, this time as the door opened a soldier entered, stood to one side and bellowed, "Julias Patricius." A young man entered dressed elegantly with a purple cloak and a thin gold crown upon his head.

It soon became clear that this was a low-key, secretive emergency meeting. Unfortunately for Darinus he understood very little, as much of what was spoken was in Greek.

It just so happened, that outside on that particular day many people were gathered in the Augustaion square, facing the Imperial Palace (which lay next door to the Curias house). They were there to protest against Patricius' unlawful marriage to Emperor Leo's daughter, making him the heir to the throne. This did not go down well with the people of Konstantin polis (especially the sleepless monks who were the main instigators for this rally) as Patricius was an Arian, and it was not permitted by Roman law that an Arian should rule. This had made Aspar doubly unpopular as he had persuaded Leo into accepting this predicament. Only a year previously a violent riot had erupted in the Hippodrome (the other side of the square) due to this fragile situation.

The public were unaware Flavius Aspar and Patricius, were presently in the Senate house, and were aiming their ongoing frustrations toward the Imperial Palace. The crowd was growing and getting more and more vocal.

As time wore on the discussions in the house got more heated, with Aspar screaming louder every time he mentioned the name Zeno. They must have been planning something big with Marcus Semis (the money man) present. He kept just shaking his head and was clearly in disagreement with Aspar and Ardarbur. He was walking backwards and forward with his hands behind his back, until at one point he stood facing Darinus.

Unexpectedly, he stopped what he was saying and turned completely white as if he had seen a ghost. He just stared at Darinus, who felt rather uncomfortable. He then hung his head and in Latin uttered in a low voice "Commander Darinus, is it true? I knew you were blessed by the gods. You have not aged a day. I had the honour of serving under you in the great war for the Island." He then took the Roman General's hand and kissed it, for Darinus had been greatly loved by his men.

Darinus was horrified, the last thing he needed was to have his cover blown. Sternly whispering through his teeth Darinus replied, "Yes it is I. Calm yourself. Acting this way will surely have me killed, all will be revealed."

Marcus instantly recollected himself and moved away; luckily the rest of the audience, thinking the old man was a bit eccentric, ignored this outburst.

Darinus glanced around the room to make sure he had not been exposed. He noticed one of the guards who had entered the room with Aspar and Ardarbur was signalling to him with his right hand. Darinus realised the guard was none other than the assassin Tariusas-Tolia; naturally it just so happened he was the closest to his targets.

When Tariusas and Darinus had disappeared into the canal system underneath the city, Julian and the two bodyguards had found their way to the Augustaion Square, where they made their way through the ever growing crowd gathered outside the Imperial Palace, to the front far left hand side of the square, nearest the Senate house.

In front of the Chalk (the area in front of the palace) two rows of soldiers were lined up, ready to keep the crowd at bay if any violence erupted. But only a handful of guards were situated outside the Senate house, as even the soldiers were unaware of the goings on behind the large senate house doors.

A couple of hours passed by, before Julian decided this was the right time to put their part of the plan into action; besides the crowd was getting more and more rowdy. So he gave the other two the nod. They had been given the task of informing the crowd who were actually in the Senate.

Julian tugged the sleeve of one of the sleepless monks (who gave him an abrupt glare) and continued to tell him, shouting, "Flavius Aspar and Patricius are in the Curia."

The monk just stared blankly, as he did not understand a word of Latin.

But fortunately this conversation was overheard by a Latin-speaking member of the public standing directly behind, and he tapped Julian's shoulder. "Is this true, sir? Are Patricius and Aspar in the Curia?"

Julian sharply replied, "Yes. Spread the word as I tell you the truth."

The word spread rapidly through the crowd, and slowly they turned their attention to the loosely guarded Senate house.

Inside the Senate house the jeering of the crowd in the square could be heard getting louder; nevertheless the meeting carried on regardless.

As far as Tariusas was concerned the plan was going smoothly and it was now time for him to move into action. Casually the assassin moved unnoticed, walking down two levels. Swiftly from behind he grabbed Ardarbur (who was nearest to him) and with his sword drawn pressed the blade tightly to the Arian's neck.

Swords were drawn from all the surrounding guards. Tariusas bellowed out in a fluent Greek accent, "Any person moves nearer and Ardarbur will pay with his life." Of course the argumentative atmosphere in the room abruptly changed.

Aspar turned to the centurion in charge of the guards and spluttered, "Who let this rouge conspirator in?" He then turned to Tariusas. "If any harm comes to even a single hair on my son's head you will die a slow and painful death, and your remains will be distributed to the four corners of the empire. Reveal to me who you are, coward."

Unfazed by this threat the assassin replied, "I am Taruisas Tolia the Isaurian."

Aspar's jaw dropped for he knew the legend that went before this mercenary. Collecting himself he spoke, "Who sent you? Zeno? I will double their price if you leave now."

Tariusas said, "Yes, Zeno is my fellow countryman, but I tell you it was not him who sent me. Now I have little time, as you can see I believe the crowd want to speak with you." The crowd at this point were just the other side of the door.

This is where Darinus stepped forward, and said in his firm voice to the senator "Marcus, order these doors to be opened immediately." Marcus froze. After all he could not override Aspar, if he did not permit this.

Aspar and Patricius began to panic; Aspar throwing his hands in the air shouting, "Let's have some order here! Who in the name of Caesar is this western soldier?"

Darinus exclaimed, "I wish not to be identified; I am a servant of Rome."

Then once again Darinus gave his order, Marcus this time chose to obey; after all he had much faith in Darinus, and very little for anybody else in that room. So he ordered the two slaves to open up, to the dismay of all the important people in that Senate room that day. This all happened so quickly; as the doors opened Tariusas forced Ardarbur across the marble floor toward the main door.

Like a stampede, the crowd flooded into the Senate room. The assassin let go of Ardarbur and rushed over to Aspar, who had stopped for a second in sheer shock of what he was witnessing. Tariusas chose to use his two trade-mark daggers for the job, cutting straight through the Magister Militum's chest.

Ardarbur's fate was soon sealed as the Roman general drew his sword and plunged it into the coward's stomach. Maybe this was a fortunate end for the Arian, and his father for that matter, rather than the angry crowd getting hold of them.

It was mayhem in the Senate room as more and more people poured in.

The Roman guard, upon the command of the centurion, had moved to the back of the room and were ready to defend the doors at the rear, as the Senate house was joined at the back to the Imperial palace.

The sleepless monks were uninterested in lawlessly attacking the soldiers.

Tariusas and Darinus made a sprint to the back to escape but were stopped by the guards, who refused to let them pass, until out of nowhere Marcus Semis, now being swamped by the crowd, gave the order to let them through. The slaves opened the black doors slightly, enough for both men to slip through. Just before Darinus left the room he turned back to thank Marcus, and out of the corner of his eye he saw a raised sword come crashing down on his faithful comrade. He realised the perpetrator to be Patricius, who after killing Marcus screamed to the centurion, "Arrest the two conspirators." He never got to finish the rest of the order as the crowd got to him.

Obediently the centurion took up the request and taking several guards gave chase.

Tariusas heard this order (which was given in Greek) and urging Darinus to make haste, they managed to gain a head start. They turned the corner and raced up the corridor, once they reached the correct pillar, the assassin got down on his knees and after fumbling around, found the correct stone, using a great deal of force he pushed the stubborn stone, just as the guards led by the centurion entered the bottom of the corridor. The pillar began to move (somehow this time it seemed to move even slower). Just as it opened enough for one of them to squeeze through Tariusas disappeared into the dark passage, and Darinus found himself back against the passage fending off the centurion, who had drawn his sword and was raining down, some heavy blows.

Tariusas wasted no time in finding, and relighting the firelight torch. He shouted up to Darinus, "make haste." Darinus didn't need to be told twice, he darted down the passage after the assassin, down the stairway and into the tunnel, with the centurion closely on his tail.

Darinus jumped down onto the narrow path that ran next to the canal, the centurion followed. He then swung his sword forward. Darinus knew this would happen and fortunately ducked in the nick of time. He turned to face the centurion; as their swords met the force knocked them both off the ledge and into the water, which was actually waist deep.

The centurion was incredibly strong and currently fitter than Darinus. The fight continued for five minutes. What made the fight take longer was the ceiling being low, preventing them from being able to raise their swords up high. Also being in the water gave them a lack of movement in their legs, so due to these obstacles all the two fighters could do was slog it out. Just when it looked like the fight was heading for a stalemate, Darinus dropped into the water and upended the centurion, who lost his sword and fell backwards, splashing into the canal. When he surfaced, Darinus with his sword raised ordered him and the guards to leave.

The beaten centurion, along with his men disappeared up the dark passage, and the out-of-breath general followed the Assassin. They plodded on for what seemed hours, not much was said, and this particular tunnel curved to the right, and ran straight till eventually they saw light at the end.

Blinking they climbed out of the entrance, which was disguised to look like the beginning of a small cave from the outside. They found they had reached the Golden Horn harbour, where a fleet of Roman ships were docked around this beautiful huge natural bay. Wasting no time they scrambled up the rocky bank above the cave opening. At the top they came out next to the Bucoleon (house of Justice); crossing a road they entered the Tz-ykanisteria (the polo field), and waiting for them was Julian and the two bodyguards who had left the crowd before they had entered the Senate house.

All five keeping a low profile made their way, avoiding Augustaion Square, out of Konstantin polis, and back to the assassin's tent.

Tariusas was appreciative of the Roman's help, but being the proud men he was he never said thank you.

The mission had been completed with no complications. The Emperor Leo was pleased, as Aspar and Ardarbur had been executed, without the people knowing an assassin was responsible; they just suspected he had been murdered by the rioting crowd. Patricius actually survived (although he was badly injured), he never became Caesar. Zeno was made Magister Militum.

Darinus was more than impressed with Tariusas Tolia the master of disguise, mercenary and assassin, and he offered him a square on the floor of the Caledonian courtyard.

Tariusas said, "Yes, but it will come at a price."

At which Darinus replied, "Yes, remember to pay me my share from your mission as I was the one who slayed Ardarbur; once you have paid we can negotiate."

Well after some kind of good-humoured bartering, a deal was thrashed out and Tariusas agreed.

Darinus and his men stayed two more days before moving on. They followed the road west and then down to the coast, where they looked to leave the great Byzantine Empire.

A CANYON A COYOTE AND A FEATHER

With the skins full of fresh water, and fruit stocked up and lying loosely in the bottom of the canoe, their vessel was pushed out to sea, they set off northward bound.

Once more Adrien took out the scroll and opened it up to take a look at the map; the great pass was still an extremely long way off. They were currently close to the bottom of the northern continent, further on up the canvas showed a long peninsula, at the top of which a river ran through the heart of the massive northern continent. Adrien, being inquisitive, decided that they would take this river to break the monotony of the boring ocean route; after all it looked like roughly the same distance (maybe a bit longer) than just following the coast.

The two Polynesian rowing machines powered on, pushing the boat through the calm turquoise sea that was gradually beginning to change to a deeper blue. They stayed close to the shore as much as possible, although at times they were forced further out due to the high surf.

A day or so later they arrived at the bottom of the peninsula. Taking the right-hand side, the men continued north, at night time stopping on a couple of the richly vegetated islands to get some sleep. Another three days and they reached the mouth of the river shown on the map.

Rowing along this new unpredictable river was a bit of an experience, for one they were now rowing against the current flow. In more calm, serene places the water became mirrored, reflecting the big light blue sky; this northern continent was a rugged place with sparse unfertile open spaces, and the travellers were in awe of this vast wilderness that surrounded them. They raced on, passing through rocky gorges; one would guess that in rainy seasons this bubbling river would be very unforgiving.

One particular morning after breakfasting (once again rainbow trout), they found that they had entered the beginning of the most amazing gorge, which had gone unnoticed the previous day because as they pulled the boat in, the sun had already set. A little further in, Adrien decided that it would be nice to stop, enjoy the surroundings and do some exploring. This gorge was marked as a reddy brown, jagged hole in the ground on the canvas map.

Again they dragged the canoe up the shore away from the river, and started to walk up the steep gorge; this time the Polynesians were invited to accompany the Saxons. In some places the walk became more of a climb. Almost an hour later they reached the top, where they all sat breathless, with legs dangling over the ledge, admiring the tremendous view, which surely was a visual treat - the immense Grand Canyon stretched far off into the distance, a vast chasm cut out of the ground. Deep below the river ran like a silver snake slithering through the rocky bed of this great canyon. Beyond the canyon on the higher ground was a vast plateau with great stones; as the sun moved higher, shadows danced away from their hiding places between these pastel-coloured stones.

As they sat relaxing, black figures were spotted moving towards them. Coming out of the basin of the canyon they started out looking like tiny black dots, but as they drew closer these figures grew bigger and bigger, next thing the most awesome condors (some with wing spans of up to nine metres) circled round just below them, before flying out and gliding around above the travellers' heads. Comically the quick-witted Eals remarked, "I never knew they made crows that big."

After some time spent admiring the condors, their attention was soon diverted back down into the Canyon, where a woman a hundred feet below was seen casually wandering along a flat ledge, freely swinging her arms by her sides, a wolf-like dog comfortably walked beside her, and both looked very content in each other's company. They had not seen the four travellers, lounging around up above in the morning sun.

Adrien put his finger to his mouth, and whispered, "Shush," to his men. Slowly he rose to his feet. He decided he was going to follow the woman; the others copied the Saxon leader and all started quietly clambering down the steep jagged route they had climbed up just a while earlier. After stalking the young woman for some time she came to a stop at the base of the canyon not too far from the river to take a rest. Adrien and his party managed to hide without being seen just a short distance away behind a rock jutting out from the side of the canyon wall. It soon became obvious that the woman and her dog (which was a coyote, an indigenous dog to the northern continent) were actually tracking something themselves.

Adrien, peering round the rock, could see this petite, pretty, tanned-skinned woman much clearer; she had dark brown, short hair, on her tiny feet she wore sandals woven from yucca and hemp, her clothing was made of bison fur, accompanied by a thick leather belt. Round her neck hung a simple necklace brightly decorated with small sea shells, which was unusual as this canyon was so far away from the ocean. On her head sat a thin band adorned with a single dyed purple feather. She sat staring at a bush as if waiting for something.

One of the Polynesians coughed, a low gruff cough, and the coyote's pointed ears pricked up. It swung its head around looking straight in the direction of the travellers' hiding place behind the rock, and its eyes met Adrien's, who was still peering round. The coyote became unsettled, but right at that split second, distracted by whatever it was she was tracking, the slight young woman rose to her feet.

Adrien then saw a greenish bird fly out of the bush; as it took off its feathers glistened and flashed in the light of the bright sun. It flew a few yards to another bush, and the pretty girl followed. Blinking its lazy eyes, the dog, taking away its threatening glare from the Saxon, turned and padded on after her.

Once out of earshot, Adrien breathed a sigh of relief. He pointed at the noisy Polynesians, signalling for them to go back to the canoe. Adrien and Eals continued their pursuit, whilst keeping a safe distance away.

The woman followed the cheeky bird, which actually appeared to be teasing her, perching just out of reach, then as the women drew near, the magnificent-coloured bird would let out a shrill chirp and fly on again. This process carried on.

The Saxons stayed on the trail, dodging and hiding behind small rocks and bushes, the midday sun was now high in the sky, thus making the Westerners sweat profusely (although on the journey since leaving Britannia they had had to quickly get used to the hot continents), causing the salty sweat to drip from their foreheads annoyingly into their eyes.

Eventually the native girl came to a barren clearing between the wall of the canyon and the roaring river. The beautiful bird had settled on a dead, white-barked tree, whose naked branches had distinctly yielded neither leaves nor fruit for many years, and was currently just a skeleton. It stood smack in the middle of the clearing, surrounded by orange sand with the odd lone rock jutting out of the ground.

Strangely enough the girl stopped ten feet away from the skeleton tree; she stood as if she was frozen. Adrien had noticed that all the time they had been following her she had never got too close to the bird. Clearly the truth of the matter was although she was drawn towards the creature, she was actually scared stiff of it.

From behind the bush in which he was hiding, Adrien stood up, and boldly walked into the clearing, raising his hands up just above his shoulders to show that he came in peace.

On seeing the white Westerner, the shocked girl cowered behind the coyote.

As Adrien approached, the canine bared its teeth and growled before breaking into full-on loud barking, which vibrated against the limestone wall of the canyon, sending an echo all around. Adrien passed by the girl and, unfazed by the baying dog, he strolled on to the tree where the bird was. As he got within arm's length the bird leaned forward from its perch and annoyingly let out an almighty screech, much higher than the squawking screech it had been using whilst teasing the woman earlier.

The Saxon stopped and paused a couple of metres away to admire this lovely creature; its plumage was distinctively beautiful, having a brilliantly mixed orange, red and yellow head with a thick, sharp, hooked beak; its body was green with wings tinged at the tips with the same colour as its head. This exquisite bird was roughly 33cms long. But the most striking feature was its long, pointed tail; one particular feather shone out brighter than the rest, it was also longer, as the creature moved, the colour of this feather flashed iridescent, shimmering with many colours from green through to bright gold, depending on which angle you looked at it.

Not knowing why, Adrien very slowly and curiously moved even closer towards the bird (which is known today as the now extinct Carolina Parakeet), which seemed unfazed by the Saxon. Just as he was about to make contact he felt something whiz by his head and with a thud the bird fell to the ground. Adrien knelt down over the now dead corpse of the parakeet; to his horror a thin arrow had pierced through the bird's breast and was still there, so he gently pulled the stick out. The neatly grafted arrow, had a smooth flint tip, and was decorated with red feathers at the end.

Adrien felt a gentle hand tenderly touch his right shoulder. Glancing up he saw the native woman standing quietly next to him, with tears flowing down her tight cheek bones. Plainly the death of this beautiful creature had upset her.

Wasting no time, and without thinking; Adrien automatically plucked the iridescent feather from the tail of the parakeet and tucked it in his belt. Fortunately the annoying bark of the coyote had ceased. Sensing danger the Saxon grabbed the girl's hand, and briskly led her out of the barren clearing and away from the skeleton tree, crouching low as they went, to where Eals was still hiding.

Adrien now had time to look up as he guessed the arrow had been shot from high up in the canyon, but there was nobody to be seen. He decided it would be wise to get away as soon as possible, so they rapidly went back to the boat, and all the way the young native woman followed the Saxons without resistance, still grasping Adrien's hand tightly.

Once back at the boat they joined up with the Polynesians, who had lifted the canoe back onto the water and were ready to go. Adrien reached for the cool fresh water, from the water skins; after he had drunk he offered the skin to the woman, who was evidently glad of his generosity.

Close up he could see how pretty this native girl was; her attractive eyes were enchantingly deep brown, along with long dark lashes, upon her face she wore a mischievous smile. Standing on the bank of the river she pointed to the right for them to head further up the great river deeper into this mysterious canyon. They all boarded the canoe along with the coyote. Just up the river the current flow slowed.

Adrien took the long exquisite feather from his belt to inspect it; running it through his fingers it felt like soft silk. He showed it to Eals who also admired its beauty, and he passed it toward the native girl, who cowering away, shook her head, and refused to touch it.

The peace was soon broken, as out of nowhere three canoes appeared, racing up the river from behind them. These canoes were different to the Polynesians' simple sturdy seaworthy canoe; they were thinner and more pointed, woven out of reed and decorated with coloured pictures of animals. Four men rowed in each vessel; they had painted symbols upon their faces and semi-naked bodies.

On the second canoe a threatening looking man stood upright, with his arms folded, in the centre of the canoe, facing towards them as he passed. Upon his head he wore a head piece adorned with white feathers, along with the odd red feather thrown in. He had wide holes in his long ear lobes and through his pieced nose was a narrow metal object. From the waist down he wore ragged, knee-length trousers made of bison leather, a small tomahawk was tied loosely to his side with a short wooden handle, and a sharp head made of bone; hanging over his left shoulder was a quiver with red, feather-tailed arrows inside, which immediately gave away the fact that this was the man who had shot the arrow that had killed the exquisite bird. But right now this man had a look of anger on his solemn face.

The three canoes slowed down until in line with the Polynesian vessel, which they had been rowing along at a leisurely pace. The canoe at the front swerved in to just ahead and the one at the back pulled in at the rear, sort of jamming the travellers' canoe in. The man in the middle canoe just stood staring.

A mile or so up river the boats started to pull in to the right hand side. Eals, who was sitting directly behind Adrien, whispered in his leader's ear, "Shall we ready to fight, master?"

Adrien replied, "Keep your hand near your sword and wait."

The natives on the three slick, streamlined canoes directed the travellers into a small quaint cove with a stony beach; all the vessels were dragged out of the water. Adrien, checking out these native men, counted twelve in all; they were all semi naked, and all wore moccasins the same as the pretty woman. The chief who was obviously the angry looking man with his arms crossed, sharply yelled at the young woman in their native tongue with just a few sharp words, which she meekly replied to, and reluctantly went over to join him; her coyote had already bound over and was licking the chief's hand.

Adrien noticed that the native men were not really interested in his or Eals or the Polynesians foreign appearance; they all had their eyes firmly fixed on the long iridescent feather tucked in his belt. They all in turn bowed and in an unusual way touched their foreheads with their fingers and thumb on one hand.

After referring with the chief, the slight woman turned back to face the Saxons, whistled and winked at Adrien and nodded for him to follow. Adrien thought it best to bring the two burly Polynesians along, just in case they were needed for back up. So cautiously they followed the natives as they walked up a neatly cut narrow path.

Adrien had mixed feelings, but trusting his own instincts he chose to obey. He somehow knew in a strange way that as long as he held the feather then they would come to no harm.

Up and up they climbed. This climb was much harder than earlier, after all they had already climbed and walked a long distance. Eals became aware that his master had begun to limp, due to the injury he had picked up from the snake bite earlier in their journey. Eventually they reached the summit of the great canyon for the second time that day.

If anyone reading this book has ever climbed up inside a canyon that size, you will understand that just once let alone twice in one day is exceedingly hard work, especially when the sun is blazing down.

Once at the top, they arrived at the native's camp. There were two extraordinarily shaped tents stood either side of the camp. Long wooden poles had been bound together in the shape of a tripod, covered by stitched-up bison skins. These tents were indeed tepees. The skirt of the bison leather was decorated with simple drawings inspired mainly by hunting and animals.

In the centre of the camp was a tall, carved, wooden totem pole; the carvings were quite intricate, and if you looked for a few seconds you could make out the shape of a bird with its wings spread out at the top.

But these native tribesmen were not alone; beyond their camp dotted around the vast plain were several or more other temporary settlements, each with much space between them.

I will tell the reason why all these groups were gathered here for shortly.

The natives had remained quiet on the tiresome walk up the steep trail. Now at the camp they began to quibble and chatter, twelve to the dozen. The chief opened up a flap to one of the tepees, and gestured to the travellers to come inside. As Adrien and Eals entered, Adrien signalled for the Polynesians to stay outside on guard.

The two Saxons were glad to get out of the relentless sun; once inside they were surprised of how the tepee appeared to be bigger and more spacious than it had from the outside. The floor was decked with leather and furs. The Saxons were given water and made to feel comfortable. Although the native men looked hard and expressionless, Adrien no longer felt as threatened as he had done earlier. The chief had not entered the tepee, but the slight, cute-looking woman, her coyote and four tribesmen had, and every time one left or entered, they would face Adrien, touch their foreheads and bow before glancing at the feather.

Eals said to Adrien with a wry smirk upon his face, "I see they think you're a god. You know how mad some of the foreign people we have met along the way have been."

Adrien in a more serious tone said, "No, Eals, my faithful Althing, I feel there is something sacred about this feather; if you watch them they always look at the feather."

After a while the Saxons were left alone to get some rest.

Late afternoon the Saxons were awoken from their nap. Adrien felt he could have just stayed there, as he had fallen into a deep sleep and had started dreaming of Britannia. Once out of the tepee they found the solemn chief, who was outside waiting for them. He summoned them to follow. A way off, a crowd was gathered; getting closer they could see that the crowd was made up of different chiefs and leaders, obviously representing different tribes.

The solemn chief guided them towards the gathering; all the way he kept glancing enviously at the shimmering iridescent feather. Only two native men accompanied them whilst Adrien only brought along Eals.

The crowd was gathered around in a big half-circle outside a small wigwam (probably only big enough for one man). As soon as the strangers arrived the chattering fell away. Adrien made no eye contact with these native men, instead he just gazed at the floor and followed the chief, and distinctly the main attraction was now the feather.

An old, old man appeared from the small wigwam. He bowed, then gestured to Adrien to come and sit on a wooden stool, next to where he stood, just outside his tepee, facing the crowd. When the Saxon was seated, the most unusual noise came from the old, old man's mouth; it was a sort of wailing sound, and the people gathered began to sit on the floor.

Now it is hard to explain these different people. Most were like the early North American Indians, Inuits and Anasazis, others had just migrated from up near the great northern pass.

The reason they were all gathered on this great plain next to the almighty canyon, was that for many years the tribes had been in conflict with each other and sometimes even wars would break out. Much of the disputing was due to the high levels of migrating people, stealing livestock and claiming new land that already belonged to existing groups.

For generations it had been told that one day a bird would appear with the most amazing distinctive gold feather, and whoever caught this beautiful creature and plucked the feather would inherit the lands to the sky and all the cattle and bison, and they would instantly become the ultimate chief over all the tribes. Most people thought this to be an old wife's tale, until recently the bird had been seen near the huge canyon. News of its appearance spread like wild fire, and the great search had begun.

Well it just happened that Adrien had plucked the feather, and in doing so this had unknowingly become the ultimate chief, which explains why everyone kept bowing.

The old man carried on his wailing, which the Saxons actually found quite soothing and relaxing; it felt as if, listened to long enough, it would send you into a long trance. Adrien found his eyes transfixed on the sky; grey blustering clouds billowed and raced up above and, although still warm, a westerly wind started to pick up. It looked like it wanted to rain. Adrien found he could make out the shape of wild horses running in the clouds.

Then quite abruptly the old man's wailing ceased, all eyes were on him and Adrien (who was in prime position), with his loyal Althing Eals sitting cross-legged next to him on the floor. Adrien was thinking to himself, this has got to be the oldest man he had ever seen, with his wispy white hair and wrinkly bronze skin. This man was from the old Anasazi tribespeople. He had a warm frock robe made from turkey feathers wrapped around him.

The old, old man started to speak; his deep voice was strong and warbled as he spoke. The Saxons did not understand a thing. He told ancient native stories of that land, and these are just a few:

The girl who married a pine tree.
The snail that tricked the beaver.
The porcupine and the wolf.
The discovery of the upper world.
The journey to the island of souls.

And finally, the girl who became a bird, which many believed to be linked to the bird they had all been searching for.

The old man was very theatrical in the way he told his stories, whispering, crawling, growling, and moving around.

All his actions kept the Saxons more than entertained. Whilst he had been talking, a fire had been lit (this is one thing that had amazed Adrien that through all the lands they had travelled, fires were lit by all races) and a peace pipe was being handed around, which had a long wooden stem bound to a carved stone.

Shortly afterwards a flagon was passed round, containing a cloudy drink made from cactus juice. Eals took a big gulp and it felt like it would burn his throat out; it was as potent as the drink they had tasted in the Orkney islands a year or so previously, and was extremely alcoholic. Adrien leaned over to Eals and warned him, "This is not the time or place; we learnt that lesson the hard way before."

After many hours the old man finished his stories and disappeared into his wigwam.

Adrien stood up. His legs felt stiff and his injured leg was beginning to ache; maybe this was down to the amount of walking earlier in the day. As he had stood, so did all the other people. At a count there must have been roughly forty or so people gathered. Adrien was now well aware of the power of the feather.

Back at the camp, the remains of a small fire dwindled, the rest of the natives had retired for that day, so the two Saxons climbed back into the tepee they had been in earlier and settled down for the night.

It took Adrien some time to get to sleep; from where he lay he could see the glow of the fire, as the flap to the tepee was slightly open. Just as he was finally drifting off to sleep, he was interrupted, as a figure entered the open flap and lay down beside him. He knew who it was straight the way, it was the pretty woman with the coyote.

She lay very close to Adrien. The Saxon was a bit taken aback by the situation. He could feel her sweet warm breath against his left cheek; she tenderly touched his face before slowly running her gentle fingers through his hair. He in return affectionately stroked her arm, her tanned skin was soft and smooth to touch.

Adrien thought this must be a dream, he felt relaxed for the first time in ages.

Then like a thorn piercing his heart he stopped; no, this was wrong. He loved another, but the temptation was so strong, after all his love would never know! But this woman was so attractive that any man in turning down her seductive advances would be out of their mind.

The battle in his head continued; in the end his conscience got the better of him; he kissed her forehead and got up and left the tepee. He went and lay down in the open air by the fire. Out from under his tunic he took the lock of hair Freyja had given him and held it close to his heart. So with the lock of hair in one hand and the other on his belt guarding the sacred feather he fell in to a deep sleep.

With a start Adrien was woken by one hell of a commotion.

It was still dark. Beside him was a different chief on his knees writhing in pain clutching his right wrist. Stuck through his hand was an arrow, with a red feathered tail; it doesn't take a wise man to guess what was going on. Whilst the Saxon was sleeping, a chief from an opposing tribe had come with the intent to rob the feather, but he had been caught red handed (in more ways than one).

Adrien realised the solemn chief had been watching over him, as he appeared and drove away the imposter.

At sunrise the chief took Adrien (who since the commotion had barely slept a wink) with him, and they walked back down into the canyon; the coyote had taken a shine to Adrien and had invited itself along for the stroll.

The Native chief took the white Westerner to a set of secluded caves set into the wall of the canyon halfway down. They entered one particular cave opening, and here they were greeted by the most fantastic art work. Over a period of many years these had been carved in to the wall and coloured in with different dyes.

What Adrien did not know, was the significance of these carvings - many were prophecies. There were pictures of horses, which felt completely normal to the Saxon, but what he did not know was that there was not even a single horse on that continent yet. The old native wise men had seen all this in visions along with many other things, thus inspiring the scripts of wonderful artwork.

But what caught his eye was a carving of a chess board no more than thirty centimetres square. Looking closer he saw that pieces were carved onto the board, but they had worn over time and were now hardly recognisable, but two pieces on one side had not faded. One was the king who sat on a white square, and two squares over to the king's right was a man on a horse, with a bow slung over his shoulder. This was a miniature replica of the chief who stood directly in front of him at that very moment, and the king was a replica of himself. Adrien had not a single doubt in his heart that indeed this man was to become one of his equus (knights) as had been foretold in this strange land. This was a unique position to be given on the board, and could cause much devastation to the opposing army.

As Adrien pointed at the board the native chief bowed his head slightly to acknowledge him, for he knew that as the elder had prophesied, he would follow the Saxon and join him when the time arrived.

Adrien then did something unexpected. He took the feather from under his belt and handed it to the chief, whose actual name was Huite (which means bowman amongst his people). Huite humbly received the iridescent feather, and for the first time a huge grin appeared along with deep dimples upon his solemn face and his large brown chestnut eyes lit up.

Adrien felt a great weight taken away from him, as he had no desire to lead such an unruly, disorderly bunch of tribesmen, and he knew Huite would be just the man for the job. Collecting his commander and the two Polynesians, they all slipped away unnoticed, back down into the canyon to the river, lifting the canoe back into the water, and off they went toward the great northern pass. The coyote that had followed to the edge of the river, stood and barked at the canoe until it was out of view.

THE GREAT NORTHERN PASS

The two Saxons and the rowing Polynesians sailed on. There is only so much tranquil, beautiful scenery you can enjoy whilst lazily relaxing in the back of a canoe.

Since Adrien's encounter with the cute coyote girl, he wondered, should he have given in to her advances – after all it would have been good! But this dark thought only prompted him to think more and more about the beautiful Freyja. Would he honestly ever get to see her again or would she marry another? Besides he was on the other side of the world.

The canoe sped onward. In those days the network of rivers on that continent nearly all joined up. Following the Colorado River north east, it soon came to a fork where they took the left hand side, joining the green river. They witnessed some fantastic sights, massive herds of bison and buffalo coming down to drink from the river, majestic redwood trees that were so tall the travellers became concerned they had entered a land of giants.

Weeks later the canoe at long last sailed out to the open sea. The two Saxons had never been so pleased to see the great ocean once again, the smell of salt filled the air, and the sound of seagulls circled up above. Further north the sight of a dark green island came vaguely into view upon the horizon. They entered a large bay, sort of in the shape of a half moon, where lodged on the shore in the centre of the bay was a noticeable white rock, which looked somewhat out of place, stuck all alone on the beach, as if it was a kind of landmark for something. This was marked on the canvas, which indicated they had now entered the far north. So they were gradually nearing the great northern pass.

They followed the route between the mainland and the dark green island, which was so huge it took a matter of days to pass, the further north they advanced the colder it began to get. At one point one of the Polynesians leant over and touched the cold water, and gave Adrien a worried look before shaking his head; these men from the southern seas were not made for such bitter weather.

So Adrien decided to call them in to shore on the main land. They stopped for a couple of days in the forest where they set traps, catching mainly moose, which they fed on and used the skins to make warm clothing. They also covered their leather soled shoes (which Taung had given them) with fur to stop their toes from getting cold.

Back out to sea they sailed onward.

Adrien had decided at a convenient location, he and his Althing would say goodbye to the Polynesians, and continue on by foot; after all he could see the colder it got the more miserable the southern sea-faring men became. So at a suitable place, next to an estuary entering a small river, he signalled for them to bring the canoe in (they were now much nearer to the pass). The Saxons disembarked into the shallow waters, and Adrien then placed his right hand firmly on the bow of the canoe, and shaking his head, he pointed south, clearly demonstrating for the Polynesians to go home. It was an unusual moment for the Polynesians who looked a little lost, as they had got used to taking orders from Adrien and this, to their delight had come unexpectedly. So both with a wry smile turned their vessel round and headed back south and were soon out of sight.

Wading to the shore the two Saxons pressed on, following the winding river inland for a few miles before it turned north. On that first day they covered some good ground. That night they camped, it felt good to be back on solid ground again.

The following day it was a crisp morning, they were up nice and early to the sound of the birds up above. They could see the smoke of their breath in front of their faces, lingering in the cold air. Rising high up ahead there were white mountain's thick with snow.

Following the bubbling river (which lay to the right), the path at one particular point was blocked by a low branch. Just as Eals was about to push it out of the way, he stopped in his tracks, as they were both distracted. Several yards away in mid-river they spotted three brown, grizzly bears frolicking in the water - a mother with two cubs. Crouching down the Saxons decided to watch these awesome creatures.

At this specific place was a short waterfall, and the mother's eyes were transfixed on this waterfall, as if she was concentrating hard on something, whilst the two cubs were more content to play fight between them, which was a heart-warming sight.

Then something sprung out of the water. Whatever it was the mother bear tried to catch it with her paws, but missed. This happened a couple of times. The strange objects springing out of the water were weirdly going up river against the flow, trying to get up the waterfall. Eals whispered to Adrien, "I do believe they are flying fish." Adrien replied, "Fish with wings – don't be ridiculous."

Then astonishingly the mother bear caught one of the objects with her mouth in mid-air, and the travellers could now see it was a fair-size fish; in fact autumn was prime time for bears to go salmon fishing.

Quietly Adrien and Eals slowly crept by. Just upriver the water changed colour to a dullish orange and, taking a closer look, they found scattered on the shallow river bed specks of copper. Further up, snow was on the ground which, as they walked, got deeper as the ground gradually got higher. Now it being mid-autumn there had already been quite a bit of snowfall.

Eventually they left the river and followed a path upward through the snow. Adrien stopped to consult his canvas and came to the conclusion it would be far quicker to go straight, which led up through the mountains, rather than all the way round the bottom of the mountain range. Not realising the harsh reality of his decision to take the short cut, they pressed forward; if he had only known the ruthless terrain that lay up ahead he would never have even attempted this route. Plodding on, at first the trail was effortless, but slowly it became steeper and steeper. Anyone who's ever climbed a mountain will know that you can walk for ages and never seem to get anywhere. As they walked the endless snow stretched out for miles before them and the bright glare of the sun on the crisp snow was causing the Saxons to squint.

Throughout the quest Eals had composed a song, and to keep spirits high it had become sort of an anthem they sang at times on the long journeys. Right now through the boredom, and to keep them going, they began to sing, and this is how it went:

Yay Saxon sword lies straight,
O Saxons shield is round,
In the realms of battle we will cut the Romans down,
We will take the land,
And Yay Old Saxon will hold the crown!

Mid-afternoon they reached a ridge where the ground levelled, further up ahead the peaks rose higher and higher. From this point they were now facing a new hazard: crevasses. Not just normal crevasses but little hidden nasty crevasses, which could not be seen until you were right upon them. These conditions made both Adrien and Eals more cautious. The silence was now deafening and incredibly eerie and the air was beginning to thin.

Then to make matters more unpleasant, the weather took a turn for the worst, as it often can in a split second when venturing through mountainous regions. The wind picked up and became stronger, whipping up the icy snow from the floor and swirling it round the Saxons' faces, as if it were warning them of the dangers ahead. The wind became so strong that the constant specks of ice actually hurt as they made contact.

This made visibility slightly poorer, and further on the crevasses became wider and deeper. In places they had to tiptoe past the slots; fortunately the moose skins were doing their job and keeping them warm as the temperature had dramatically dropped.

The mountain once again started to slope steeply upward. At one point Adrien nearly suggested they retreat and go back down, but he was stubborn and certainly no quitter. Besides, they had come this far it would be unthinkable to back out now!

On and on the determined Saxons pressed. It had started to snow now, creating a blinding blizzard, and then as if someone commanded the weather to stop, the wind ceased and the snow stopped falling, giving the travellers a break, making it easy for them to see the crevasses properly, which became less frequent the higher they got. This landscape was surely an unforgivable environment. Then just as the Saxons thought things were improving, something happened straight out of the blue to change the whole direction of the journey.

Far up above the mountain it looked like it began to move, and there was a sound of rumbling deep below where they stood. The events that took place next happened very quickly. The ground began to shake. Both looked at each other in disbelief for this was not good, they were far from being familiar with hiking up mountains let alone what was about to occur. The word avalanche strikes fear into even the most hardened mountaineers, and this is what they were about to encounter.

Looking up they watched, as in the distance the snow began pouring down the crisp peaks, gathering momentum and speed as it hurtled toward the two bewildered travellers. Aware that there was no time to even consider escape, in true Saxon style these two brave fearless warriors did what they did best and automatically drew their swords and stood firm.

The avalanche hit hard, swallowing them up; there was not even time to think of uttering a single farewell. The force of the landslide winded Adrien so hard. He had never felt such unbelievable power! Engulfed in the moving snow he found himself hurtling down the mountain, being thrown around like a straw doll and in complete blackness occasionally smashing his head upon the floor.

Then unexpectedly he hit the edge of one of the dreaded crevasses feet first. Next he found himself awkwardly falling, but instead of falling through thin air he slid down an icy wall, until with an almighty thump he hit the bottom. He felt a searing pain, not in his feet but his side. Through the whole ordeal he had kept his sword in hand and, as he hit the bottom of the crevasse, the handle had smashed into his left side, piercing his skin and no doubt breaking another rib. Holding his side the Saxon writhed in agony.

For a while he lay stunned in the darkness. Up above was a thunderous noise, which could be best described as like the sound of a hundred horse and chariots galloping overhead. Being in the dark Adrien was totally disorientated. He knew he had fallen down a gap into one of the dreaded crevasses. Up above the excited snow kept on bellowing down the mountain slope as if it were alive and ignoring the gap, as none of it was flooding into the crevasse opening. Shortly the rumbling overhead ceased, and a weak ray of light poured through a five-foot gap into the cavity. Adrien realised he had fallen almost thirty feet; this in itself (apart from surviving the avalanche) was almost a miracle.

He lay on an ice ledge barely two metres wide.

Peering over the ledge he was faced with a sheer drop spiralling down to what looked like an endless black hole. He was in an icy chamber, like a pear shape that narrowed as it got nearer to the opening at the top.

All this time he was struggling with the horrendous pain in his side, underneath the moose fur he was bleeding, whilst constantly trying to catch his breath. A couple of cruel painful hours passed before the dazed Saxon managed to collect himself. His two main concerns were, firstly, how to escape, and secondly, where was his friend Eals?

To scale this ice wall was to be a feat in itself, especially in his condition. The odd narrow ledge high up jutted out, but apart from that the walls were smooth and too slippery to even attempt to climb. So he would have to devise a logical plan (which wasn't easy in his emotional and physical state) of escape.

Dotted around the bare ice chamber, were unusual long thin sharp icy objects, some hanging, whilst others were pointing upwards from the floor. Fortunately he had missed these as he had fallen; they were in effect stalactites and stalagmites. If he could break these off, then he could somehow wedge them into the ice wall and then use the spikes to climb, which seemed like a feasible plan.

So using his sword he cut some of the thicker ones down to use, as the thinner ones just easily shattered. But his feeble attempts to hammer them into the solid ice made the disillusioned warrior soon give in. Besides the pain in his side was sapping the strength out of him.

Through the opening in the crevasse the light began to fade and so did Adrien, barely able to move, although the moose skin kept him warm, his fingers and the tips of his toes were feeling the biting cold. I should imagine most of this was down to bad blood circulation through his body.

The night passed and daylight funnelled through the gap. Shivering with the cold Adrien knew he had to move to try and warm up, so trying to be positive he mustered up as much strength as possible, but this soon faded as his hands were beginning to cramp with the cold. He did manage to get three of the pointed stalagmites in to the wall though, but then slid back down.

To try and raise his spirits he started to mutter the words to the Saxon tune. Nevertheless his new-found confidence was soon quashed, and a dark depression entered his head. By the looks of things it looked like this time he was doomed; clearly there was no possible way of climbing out of the gap, way up above.

Sitting back down, for the first time in his life he actually felt sorry for himself. This was much worse than being locked up in the Viking jail; at least there he had had his friends. He had come so far over the last few years, whilst on his quest, enduring the fierce southern seas and surviving the great snake bite. But as well as these wretched circumstances, this loneliness he was feeling was too much, as during his life he had never been on his own.

With overwhelming anxiety he began to sob tears of utter despair. In his hand he held Freyja's lock of hair. There was also the not so small matter of his trusted friend Eals. What had become of him? Surely he would have perished in the deplorable avalanche?

As the time wore on during the course of the day, he was hit with another peril - hunger and incredible thirst. So to quell his thirst be began to lick the icy wall.

Another night came and went. In the darkness he started considering sliding off his ledge and ending it all by throwing himself into the abyss below. Well, what could he do as he was beginning to become more and more delirious?

As the first slither of light entered the gap he had made up his mind. It had started to get so cold the deposit seeping from his nose had begun to freeze. So in a haze and physically wounded he decided this was the end. Giving up he peered over the edge. "This is the end, Adrien, King of Britannia," he muttered, and effortlessly he slipped over the edge and into the dark void.

He fell, spiralling down into the black hole, the hollow did not drop directly downwards. Instead he entered a narrow tunnel inclining at 45 degrees. Unable to see a single thing, the only thing that was apparent was the fast rate he was travelling. Rushing down the icy tunnel and gathering such velocity Adrien was unable to prevent the fall, and then to his sheer amazement he came flying out of a hole further down the mountain and into the fresh air, skidding down on the freshly fallen snow before grinding to halt on a small rock. Out of breath and somewhat delirious, Adrien sprawled out on the snow, lying dazed and absolutely exhausted; what an incredible escape!

The thought he had cheated death in such extreme circumstances was overwhelming and he bellowed out in a rather croaky voice "I am alive, I am Alive."

Raising his head he took a good look around him, and reality struck, yes he had come down a long distance but he was still fairly high up and as far as he could see was crisp white snow. He soon felt weak and physically drained. Finally he gathered enough strength, and, getting to his feet, he began to stagger down the slope with pure determination. He managed to stumble a fair distance, before falling into a heap, and he just lay wearily staring up at the white sky.

Time ticked by. It must have been mid-afternoon when Adrien noticed a shadow appear. A face, the like of which he had never seen before, came into view, blocking out the pale sky. Adrien had not even heard the man arrive, but still a herd of elephants could have thundered passed and he would not have realised a thing, in his delirious confused state.

The man had narrow cut eyes and an orange complex, he wore a hood, the edge of which was laced with thick white fur, as were the end of the sleeves to his thick wolf's fur anorak. He cocked his head to one side, and then started to prod Adrien's face with his stumpy little finger; as you could properly have guessed he had never seen a Saxon before.

Seeing Adrien was distressed he stopped his prodding. Grunting, the man proceeded to put his arm under Adrien's shoulders and levered him up to his feet. Somehow Adrien now managed to muster enough strength to walk. Mentally now knowing he had support spurred him on, although it was uncomfortable as the man was much smaller than the Saxon, but this sturdy man steadily guided them down the hill, which was much harder than you could imagine as the snow was quite deep (and sometimes climbing down a mountain can be harder than climbing upward).

For an hour they staggered on. It was now snowing heavily; there was no pathway, and they had come to a high-up ridge next to a rocky cliff on their left-hand side which they followed. It wasn't too long before they were hit by a blizzard, making it impossible to continue. The man found them shelter just below the ridge under the protection of a huge rock.

Here the man left Adrien and disappeared back into the snow storm. He reappeared sometime later, bringing water (in a seal skin) along with strips of tough meat which he gave to the hungry Saxon. Having not eaten for four days Adrien was more than grateful to receive any provisions given. They stayed under the cover of the boulder for the remainder of the day and that night.

At sunrise, and with the weather now calm, they ventured out. Adrien was slightly stronger and could move unaided. The man led him westward and away from the dangerous mountainous regions. After a couple of days, they crossed sparse flatlands, and a little further on they, reached their destination, next to the sea on the underside of the great northern pass.

Before them were five unusual dome buildings clumped together like a small hamlet all made out of snow. Adrien was intrigued, although he was used to snow during the winter months in Britannia, he could never imagine people physically living in it.

Adrien was soon acquainted with the locals, who were a family made up of two senior figures (parents) who had three sons; two of the sons had young wives. One of these couples had a baby. Adrien's saviour was the oldest and only single son whose name was Amorak (meaning wolf). On meeting the other family members, they were timid and withdrawn. All the men were dressed in wolf and bear furs, whilst the women were dressed in caribou skins (reindeer).

The fascinating snow buildings were igloos made from skilfully cut ice blocks. This settlement was a temporary residence for this tribal family during the Arctic winter months. Three of the igloos were used for sleeping and socialising quarters. One was used for storage and the fifth was for the dogs, as the family owned eight handsome-looking husky dogs, but these were not pets they were purely working dogs.

Adrien was still in a bad way. He was taken to one of the igloos, where he lay on an ice block (covered with animal fur) to recuperate. Inside the interior, thanks to the warm skins, was quite a comfortable dwelling. He rested for two solid days and on the third day he got up from the ice block and stepped outside the igloo. He was given a neat hooded coat made from bear fur to wear which was much better made than his moose garments.

The surrounding landscape was completely barren, with just miles of crystal white snow. The days here were incredibly short, with only several hours of daylight. The men spent every precious hour out hunting.

The family members had gradually warmed to the strange white Saxon. As he was wandering around, he was suddenly distracted by the women, who started jigging around and he soon saw why: the men had returned dragging along a massive seal.

One of the women, who was holding her chubby bouncing baby, turned and passed it to Adrien to hold before speeding off, with cries of excitement, to help the men. The surprised Adrien wasn't given much say in the matter. He had little experience with babies; as a young child he had been allowed to hold his cousin Godfrey for a few seconds but that was all.

Amorak had killed the seal using a lethal-looking harpoon (which he had slung carelessly over his shoulder). It looked extremely hard work dragging the animal along.

The baby seemed more than content being held by Adrien and began amusing itself by poking his fat little fingers up the Saxon's nose; getting bored with that he started to rub his nose against Adrien's, thus giving him an Eskimo kiss.

After hoisting the seal close enough, Amorak drew a knife made from animal bone and started to cut chunks of rubbery meat from the carcass, some which the mother fed to the delighted young baby, which made Adrien's stomach turnover.

That night the whole family were in good spirits due to the day's huge catch; a seal of that size would feed the whole family for days. The only obstacle for Adrien was eating the raw meat, but the reluctant visitor gave it a good go; after all it would be plain rude to show discourtesy, after they had saved his life.

Before long the whole sky was lit up. Adrien had witnessed the aurora borealis before, on that sad night when he had pushed his cousin Godfrey on the burning barge, out to sea away from the beach, in the land of the Vikings. But now what hurt was the loss of his dear friend Eals.

He watched the mesmerizing northern lights (they were different colours as well as green reds and pink) as they danced across the sky, with the reflection glistening off the sparkling snow. It was like a fantastic show, the beauty of which far excelled anything the sad Saxon had seen on his quest.

This show was a fairly regular occurrence this time of the year for the northern family. The two excited young women faced each other; one formed a tube with her hands and started chanting into the oral cavity of the other women, which was regarded as a vocal or breathing game rather than a form of music. Then, holding each other's arms, they began to dance, inhaling then exhaling, before falling in a heap, laughing uncontrollably.

The husky dogs were left to roam and could be heard howling to each other as if trying to sing. For the Western visitor somehow this was quite a magical night, he felt humbled by the simplicity of these content people.

Adrien stuck around for a few more days, until fully fit. One day, Amorak rounded up the huskies and tied them together in order, before tying them to a sled made from whale jaw bone put together with wood fixed with skin belts and he gave Adrien a lift. Storming on at a good pace they crossed the great northern pass. Mile after mile they skidded. Adrien contemplated whether to give Amorak a place; would his qualities be an asset? After all he was an exceptional huntsman, but more importantly his tracking skills were impeccable.

Adrien owed him for saving his life, so he decided he would give him his own square on the Caledonian courtyard.

To the grateful Saxon's surprise, Amorak and his huskies took him much further than he could have wished for.

THE SECRET SOCIETY

Journeying southward, this time Darinus and his band of men decided to push the dreary camels through their paces.

A week or so later they entered the city of Adalia, which lies on the edge of the Mare Nostrum gulf. Here they gladly sold the miserable camels to a local market trader, before making their way to the port, as the plan was to sail to Alexandria, the famous city founded by Alexandra the Great. They were in luck as almost immediately a merchant ship was set to sail directly to Alexandria. So paying their way they all clambered aboard. It was the month of July and incredibly hot.

Darinus, from a young age had been obsessed with the legendary King Alexandra. As a child he would pretend to be his hero, and used to re-enact the famous story of the king taming a horse as a ten year old, when Alexandra had detected that the horse was afraid of its own shadow and eventually where everyone else had failed he tamed the horse. Many generals throughout the world compared themselves to Alexandra's military academics and copied his tactical exploits. The reason Darinus decided to go to Egypt was to see if he could learn more about his boyhood hero, whose legacy had still lived on centuries after his death.

The merchant ship sailed on for several days, and the beautiful Mare Nostrum remained calm throughout. Then late one night as Darinus leant forward on the side of the ship, resting his chin on his crossed arms, he spotted ahead in the distance on the horizon the flicker of a fire, many miles away, a signal which had come from the shore which meant they were finally nearing land. The burning fire came from the famous Pharos (Alexandria's light house). At that time this was one of the tallest manmade structures in the world, and the reason the fire flickered so brightly was that on the top of the Pharos behind the fire stood huge mirrors reflecting the firelight out to sea for many miles.

The ship remained out to sea until the following morning. Sailing in toward port they passed the Pharos. The magnificent structure was constructed from large blocks of light-coloured stone, and was a tower made up of three stages, the lower a squared section, the central core an octagonal section and the top circular. At the apex was positioned a mirror, reflecting daylight during the day and fire at night. In all it stood at an impressive 138 metres high.

Arriving into the port the ship's anchor was thrown overboard and the seven Romans disembarked. Darinus breathed a long sigh; now this was part of the adventure he was looking forward to. Stretching out his arms he checked his surroundings. Next to them away to the right was a mole, a man-made peninsula a mile long leading out to the lighthouse. The impressive city rose up in front of them. Up on a hill standing at the highest point proudly stood Pompey's pillar made of polished red granite; this signified the might of the Romans with the remains of this triumphal column.

Just as the party were about to make tracks into the city, Julian, without looking, accidentally bumped into a barrow one of the merchant sailors had been using to unload sharp tools such as spades with wrought-iron blades and such like. He lost his footing and fell face first into the open barrow. Barely able to use his arms in time to break his fall, the Roman centurion was left sporting a terribly deep gash just above his right eye. In fact the cut was that severe that the bleeding refused to cease, which still did not deter the angry Roman cursing the much-apologetic sailor. A passing Jewish man, who had also caught the merchant ship, stopped and advised, they should head for the School of Medicine to seek the aid of one of the physicians to fix the terrible wound.

A wide road ran from the end of the mole in toward the centre of town, it must have been at least one hundred feet wide, and at one time this road would have been paved with gold. The city had been laid out as a rectangular grid of parallel streets each of which had an attendant (subterranean canal). The city had been split into three regions: the Brucheum, which was the Hellas quarter, the Jewish quarter, and the Rhakotis, which was the oldest part of the city. But sadly the city was at this time very much in decline and just a shadow of the glittering metropolis it had once been. Nevertheless it was still an impressive place, with its granite-paved but somewhat faded colonnades and its many neglected monuments. The city was flanked with theatres, markets, lecture halls, and giant temples along with a zoo and coin mint, but various earthquakes and a Tsunami had battered the city, leaving her a shadow of her former self.

The Romans took the advice and had found their way to the School of Medicine which lay in the Brucheum quarter; it was a one-tier, typical Egyptian-style structure. But this was not the original medical school of Alexandra that had been destroyed by the great fire which had also been responsible for destroying the famous library that stood next door, one hundred years previously. This School of Medicine stood on the old original site, and was very much operational and in working order. And it too was a fair size.

Darinus playfully commented to Julian, "Centurion, you bleed like a man well beyond your years. Luckily we are not on the battle field as I am not sure you would survive."

The doors to the school entrance were open. Darinus ordered his bodyguards to wait outside, while he went with the wounded centurion to find help. Inside the school appeared to be empty, the first room was set in a hexagon shape with corridors running off at each angle. The two Romans took the corridor directly in front as they could hear a strong voice coming from that direction. The corridor was only twenty metres long leading to a high, open doorway (as were all the doorways in this building).

No wonder the rest of this place was empty as the room at the end of this corridor was packed and it wasn't very big either, roughly ten metres long by five metres wide, surrounded by pillars sunk into the walls, and to the side of the room was a long, firm wooden table. Standing the other side of this table was a physician giving a lecture whilst dissecting a pig using a sharp knife.

What struck Darinus was the audience, who were made up of different races and religions, all learning peacefully side by side. But he didn't have much time to stop and take all this in, as Julian stumbled into the room like a bull in an arena, demanding help and totally disrupting the lecture. Everyone present turned to see the distressed centurion (who was about to collapse) as he blurted out, "Can you see I am a Roman Centurion and I need immediate attention for this cursed wound that ceases not to bleed?"

At this statement many of the men in the room looked a bit baffled; clearly this declaration would have held some kind of clout had it been uttered two hundred or so years prior to 471AD.

The lecturer stopped what he was doing, and seeing the severity of the gash, turning to one of his students, and speaking in Greek, instructed him to take them to his private room, before turning back to the injured Roman, and in broken Latin said, "Go with student, my room lie on stool, stop is more loss... of blood and wait." Then he raised his voice in a kind of warning tone whilst looking at Darinus and pointing at his own eyes, "Not hand anything."

They followed the allocated Jewish student back down the corridor to the hexagon room, and down the next corridor to a room on the right-hand side. This particular room had a door that the student opened. Letting the Romans in he handed Julian a leather cloth, before leaving and closing the door behind him.

Inside, the fair-sized square room had the usual high ceiling. There was a low flat table, covered with a woven mat; this is what the lecturer had referred to as the stool. Two of the walls were made up of shelves piled with papyrus scrolls from the floor to the ceiling. The stool was a foot or so from the right-hand wall, where the shelves were stacked with glass and clay bottles of all shapes and sizes containing different types of coloured potions and medicines. Facing the wall next to the door was a desk accompanied by a lattice stool with rounded legs.

Perched on the table was a statue of a head. Darinus recognised it as a replica of Alexandra the Great. It had been carefully painted giving the king golden-coloured hair and distinctly different coloured eyes, one brown and one blue. Next to the icon was a patasos (a wide-brimmed hat used for protection from the strong sun). Also sitting on the desk was a long, partially opened papyrus scroll.

Julian lay down on the flat table and held the leather cloth on his wound, thus stemming the flow of blood and waited. Half an hour passed. The inquisitive commander decided to take a closer look at the statue, uttering, "Maybe the physician will be able to lend some information on Alexandra the Great."

Julian replied, "What does the papyrus mean?"

Darinus had chosen to obey the physician's word and not touch anything, but evidently this did not apply to the disobedient centurion, who took orders from nobody except Darinus, and even then he frequently disobeyed. So he leapt up from the short table and started to unravel out the scroll.

On the papyrus was a series of drawings and diagrams, and all the writings were written in Greek. Both Darinus and Julian understood Greek as it was a popular language spoken in Rome. On top of the papyrus was the heading: THE SOCIETY OF OUR LOST MASTER ALEXANDRA THE GREAT. This title instantly prompted the Roman commander to take note. Reading on it explained that in two days, it was to be the anniversary of the great leader's death, and that the society was to meet at his tomb. On one of the drawings was a map showing the location of the tomb. At a location in the great desert, just eastward, a little way off the road that ran between Alexandra to Memphis, the only mark signalling the way was a granite boulder.

All this excited the Roman general, because it was common knowledge that Alexandra's body had disappeared nearly a century ago. Then a drop of Julian's blood fell onto the papyrus. Frantically he tried to wipe it off, but it just smudged making it even worse. Footsteps were heard outside the door, so Julian quickly lay back down on the flat table, whilst Darinus attempted to partially wrap the scroll up, before venturing to the other side of the room, just as the door opened.

In walked the lecturer, who was a short, stocky, tough-looking man with a high complexion, short, with mousey brown hair and his face was clean shaven, he had the most distinctive piercing eyes: one brown and one blue. He wore a full–length, dyed brown exomie, which was a linen tunic with material draped over his left shoulder.

Walking over to Julian he took away the leather cloth and lifted the centurion's head up to examine the wound. Shaking his own head and breathing in a deep breath, he gently placed Julian's head back down on the woven mat. He then took a thin, bronze, sculptured needle and a thread made out of horse hair from his desk, before taking a bottle of clear potion from one of the shelves, which he poured directly onto the centurion's cut, and with the leather cloth, he wiped it round his forehead.

Julian felt his forehead and the surrounding areas go numb, for the potion was an anaesthetic.

The physician then got to work, neatly stitching up the wound. As he did this he asked the Romans, whom he now addressed in Greek, "Why in Alexandria?"

There was a pause. Just as Darinus was about to speak, Julian croaked, "We have come to gather information about Alexandra the Great."

On hearing this, the physician stopped what he was doing and glared up at Darinus and answered abruptly, "why?"

Darinus had been going to put this in a more tactful way as it now looked as if they had been snooping around the man's office. Softly he replied, "Sir, I have since my youth been a distant admirer of the Great Alexandra, and while we were passing through this city would appreciate finding out more about him. Coming here today I cannot help but observe you yourself are also an admirer, as the statue of the Macedon on your table would suggest."

The physician now seemed to be agitated, as he began to pull the stitches harder and faster. He chose to ignore the Roman general, and soon finished, saying, "You now leave, not forget to pay your taxes while you in Alexandria."

Julian thanked the medical physician and they left.

Once outside they met up with the waiting bodyguards, and just as they were debating where to go the physician walked out of the building. He whistled two low-pitch whistles and a grey horse trotted around from the side of the building. He swung himself up and galloped off up the road. Darinus noticed him glance round and scowl before disappearing out of view.

Later that day the party of Romans found a tiny inn on the edge of the once Jewish quarter, that was now really run down.

Out the back of the inn was a tiny courtyard, set around an old olive tree, which is where the Romans congregated to decide what they were going to do next. Having seen the papyrus in the physician's office the general and the centurion's minds were made up: they were to go out to the desert to try and find the tomb, on the anniversary of Alexandra's death.

When the sun disappeared from the sky all the Romans except Darinus retired to sleep. He decided to purchase a morsel of wine from the inn keeper. He had a heavy heart because sometimes he would feel dispirited by the constant travelling and terribly missed Ki-Sui.

The inn keeper was an older man, with quite a unique character. He seemed to spend most of his time in the courtyard at the back smoking on an unusual looking pipe attached to another instrument containing water. Darinus got talking with the man who was of Greek Jewish descent, whose dark skin was tanned and leathery.

In Greek, Darinus asked, "Old man, can you tell me of Alexandra the Great?"

The man replied, "This place is only Alexandria by name; the great king died a long, long time ago." The inn keeper was incredibly laid back and relaxed.

Darinus continued, "Do you have knowledge of The Society of Our Lost Master Alexandra the Great?"

No sooner had he finished the sentence, than the inn keeper put his finger tightly to his lips, before sheepishly looking around, making sure nobody was listening. He moved close to Darinus and began to whisper, "Roman, do not speak those words out here in the open, let us move inside the inn before we talk further."

Darinus followed the inn keeper further inside, where he lit a candle and took him to some steps that led to a cellar underneath the building. The cellar was only a pokey little room, surrounded by thick walls with a thick solid door; here the men could now talk without fear of being overheard. With the door firmly shut, the Roman commander told the old man of the day's events and what he had seen on the papyrus in the physician's private room.

The inn keeper listened intently to every detail, before giving his own conclusion. "Young Roman, you must solemnly promise you never repeat what I now tell." Darinus replied with his hand on heart, "You have my word."

The inn keeper, holding both hands on his face, lowered his voice. "Your life may be already in danger. Nicomachus Atas is the name of the physician you encountered, and he is of Macedon descent from the direct line of Philip II, the father of Alexandra the Great.

"As well as being a physician he is a scholar and mathematician, and although it is the worst-kept secret in Alexandria, he is almost certainly the most powerful man in the whole of Egypt. People say he is identical to Alexandra the Great, in stature and build; he also has one brown eye and one blue eye. He hates foreign invaders, above all Romans, who year after year send explorers on missions to find Alexandra's body. All of course search in vain."

The inn keeper spoke quickly, sometimes whole sentences without stopping to take in air.

"Until a time not so long ago when a young man, in line to be the next Caesar to the Byzantine throne, sailed to Alexandria where unusually he set up tents just south west of the city in the desert. He brought astronomers and navigational men along with slaves and guards, and word spread they were close to discovering something. Then one morning the whole party was found dead; most were still in their beds, but strangely not one had a single mark on them.

"The only link to this mystery was a man seen on a grey horse galloping back up the desert road from the camp the night before. There is only one man this could be, Nicomachus

Atas. Rumour has it he used a supernatural, invisible chemical to cause the atrocity. This has never been proven, but you see this is the only conclusion it could be.

"Nicomachus Atas is the leader of the society; it is a secret society people dare not mention, but I understand they are planning to take Alexandria back from the Egyptian leaders and restore the city to its former glory. I doubt not that Nicomachus Atas is willing to recapture Persia and recreate the great empire once more."

Slowing down the inn keeper, continued, "Young Roman, I know not what your intentions are, but you must tread carefully while you are here and not breathe a single word of what you saw or have heard."

The old man offered to help Darinus, but starkly warned him if he found the location of the tomb then it could cost him his life. This was too good an opportunity for the Roman to resist. So on the day of the anniversary it was agreed that the inn keeper would arrange for seven horses to be saddled and watered and ready waiting at the edge of the desert.

The final thing Darinus said to the inn keeper that night was, "Tell, no disrespect how such a learned man as you become a simple inn keeper?"

With a wry smile the man replied, "Young General, things are not always as they seem." Puzzled on that note Darinus asked no more questions and bid him goodnight although he thought to himself, that man looks familiar in a canny kind of way.

The following day the party of seven kept a low profile. Darinus kept the previous night's conversation quiet. He just warned his men, especially Julian, not to talk about their reason for being there. During the course of the day Darinus felt paranoid and could have sworn they were being watched. That evening he briefed his men about the following day, as the inn keeper said they should leave before sunrise.

Before he retired to sleep he held counsel with the inn keeper down in the cellar. The old man reached for Darinus' right hand. "If you survive this then you are blessed. When you arrive at the catacomb beware and move slowly; use your instincts as one false move will result in certain death. There is one more thing, remember the horse! You will understand, now go get some rest."

They rose before dawn and left the city; sure enough at the edge of the desert were seven horses saddled and watered by a young lad, who had been given the job.

The route was easy as only one sandy road ran south through the desert. Under other circumstances Darinus would have been reluctant to cross another desert but to him this price was more than worth it. They galloped hard till past noon, eventually they arrived at the granite boulder, and this was the only object they had seen since leaving the city.

Julian joked, "Looks like the Franks have got here before us looking at the size of that obelisk." He was referring to the boulder that did actually resemble an obelisk.

Here they took a right turn, as the papyrus in the physician's private room had instructed. This felt rather daunting as all that lay before them was miles of untouched sand and more sand. After a while the desert became hillier, then hidden away in the dunes they stumbled across a picturesque oasis surrounded by palm trees, two clay watering vessels sat beside the water, proving humans had been here.

Julian then recalled how he had seen a pool marked on the papyrus just south of the entrance to the tomb. So they turned north and rode just a bit further. As they reached the top of one of the sand dunes, they saw in the sand valley below them the figures of two massive sand statues. Although a way off from them, they could just make out giants with dog's heads. Putting the size of these figures in perspective below stood two guards either side guarding the entrance.

So this was it! They had found the tomb of Alexandra the Great. The hardest part was over, well at least so they thought. But as we all know assumption can more often than not lead to the wrong conclusion.

Julian wished to ride straight down there, split up, and take the guards out, but the calm Darinus had a gut feeling. Retreating back to the oasis and waiting for night fall was the best option.

They lazed around at the oasis. As Darinus sat with his back to a palm tree he opened out the canvas map; astonishingly the map had disappeared and had been replaced by an extraordinary diagram, the full length of the canvas. Darinus soon worked out that on the left side of the canvas were the figures of the dog giants (clearly the entrance); on the far right written in bold letters was the word "tomb". In between were three squares separated by long thin lines. Darinus was not aware what these were, but squares represented chambers and the thin lines were the passageways between the chambers.

A LONG LOST SECRET FOUND

Just before darkness threw its shroud over the land and whilst there was still a glimmer of light, the Romans left the oasis, leaving the horses behind. They scrambled up the high sand dune and peering over they observed the guards were no longer there. Carefully they trod downward, with their feet sinking into the soft hot sand. The dunes were higher than they looked. At the bottom the dog-headed centurion statues were huge, and looked rather daunting.

Darinus assured his men that he was making the right decision, once again walking into the unknown. Each side of the great sand-stone effigies, the sand was piled high, behind these fearsome relics ran a long walkway.

All the Romans held their hands onto the hilt of their swords and spread out in rows of pairs, six feet apart. With the general at the helm they pressed cautiously forward, passed the first dog-headed centurions, and then more statues which stood side by side each identical to the last. Darinus later referred to them as the sleeping guards of the desert.

Further on, the heads on these relics changed to pharonic eagles. The walkway must have been about forty or so metres long. As they reached the end the sun had almost gone.

Here they were met by a six-foot high gaping hole in the sand, surrounded by two stone serpents, whom were wrapped around the side of the opening, with their menacing looking heads at the top of the opening facing the visitors, with long forked tongues and stone cold eyes looking like they could strike into life at any given moment. Either side of the hole were two stakes next to two buckets of fire. And a line of fire ran along the floor to the entrance to the gaping hole. Inside it looked pitch black but with the faint flicker of the flames, the ground inside looked like it was moving.

Darinus picked up one of the stakes, lighting the tip in the bucket of fire. He shone it into the gaping hole. Julian lit another stake. And they decided to head into the darkness. The general stepped over the line of fire, and was instantly met by a barrage of hissing, as the whole floor was covered with snakes. Before he could take another step a cobra lunged forward. Just in the nick of time Darinus turned and literally dived back out of the hole. For some reason the snakes stayed away from the fire, the hissing noise from inside magnified, and it became almost deafening.

Julian said, "Sire, only a mad-minded fool would enter that forsaken hole; I strongly suggest we return to Alexandria at once."

Darinus unravelled the canvas, for some kind of assistance. Now written on the first square (chamber) were the words "Slay the red eye, all will obey".

He hesitated, in order to think for a minute or two, before taking his torch and shining it back into the opening, where the snakes were going berserk and relentlessly hissing. One particular cobra was persistently throwing itself toward the fire; its burning red eyes were bulging out of its head, it was twisting and turning with its fork tongue flickering back and forth, then it started to violently spit.

Then Darinus figured it out. He realised the meaning of the script, drew his sword, and lunging forward he plunged his sword through the flames and through the neck of the red-eyed cobra, burning his hand in the process. As the cobra fell, slain to the ground, the hissing from inside stopped.

Waiting until he was sure it was safe, Darinus stepped over the fire and into the first chamber. The snakes moved aside, leaving a clear path for the Romans to walk through. The chamber was reasonably wide with a low ceiling. The walk through was only several steps. Here the chamber narrowed into a thin passage that became so thin they had to walk single file.

A way along the passage Darinus again chose to consult the canvas; it now showed a picture of a cymbal, followed by pictures of three axes, each with a caption below.

The first read: on first cymbal tread five stop.

The second read: on second cymbal tread five lie down.

The third read: on the third cymbal tread five be wise.

The passage was so tight Darinus could hardly turn to address his men. So he called out, "Men, when you witness the sound of a clanging cymbal fix your eyes upon me and follow my actions upon the clanging of each cymbal."

No sooner had he taken two more steps than Darinus saw set into the wall next to where he stood two gleaming metal cymbals, but he had no time to stand and admire as they smashed together making the most almighty crash; you can imagine the horrendous sound in such an enclosed area.

Without delay the Roman general took five paces forward and stood still, then, in the distance he had just walked, a double-bladed axes swung from either side of the passage, several times inches from his nose. Without turning to look back Darinus felt the breeze of the axes, just behind his head. He called out, "Julian, follow my footsteps on the next cymbal."

The second cymbal smashed, and Darinus took five paces and lay flat on his stomach. Again axes fell from the ceiling; this time so close they slightly cut through his clothing.

On the third cymbal he leaped up, this time remembering what it had said on the canvas, so he knew he had to do something different. In the flicker of his torch he saw two ledges either side of the passage a foot up from the floor. He jumped up each foot on the ledges before two razor-sharp blades cut through the sand from below, reaching up just underneath his crotch. Jumping down the general breathed a massive sigh of relief; fortunately all the other Romans made it through unscathed.

Again checking the canvas, which now showed a chamber with just a set of eyes, with a caption reading "gaze into the eyes not".

The passage ran into the second chamber, full of cats, Darinus realised what the caption read as he ordered, "Do not look into these feral creatures' eyes." This exercise was harder than you would imagine. Things were going ok, as they passed through; this chamber was similar to the first, just a bit higher. The slender cats with their pointed ears seemed unfazed as the strangers passed; in fact some of the cats showed affection by rubbing against the humans' legs; once more the chamber narrowed into a passage.

As they were exiting the chamber, Julian decided to see what would happen if he took one look in one of the creatures' eyes, so he stared down into the glaring green eyes. The reaction was instantaneous – the cat pounced up, its sharp claws extended, making the most bloodcurdling screech. Darinus knew somewhere along the way the centurion would not be able to help himself and disobey the order, so as he aggravated the cat, the general unleashed his sword. All the Romans rushed down the next passage before any of the other cats reacted.

Darinus scolded Julian, "Centurion how many times?"

Once more he opened up the rolled-up canvas. This time what he saw made his heart jump, for covering the entire canvas was the diagram of a chequered board, like that of the Caledonian courtyard. With the script beneath reading, "Use the method you have learned to accomplish reaching the opposite side".

The passage was short, and the Romans found they were entering a much larger chamber, the entire floor of which was covered with a perfectly square chequered board. On either side, in banks of two lines, stood life-size pieces, carved from granite stone. On one side the pieces were cut from black stone and the other from white.

The Romans entered the chamber directly behind the black figures. Looking closer, they could see that the black pieces were sculptured in the shape of Macedon soldiers, and the opposing white were sculptured with the back line of Caesar and major Roman characters, and the front row made up of Persian foot soldiers.

Darinus gave the order not to step onto the squares. The chamber was lit up with fire baskets hanging from the ceiling. Darinus put his right foot forward onto the white square the Macedon king was perched on. As soon as he touched it, the whole square dropped beneath him. Julian grabbed his commander's shoulder, and Darinus pulled himself back. The square spun all the way round (as it must have been held by a kind of pivot) so quickly the king standing central hardly moved.

Gathering his senses Darinus carefully leaned over and placed his foot on the back of the Queen's square without putting any weight down, but the same thing happened again. This time he had a glimpse beneath, though all he could see was black darkness. Below was actually a horrifically high drop.

Scratching his head Darinus recalled the last words the inn keeper had spoken. "Remember the horse," so this time he moved over to the square where a knight was perched on a horse two squares left of the queen. Gently he tapped his foot on the back of the black square. This time nothing happened. Satisfied it was stable, he put his full weight down.

As Darinus stood waiting, the pawn in front of the king moved two squares forward, followed by various other pieces on either side. Then everything stopped. Darinus figured that it was now time for him to move, so he tapped his right foot on the black square diagonally in front. Once more the square dropped.

It suddenly dawned on the Roman general which square the knight could move on to, as it was obvious he was involved in a game of chess, and to get to the other side he had to get moving. So bravely he stepped one square forward and one diagonally to the right. Sure enough he had remembered the correct move and the knight followed him. Again the pieces moved around him, until it was his time to move once more.

This time the square he wished to move to had an opposing Persian foot soldier standing upon it, so he stepped one square forward and one diagonally. Just as he was about to place his foot onto the black square, the square dropped and the Persian pawn fell through into the deep dark pit below. The square spun round and the reluctant general and the knight replaced the Persian pawn.

Over again other pieces moved. This time Darinus noticed the white queen had moved, putting himself and the stone knight directly in her firing line only three squares to the right; it was time for him to move and imperative he did so swiftly, so he moved diagonally one and one to his right, but his calculation appeared to backfire as he found he had stupidly moved right next to the Roman queen. He stood sweating, the situation was now out of control, and he was surely doomed.

Then, surprisingly, the white queen shot forward across the board and eliminated the Macedon queen. The game was now well under way - Roman lords, Persians and Macedon's carved stones were falling in all directions.

When it came to the Roman to move again he noticed one of the squares in the midst of the Roman and Persians ranks was vacant. He could see no on-coming threat from any of the enemy pieces. He moved one square to his right then one diagonally to the safety of the empty square, followed closely by the knight.

Mysteriously, the fire lights above began to flicker. Without knowing it he had cornered the Roman king (Caesar) into checkmate. Initially he had meant to take the rook (castle) with his next move. The replica of Caesar could not escape, as the only empty square for him to move to was covered by a Macedon bishop. Way up the board, the square below the Roman king fell and the replica disappeared, and the game was over.

Darinus waited but nothing else happened, so he moved over to the now spare king's square, and stepped off the other end of the chequered floor. Although the figures were made from stone Darinus felt a pang of guilt fighting against his own kind.

The Roman commander from this point went on alone as he was not willing to risk losing any more men. Especially on the perilous chequered ground. Besides, the canvas had shown four chambers; therefore there was only one left.

Alone, the solitary warrior pushed on. He found himself wandering down an eerie passage, the walls made out of massive sand stones two-and-a-half feet deep. Inside the walls, roughly the height of his shoulders, were cut notches holding papyrus scrolls all the way along the length of the passage. These were not ordinary scrolls, but many of the scrolls that had been saved and retrieved from the famous Alexandria Library when it had perished in the fire of 389AD. Most of this papyrus was thought to have been lost forever but they still lie to this very day, underneath that desert in the corridors of that secret tomb.

Although Darinus was tempted to take a quick peek at a couple of the scrolls to nose through, he felt compelled to swiftly venture forward. Moreover the passage was about twenty metres long. Reaching the end he entered the final chamber, which was different to the others. It was circular in shape and the ceiling spiralled up in the form of a dome. This place needed no introduction for this was indeed the tomb.

Darinus felt completely numb as just yards before him lying on a gold casket in all his entirety was the body of Alexandra the Great. The Roman general had a lump in his dry throat. Unaware of his surroundings and smitten with overwhelming awe, he slowly shuffled forward. He had come to Alexandria to seek inspiration and to learn of the legendary king. Never in his wildest dreams had he dreamt he would now be standing before the lost royal corpse.

The body had been so well preserved over the ages; it appeared that Alexandra was just sleeping. The only defect in the king's white face was that the end of his nose had been removed. Amazingly the king was wrapped in his famous purple cap, with yellow trim underneath and he wore a gold breastplate. On his head he wore a thin gold crown and on his finger he wore his lost ring. As the stories had been told, these precious relics had been robbed by various emperors and kings etc. But Darinus was unaware that the Society had made it their quest and had searched high and low, far and wide, to return the precious belongings back to the king.

Darinus knelt down on one knee and bowed his head. After a time he stood back up and reached out to touch the great king's hand, when all of a sudden the silence was broken by a voice on the opposite side of the gold casket. "Halt you no move, how dare you touch with filthy Roman hand?" The Roman general froze. Before he could answer he was struck on the back of his head, a blow so hard that it knocked him clean out.

He woke to the splash of cold water being hurled over him. His head was throbbing. He opened his eyes, seeing the world from a different angle he realised he was hanging upside down, with his right leg clamped to a chain, connected to a metal plate fixed to the ceiling. He was being held captive in a dingy underground chamber, which was poorly lit by a small fire basket laid upon the floor. The man responsible for throwing the water disappeared.

The first thing he noticed was his sword had been taken. Darinus lifted the weight of his body up, and using his hands grabbed his ankles, this relieved the tension in his banging head, but as you can guess there is only so long you can hold yourself in that position.

Then a familiar person appeared. Darinus had wondered how long it was going to be before he encountered the physician. With a violent approach, Nicomachus Atas spoke, "I wondered how long till you appear when see blood on papyrus. How find tomb?" Darinus remained tight lipped.

The Macedon knelt down next to the Roman's head and repeated the question; once more the stubborn Darinus ignored him.

Darinus was preparing his mind to deal with what he expected: imminent torture.

Nicomachus Atas spoke, using a softer tone, "Impostor, I despise you kind, but I no condone torture. I rather kill than hold a dog in trap." And leaning over, he unlocked the chain and the helpless Roman fell in a heap on the floor.

Nicomachus Atas proceeded to talk, "Impostor, it impossible to enter tomb, without being slain. I designed, placed dangerous obstacles in way. I the only human alive who knows passage through. I desire know how you got to tomb. Impostor tell me reason why I shall kill you not, for you only Roman to have seen master in sacred tomb."

Darinus decided to tell the truth; after all it might be the only way out. So he told the story since he had landed in Alexandria (sidestepping the part of the story that included the inn keeper).

The secret society leader was dumbstruck by what he heard, although he did not understand word for word he got the main gist of the story. Gathering himself he asked to see the map, so Darinus handed over the canvas, which had returned to its normal state showing the map of the world. Darinus took the opportunity to briefly tell the Macedon of his quest; deep down he was dying to offer Nicomachus Atas a place in his army.

But he didn't even have to ask as Nicomachus Atas the Macedon solemnly exclaimed, "I join your ranks. Use this as training exercise, then return take back Alexander's empire. Will my horse fit on courtyard floor?" Darinus without hesitation replied, "Yes. Naturally I will give you the honourable position of my second knight."

Nicomachus Atas was tailor made for this position, as he was extremely gifted in many areas, and had already great knowledge of the game of chess. Also he was a Macedon, automatically making him an exceptional horse rider. So it was agreed for him to take his place at Caledonia for the beginning of the game. Darinus was given his sword back and was sworn to secrecy to never mention what he had seen.

Julian and the rest of the bodyguards had been stuck back in the chamber, and what's more the fires lighting the chamber had gone out so they had been left in the pitch black (thankfully none had stepped onto the chequered floor and fallen through). So when the party was rescued and shown out by some Macedon guards (accompanied by Darinus) Julian was red faced and furious.

Collecting the horses at the oasis, they were shown the way back to Alexandria. They started the trek back in the early morning and, travelling at a more leisurely pace than before, arrived back in the city in the early evening. Deciding to stay one more night at the inn, to their utter surprise they found where the cosy little inn had been stood just a rundown, uninhabitable shack that had not been lived in for many years. And as for the inn keeper, he was nowhere to be seen. How odd.

Finding another inn they spent one more night in Alexandria before it was time to move on.

THE DARK PIRATE PRINCE

Darinus was glad to leave Alexandria and not get too involved with Nicomachus Atas and his secret society.

This time the Roman party followed the coast eastwards; it was a treat to all be riding these well-trained racing horses, which allowed them to cover a lot of ground at pace. Darinus would have liked to venture further into the vast land of Africa but time was not on their side. The kingdom of northern Africa was mainly a barbarian wasteland; the majority of the barren ground under foot was covered with aracia. The party of seven rode for thirty days, during which time they rode through into 325AD; the one thing that never changed whilst crossing these time changes, was the location.

The next point outlined upon the canvas was Tripolitania, a city set on a major port, on the western side of an easily defensible peninsula. Just a couple of miles from the outskirts of Tripolitania they found themselves looking down across an unusual kind of settlement. Shabbily lodged down the steep cliff that led down to the sea were tatty looking old tents, some wedged between boulders and jagged rocks, but all huddled close by each other. Drawing closer Darinus and his men realised that this was a dreaded leper colony, and was full of people who had contracted the horrible disease, therefore had been banished and expelled from civilisation.

As a mark of respect Darinus ordered his men to dismount from their horses and hang their heads low as they passed by. A few of the lepers who were out from their tents hung their heads in shame and turned away.

Remounting upon their horses and just as they were about to gallop on, Julian croaked in a low voice, "halt," the reason being a woman had appeared to the left side of the camp coming over a small hill. She was dressed in bright orange, and under her arm she had a long brown cloak made of sack cloth.

She was about one hundred metres from them; they could see she had bronze skin with long black hair. As she approached the colony she put the sackcloth on and pulled a hood over her head covering her face, and then she stopped in her tracks as she looked up and saw the gawping Romans. Turning around she briskly walked back up the rugged hill.

Julian commented, "With great hope I desire that the women of this land are as fair as she."

Darinus said, "Men, let us ride forth. This doomed domain is one I think we shall forget."

No sooner had they ridden twenty or so paces, when one of the Romans glanced back and alerted the others. There, hidden away in a tiny cove, was a handsome-looking ship with a big sail. High on the mast flew an unfamiliar looking flag, adorned with a prominent black lion walking from left to right on a white background. Darinus, without question, knew this to be the ship of a pirate which had no doubt been stolen from some unfortunate crew. But the Romans didn't have time to hang around.

Although it was early summer, the light breeze from the Mare Nostrum gave a refreshing feel all around. It was midafternoon when they rode up to the fortified city of Tripolitania which was currently under Roman rule. They were stopped by the guards, who acted more like guides than guards. They told Darinus where to find the legate (the Roman officer assigned to oversee this part of the Empire).

Darinus was relieved to find Tripolitania under Roman rule at that time; clearly it had been ruled by the Greeks, and numerous other nations had left their stamp, which gave a nice unique blend of mixed cultures rolled into one kind of place.

Darinus made an executive decision to stay here for three nights and gave his faithful men some time off for themselves, providing they stayed out of trouble. Surprisingly the Romans had not spent as much money as you would have imagined considering the amount of time they had been travelling.

Although the place was under Roman rule the atmosphere was very casual and relaxed. This sea port and economic hub was a marvellous tangle of narrow streets enclosed by the Roman-built, fortified walls with labyrinthine dark lanes; it was a commercial port city bustling with many different peoples.

Darinus and Julian took a walk before deciding to go in search of the legate. They came to a fascinating market, selling almost anything you could dream of, from exotic wild African animals to human slaves; much of the merchandise sold here would be sent off to Rome, as this city was a major player on the Mare Nostrum trade route.

After browsing round the marketplace, the general and the centurion searched and found the legate's quarters almost in the middle of the city near the Arch of Marcus Aurelius. The arch was over one hundred and fifty years old and situated at the cross roads of Cardo Maximus and Decumanos; this relic gave an impressive welcome to the city. It was a large archway with notches inscribed in the pillars containing statues of Marcus Aurelius.

It was not hard to distinguish the Legate's house as two armed guards stood below two pillars either side of a door outside of a typical Roman building. As Darinus and Julian approached one of the guards stepped forward. In any normal circumstance both guards would have saluted both Darinus and Julian before stepping aside, but this guard looked slightly perplexed at what they were wearing as they were dressed as normal Byzantine foot soldiers from 560AD.

Darinus forgot how he was dressed and ordered an audience with the legate. It became apparent by the authority in his voice to the guard that he was of a much higher rank, so the two visitors were taken through the modest-sized building to a pretty, well-kept garden. The whole house had been built round the garden space, which was surrounded by pillars holding up balconies all the way round overlooking the garden, every inch of space was covered with many shades of flowers, and in the centre was a lovely stone fountain.

Here they found the legate pottering around, totally engrossed in tending to his flowers, seemingly unaware of the visitors now present. Julian took it upon himself to distract the man and let out a deep cough. He succeeded, as the legate stopped what he was doing and turned his head round. Being an eccentric man on the wrong side of being middle age, the first thing he said was some comment on the lack of water they had had so far that year.

For the next five minutes he just went on about his beautiful garden and the bees, before he suddenly snapped out of it, and directly said, "What is an honoured general and a centurion from Rome dressed in unfamiliar foot soldiers garments? Are you on an undercover mission, what brings you hither? I have not been informed and have no record of your arrival."

Darinus was astounded by this legate's discernment, and replied, "Yes, sir, we are here on an undisclosed mission and have ridden all the way from Alexandria."

The legate's name was Justin Pilot and he invited the visitors to sit with him in his tranquil garden, and called for a servant to bring them some red wine that was served in silver goblets. They spent a good couple of hours talking, and found out a bit about Tripolitania and that Justin Pilot was very forthcoming with his love for wine, entertainment and loose local women of whom his favourite was a foreign Nostrum woman called Leila.

But Pilot's main concern at that present time was the disruption of trade that was currently taking place out to sea by a ruthless pirate who was robbing and pillaging merchant ships on course for Rome. He told of what he knew of this pirate, describing him as a small, dark, egotistical, wretched fool with locks as bushy and black as a raven upon his head. This man was an absolute menace for Pilot, as he had proclaimed war on Tripolitania's merchant trade and, with the city being under Roman rule, this was seen as a direct attack on Rome herself.

This rogue had not just attacked by sea; the first the legate had heard of him was months earlier when he had ransacked the market setting slaves free and releasing captured animals and taking with him most of the expensive ivory. All that he had left was a life-size rough carving of a lion on a nearby wooden door. Pilot and his mentors had thought this a one-off attack, until less than a week passed and he had the audacity to return in the dead of night and with a band of accomplices stole Pilot's very own galleon called Lipitor and sailed away unchallenged into the dark.

Pilot was enraged and sent missions up and down the coast but to no avail as the galleon had disappeared. Well, so everyone thought until days later a galleon appeared in the hands of some vicious pirates and attacked a merchant ship carrying slaves amongst other goods to Rome. The ship was stripped bare. By description Pilot knew this to be his beloved galleon which had been revamped and now sailed under the flag of a black lion on a white background. Both Darinus and Julian glanced at one another; this was definitely the galleon they had seen hidden away near to the leper colony. They kept quiet and just listened as the legate continued. "The attacks have only been vented toward select vessels at certain times and somehow he knows which vessels to attack, and after each assault he disappears. Some slaves have even joined the pirate." These men were thought to be particularly dangerous as they are willing to give their lives for their new leader. Pilot had sent word to Caesar Crispus in Rome but due to the Hellespont battle out to sea against the eastern Byzantine a year previous, many of the vessels had been damaged so no help had been sent.

Darinus then quizzed Pilot, "Do you know from whence this rascal came?"

Pilot replied, "Reliable sources conclude he is the son of the King of Ethiopia, and he radically opposes the use of humans for slaves, one only knows why."

This pirate was a thorn in Pilot's side and Darinus could see how distressed he got every time he mentioned the pirate. He admitted the only person he discussed the pirate with was his favourite whore Leila, whom he said was always interested. Julian asked a bit about this Leila as he was always fascinated to hear about any female.

Pilot said, "Although she is a prostitute, she has a good heart and even goes out of the city to take food to the leper colony."

Darinus didn't hear anything else the legate had to say as it had dawned on him what was happening here and he interrupted Pilot mid–conversation. "Legate, your request has been heard in Rome, for me and my centurion have been assigned to answer your request. We came by land so as not to arouse suspicion."

Julian's jaw dropped. What in the name of the gods was his commander up to now?

Justin Pilot offered the visitors accommodation in his house whilst preparations were made.

Later when the two Romans were alone Julian asked his commander, "Darinus, tell me, what is your plan?"

Darinus replied, "Why, centurion, do you not perceive, the boat we saw was Lupitor the stolen galleon seized by the pirates now flying under the lion flag, the woman in the orange at the leper Colony was the traitor Leila, the whore who is taking information straight to the pirate, using her disguise in taking provisions to the lepers? We must locate her and you will have to take the proposal further."

Julian liked the sound of this and a new plan was formed.

Just before dark the two Romans left Pilot's house and wandered over to Marcus Aurelius's Arch, and sure enough, as the legate had told, under the faint light they saw a woman dressed in orange clothing kind of like a sari. Anyone could see she was not short of wealth as she had plenty of jewellery on show with a gold chain hanging from her left ear to her nose.

As they drew near the Romans could see she was strikingly attractive although she wore a cold, hard look upon her face, and had a distinctive mole on her right cheek. They knew exactly who she was, as she stepped out from under the arch, and the sweet aroma of her perfume filled the evening air. She introduced herself and in a very becoming sweet voice said, "Would you two strapping soldiers allow me to seduce you this night?" Her Latin was perfect (although not her first language).

Julian didn't need to be asked twice, as he took her hand and gave it a tender kiss. At this Darinus, embarrassed, thought, oh no what is the deluded centurion doing, kissing the hand of a whore?

The scarlet lady continued, seemingly pleased at Julian's introduction, "My name is Leila, queen of the night."

Darinus interrupted. "Comrade, I have much to occupy myself with this evening. I will meet with you later."

And that was that, the wheels of the latest plan were in motion, as Julian was led away by the lady of the night.

To Darinus' disapproval Julian arrived back at Pilot's house the following morning looking rather jaded, but with a smile upon his face from ear to ear like an Egyptian cat. Darinus had ordered him to return the previous night. But the good news was that he had sown the first seeds of Darinus' plan. Acting ignorant he had told Leila that there was a merchant ship bound for Rome set to leave in two nights' time. On it he said that there were some of the finest slaves from around that part of the world, along with boxes full of ivory for Caesar himself.

So if the scheme worked, the conspiring prostitute would go and inform the dark pirate, and this strong haul would be too much of a temptation for him to ignore. Julian also told she had left in a hurry that morning as she had to take food to the leper colony.

Darinus went to Pilot and asked him for a ship to use for his mission, to which Pilot agreed and offered as much help as he would require. He was given a large trireme-like ship along with rowing slaves. On the ship were placed big empty boxes to indicate much merchandise was on board. Julian was sent to find the other soldiers, whilst Darinus was taken down to the harbour to inspect his vessel.

The evening before they were to set sail, Julian was again sent out to see Leila. But before he set out he had complained that last time he had seen her he had spent most of his silver coins. Now though, he was on a different errand. Sure enough, as he arrived at the arch, she was in exactly the same place as where she had stood the previous evening. But this time another man fashionably dressed in wealthy looking clothing was chatting with her, obviously about business.

Julian marched straight up to the pair and ordered the wealthy looking man to leave. Seeing that Julian was deadly serious, the man muttered something and left. The centurion said to Leila, "You must come."

She remarked, "I like a masterful soldier."

He took her down one of the extremely narrow lanes, grabbing her by the left arm he hissed, "Leila, I know you're a poisonous whore, with a loose tongue like a double-edged sword and a betrayer of Rome. I will spare you your wicked life if you tell me what I desire."

Leila gave a vacant look. She lifted her other hand up to Julian's chest. "Oh, dear Roman, you are so delusional."

This is the point where Julian would usually give in to a woman's seductive charms, but he stood strong. He drew his sword and held it to the scarlet woman's naked neck, as this was the only way he was going to prise the truth out. Eventually she did admit that she was the spy and the dark pirate was Prince Axana of Ethiopia and that he paid her handsomely for her services. One thing he did get out of her when he pressed for it was Axana's weakness, that even though he was an exceptional seaman he was absolutely terrified of water.

After the not so friendly meeting, Julian marched Leila back to the arch, where they bumped into Pilot, who had been discreetly wandering around the arch. On seeing Leila he acted surprised to see her, before inviting her to accompany him back to his house for the night. He didn't seem to notice Julian. As Leila walked past, she stamped hard on the top of the centurion's foot.

Julian was relieved that Pilot had taken her away; at least she would not have the chance to get back to tell the pirate and scupper the plan entirely.

It was late afternoon/early evening when Darinus and his band of men boarded the boat which they had been allocated. The rain was lashing down and the wind was blowing hard, the waves below were lapping up the side; was this really a good idea after all? Julian shouted over to Darinus, "I think the gods are telling us we will perish this night."

The slaves dropped the oars and the anchor was pulled up.

They turned right out of the harbour and out to sea where the thunder and lightning had been waiting and crashed through the sky. They rounded the peninsula, and sailed roughly half a mile from the coast; because the waves were so choppy the ship went slower than it would have on a calm night. Up one wave and down the next the Romans had to hold on.

The lightning was now too close for comfort for as soon as the deafening thunder roared up above then the lightning flashed instantaneously. Darinus had his eyes fixed toward the shore as when the lightning flashed it lit everything up.

Half an hour passed, then, as the lightning lit the shore, unmistakably he saw what they had come in search of: Lupitor, Pilot's stolen galleon. In that brief second it looked incredibly scary and intimidating.

Then it was swallowed up by the darkness of night. Darinus screamed out to his men who were all on the lookout from different angles, "Men, we have company, all below deck." They all crammed in below the stairs as Darinus gave his orders, "Men, I have seen Lupitor. It will give chase, as it draws near I urge you all on my command over board." (They had already prepared for this earlier that day and a rope was tightly fastened round the side of the deck.) After the speech they returned to the deck; all they could do now was stand and wait as no one knew when the pirates would appear.

The storm was easing, although the wind and rain were still strong. Darinus gazed back toward the shore. The next flash of lightning revealed that the pirate ship had completely vanished. They were surrounded by pitch blackness and time was slowly ticking by. There was no sign of the ghost pirate ship; in fact Darinus thought the plan had failed. Then an almighty thud shook the ship throwing the Roman's sprawling all over the slippery deck in all directions.

So out of the darkness Lupitor had arrived, shunting its helpless victim with its long battering ram that had been installed following the modernization since its takeover, smashing into the stern, leaving Darinus' borrowed ship partially disabled and at the full mercy of the pirates.

Lupitor withdrew. Darinus was fully aware it would reappear and if his judgment was correct it would be alongside, away from the coast, on the portside so it could force the crippled vessel toward the coast, so he gathered his men on the starboard side. Sure enough Darinus was right. A while later their ship shuddered as it was thrust violently from the portside. He gave his men the signal and they all leaped over the side and hung onto the rope. There was enough of a gap so they could just spy under the railings onto the deck. All along the far side, faintly upon the horizon, dark figures of the hijacking pirates could be seen jumping on board the now captured merchant ship.

At that moment the moon peered out from behind the black clouds so the Romans could vaguely see what was going on. The pirates swamped all over the deck like ants and stripped everything in sight, wrenching the wood off the empty boxes.

The figure of a smaller man appeared on board and his subjects cleared out of his way. By their reaction and the way this pirate was acting, Darinus knew this to be the pirate prince who was furious, realising that he had been set up. He ordered the rowing slaves from below to be brought up. They were pushed, shoved, punched and even spat on as they were assembled into a line near the front of the boat.

All the Romans could do was hold tightly on to the rope which in itself wasn't a comfortable exercise to say the least.

The pirate prince with a burst of energy ran a few steps to the front of the ship and athletically leapt up onto the bow and balancing on the top he crouched and, holding his chin, he looked down. Maybe this gave the smaller man a feeling of authority as he looked down upon the rowing slaves.

Darinus was getting ready to intervene in case any harm came to the rowers as he felt a sense of responsibility toward them, but everything changed in a few seconds as the dreadlocked pirate disappeared overboard; it looked like something had pulled him over from behind. The bodyguards hanging next to Darinus said, "Julian, sir." He had fearlessly hitched his body round clinging onto the rope, and as the pirate had sprung up onto the bow he was in the centurion's grasp, and knowing the pirate was terrified of the water and could not swim, he decided to go for his Achilles heel and pounced, grabbing him from behind, and they both spiralled down into the swell below.

Without a second to spare, Darinus, followed by his men, launched themselves back up on to the deck. Axana's men were hysterical and had all pushed to the side to look overboard, so the Romans arrival on deck went unnoticed.

Ropes were dotted around the deck tied to the sides. With no time to waste Darinus grabbed one of these ropes and, surrounded by his men, who cleared the way (there was no resistance from the pirates as without their leader they seemed lost) he rushed to the side and tossed the rope out into the sea.

As Julian fell down roughly four metres into the choppy water below he held onto one of the pirate's feet. He found himself swallowed under the waves; everything seemed to go in slow motion. Whilst he was engulfed in the water, he had time to think, What have I done? This is a more crazy thing than even his commander Darinus would do.

But then he surfaced and was thrown around by the harsh waves. All this time he had clung tight to the pirate's foot, who was thrashing around and Julian took a couple of good kicks to his head. Fortunately he had fallen right next to the ship and the swirling current was pushing them toward the boat. Through the torrid sea he could see the faces gazing over from the ship and he saw out of the corner of his eye Darinus throw the rope overboard.

The rope dropped just a couple of metres away, which doesn't sound that far but it is when amongst the waves. Julian was a relatively strong swimmer but he had Axana to contend with and the pirate was panicking like mad and was furiously grabbing at Julian, so the centurion screamed, "Wretch, be still and I will save your life." The pirate seemed to go into shock and became motionless, realising that if he did not listen then he would die, so Julian twisted him round onto his back and took him by his chin.

The new problem he had was, whilst he was doing all this, he had floated further from the rope so he began swimming as hard as he could using just his right arm, but he only succeeded in not drifting further, and all he was achieving was sapping his strength, and if he didn't manage to get to the rope soon the results would be fatal. So he decided to go under water and taking the plunge he took them both downward under the swirling waves.

From up above Darinus was getting more and more anxious as Julian was underwater for so long, then he surfaced amazingly within a foot of the rope. Julian went to grab the rope and completely missed it, and disappeared below the waves. Darinus felt his heart tear. For once he was absolutely helpless. To see his friend on the verge of such an act of bravery disappear before his eyes was cruel; he just stared frozen at the swirling waves below.

The moon decided to fully come out from of its hiding place behind the dark clouds. Then out of nowhere Julian's arm reappeared out of the torrid sea and this time he grabbed the rope fast and hoisted his body up. All this time he had held the spluttering pirate, who had come back to life, and they both slowly climbed up the rope. On deck the Romans pulled it up from the top, even some of the pirates lent a hand on seeing their leader alive. But as they got to the top Julian shouted, "Darinus, stop the rope." Somewhat puzzled by this demand Darinus obeyed.

Julian seized hold of Axana's shirt and said, "Pirate, before we enter back on the deck there is one thing I request that you give me your word on; if you refuse then I will take us back to perish in the waves below."

This really gave the pirate no option but to obey and the pirate prince replied in broken Latin, "Agree, but you give I my word."

Julian agreed he would honour the pirate's request also. So the centurion spelled out his appeal. "Pirate. I demand you to travel to the Caledonian courtyard and take your place in the extraordinary army under my commander's rule."

Axana surprisingly agreed with no reservation; no doubt he just wanted to get back onto the deck.

On hearing this Darinus was enraged. His mood turned from elation on the rescue of his centurion to anger. How dare Julian choose his warriors? As the exhausted Julian was helped back on board Darinus turned away and walked to the other side of the ship.

The wringing wet Axana called out to the centurion, "Now my word." Julian was bound to his word and had to obey. The pirate signalled for him to come over and said, "Kiss feet, kiss feet." After all Julian had somewhat humiliated the pirate in front of his subjects, so embarrassingly he knelt down and kissed both of the prince pirate's feet.

When Darinus could bring himself to talk to Julian he took him aside and gave him the biggest scolding the centurion had ever received from his commander. Julian was a bit bemused by his leader's reaction toward him as he thought he was doing the right thing.

Darinus assured Axana that they meant him and his band of pirates no harm; Darinus also saw this as an opportunity and seeing that Axana had agreed to join his ranks at Caledonia asked if he could transport him and his men over the Mare Nostrum (Mediterranean).

So the Romans were invited onto Lupitor and sailed under the pirate's flag for a few weeks. During this time Darinus spent some time with Axana and found him to be an interesting character who held some very interesting principles. He prayed to Jar - the name he called God by. Being a prince he had travelled a lot and smoked a lot of a herb which he had found whilst in the mountains north of the Gupta Empire; he applied oil daily to his thick dreadlocks, and entertained himself playing some small drums with his hands while they were out to sea and the other pirates would sing along.

Darinus forgave Julian and was pleased to have the pirate in his army.

ADRIEN'S YOUNG APRENTICE

Shortly after saying farewell to Amorak, Adrien crossed over to autumn 700AD.

This particular day the weather was calm with just a slight breeze. Strolling onwards, the traveller, for some reason, was feeling rather jolly and had a spring in his step. After a while he stumbled into a clearing, where he paused, as ten yards or so further on was a woman standing next to a neatly built stone well. With her was a young lad of roughly five or six years old.

The woman had lowered an empty bucket down the well on a piece of rope and was struggling hard to pull the now full bucket back up. So Adrien decided to intervene and lend a hand. He drew his sword and hid it behind a nearby larch tree so as not to alarm the woman and her child. Marching over to the well he approached the woman and taking the rope attached to the bucket hoisted it up.

He could see the woman had been crying, and held sadness in her melancholic eyes. Upon her head she wore a white head scarf, accompanied by a long, dowdy, pale blue dress.

On the ground next to them was another empty bucket, so Adrien picked the second bucket up and tying the handle to the rope he dropped it back down into the deep water below. With the bucket full he hoisted the rope back up. The woman faintly nodded showing a little gratitude, lifted both buckets and tottered off with the infant in pursuit.

They went in the direction of a village just over a clean-cut meadow; it was obvious she was straining under the weight of each bucket, so after watching for a minute he decided to go lend a hand. So chasing after her the Saxon took the wooden handles. At first the sad woman refused to loosen her grip, but soon gave in and let go.

They walked through the village (the lad contently ran next to Adrien just grinning at him), which was a quaint place with small, rounded grey stone houses with spherical sloped roofs, the road (if you could call it a road - more like a wide muddy pathway) led directly through the village. Once the other side, the path rose upward, and there, perched upon a small green hill was an old, shabby, one-storey wooden house, surrounded by a weathered wooden veranda. Beside the house (on the near side) almost twice the size, was a big lofty barn, also put together with wooden slats. These two buildings were surrounded by rolling lush green hills.

Sitting on the veranda was a middle-aged man, with a hat on his head, sharpening the blade of a sickle; he looked up as they approached. For this was the farmer and the woman at the well was his wife; their small child ran to greet his father, who instantly put down his sickle and lifted up his son. He gave the strange traveller a vacant look as Adrien placed the two buckets next to him on the veranda, and turned to walk away.

As he ambled back toward the village he heard someone yelling, and turned to see the farmer calling and waving him to come back. He didn't have a clue what the farmer was doing, but he understood the gesture to return, so he obeyed and walked back to the veranda. Adrien was given a shallow wooden cup filled with cool water from the well, and a lump of bread.

The farmer, like his wife, had an expressionless face. He then signalled to Adrien, lifting up the two now empty buckets. Adrien understood the farmer wished him to collect more water from the well. He thought, if I do this a couple of times then maybe I'll get some more food and somewhere to rest my head for the night. So he obliged and collected six more bucket loads; the little lad faithfully followed him on each trip.

The Saxon was right. He was rewarded with more bread and a comfy straw bed for the night out in the barn; he was given a candle and proceeded through the large doors. Inside the barn was filled half full with hay, and two undernourished looking oxen. Up on top of the hay was the figure of a man fast asleep, so without any reservation he blew out the candle and lay down on the soft hay himself.

Adrien woke to the crow of a cockerel, a recognizable sound he had not heard for some time. Then he felt something shake him. Automatically he jumped to his feet. There before him stood the tallest man he had ever witnessed; it was the man from the previous night who was asleep on the hay and he was enormous, in fact he was eight foot one. The man took the two oxen out of the barn and lifted up a heavy yolk on to their backs, and then he took some more heavy-looking equipment, and set off.

Adrien was still a bit sleepy and his brain was not really registering properly, yet instinctively he followed the tall man. Outside the stars were still high in the sky, but the sun was rising in the east. Curiously the traveller followed the giant. They passed through the village, and at that time of the morning anyone who had any sense was asleep so the village was deserted.

The tall man was in his youth, and was the eldest son of the farmer. Unfortunately he was deaf, and nobody had ever heard him speak so he was presumed to have no speech. Sadly his father was ashamed of his eldest son and would not have him either eat or sleep in the farm house, and had banished him to the barn. He was just employed (if you count working to sleep in the barn as employment) to work the land.

He had fair hair and a light complexion, and extremely broad shoulders. He wore an old ragged tunic with a piece of old frayed rope around his waist and on his big feet he wore old leather boots that were falling to bits.

Once through the village they crossed the meadow and passed the well, where they turned off at a fork in the muddy road to the right. One thing that was noticeable was that the land was well kept and the fields pleasantly cultivated. The oxen obediently followed the silent giant, until they stopped at the edge of a field. The sun had replaced the dark night and the giant was ready to start work. The two oxen stood still as the giant prepared the iron-tip plough. When the plough was securely fitted and they were all ready, he steadily led the beasts forward, following him in a straight line.

On the fourth line a major problem occurred, one of the oxen smashed one of its front legs on a sharp, jagged rock sticking out of the ground. The ox stopped and yelped with the pain. Rather than letting the poor oxen limp on, the big man lifted the yolk off the beast's neck and walking slowly took the injured oxen to the edge of the field.

Adrien was amazed how the two animals reacted to the gentle giant, who returned to the healthier ox and lifted the redundant side of the yolk up to his stomach and proceeded to carry on where the injured oxen had left off. The Saxon could not believe his eyes. To plough a field instead of an ox would take almost super-human strength. The spectator decided to lend a hand instead of watching, so he walked ahead of the giant and the ox checking for rocks and throwing them out of the way. Row after row the giant ploughed alongside the ox, until noon when the man stopped working, and unleashed the oxen and put the heavy yolk down for a rest.

On the far side of the field was a single hedgerow. The giant wandered over to a yellow leafy hedge, while Adrien moseyed on behind. As they drew near he soon came to an abrupt stop as flying around in all directions were many bees; he could now see a bees' nest neatly placed in the now nearly bare hedge.

The colossal man advanced to the bush unfazed by the now swarming bees, he put his hand right into the nest, then withdrawing his hand (without receiving a single sting) he licked his fingers; placing his hand in a second time he waved the reluctant Saxon to come closer. This time after he plucked his hand from the nest he urged Adrien to taste. Adrien felt a bit weird licking the silent man's fat fingers, but he found the sweet taste delightful and rather moreish.

They lounged around the well for a while with Adrien pondering. This giant of a man had him mesmerized; imagine how strong he would be with a sword, at this he remembered his own sword was still hidden behind a tree nearby. So he went and collected it; the man didn't take a blind bit of notice.

They worked on till near on dusk, before wrapping up and heading back. They walked at a particularly slow pace as the silent man patiently waited for the injured oxen. Adrien liked this giant and his gentle nature, and he decided he would stay around for a few more days.

As they sauntered through the village (there were a few people around) their peaceful walk was rudely interrupted, as a rotten tomato was thrown as they passed a certain house, hitting the gentle giant square on the chin, then an egg hit the side of his cheek slithering down his face. Then the sound of cackling children was heard shouting, "Nielub, Nielub, Nielub," this meaning in the local language, 'not loved'.

At this act of persecution the gentle giant did not even look up or flinch, he just concentrated on helping the injured ox. Back at the barn they never saw the farmer. They did see the farmer's wife though briefly as she brought some food in: a couple of turnips and some bread, along with some warm milk.

The next few days were very much the same, except at noon the injured oxen was left in the barn to recover.

Adrien found two sturdy staffs relatively the same size. He held one and the other he gave to the gentle giant, whose real name was Syziaslav. Over the next few days during break time he encouraged the silent giant to pretend to sword fight with him, and then they would work in the afternoon and return to the barn at dusk, passing through the village on the way, where Syziaslav would receive the same abuse daily from the local children, but never once did he retaliate. Years of abuse had no doubt wilted any confidence he had once held, if he had ever had any.

All this time he stayed silent, Adrien never heard him utter a single word. He had a unique bond with animals and when he ploughed the field, birds would regularly perch upon his shoulders.

The Saxon leader taught him to fight with the sturdy staff. Syziaslav was a quick learner.

Early one afternoon they finished ploughing the field, and returning to the farm, no one was around, so Syziaslav took them both into the house. Inside there wasn't much space: there were two rooms, one was the kitchen and dining area, the other was sleeping quarters, the front door opened into the kitchen where most of the space was taken up by a large pine table surrounded by three pine log stools, the ceilings were low held up with old thick beams, the main feature was a large hearth.

The giant went over to the hearth where, just above, hidden on a shelf was a long thin object wrapped in a cloth. Syziaslav took this and they left and went to the barn. Once in the barn, he unravelled the cloth, revealing a shiny looking sword made of Rus steel. The handle was huge, along the edge of the sword in the middle there was a hollow, the crossover and the top were decorated with a silver pattern and it was one metre in length. This was the farmer's weapon. He had once fought in the Slav battles defending their new land against the Norsemen from the west and the Byzantine armies from the south before he had taken a wife and retired to the farm.

The following day they took the sword with them. At noon for the first time Adrien put Syziaslav to the test with a real weapon, putting into practice what he had taught his apprentice. As they fought Adrien had to up his game, for it was like fighting an experienced warrior. The man was much bigger and stronger than himself, and after a while the blows were so hard that the Saxon had to retire almost exhausted. The truth was he wasn't really used to play fighting for any length of time, as in a real fight he would go straight for the jugular.

This went on for two more days and Syziaslav improved dramatically each time. On the third day they returned back to the farm as usual just before dusk. As they passed through the village the place was oddly deserted. Arriving at the farm house they found six horses tied up outside, and two soldiers were standing on guard.

They quietly crept in to the barn with the ox. Adrien insisted the gentle giant unravel the sword, then they tiptoed round the back of the house. As they passed the first window Adrien peered inside where he saw the farmer perched on a stool, with a soldier holding the point of a curved sword to his neck. There were four soldiers in the kitchen; two were guarding the door whilst the other was rummaging through the farmer's possessions. The farmer's wife was on her knees, with her hands pressed together, pleading.

In those days, Bora the Knyaz was the ruler of the land. He was an eastern Slav from the new city of Novgorod, set on the banks of the Volkhov River. Having increased taxes fourfold on wheat, farmers were literally being bullied out of their livelihoods by these crippling taxes. This particular year the crops had yielded less than expected, making it impossible to meet the given deadline. The soldiers were here collecting for the greedy tyrant ruler. If the farmer refused to pay or could not, then the soldiers had been told to deliver their own punishment, and in some cases they had been known to torture, or even kill the subjects.

The Saxon and the giant, with their heads down, continued quietly round to the front, where they ambushed the two guards; they acted so swiftly that the guards did not see them approach and were not ready. In reality it was Adrien who drove them away whilst Syziaslav watched. Using the flat of his sword he winded both men and forced them to flee; they ran off into the distance, and disappeared. They then crashed through the farm house door.

For the first time Adrien actually saw emotion in the gentle giant's face, when he saw his father being threatened, sending him into frenzy. The invading Slav soldiers were taken by surprise by the new arriving warriors. Syziaslav grabbed the two guards standing either side of the doorway, one in each hand, lifting them both off the ground, smashing their heads together, knocking them out instantly, before throwing them out of the open door.

The other two soldiers drew their scimitar-shaped swords and turned to face them. In a rage the silent man flew at the man oppressing his father, whilst Adrien faced the other. Both the Saxon and his apprentice made light work of the intruders, driving them out of the house where they, too, fled over the rolling green fields. Out of embarrassment they never returned. Adrien was so proud of his apprentice for the unbelievable pace and strength he had used to dispose of his opponent.

The farmer was absolutely speechless - his useless son, had come to his rescue. He had not even realised his sword, his own precious possession, had gone missing, and under any other circumstances he would have scolded the giant.

That night they celebrated by slaughtering one of pigs, and for the first time since he was a small child the farmer called him by his first name Syziaslav. He also became a hero in the village, as the farm supplied them with food; surely with the farm threatened the village would have also suffered?

It was soon time for the Saxon to get moving. Syziaslav and his younger brother gave him a lift in the horse and cart. He made the decision to go south as the winter was coming and the Northern provinces would be a treacherous place to travel.

It was agreed that the giant apprentice swordsmen would come to Yeovil castle to complete his training in a year's time before taking his place on the Caledonian courtyard.

A MAN ON THE ROAD TO RUIN

Adrien could now sense he was on the final leg of his incredible journey, which was making him feel more homesick than he had for a few years. Although, before returning home he was intent on taking a detour north, to see a certain person! Up to this point he had gathered and filled all the places, except one of his interesting army.

Adrien had been dropped off by Syziaslav deep inside the land of Germania. Studying his trusty canvas it showed he was not too far from the top of the mountainous region Gallia Cisalpina in the south, so he now needed to head west to the great Renos River. Being aware of which direction he had been travelling, and knowing the sun rose in the east and set in the west he turned west.

One night as he slept, once more he crossed over another time change, this time right back to 45AD. Unaware of the year change he pressed forward. The route he took was away from any of the roads or tracks. He crossed unspoilt pastures, through woodlands over hills through valleys and over streams. He lived on the land for weeks until reaching the Rhine and the Roman road on the border of the Roman Empire. Here he turned right towards the north.

It soon became apparent that there was a strong Roman influence on the road, which made the single travelling Saxon feel uneasy. Every hour or so, a battalion of Roman soldiers would march past as the road was fairly busy. After a time he glanced across the road and saw a man alone wandering in the same direction, walking at the same pace that he was. An hour passed and the man was still across the road, walking level with him. For some strange reason Adrien felt compelled to cross over and talk with the stranger - maybe one of the reasons he crossed that road that day could have been due to the fact he had not spoken to another human being for a number of weeks. Or was the reason much more powerful?

This man held an unusual aura about him; he wore a simple white tunic, and slung over his right shoulder was a dark green cloak and he wore no shoes upon his bare feet. His hairline was receding and his face was covered with a long but well-groomed beard; in his right hand he held a solid wooden staff. As Adrien approached he suddenly felt completely tongue tied and somehow humble in this man's presence, so he just walked besides him for a good twenty minutes, before whispering, "My name is Adrien."

The middle-aged fellow replied, "I am glad for I am Simon Zelotes."

Adrien then blurted out, "Do you care if I walk with you? I have not spoken to a single soul for a time."

Simon answered, "I would be glad. You are indeed a Saxon no doubt, I have a lot to tell in return."

As they walked the two talked a great deal. It was not long before Adrien encountered his first Roman checkpoint, where the Roman guards questioned where they were from and what business they had travelling along that road. At this point Adrien was so glad he was not alone as Simon the Zelotes spoke, "I travel to tell the message of peace on earth and good will to all men." The Romans looked confused by such a strange statement and waved both the travellers on through.

Adrien spent three days with Simon the Zelotes, who was from the land of Cana, south east of the Sea of Galilee. You could see that in his youth he had been a fiery figure, and he told how he was a revolutionary fighting for freedom against the occupying Romans in Jerusalem. But he had met a man who came from the kingdom of heaven, and who had cruelly been hung upon a tree to die. He had become a close friend, and spoke dearly of this remarkable man. And knowing him had dramatically changed his view of the world.

Simon the Zelotes spent a lot of his time fasting and praying. He told Adrien some amazing stories of miracles and other happenings, but to find out more about them you would have to read another great book. This encounter had a profound effect upon the Saxon, changing his whole outlook on life.

Adrien was thinking during the time he spent with this old ex-revolutionary that he ticked all the boxes to take the last vacant square at Caledonia; he had the quality to be a leader and an adviser. He also had an unworldly sparkle in his eye. So Adrien decided to put the question to him.

To Adrien's surprise, Simon the Zelotes point blank refused. His response was, "I am here on a far more important quest, to save the souls of men and show them the way to the eternal kingdom of heaven."

And that was that, as it was time to say their goodbyes as Simon Zelotes wanted to head into a nearby town and Adrien needed to press on. Little more is known of Simon Zelotes, but he took his own quest to Britannia, where some historians have written that he went to Glastonbury. Maybe this was due to listening to Adrien, but sadly he became a martyr, dying for what he believed and taught.

Adrien felt different; he had a buzz about him as if he had been injected with new life. He was now closer to home and started to move with a spring in his stride. Then, after another night's sleep, he crossed back into the year 426AD. Fortunately for the Saxon he didn't have to walk the long Roman road on his lonesome.

Waking up with the wet morning dew on his nose, on the soft bank next to the road, it instantly occurred to him his surroundings had changed. But the hardened traveller carried on regardless. Mid-morning he came across another Roman checkpoint, but this one was deserted and appeared to have been abandoned for a number of years, as it had clearly been vandalised and burnt out. An old pole was all that remained of what had once held the proud Roman crest.

Adrien didn't linger but quickly passed by. Two more days on he came to a Germanic settlement, just off the road, where he found a tavern - an old travellers' watering hole. It was run by an older couple, politely he asked if he could sleep here for one night, but as always he had no money, so the woman (who was noticeably in charge) said he could go and assist her husband rounding up their cattle.

Since the demise of the Western Roman Empire, travellers on the road had become scarce, mainly due to bandits and robbers roaming freely.

Adrien gratefully went with the older man, and rounded up the cattle. That evening he was given a chunk of cow meat and a clay goblet full of warm, misty brown ale brewed from locally grown hops. The tavern had once been a busy thriving place but now sadly only a few people dropped in and most of them lived locally.

This square building was made up of two rooms, one was the sleeping quarters, and the other was the watering hole which was a large area; dotted around were quaint wooden tables, along with wooden stools. A roaring fire was the main attraction set in a grand ingle. Low wooden beams held up the flat wooden ceiling that was made up from neatly bounds logs. On the flat, hardened mud floor was neatly laid fresh hay. It would match up to any modern tavern of that day.

Whilst Adrien had been out cattle herding earlier that day the old man warned him of a once-famous warlord called Gregor, who would occasionally enter the tavern, and stay all night drinking till he almost passed out. The old man went on to tell of how years previously Gregor had been a fearsome warlord; he had such influence throughout the land that he had gathered a formidable army of one hundred thousand men and marched down to conquer Rome.

His army had defeated a watered-down Roman army at the edge of Gallia Cisalpina. Then he received word that a rogue Roman legion had destroyed his village, butchering all who lived there, including his parents and family. At once he turned back and marched with his weary army back to avenge his settlement, but somehow he was out-witted by the Roman force, which passed him during the dark of night, thus escaping his wrath. On returning Gregor found his home utterly destroyed; he lost the will to live, and even contemplated suicide. His mighty army that he had gathered dispersed, some returning to their villages, others joining other armies.

The man told how he witnessed that fine army before it started on the journey to Rome. The proud warlord at the helm was a born leader, saying in his own words, " I ponder wither an army as fierce will ever be assembled again; it was Gregor's time to seize the dying Empire and sadly it passed him by."

With compassion he took pity on Gregor, and for a time let him drink his ale without charge.

As time wore on Gregor lost his respect for the tavern owner and his dear wife, and having violent outbursts and becoming unpredictable like most drunks do, caused the tavern to lose valuable business.

Adrien was relaxing, watching the flames of the roaring fire dance; he didn't care much for the local ale but drank it anyway. Then through the wooden door entered a large guy, needing no introduction whatsoever, for this character was unmistakably Gregor the retired warlord. He wandered in and plonked himself down on a stool in one of the dark corners, placing down on the table a rather heavy-looking sword, and placed his large round shield upon the floor. His shield was made from oak wood with a metal rim and on it was a faded painted picture of a black crow.

Immediately the old tavern woman ran over with a goblet of ale putting it down on the table next to him. He picked up the ale and opening his mouth he knocked it straight back, and placed it back down. The woman quickly replaced it and this cycle happened four times before the warlord decided to drink at a normal and reasonable rate.

Adrien asked for another goblet, as he had decided to stick around for a while, and see if what he had heard that day regarding Gregor was true, though he doubted the old man would make up tall stories. If he got the chance he would like to in some way interact with the lost warlord, but for now he thought it best to be a spectator and keep his distance.

As the evening wore on two local men entered the tavern. They were very loud and were laughing and joking amongst themselves. They took two stools near the cosy fire, and the tavern woman brought them over two goblets of ale. Then one of these merry fellows glanced over in the direction of Gregor, and the look of merriment upon his face turned to dread. He nudged his friend with his foot under the table, and discreetly nodded his head that way; his companion too saw the ex-warlord in the corner. The chatting and joking ended and they sat in silence as they swiftly finished their ale, before leaving.

Adrien thought, how odd, there's more that scratches the surface and this Gregor is clearly a fearsome character with a dark reputation. Watching the warlord's actions Adrien could see he was a troubled man and was suffering incredibly. He had broad shoulders, slightly thinning, light mousy-brown hair upon his head – it was easy to figure that by the length of his beard that it had not been cut for a considerably long time, but anyway he could drink like a lord. He wore a thick black bear fur held in by a wide old leather belt around his waist, and on his feet he wore tatty sandals that looked like they had seen better days.

As time passed Adrien noticed the more Gregor drank the more agitated and uneasy he became, starting to chunter under his breath in his Germanic tongue, whilst fingering the handle of his heavy sword. He then became more alert, and getting himself together gulped down his drink, spilling half of it down his bear fur. Then after he had consumed more ale than Adrien thought it physically possible, he grabbed his sword, and, stumbling to his feet he raised the weapon up till it hit the ceiling whilst shouting, "Romans, Romans", before bringing it crashing down and splitting the table before him in two. The worse for wear ex-warlord then left the tavern through the door and stumbled into the dark night.

The colour returned to the tavern owners' faces as they both breathed a sigh of relief. The observant Saxon went and talked with the owners as he still had many questions to ask. The woman spoke saying, "I am glad Gregor held good humour tonight."

Adrien asked if the man would take him to where Gregor lived or resided. At this question he looked mortified and shaking his head refused, quivering that this would cause him and his wife nothing but trouble. But the Saxon could be a very persuasive individual when he wanted things to go his way. He promised to try and help the troubled unstable warlord.

The tavern owners were flabbergasted at such a proclamation; why would he even attempt such lunacy. But after much conversation and partially explaining why, the owner agreed. Besides, Adrien did not speak the Germanic tongue and needed a translator, as you would very much doubt the Frank Germanic warlord would utter a single word in Latin.

Up early as the sun began to light up the eastern sky, the two men left the tavern. A thin frost had covered the ground and the cold blue sky was crisp and breezy. This region was surrounded by much forest. The decimated settlement Gregor came from was roughly two miles away. The tavern owner admitted he had not ventured near the tragic scene since the horrific events of that fateful night that had taken place six years previous.

The stroll was rather pleasant. One hour later, the significantly now forlorn tavern owner indicated they were about to approach the settlement. He began to act nervous, when he spoke his quiet voice started to tremble. "We are here, I do not know if we will find Gregor."

A few yards forward and they stepped out into a sizeable clearing within the forest. Here before them stood the desolate remnants of what had once been a trouble–free, self-sufficient settlement. Located in the centre of this settlement had once been a farm, with other buildings dotted around, such as living houses along with granary and storage buildings; many of these simple people lived with their livestock within their houses. The buildings had been made of timber cut from the surrounding forest.

But now all that was left were burnt-out remnants. Some of the houses had been burnt to the ground whilst others were just blackened shells, a few charred walls stood in random places scattered around. Tall wild weeds had grown and swamped the floor of this part of the forest, as though they were trying to hide the atrocities of what had become of that sad settlement. The vision of this sorrowful place, even six years on, was still a harrowing sight. Adrien's heart was full of remorse towards the perpetrators responsible for such a cold-blooded act.

From what the tavern owner had explained, Adrien figured that this was the work of his very own enemy Darinus and his men, which sickened him even more. On the flip side of the coin, if Darinus had seen the shameful cruelty Julian and his own bodyguards had inflicted on that tiny settlement, his punishment would have been far greater than just the verbal scolding which he had given.

There was actually one building still intact, which stood a way back from the rest; this had been used as a sick house, for sick humans and animals. Adrien and his accomplice soberly sauntered over to the sick house, cautiously tiptoeing as they went. Peering into the dark, single-room hut, they could vaguely see the outline of a man lying face down on the floor, asleep with his arms and legs sprawled out beside him. In his left hand he held the handle of a heavy sword, and in his right he held his huge shield. They knew him to be alive as he was softly snoring and also his identity was recognisable due to his heavy sword which he had carelessly wielded in the tavern the night before.

This was Gregor, still drunk no doubt from the amount he had poured down his gullet hours earlier. Adrien gave his leg a relatively hard kick. The ex-warlord stirred, mumbling something under his breath and eyes still shut he turned on to his back.

Again the Saxon kicked his leg, this time a little harder. This time he opened his eyes wide and stared directly upward toward the ceiling before letting out an almighty roar and clambering to his feet. The scared tavern owner cowered behind Adrien.

Gregor, with glazed-over eyes, stared at Adrien; it appeared he was looking mysteriously straight through him. Being so close to the unwashed Gregor wasn't the most pleasant experience as the ex-warlord didn't smell too good.

Adrien chose to retreat back outside. Turning to his accomplice he asked, "Can you translate what I say into this ragamuffin's words?"

Gregor had also stepped outside to face the new day, but he completely ignored the other two. Whether he chose to or not remained to be explained, or was he just in denial, who knows.

Adrien urged his translator, "I am the future King of Britannia, therefore I order you to listen to what I have to say." But these words fell on deaf ears as the Germanic Frank showed more interest in clicking his stiff neck. Adrien continued, changing his tactics to try and get a response, "I have come face to face in battle with the Roman responsible for the destruction of your settlement, and I will engage with him again."

The poor translator became increasingly nervous, but after a brief delay obeyed.

Gregor frowned, a deep frown bringing his thick eyebrows down over his eyes, so he obviously had heard what had been said.

The petrified tavern owner (whose name was actually Trix) started babbling on, clearly apologising to the ex-warlord for disturbing him and bringing the Saxon hither. But the torn Gregor hung his head and wandered away.

The relentless Adrien followed. Placing himself directly in front of Gregor he drew his sword and holding it out he pointed it directly at the man's heart. He saw something stir in the broken man's eyes, as he slowly raised his bowed head until his eyes levelled with the Saxon's.

Then, with razor-sharp accuracy, he disarmed the shocked Saxon, who had wanted some kind of reaction but was not ready for the speed at which he received it. A loud twang was heard as steel met steel. Adrien's weapon flew out of his hand and landed a few metres away, and he automatically darted out of range.

Fortunately Gregor did not retaliate further, as the astonished Adrien lurched for his sword. His hands were still ringing with pain. From that moment Adrien knew even though he was in dire condition he had found his last man; all he had to do now was convince him to pull his act together.

Adrien ambled up to walk a while next to Gregor, who seemed to be stuck in a trance. The Saxon felt a pang of sadness inside him, for this was a man whose life had been so smitten with grief and so consumed by hatred and revenge that he had lost his way. But he was still alive and whilst he remained alive then there was hope.

Then the most extraordinary thing happened, Gregor fell on his knees and started to sob. Clearly what Adrien had said to him had had an enormous effect on him. He had waited for a chance to avenge his family and as far as he was concerned he could kill as many Romans as it would take but to find the guilty one was virtually impossible, as he did not know who had wiped out the settlement. Then, out of the blue, this Saxon turns up with the information.

Slowly this wreck of a man fell apart. Adrien felt a bit awkward, so reassuringly he knelt down next to him and placed his hand on his shoulder.

After ten or so minutes Adrien said to Trix (who was just astounded by what he was seeing). "Man, will you transfer my words?" and he said, "Gregor, it is time for you to mourn and be sad no longer. I need you to come with me and lead part of my army. We shall leave this Godforsaken place now, and you will get the revenge you want against your enemies, who are my enemies also."

The ex-warlord rose to his feet and heeded these words, and followed his now new leader.

They all went back to the main road where Adrien pointed to the great Renos River. Gregor needed no explanation; he climbed down the bank and dived into the water to cleanse himself, something that clearly he had not done for quite some time. He was down there for a while as he also decided with his sword to take off his unkempt beard. When he returned to join the other two they were amazed at the transformation as once again he looked like the great warrior warlord he had once been. Trix's eyes were filled with tears; he could not believe what he had seen that day. And Adrien was in complete awe of this man.

Leaving the happy tavern owner behind, they left, taking the road north.

DID HIS QUEEN WAIT?

Adrien's journey had become much more interesting travelling along with Gregor, who was almost unrecognisable from the man found lost the previous day. Neither of them could understand the other, as they both spoke different languages. All the same Adrien was glad of the company as he could not stand being alone.

Soon they left the Rhine river and headed more north west; the land of the Vikings was still a considerable way off. Adrien felt that on foot they were making little progress, so needed a quicker mode of transport. A day or so passed when an opportunity arose that he could not resist as they passed an isolated farm.

Next to the farm was a fair-size paddock, surrounded by a neat fence. In this paddock was a small herd of well-groomed horses. The problem was that the Saxon had no money and nothing to trade with. The other thing he had to consider was, did this barbarian even know how to ride a horse?

So under the cover of darkness they crept into the paddock and stole two of the bigger horses which appeared to be fairly tame and approachable, and yes, for once, Adrien felt a pang of guilt. But still it was only two horses and there were more left (luckily Gregor did know how to ride). They happened to find some rope and with Adrien's knowledge they managed to make two bridles with reins - there was no option but to ride bareback.

The language barrier didn't cause much of an issue; Adrien showed the map to his new comrade which at first seemed alien to the barbarian, but slowly as he learnt to understand it he showed some interest. And Adrien taught him to sing the Saxon song as they rode.

Although uncomfortable, they now travelled much quicker, and in a matter of weeks they reached the top of Germania (known today as Denmark). Reaching the sea was a refreshing relief for the tired Saxon, it was all that lay between him and his beautiful Freyja.

Following the shore and riding on the sand they came to a tiny port, which was marked as a dot with a ship next to it on the map, shown at the most narrow of crossings onto the bottom of the northern continent of Norse land. This is where the Frank Germanic warlord became of some use, by negotiating with the locals, as there was a merchant ship sailing within two days. Adrien could not understand what Gregor said, but he did manage to get them and both the horses onto the long merchant ship.

Sailing on that boat in the north was much smoother than when Adrien had sailed those great distances on the perilous southern seas in the long canoes. Although one would think that the cramped horses enjoyed the experience very little.

Once the other side, the journey continued on. Adrien took the most direct route; that sometimes turned out to not be the best. Much of the first part of the trip was barren marshland, and then the landscape gradually turned hillier and more picturesque, with spruce woodlands, the chill of autumn lingered in the clean fresh air. Along the way they entered 793AD.

Further on up they reached the amazing fjords, where some places the horses had to swim to cross the waterways.

Adrien had been growing his beard for a time, hoping that when he arrived in Tonsberg he would fit in with the bearded Norsemen, but to be truthful he was kidding himself as in reality he would stick out like a sore thumb.

After crossing the final fjord they entered the outskirts of Vest fold. Adrien decided to leave Gregor at a point where the great fjord entered the sea; it was too much of a gamble taking him into Tonsberg. Thankfully the barbarian was more than grateful to stay and rest, so alone on horseback the lovesick Saxon jogged the last two miles.

Late afternoon, after riding up to the top of a hill, he found himself looking down over the town of Tonsberg with the impressive harbour behind; there appeared to be a lot of long ships of all different sizes in dock. He tied his horse to a nearby tree, with his heart almost beating out of his chest he curiously walked down the hill, constantly thinking to himself, what if Freyja has forgotten me? For his own sanity he needed to see her.

Entering the town it soon became apparent that some kind of important event was about to take place, as there were crowds of people rushing to and fro. Down the left side of the road outside the small huts, were tables with clay jugs lined up with drums full of beer ready to be poured when the celebrations got under way.

Where should he go to first? The town was not very big, and its main attraction was its harbour and the striking fleet of Viking ships within it. The Norsemen were more intent on sailing and exploring faraway lands than staying put and building a lavish kingdom at home.

Not one person gave the stray visitor a second glance as he mingled in amongst the crowd. Although nowhere looked familiar, there was one place Adrien did spot that sent a shiver down his spine, the rugged gates (which were slightly open) to the courtyard leading to the jail where his beloved cousin Godfrey had lost his life.

Anyway there was no time to reminisce. Where could he find Freyja?

Through the busy crowd Adrien found what he was searching for, the Royal Fortress. The Royal residence of Vest fold was not an over-elaborate palace, like usually associated with royal homes although it was a fair size, and was a dull, two-storey building, made out of tall trees bound together with the outer side covered with mud. High up on the first floor there were wide windows with wooden shutters, whilst the windows on the ground floor were considerably narrower. Dug out around the edge of the building at the bottom was a ditch. This was definitely a unique building to that part of the world at that time; many of the buildings in Norse land were built in a similar fashion.

There were two burly berserkers guarding the front entrance. Both held long double-edged axes. On their heads they wore iron helmets with horns sticking out of each side. They appeared to be all twitchy and fired up. Adrien had to hatch a new plan. What were his realistic options? He could maybe wear a disguise and try to get past the monster-sized berserkers without being caught out, or he could draw his sword and fight his way in, but the odds were highly stacked against him, and if this failed he risked being executed or sent back to the dreaded jail.

It was then he observed out the corner of his eye (and out of view from the berserkers), a tall tree off to the right of the fortress which ran parallel with the building and, better still, it appeared to be next to the only window with its shutters wide open. Discreetly he crept round until he stood beneath the old maple tree; underneath it looked far bigger than it had from a distance. Crisp yellow leaves were scattered around the floor and a family of geese were pecking through the dead leaves looking for food.

Checking left and right to make sure he wasn't being watched, the lovesick Saxon hoisted his body up on to the lowest hefty branch. After a bit of a wobble he steadied himself on the first branch. Lower down the tree, the branches were thick and sturdy, and he climbed up as slowly and carefully as he possibly could. Being autumn the tree had already shed a lot of leaves, so if any one looked up for long enough they would easy spot him, but luckily the public and the berserkers were otherwise occupied.

Adrien scaled up the tree until he was level with the window (roughly twenty foot high). From that point the maple tree was further from the side of the building than it had appeared and the dense branches were much thinner. Higher up, a long thin branch reached out - the nearest to the wall. Adrien thought if he climbed out along this branch then it would bend down toward the window and he could make a jump for it.
So that is exactly what he did; he scrambled up to the branch then edged his way outward, but his calculation was slightly out, and the branch bent downward more than he had anticipated, and to make matters worse every time he climbed a bit more the branch began to creek more. Just as the crazy Saxon reached the end, the branch snapped, and he was forced to make a jump for it. Fortunately he was only two metres from the window and, although he had to jump upwards, he just managed to grab the sill with his fingertips.
He clung on for dear life. Hanging for a good minute he caught his breath, then using all the strength he could muster he managed to hoist himself up on to his forearms. He could see directly into the window, and was astounded at what he saw: just a few feet away, kneeling down, facing the window was an attractive blonde-haired woman.
She had removed the clothing just above her left breast revealing, bare lily white flesh. She was clasping something with both hands just above her head, her eyes were closed so tight it screwed up her face. Adrien realised that this was his beautiful Freyja and alarmingly she was holding a sharp ivory bladed dagger and by the looks of it she was about to drive it into her heart.

Exasperated, the Saxon urgently yelled out, "My love! No! Stop!" Abruptly she opened her eyes, and seeing the unkempt intruder hanging from her window sill automatically screamed out with a high-pitched screech and dropped the dagger. Her screams were heard by a member of the public who looked up and saw the bedraggled Saxon hanging, and alerted the berserkers.

Freyja in a flash seized her bow and armed it with an arrow. Adrien pulled himself inside, and sat panting out of breath on the inside ledge of the window. Freyja stood speechless, an arrow aimed at Adrien's head. She recognised the stranger to be the man she had waited for. She stood frozen in that position for what seemed like an eternity, then the bow fell to the floor as she ran to embrace her long-lost love, and they both wept tears of joy and happiness.

If Adrien had been a few seconds later he would have found her dead.

There was no time to waste as the berserkers and guards would be on Adrien's tail.

Freyja changed out of her shoulder-strapped linen dress into her warrior clothing that was made out of short cut grey animal furs, and put on her fur boots. Whilst she did this the Viking princess quickly told how her brother Olaf (who was now king following the death of their father Gudrod the hunter) had given her away against her will, to Dork, king of Hvinisdair, another Norse kingdom, and she was to marry him in Tonsberg tomorrow. This would explain what all the preparations in the town were being made for. Money had already exchanged hands as was a custom between both the groom and the bride's parties. So the heartbroken princess had chosen to take her own life.

Her room was quite empty; on one of the walls was a large, faded tapestry. While in the centre was a big bed, that wouldn't look out of place today. It had intricately carved bed posts, depicting some Viking god, and on the bed was a linen mattress stuffed with straw. Next to the bed, on a tiny wooden table, sat an oil lamp carved from soap stone, sitting next to the lamp was an object Adrien had seen before, in fact he hadn't just seen it before for he had made it, it was indeed the little straw boat he had made for her whilst he was in prison, many moons ago.

Freyja slipped on her cherry-coloured cloak that was held together with a brooch, and strapping her quiver to her back, she grabbed her bow and they left the room.

The guards had already alerted King Olaf that someone had broken into his sister's quarters, but before the guards had arrived to check, Frejya and Adrien had slipped out by the back. They were spotted as they made their escape up the hill, but by the time the guards and berserkers had time to follow them, they had reached Adrien's horse and together they galloped out of sight.

Between the two of them there was a lot of catching up to do. It suddenly dawned on Adrien that she was speaking in Latin. Freyja described that she had made it her passion to learn the Latin language so when he returned she could speak with him.

The princess had a childhood friend whom they could go to who would be able to arrange for a ship to take them back to Britannia. So on the way they found Gregor who had waited patiently and rode to her friends.

A few days later they sailed for Britannia. As they crossed the rough northern sea they crossed Adrien's last time change back to the summer of 426AD.

As the island came into view Adrien felt his heart warm, for he had finally returned. Many times during his long quest he thought he would never again see the coveted island with its green woodlands, rugged peaks, and rolling green hills. He had seen and learnt so very much in his lifetime already, and was a very different person from the one who had left the shores of Britannia over six years previously.

Disembarking from the ship he knelt down and kissed the soil.

A couple of weeks later and he arrived back at Gifle Castle, but he did not receive the welcome home reception he expected. He jumped off his horse and walked over the open draw bridge, where he encountered a lone servant carrying a cask of water, who on seeing the Saxon leader turned white, as if he had seen a ghost, and dropping the cask stammered, "My lord, is it you? Are you alive?"

Shocked by this question, Adrien, somewhat annoyed, replied, "Of course I'm alive."

Without delay the servant shouted, "Adrien, our beloved leader is alive! Adrien, our beloved leader is alive!" Then he was seen by the slumbering guards under the keep, and on seeing this for themselves, continued the shouting and this echoed throughout the whole castle. And the trumpets on the tower blew to signal his return.

That night there was great celebrations all over Gifle castle, Mercia and beyond. As the night wore on, Adrien was outside sat in the courtyard with Freyja when he saw a lowly man walking toward him. He recognised that swagger a mile off. Shakily he got to his feet. Could this be true? Yes, it was. It was his trusted lifelong friend and companion Eals. They hugged each other with disbelief, as both thought the other had perished in that fateful avalanche on the great northern pass.

It just so happened that Eals had been miraculously carried on the top of the falling avalanche all the way to the foot of the mountain and had survived. He had found his way home arriving just one week ago (having had his own adventures), informing everyone of Adrien's certain death.

Now the only person who could have said this was not true was the Druid Mahours, who had not been seen for weeks, even months.

Adrien started to make preparations as the battle at Caledonia was to commence in six or so months' time, so he trained hard and spent time with Eals playing chess.

He married his beautiful wife Freyja in a small, low-key affair in the castle. Shortly after the wedding Adrien was crowned king of the western province of Mercia. And Freyja became his queen.

His apprentice Syziaslav arrived to complete his training.

And word came from the far north that Killgore had returned home.

One thing that did concern him though was the disappearance of Mahours, so he went down to his cave in Cornwall, where he found the illusive Druid. Here he got a frosty welcome and was accused of being disobedient and turning away from his roots. This was a bit of a worry as Adrien needed Mahours' judgement and guidance to take with him to Caledonia.

CROSSING THE PYRENEES BY SNOWBOARD

The trip across the Mare Nostrum with the Dreadlock Pirate and his crew was the most chilled but entertaining journey, helping the travel-weary Romans to relax and recoup a little.

During the night before land and their chosen destination came into sight, the date switched to March 412AD. In doing so the temperature dropped radically and most men on board woke up with chattering teeth.

The rugged Iberian coastline was spotted as the first rays of morning appeared. Axana's acute navigational skills had taken Darinus right to the position he had pointed to upon the canvas, where he had wished for him and his men to be dropped off, just up from the north–east, Roman-owned town of Barcino.

Drawing closer, the jagged shoreline suddenly didn't look as inviting as it had from afar; the men were met by the stark reality of this dangerous coastline, as the daunting picture before them revealed the pirates' darkest nightmare – a shipwreck was washed up on the merciless rocks. It was an unfamiliar ship, an old vessel from a past age - it was in fact centuries old.

The freezing cold had already thrown a depressing atmosphere over the usually cheery crew. From their mouths their warm breath could be seen against the ice-cold air. Most of the miserable sailors who had any brains stayed below deck trying to keep warm. Darinus understood that Barcino had belonged to the Western Roman Empire, but due to the sudden change in the weather, which proved that they had most likely crossed another time change, Darinus felt unsure that this town was still a safe place for him and his men. So the Romans disembarked just up the coast. Axana wasted no time in turning his ship round super quick and full-steam ahead he and his pleasant crew disappeared over the horizon, back to the south and the sun.

Climbing the rocky bank to level ground, the Romans followed their leader, who was moving at quite a pace, for the bitter weather conditions were deteriorating, and drizzle made visibility poor, the thin Eastern-made Roman cloaks gave little protection against the cold conditions. So instead of going south west Darinus took his men north. He had originally planned to go into the city of Barcino (which was widely known across the Empire for being a tax-free haven for higher ranked retired Roman soldiers). It was the ideal retreat with its calm quiet flat landscape, and the serene purple silhouette of the Pyrenees mountains in the background.

Forward the troops marched. Hours later the drizzle turned to rain, which rudely continued for the duration of that miserable day, before the dwindling sun sulked away, and the party found refuge under the shelter of a huge rock. Because of the dark, the travellers were unaware of their surrounding; they had actually arrived at the foot of a huge, multi-peaked mountain. Tired and wet, they all lay down and fell asleep.

Thankfully the following morning the rain had ceased, although it was crisp and the chilly sting of winter still lingered, but at least they could now clearly see their surroundings. So, stepping out from beneath the rock they saw that they were at the foot of a multi-peaked mountain, with peaks rising up to one thousand metres high. The rock that made up this impressive jagged mountain was composed of striking pink conglomerate, a form of sedimentary rock. Below the rock the land was fairly flat and was covered with low wild bush land, most of which was hidden under melting snow.

Darinus was in a bit more of a sombre mood, as he was considering whether he had made a mistake in passing by Barcino, as perhaps all the tools and transport he needed for the final leg north could be found in the city. Besides the road north looked quite bleak especially the other side of the mountains and into Gaul, making it less likely that they would meet anyone of worthy pedigree who would meet the requirements for his chosen elite army.

As he started to propose his new plan to his men, unexpectedly the morning silence was shattered by an excited shrill from up high. Looking up, their eyes were met by the wackiest of sights imaginable coming from a rounded ledge two hundred metres up. At first it appeared that a giant bird had just been thrust out of its nest. But this flight was far from gracious and it took the Romans seconds to realise this was no giant bird but an eccentric human being, imitating a bird, using a pair of gigantic manmade wings attached to his arms.

With wings flapping like mad the figure hurdled straight toward the ground, then several metres from the ground he levelled out and gently glided like an albatross for a good fifty or so meters, and was looking confidently graceful. But this wasn't to last as, like a stone, gravity grabbed hold of the human bird, and pulled him directly toward the floor and so he disappeared into the bush land over yonder. Intrigued and wondering whether this rare man had injured himself, and unsure of what they were about to encounter, the Romans jogged over to where he had fallen.

And this is what they found - a jolly, middle-aged, bald-headed fellow huffing and puffing and muttering away to himself. What is more he was looking rather pleased with himself on his back, laying on a thick bed of fresh hay, for the man had evidently planned to land at that particular place. Subsequently the man looked up to see the gawping Romans, and briskly sat up and started to undo the leather straps that fastened the long wings to each of his arms. These long, feathered wings spanned seven metres tip to tip; although relatively heavy they were robust and very well designed, with real feathers stuck to a thin leather material. After undoing the leashes from the wings he had more straps wrapped round his ankles to undo, fixed to a triangle shape object that would have worked in a similar fashion to that of a bird's tail.

Darinus felt compelled to lend him a hand and ordered Julian to help him get the man to his feet; at this the centurion looked rather cross and, passing the buck, ordered one of the bodyguards to do the job instead, as after all this was below him.

At first the flying man frowned and resisted any help; he clearly was a proud, stubborn guy. But on realising that the Romans were only trying to help, he held out a hand to shake Darinus', which slightly shocked the general as he had only ever used this gesture in an act of combat, but he did it anyway. This man worked hard, for his hands were terribly coarse and rough. This bald-headed fellow had long thick eyebrows which were pointed at the ends, on the tip of his thick nose he had the biggest mole, the kind that you can't help but get drawn to. Now standing upright he was only short and plump.

To the surprised Romans he spoke with a sure Latin tongue, which made Darinus feel a bit uneasy. He introduced himself with much pride as Leighton the Visigoth from the barbarian tribe of the Visigothi people.

After chatting with this unusual fellow they soon learnt that this was now an unfriendly place for the Romans to be, which proved that Darinus' initial discernment had been correct and that a change in direction in going to Barcino could have had disastrous consequences.

Barcino had recently been taken by the Visigoths who had ruthlessly banished any young Romans from the province in case of any revenge attacks, and strict orders had been given that if any Romans were seen intruding they were to be executed on the spot.

The eccentric flying man told Darinus that fate had smiled upon him and his men. And he commented that fate had also smiled on him to, as he now had help to carry the giant wings. Who knows how he had originally got the wings up to the ledge. The Romans were invited back to the Visigoth's home, the deal being that they had to carry the giant wings.

Leighton lived in the vicinity, hidden under the shadow of the jagged mountain. On reaching his home Darinus was flabbergasted, for this was a modern grand design dwelling. The house was partially built into the side of the pink mountain; the front was raised up on thick wooden stilts, which kept the house level from where it protruded out of the rock. The base and the frame of this contemporary structure were made of thick wood, however the walls were made from a clear substance totally alien to the Romans, but what we know today as glass. But this was far from the clear glass which we are familiar with; it was lots of clear, round bottle-shaped objects all cleverly fused together and built up like a jigsaw to make walls. The glass wall at the front was built only partially up half way, giving whoever was inside the chance to look out.

The smoothly cut stone roof sloped from the mountain wall right to the front of the building where it overhung by a metre, as a result protecting the structure from all weather conditions. At the end of the roof hanging just underneath was a kind of thin wooden guttering that very gradually tilted down at an angle to the right-hand side; a few metres downs on the ground was a large clay bucket, that cleverly caught all the fresh water from the roof.

Leighton instructed the Romans carrying the large wings to put them underneath the house as there was plenty of space. "Welcome, welcome, Romans to my nature-friendly abode," said Leighton, as he encouraged them to follow him. He ventured further under his house, where he stopped and tugged on a loose hanging rope. A trap door above opened, and a set of ladders lowered down, showing that this was the entrance to this jolly little man's bizarre designer house. Climbing up first he then invited them to join him. As per usual custom two of the soldiers remained outside on guard.

Darinus was the first to scale the steps. As he reached the top he thought he had entered another world. Inside the place was much bigger than it had appeared from below, and at the far end another room had been cut into the rock. The hatch opened up into the centre of the house; on one side was a big open fire place built out of stone, on the shelf above sat a big clay pot, just above was a kind of chimney to vent out the smoke. From out of the side of the clay pot ran a clay pipe that ran downward at a slight angle around the whole room. When the fire was lit the pot would be gradually filled up heating the water inside flowing over and into the pipes, which actually created a simple but unique heating system to warm up the nature house during the cold winter months.

The whole place was very untidy with weird and wonderful gadgets dotted everywhere, as the inventor would start one project and another bright idea would pop into his head and he would go on a tangent doing something else; in fact it's a wonder he ever finished anything. He had a go at designing everything you could imagine from sundials to a wooden ski, a mini cross bow you could hold in one hand (so effectively he could fire one in each hand), and he was obviously in to blowing glass as there were many weird and wonderful glass constructions dotted about.

Near the front of the house sitting upon a stone table, was a miniature version of the giant wings in which he had just used to make his ambitious flight with; the only difference being that the miniature version was made from leather. He had little wooden tools we know to be similar to that of a ruler and a protractor used to carefully measure these wings on a much smaller scale.

In the corner of the room near the back was a cage with a lizard in it but the thing that caught Darinus' eye was the simple cross hanging from the ceiling; at once he recognized the Visigoth to be a Christian. But the most impressive thing of all was the fantastic view from over the half-built wall; on a clear day you would be able to see for miles.

It didn't take too long until Julian had something to say, "What in the name of the gods possessed you man to foolishly jump from the rock? You are fortunate to not end your days."

Leighton wiggled his finger at the centurion. "You see not that the birds in the sky fly, there will come a day when men will learn to fly, my strategy has taken many days and nights, and today was a triumph."

Julian shrugged his shoulders and under his breath uttered, "Man will fly – what next, horses?"

All Darinus could think about was a few years previous when he had looked into the future pool with the monk Ravarda and had seen giant metal birds flying in the skies. Everybody else thought this guy was crazy but Darinus, on hearing the man say this, had an unusual feeling down in the pit of his stomach.

Leighton asked inquisitively why the Romans were in the province. "Have you been sent by Honorius in pursuit of our leader or are spies?"

Darinus responded intently, "Caesar Honorius may he be blessed is still alive and well in this time then. I come by neither request and have fallen from Caesar's favour, will you tell of your tribe, and how they come to be in this land?"

But just before the bald Visigoth replied he was distracted by a thud as a tiny flap next to the fire place opened and shut. He proceeded to walk over and pick up a freshly laid egg that had just fallen through. It just so happened that on the other side of the wall was built a little balcony where two chickens lived; when it came to lay eggs they sat on the hay which was situated on the end of a seesaw; when the chicken got off the egg would roll down the seesaw through the flap and into the house.

"Right then, where was I? Yes, I am a true Visigoth, I rode alongside our great leader Alaric. As a youth a condition prevented me fighting in the army, I have a weak heart, so the only way to join was to invent weapons, so I devised the modern catapult, among other weapons, which gave our army such an advantage over our foes that we became unstoppable. By the time we arrived at the gates of Rome I had become chief adviser to Alaric himself. I was there when we sacked and decimated Rome."

At that point Julian roared, "Traitor," and drew his sword. Darinus sternly ordered him to practice restraint and put his sword away.

Leighton continued, "Sadly one year later Alaric died and his half-brother Ataulf took charge, so I followed him to Barcino and after witnessing so much bloodshed and feeling much guilt about what happened in the eternal city I chose to take refuge up here. Ataulf has changed with his selfish demands in playing the Germanic tribes against the Roman commanders. When we left Rome we stole Galla Placida, who is Honorius' sister and he is planning to marry her. This will give him a full excuse to join forces with Rome and this I fear could be the end on our tribe."

All this was a lot to take in for the bemused Romans, and Julian was livid.

Seeing he had irritated his visitors and to bring tensions down he offered to give everyone a strong drink, made of some kind of hot substance; Julian took one sip and spat the rest on the ground, at which point Darinus requested him and the others to leave and wait outside.

Once alone the calm Darinus said to the man, "There is one thing you can do if the burning feeling of guilt of ransacking Rome still lies like a burden upon you." And he commenced to explain the chequered courtyard and the game of chess at Caledonian castle. "I have a position open for you if you can create new weapons for me."

The plump little bald fellow stared in sheer bewilderment at the Roman for a good ten minutes and, realising the sincerity in Darinus' voice, and knowing that these were such unstable times he eventually accepted. Also he could see the same vision and zest in the young commander's eyes that he had years ago in Alaric's.

Now there was no time to lose, as Leighton said that the Romans should leave as soon as possible as it was only a matter of time before a Visigoth patrol would pick up the Romans' tracks from last night.

Aware that he had to cross the Pyrenees Darinus, asked if his new comrade could enlighten him on the easiest route to cross. But Leighton went one better than this. He took Darinus back down the ladder to under his house, to the darkest corner underneath. Lifting various bits of junk out of the way he pulled out several oval-shaped boards, each about one and a half metres long, rounded at each end and slightly raised up at one end. On top of the boards was animal fur and two sets of rude leather straps, one at the front and one at the back, which were used to fasten each foot to the board. Leighton explained that the Romans would have to stand on top of the boards on their way down the mountains, or, failing that, they could lie down.

He said that he came up with this invention as he travelled through the treacherous mountain range on the way to Iberia; he had made the snowboards to cut time but they were yet to be tried and tested. Plus the Romans could carry them on their backs as they were quite light. Before leaving, Leighton gave all the Romans fur gloves and new thick fur Visigoth cloaks along with fur boots, and the strangest object yet: two bits of glass placed in leather straps to put in front of their eyes to stop them getting snow blind by the bright white snow.

Saying farewell to the Visigoth inventor they set off. The mountain range was still a good way off and a good couple of days' walk. There was plenty of snow still hanging around. The landscape got steeper and the party found themselves climbing up and up; the centurion begrudging wearing the Visigoth's cloaks, but they were all glad to be warm. Eventually they crossed over the first peak and came to the first proper slope down, and this was a chance to try out the boards, so all fastened their feet to the boards and off they went. That day the furthest any of them got whilst standing upright was probably ten metres. But it did get better over the course of the next few days as they persevered, and learnt to turn from left to right, moving from their heels to their toes. Leighton the wacky inventor's calculations had been pretty accurate. And they began to make excellent progress.

A BITTER SWEET DECISION OF A NEW KING

A week or so later and the Romans had crossed right over the Pyrenees mountain range on their snowboards and entered into Gallia and the province of Aquitania. Each of the soldiers would agree it was probably the only time they had actually had fun for a whole week whilst travelling during the whole mission.

It was late March and the transitional period between winter and spring, the snow had had enough and was beginning to pack up for another season, and the whole landscape was crying out for the sun. Some of the early spring flowers were prematurely pushing through what was left of the dwindling snow. With no use left for the boards they decided to leave them behind. Darinus felt it a bit disrespectful just dumping them, so when they got the chance they burnt Leighton's new invention, and it wasn't until centuries later a similar idea was designed again, and this time became a global trend.

Whilst entering Gallia in these uncertain times the Romans were well aware that they had to watch where they went. There was a good network of Roman roads covering Gallia (Gaul) but Darinus insisted that whilst on foot they would make their own way cross country, which worked well at that time of the year as a lot of the undergrowth had been killed off by the cruel winter.

A week further on, they found that as they were crossing sets of smooth rolling hills (that seemingly stretched on and on). They strolled over the brow of one of the low grassy slopes, and the scenery in the valley beneath changed into a neatly kept vineyard that spread across the whole valley; it was huge. On a hill the other side overlooking this picturesque vineyard was a tall, handsome-looking building. This was the first time for a good couple of weeks they had encountered any sign of human life.

Before long the Romans found themselves meandering between the vine corridors, the rows ran almost perfectly parallel to one another; they appeared to pleasantly go on for miles. Soon they discovered that they were not the only people there. They came across a frumpy woman, drably dressed in a long not very attractive sack material tunic, from her neck to her bare feet. She was working, tending to the vines and she also was not alone, as there were many more women all working hard, pruning and weeding the vines in the early spring sunshine; this was a much-needed process this time of year keeping the vines in excellent condition, readying them to produce the finest wine for the forth coming season.

The Romans carried on walking. There were so many women, all concentrating and working hard. Darinus eventually stopped and stooped down next to one and politely asked, "Woman, where tell me is your master?" He received no reply.

On seeing the woman remaining mute and ignoring his commander Julian stepped up to her and leaning down shouted, "Answer the commander. Where is your master?" Clearly she could hear, as she scrunched her face and flinched but remained silent.

This only fuelled the fire for the short-tempered centurion. "Daughter of a whore, answer!"

Darinus swiftly diffused Julian's foul attitude by sarcastically saying, "Centurion, you are a fine man to speak of whores. Now leave the woman alone." This defused the situation as they burst out laughing.

The soldiers walked on (ignored by the women like invisible ghosts) toward the green hill where the building stood. The massive vineyard stretched out for hundreds of metres, no doubt in the summertime all the greenery on the vine branches would make the whole place look heavenly.

Reaching the foot of the green hill it now rose up much higher than it looked from afar; the building in fact was a fine-looking fortress, in defensive terms this fort was in an excellent location to defend from.

From where they stood they could see that the doors were wide open, and somebody was standing next to them. So Darinus and his trusted bodyguards scaled up the steep green slope. Panting hard they reached the top and the foot of the fort. Looking down the view over the vineyard with the fresh green hill beyond was pretty special; the owner of the estate would have been very proud.

This was a typical Roman-built fort with a bit of a charismatic twist obviously designed by a Roman architect with a personality. It was fairly small as strongholds go, but was well designed to withhold any kind of attack or siege keeping whoever was inside perfectly safe. The building could house up to one hundred people. It was built in the shape of a triangle with twelve-metre high stone walls on all three sides; the main feature was a watch tower erected in the centre of the fort at a height of roughly fourteen metres, and on the top of the tower was a sloping roof. As there was only one main door in, I should imagine that there may have been secret escape tunnels leading underneath the hill, who knows.

The person standing beside the open doors was a mysterious-looking woman, holding a long shepherd's crook in one hand; she had an ordinary, plain-looking face and was a brunette with horse like whispery hair covering half of her face. She too was dressed in the same drab common clothing as the women working in the vineyard but as the Romans noticed she had a fantastic slim figure.

The woman had her index finger poking in her mouth in a weird kind of provocative manner, with her hazel eyes her gaze was out to the horizon and she too ignored the Romans dressed in their Visigoth shrouds, not even flinching when Darinus addressed her, "Woman, can you inform us on the name of this abode and lead me to your master?" Again there was absolutely no reply, nothing. And before the hot-headed centurion could intervene, Darinus raised his hand to silence him.

So the brazen Romans breezed past the woman and through the doors. Their confidence was due to the fact they knew this to be a Roman building. Through the doors was a wide, lengthy walkway that led to another set of doors. The apparent reason for this walkway was in the case that enemy troops burst through the first set of doors they would then be exposed to the elements from above. The prominent watchtower rose up directly above them. Either side under the tower were two neat wooden doors which were both shut.

The second set of doors were wide open too. Meeting no resistance they wandered under the watch tower and through into a big, open-air, deserted courtyard. They were met by an inviting sweet smell in the early spring air; unbeknown to them it was the smell of wine, which made it feel, although abandoned, a very pleasant place to be in.

Right the other side was an open arch way, so they crossed the courtyard and through the archway and here the mood changed. This was the throne chamber, but it was completely overgrown with brambles and thorn bushes, that wove all around the perimeter and up the walls. In front of where they stood were two flights of long steps leading up to a throne made of stone; not that they could see much of the stone as it was covered in ivy. The room was oblong in shape and not very wide. From the ceiling hung an old wooden candle chandelier that looked as if it was ready to fall.

Julian was the first to state the obvious. "This desolate abode appears to have been unoccupied without a ruler for a time."

Darinus failed to detect the sarcasm in the centurion's voice. "You are right. Looks like this place has not been inhabited by Romans for some time. But why a throne?"

Just then Julian, who had climbed up the first set of steps and knelt down, had started brushing away the dust from the floor.

Darinus questioned, "What is it, Centurion?"

Julian replied, "I have found something, sir."

Darinus went to see what it was. Julian had found a stone tablet lying on the floor with writing carved into it and was wiping away the dust. The only problem was the room was very poorly lit. Eventually he could read what it said in Latin.

UT A ROMANORUM REX RGIS SITS IN PER VOMICA MOS LEVO.

When a Roman king sits on the throne the curse will lift.

To the Romans this made little sense, as in any case they have a supreme Caesar not a king.

So they left the throne room and crossed back through the courtyard, under the tower and back through the second set of doors. This time, looking up to the open air whist passing through the lengthy walkway between the two sets of doors, they saw a stairway that ran round the walls up above them, that looked like it started halfway up. Surely these would lead up to the watch tower? To get to them you would have to pass through one of the little doors no doubt.

Darinus decided that he had some questions, and seeing that there was no sign of life within the fort walls, they headed back outside. But the whispery-haired woman was nowhere to be seen, and looking down upon the vineyard all the working women too had vanished; this in itself was a bit unusual as they had only been inside the fort for ten or so minutes.

Darinus said to Julian, "Centurion, with two soldiers you venture that way round the walls and I accompanied with the others will venture this way and meet with you halfway, and tell what you witness."

Darinus, along with three bodyguards, followed the outside wall of the triangle fort all the way to the back to the point; here he saw below them a straight Roman road, so he reached for his map that showed that this was the Via Aquitania, the road that ran north west all the way to the sea of Atlas.

Shortly after, Julian arrived, and same as Darinus he had seen nobody, but said that there was a wood up a hill over yonder, but for all the women to have disappeared up there was unlikely. Darinus suggested that they went back to explore the fort, so they all trudged back round.

Two of the bodyguards were ordered to wait outside on guard and to keep their eyes peeled. The rest of the party entered back through the doors. As they were walking underneath the watch tower Julian whispered, "Sir, look. Do you see what I see?" and he pointed to the little door on the left hand side, which was now ajar, for this had definitely been shut tight before. This prompted everyone to be a bit more alert.

The fearless Julian tiptoed over and opened the door wide, drew his sword and cautiously passed on through followed closely by his comrades. Darinus ordered another one of the bodyguards to stand guard outside this door.

The General, Centurion and the two remaining soldiers found themselves in a large room, with very dim light but enough to make out their new surroundings; the little light that came through was from two narrow cut slit windows, one on each of the outer walls. In different areas of the room were five raised-up stone slabs about four metres square, with drainage all-round the edges, for this was the wine-making room, where the grapes would be brought in and piled up on the slabs, before being trampled down under foot until the juice would be squashed out and flowed into the drainage system and poured into large clay pots. The different slabs would be used to produce different wines. A simple yet effective method, used to manufacture wine.

This room had a warm, much more potent, sweeter smell in it than the rest of the building. A couple of broken clay vessels were lying on the floor, but there was no sign of the sweet nectar around. In the centre of the room an authentic wooden spiral set of stairs rose up to a floor above. Swords drawn, the Romans discreetly made their way upstairs. Well, they thought they were being quiet but in truth, with the creak of the wooden steps they could be heard out in the courtyard.

The next floor was completely barren; it too was only lit by the slits on the two outer walls but there were two on each wall letting in more light. This room was entirely round, with old candle holders placed around the walls. The wooden floor was cut from long wooden boards all spread outward from the staircase in the centre, forming a circle. Once upon a time this would have been a grand room which may have held banquets or some other kind of entertainment, however now it lay silent. One of the inner walls had a short archway with the obvious opening for the high stairway they had noticed earlier.

The party made their way to the opening. Stepping out onto the stone stairs was not for the faint hearted as there was no banister or anything at the sides to hold on to, and down the left side was a sheer drop; the stone steps were no more than three-foot wide, jutting out of the wall. Up above the bright blue sky gave the opening a nice roof.

From the side further up the watch tower peered down the gap, and to reach it they had to scale the staircase. Unfazed the soldiers marched out on to the steps in single file, Darinus at the helm. Up to the first corner where they turned left onto the stairs on the outer wall, up to the second corner where they turned left again and carried on up each flight, all the time able to see the doorway under another arch that led into the watch tower.

On the third corner they all of a sudden realised that the stairs turned downwards. When they reached the middle of the wall where they had seen the door opening to the watch tower, they found that there was nothing, just a stone wall. So they felt their way to the opposite corner but strangely no sign of the door.

Darinus told the two soldiers to go and wait in the centre of the wall where the opening had been, and he and Julian carried on round, past the first opening from where they had first stepped out. What they did not recognise was that that opening had disappeared too and they also didn't take into account that when they first trod on to the stairway there was only one way to go and that was upwards, and it certainly wasn't joined up from below.

Darinus and Julian turned the corner to the stair dead opposite the two others soldiers and as clear as mud they could see the doorway to the watch tower behind the bodyguards. Darinus shouted for them to go through, but from where the bodyguards stood they couldn't find it; all they felt was the cold stone wall.

Julian then chirped up, "Sir, do you comprehend we are descending?" He was right the stairs were now going downward instead of up like they were when they had passed them earlier. But the irritated commander was more intent on getting through the illusive watch tower door.

One hour passed and the miffed Romans tried everything, up and down they went and the stairs changed direction at every turn so they were not sure whether they were heading either up or down; they had also lost the original entrance. Eventually Darinus figured the only way out was to rewind and go back and back until they arrived at the beginning and back to the empty room.

Darinus remarked, "This domain is cursed as it says on the tablet in the throne room."

Back down the spiral stairs and into the grape-crushing hall. As they exited the grape hall they found the soldier on guard was no longer there, so they presumed he had gone against his commander's order (which was out of character) and gone out to hang with the two guards at the front.

As soon as the party reached the tall front doors they found the two guards were still where they had left them, but the other guard was not, and asked if he they had seen him the response was no!

The sky had turned paler and the shadows were getting longer in the late afternoon.

Darinus and Julian marched back inside to find the missing guard. What they saw next stopped them in their tracks. Placed in a row on the ground just outside the door to the grape-crushing room stood six miniature clay pitchers all full of wine; this was most odd.

Julian crouched down and dipped his finger into one of the vessels and smelt the contents. It smelt ok but he dare not risk tasting it in case it was poisoned. He then pointed out to his commander, "Sir, there are only six jugs and not seven. We are being mocked and they have taken our comrade."

Darinus sprang into action and voiced, "At the ready, men." In a flash the highly trained soldiers had positioned themselves, swords at the ready, several yards apart with every angle covered. Then he roared through gritted teeth, "Cowards, we will not leave until you return my soldier. If you value your life whoever you are you will obey immediately."

But a reply never came, just silence.

Julian spied it first and he whispered to his commander, "Sir, look up."

Slightly tilting his head, and rolling his eyes upward to the dreaded stairway he saw the silhouette of a human against the fading blue standing on the steps on the side above the front doors. He was dressed in some kind of body armour, with a pot-shaped helmet, and held a sword in one hand and a round shield in the other.

"Reveal whom you are," yelled Darinus. But the same as everyone around, they remained quiet.

Then one of the guards nearest to the open front doors screamed, "Sir, we are surrounded!" Everyone stood to their positions and waited for their master's instruction. Darinus went to check out what his bodyguard was saying.

Standing at the front entrance he looked down to see an army of soldiers advancing up the green hill from every direction, all dressed in identical armour and all with pot-shaped helmets. The armour they wore were metal plates across the breasts and stomach held together with leather straps onto harden leather that protected the sides; on their legs they wore metal leg plates, their hands were protected by thick leather gauntlets and the pot-shaped helmets had flat tops with horse hair fixed to the back of them that draped down their shoulders. With this modern armour Darinus knew they were in for one hell of a fight.

Darinus ordered the two nearest soldiers to hoist the front doors shut. So the two doors were closed and the heavy beam lifted across to lock them together.

"Soldiers, we have a battle on our hands," the Roman commander exclaimed, before glaring back up toward the mid-air staircase and to his horror the lone soldier was no longer alone, he had been joined by more soldiers covering the whole staircase all the way round, and what's more they were marching downward like robots and into the empty room above the grape-crushing hall.

The Romans were ready for the fight and counting the seconds.

Just as expected the soldiers began coming through the short wooden door. At the same time, soldiers appeared from the other little door the other side. Outside the front the advancing army were thumping with their swords against the tall doors, inside countless troops kept coming through the narrow doors.

The Romans retreated to the back of the courtyard and drew closer together with their backs to the throne chamber.

Some of the soldiers inside the fort opened the front doors and the outer troops flooded in from the back.

Now the Romans were completely outnumbered and would have to fight for their lives. As usual Darinus ordered his men to hold fast as the enemy slowly pressed toward them. These troops were a bit smaller in stature than the Romans but never the less at that moment this meant absolutely nothing.

The two forces engaged with the fighting fast and furiously, and the Romans found they were more on the defence than attack; the enemy fought efficiently and tactically, their strategy was, the front row would fight in a line for no more than a minute then the row behind would come through and take over as they peeled off and moved away from the fighting; hence the enemy were never tiring, which was making it even harder for the Romans.

Back and back the intruders were pressed. Both the commander and the centurion struck metal but failed to penetrate, then one of the bodyguards was stabbed below the lower rib cage, which forced them to withdraw through the throne chamber archway, where they held on for a while. Eventually the Romans were driven up the steps and were completely drained and fatigued fighting from three sides, and the poor light wasn't helping either.

Julian gasped, "Darinus, I understand what the tablet means. It's you, sir, your destiny to be king at Caledonia. Swiftly you must sit on the throne. It's our last chance."

The commander at once obeyed the centurion and lunged for the throne, and as his behind touched down the reaction was instantaneous as a force of unknown light shone out from underneath him and threw the enemy soldiers back.

The light disappeared as quickly as it had appeared, but in its wake all the candles round the perimeter of the room had been lit and the old wooden chandelier had now been reemployed. The brambles and thorn bushes withered and turned to dust, the ivy that had been resident on the once-redundant throne had vanished. The whole room had the feel of a throne chamber once again.

A few seconds after the amazing transformation had taken place the thankful Darinus softly said to his trusty centurion, "Julian, the best decision I ever made was to bring you with me on this perilous journey." This was one of the only times during their long comradeship that Julian had heard his commander utter such kind words. With a twinkle in his eye Julian replied, "Someone has to watch your back sir."

The enemy soldiers had made no attempt to continue the fray and the obvious leader took off his pot-helmet and shaking her long hair the Romans saw it was a woman.

If they had not been so knackered they would have realised that this was the same whispery-haired woman from outside the fort doors earlier in the afternoon. She was the apparent leader of this army. As the rest of the soldiers took off their helmets the Romans found that they had been in combat against an army full of women.

The women's leader turned to face her army and shouted in Latin, "Go, get the priest." Many of the women troop started leaving, as there was so many of them and not much room in the throne chamber. The woman then turned to Darinus and spoke, "You wait, you must not leave the chair."

Darinus was just glad to sit down. Half an hour passed and there was a bit of a kafuffle in the courtyard then the women soldiers stepped aside and an old priest in a long white tunic entered the room and walked up to the long steps. Following behind him was a natural young woman who held a white cloth wrapped over her outstretched arms. Resting on the cloth was a slender gold crown.

The priest took the crown and stood in front of the king and started chanting in a strange ancient language of which the Romans understood nothing, then some sweet music started to play coming from the courtyard.

But there was something else that had attracted Darinus as this ceremony was taking place. At the back of the chamber from whence the priest had arrived, stood two extraordinarily familiar figures that Darinus recognised. Either side of the archway, stood the Druid Mahours and Wei-Po-Yang the dark-dressed Eastern Magician.

Darinus was crowned king of a small corner of the Province of Aquitania, and now he was a king he would be ready to take his rightful place on the courtyard floor at Caledonia. After the coronation he wished to talk with the Druid and the Magician but they were nowhere to be found.

With the curse lifted the whole fort had been transformed back into what was no doubt its original state. Up above the sky was now black but inside the fort the whole place was adequately lit up all over.

It wasn't long until the empty hall above the wine-making room was fully furnished and a banquet rapidly prepared ready for the celebrations, of which Darinus was not sure whether the people were celebrating their new king, or the restoration of the fortress.

Instead of the usual long-ended table, it was nice to come together around a circle-shaped table for once. At the table were Darinus and his men (the missing guard had been returned unscathed), the priest and the whispery-haired women's leader joined by two other women who must have held some kind of important rank in her army.

The Romans were spoilt with delicious vintage wine that had been saved in a hidden-away cellar under the fort, which there certainly was no shortage of.

Darinus was interested to hear about the curse, this strange fort and the highly skilled army made up of only women.

The head woman introduced herself as Eleanor. She spoke with a soft but high-pitched voice and her Latin was impeccable. It did not take much to realise that she was from good stock. Eleanor was a Tolosate from the wealthy city of Tolosa which was not too far away. She was a well-respected, talented artist and singer and the daughter of a lord.

More than a few years previously things in that province changed. The Romans used to live side by side with the peoples of the land, but due to Rome being under attack, all the Romans were called back to defend her and left. This gave way for the barbarians from the north and west to invade Gallia in great numbers, and because a famine had hit the western world the Vandals lay siege outside of the wealthy, strong Tolosa walls, and after many months and seeing that they could not get in, they raped and pillaged all the surrounding towns and villages, killing all the men and raping the women. One writer wrote that many tears fell over the Desolation of Tolosa. Inside the city during the siege a lot of people died of hunger and thirst.

Eleanor's family died, so she chose to leave, taking with her only a sword for protection, and as she walked she saw desolation, and she came to a village, where all the women were weeping for the death of their men. Knowing that this was not the end and that it was only a matter of time until the barbarians would return, something inside told her she must do something. So not knowing why, she told the women that she had come to train them to fight, and they were to be enlisted into a new army of women; now she did know how to use a sword but not very well.

Strangely the women obeyed, as to be truthful they had nothing left, and collected their dead husband's swords or what weapons they could get. The word spread like wild fire and before she knew it, broken women who had nothing left were coming from as far up as Lyon and Narbonne, where the desolation had been ruthless.

In all she raised an army of more than two thousand women all willing and ready. And eventually they reached the abandoned vineyard, and chose to stay in this safe, hidden-away place and disguise themselves as vineyard workers.

As she continued to teach she found herself getting better and better with the sword. Ultimately so did the rest of the army, and strategies were taught. Until, as the Romans had learnt first-hand, they had become a formidable force.

Darinus also found that the fort had belonged to a popular lord. The Romans had built the fort for him as a present to say thank you for the amount of wine he produced for them. When Tolosa had come under siege by the Vandals he had rode out with his bodyguards to help defend her, but he was concerned that if this place fell into the hands of the hated barbarians with the amount of wine produced here this would prompt them to stick around, so before he left he consulted an astronomer who told him of a Roman king who would ride through this province. After hearing this the lord went to see a Roman priest and it was agreed if he did not return then the priest would throw some kind of curse over the fort. Unfortunately the lord was killed in battle and never returned.

When Darinus and his men appeared in their Visigoth mantles, this was their downfall, as Eleanor knew that the Visigoths were coming and seeing the shawls sent out the wrong signals. Therefore they nearly paid with their lives.

The wine flowed deep into the night and Eleanor decided to retire early. No sooner had she reached the bottom of the spiral staircase, than the ever-opportunistic Julian shortly followed. He caught up with her just as she was leaving the grape-crushing room. In a kind of slurring voice he said, "Ele...a...nor sha...ll we go straig...t to you.r quarters." The surprised Tolosate woman responded to this with an almighty slap round the centurion's cheeks and stormed off.

The red-faced soldier returned to the banquet hall with his tail between his legs; he wasn't used to getting knocked back.

That night after the evening had died down Darinus went alone up to the watch tower, where he stayed till daybreak. He was contemplating giving Eleanor a place on the courtyard floor at Caledonia, and not just any square but one of the most sought-after positions in the whole army – the Rook on the back corner.

The last thing he needed was any internal animosity between his chosen elite, which could potentially damage his whole army.

In the morning he asked Eleanor to come walk in the vineyard with him. While they walked he explained everything. Returning back to the fort he looked relatively pleased with their conversation.

And he told his men, "Men, I have come to a decision, nonetheless it has been hard for me. The good woman Eleanor has agreed she will follow me to Caledonia and join my elite army; she has the qualities I am looking for. She too had her own terms and because I am now king of this province it is in my interest to protect it. So, my five trusted bodyguards, it is time to part from you. I will give you this province for I wish not for you to fight with me anymore." As he said these words he bent forward and without being seen, wiped away a single tear. He had grown close to these faithful men.

Julian was angry but dare not defy his master's decision.

TWO ELITE ARMIES COME FACE TO FACE ON THE CALEDONIAN COURTYARD

Darinus and Julian were given two grey Camargue stallions; these were intelligent hardy horses, a bit on the small side, however excellent for long-distance journeys. The two turned left on the Via Aquitania which headed north east toward Bordeaux and further on to the sea of Atlas. Nearing Bordeaux they passed through many more vineyards, and gave the city a wide birth as they did all the cities along the way. Eventually they reached the rough shoreline of the harsh sea of Atlas, where they followed the coast north.

For weeks they pressed forward until reaching a tiny sea port at the estuary of the River Sequana. Here they were fortunate to catch a trade ship straight to Londinium, all for the price of three gold coins which also included both the stallions.

Darinus was thrilled to get back to the island he had yearned to return to for so long. Patting Julian on his back he said to his loyal centurion, "Can you believe we made it home? Hence we are aware our real mission is about to commence."

The journey took two days' ride to Camulodunum, the city where Darinus had spent his childhood. The few Romans who had stayed in Britannia in recent times still held a tiny settlement.

A few weeks passed, and whilst preparations were being made and they were thinking of heading north, some shocking news arrived. Eals, Adrien's Althing (senior chief) had arrived back to Britannia alone with information that his leader had perished in the unforgiving mountain range on the great northern pass.

Shortly after the news, a man called Sion arrived at Camulodunum and asked to speak with Darinus. He had worked hard and been a faithful servant to Adrien, and clarified that the news was true. Now Sion was from the mountainous west, the legendary land of dragons. He had the reputation as one of the most sought-after weapon-makers in Britannia, and had produced the finest steel-cased swords in the business.

The reason he had left Gifle Castle and the realm of Adrien's kingdom was now with his leader gone, Darinus would retake the island back for the Romans and he needed to stay in employment, so had come to see if Darinus would give him a job. After all Roman pay was much higher than the newly arrived Saxons, or the locals for that matter.

Sion was a tall thin guy, with short brown hair (well it was short but he obviously cut it with a knife or sword as it was not very neat). He wore leather clothing with sleeveless arms and high leather boots. He spoke with a lilt in his voice like he was singing. Darinus at first thought he was putting his voice on, but soon realised this was his accent. Julian for that matter couldn't look him straight in the eye without laughing at his voice.

But the weapons he made were of the most fantastic quality and he tried out every single one on various objects etc. His only request was a fire well to produce his weapons. Darinus was over impressed to say the least.

With the news of Adrien's demise, Darinus could not believe his luck. But at the same time, had his mission been a complete waste of time? Except there were a couple of good points, first and foremost he had met his beautiful wife Ki Sui-Tang, who would join him shortly, along with his chosen army, where there may be a slight problem as he had promised them all a place in the greatest battle which would now not be taking place.

However, everything changed dramatically three weeks later, as news came to Camulodunum that against the odds Adrien had turned up alive and well, at Gifle Castle.

For Sion this was a massive blow as he loved Adrien and would never have betrayed him. There was no going back as Darinus offered him the last position in his elite army. Besides Darinus, although of a hated Roman race, was not a bad man, and had offered him the only chance he could have ever dreamt of - a place in history in the greatest battle ever, so with a heavy heart he accepted.

Both kings, Adrien and Darinus, arrived at the Caledonian Castle. Before the members of their new armies turned up, they were met separately by the Druid and the Magician and submitted the names and positions of where their troops were to stand. Adrien found it quite hard as his old friend Mahours was very short with him and would not engage in eye contact, as the druid had not approved of his disobedience.

As members of the new armies arrived, they were kept separate and guided into the castle from different entrances, and greeted one by one, by the two confident black and white Kings respectively.

There were some emotional scenes, especially when Darinus met his wife Ki Sui-Tang. She chose not to tell her husband of their young son at this time, as the last thing he needed was any kind of distraction.

Finally every single character arrived and took their squares on each side of the impressive chequered marble floor. This was the first time in history such a mixture of races and peoples from all over the world had been assembled within the same place, from the count, the traitorous Hephthalite and the Viking queen, to the shaman, the astronomer and gladiator and the rest of the elite armies.

Anyone that had been there that day, and stood in the middle of that courtyard, would have been struck with such awe at the choices both the Saxon and the Roman had chosen.

It would make the hairs on the back of one's neck stand up. There was plenty of brains and brawn on each side. This was going to be a game played by wit and strength by both bad and good decisions.

The two kings were brought to the centre of the courtyard, which was the closest both the sworn enemies had ever been to each other. Two feet apart they stared into one another's eyes. As they eye balled each other the atmosphere could have been cut with a knife.

The druid spoke to them, but what he said was for their ears only.

Just before they returned to their sides, Darinus held out his right hand as a mark of respect (a gesture he had picked up from Leighton the Visigoth) to shake his opponent's hand, but the stubborn Saxon rudely turned and walked away back toward his square.

As it had done seven years previously the whole place fell silent as the Eastern Magician with his stick wandered to the middle of the courtyard and, pacing to and fro, explained how this game was going to be played, taking long pauses as once again the druid translated. Although over half of the new chess pieces did not understand Latin they somehow understood.

On the floor of each square on both sides had been placed a precious stone. On Adrien's side the stones were white diamonds roughly cut one inch by one inch square encrusted in a silver chain necklace. On Darinus' side the stone was a black sapphire cut about one inch square, also encrusted in a silver necklace. All the chess pieces on the courtyard floor were told to put their stone around their necks; each single person's stone had their initials engraved on the back to show it was rightfully theirs.

The Game was almost ready to begin.

Made in the USA
Charleston, SC
24 December 2015